Stone Cold Case

A ROCK SHOP MYSTERY

Stone Cold Case

Catherine Dilts

FIVE STAR
A part of Gale, Cengage Learning

GALE
CENGAGE Learning

Farmington Hills, Mich • San Francisco • New York • Waterville, Maine
Meriden, Conn • Mason, Ohio • Chicago

Five Star™ Publishing, a part of Cengage Learning, Inc.

LIBRARY OF CONGRESS CATALOGING-IN-PUBLICATION DATA

Dilts, Catherine.
Stone cold case : a rock shop mystery / Catherine Dilts. — First edition.
pages ; cm. — (Rock shop mysteries)
ISBN 978-1-4328-3099-1 (hardcover) — ISBN 1-4328-3099-6 (hardcover) — ISBN 978-1-4328-3093-9 (ebook) — ISBN 1-4328-3093-7 (ebook)
1. Women geologists—Fiction. 2. Cold cases (Criminal investigation)—Fiction. 3. Teenagers—Crimes against—Fiction. 4. Murder—Investigation—Fiction. 5. Precious stones—Fiction. I. Title.
PS3604.I4633S755 2015
813'.6—dc23 2015008358

First Edition. First Printing: September 2015
Find us on Facebook– https://www.facebook.com/FiveStarCengage
Visit our website– http://www.gale.cengage.com/fivestar/
Contact Five Star™ Publishing at FiveStar@cengage.com

Printed in the United States of America
1 2 3 4 5 6 7 19 18 17 16 15

To my daughter, for your unexpected and amazing editing skills, and your encouragement.

To my father, who wants it known that he is my Number One Fan.

ACKNOWLEDGMENTS

I was fortunate to attend CPR classes with health and safety instructor Adam Lucero, who made this very serious topic approachable and entertaining. If I got any first aid or CPR details correct in this book or *Stone Cold Dead,* credit goes to Mr. Lucero.

The Rocky Mountain chapter of Mystery Writers of America and our fantastic carpool group have provided instruction, inspiration, and encouragement.

Donna from Lin Ottinger's Moab Rock Shop shared her enthusiasm for fossils and minerals during my visit to Moab, Utah, where I found fun specimens of ammonite.

The Western Museum of Mining and Industry in Colorado Springs, Colorado, keeps the history of mining alive, and maintains working mining equipment. They also have two charming donkey mascots.

Faerie Tales
Golden Springs Gazetteer
Bibi's Bakery
Kruger's Auto Repair
Feed and Seed
Community Church
Jade's Aspen Gold Art Gallery
The Hot Tomato Restaurant
Mineral Springs Park
Dalton Ranch
Golden Springs Homestead Park
SPRUCE
PINE
OAK
MAIN
ROCK OF AGES
5th
4th
3rd
Temple Mountain

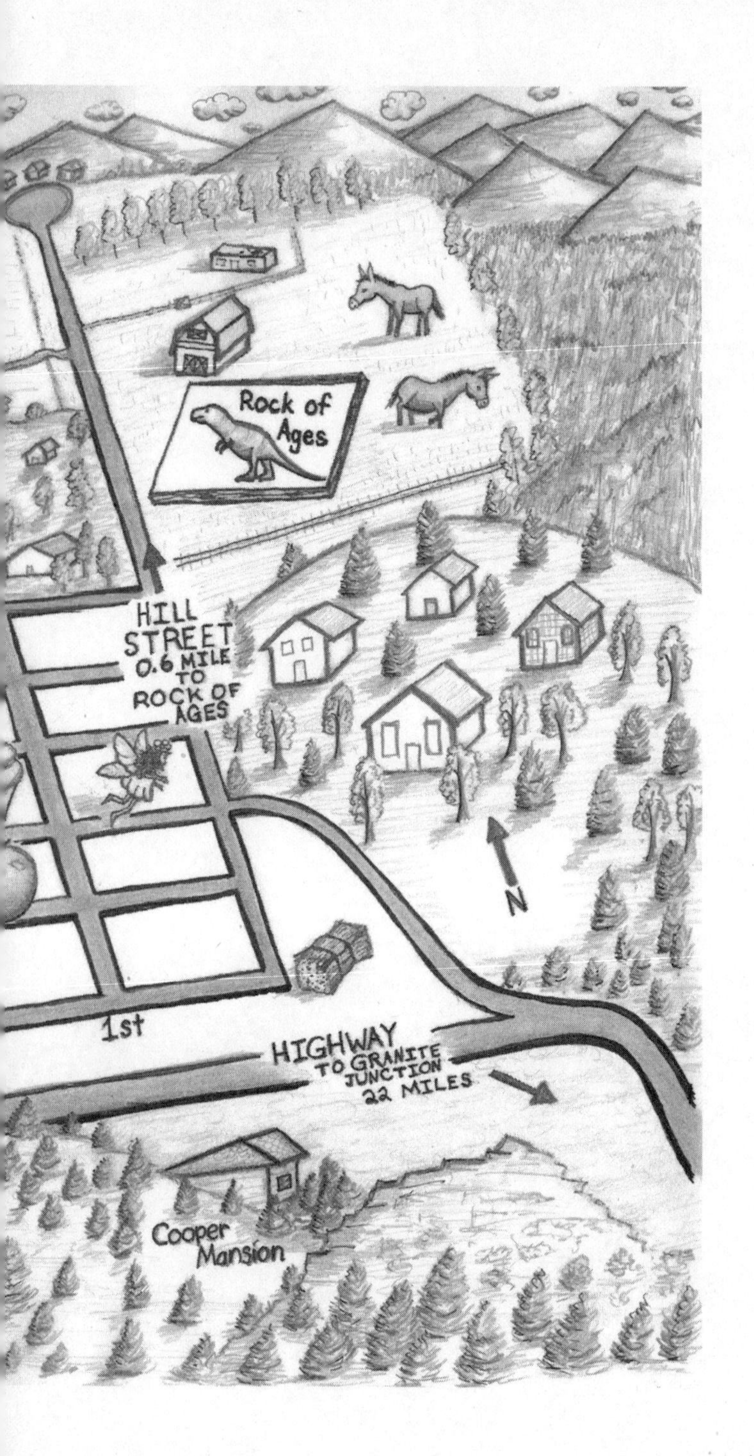

Rock of Ages
HILL STREET 0.6 MILE TO ROCK OF AGES
N
1st
HIGHWAY TO GRANITE JUNCTION 22 MILES
Cooper Mansion

Chapter One

Nothing buffered the wind above tree line. Morgan Iverson shivered and zipped up her windbreaker. Springtime in the Rockies was a rollercoaster ride. The May weather went from warm and sunny one minute to freezing the next. Half the geology class had already hiked back to their cars in the distant parking lot. When Morgan heard the brief rumble of thunder, she wished she had been among them.

"Is this fine specimen a mineral or rock?" Professor Tony Esteban slapped a leather-gloved hand against a stone outcropping abutting the steep trail.

"Rock," Trevin Pike said. "It contains a mixture of different minerals."

"What minerals do you see here?" he asked.

"Mostly quartz," Morgan said.

"Which might indicate the type of crystallization that forms gemstones." The wind tousled the professor's thick black hair. He pulled a small pick ax from a loop on the side of his backpack and prepared to strike. "Shall we dig in and see?"

"No!" Three people shouted at once.

Professor Esteban smiled. "And why not?"

"We don't have a mining claim." A white-haired woman shook her head, causing the brim of her floppy sun hat to wobble. "Digging would be illegal."

"Excellent."

Tony Esteban looked like a prospector. The half dozen

pockets on his canvas vest bulged with gear, a worn daypack hung from his wide shoulders, and his scuffed leather boots had seen many a mile. He spoke like a professor, though, repeating the rules about prospecting on private or public land as though there would be a quiz later.

The final field trip of the semester counted as extra credit. There would be no more tests, and for Morgan and an older couple auditing the class, grades had been optional. Even so, she had studied right along with the younger college students. The class was more than a fun diversion or a degree requirement. She needed to learn about geology if she had any hope of keeping the family rock shop in business.

Thunder sounded again, a long low rumbling that echoed off the surrounding peaks. Professor Esteban shielded his eyes and studied the dark clouds bunching at the top of Temple Mountain. He muttered something that Morgan's high-school Spanish classes hadn't covered.

"We need to get below tree line," he said in English, "before the storm reaches us. We are the tallest objects on this mountain, and most of us carry metallic implements, making us prime lightning targets."

A nervous classmate squeezed around Morgan, sending a cascade of stones skittering down the rocky slope. The falling rocks startled a pair of ravens perched on an elk carcass. Morgan pressed a gloved hand to the unyielding granite mountainside, seeking stability while her brain processed being above the flight of birds. A valley stretched below, the highway up Topaz Pass a narrow ribbon running parallel to a twisting creek.

Trevin touched her shoulder. "Are you okay, Mrs. Iverson?"

"I will be when we get back to tree line. Just feeling a little lightheaded."

Going uphill always took longer than the return trip, and today's hike had included plenty of stops for mini-lectures. The distinct boundary across the mountain where trees could no longer grow, approximately eleven thousand feet, was not far. The class would reach it in fifteen minutes. Still, it would be at least an hour before they reached the trailhead and their vehicles. If it began raining, the hike would be miserable. Morgan moved as swiftly as she could without losing her footing on the steep, rocky trail.

When they dropped back into the forest and the trail widened, Morgan walked beside Trevin.

"There are rock formations on your property just like the one Professor Esteban pointed out," the young man said.

"No one has ever found gemstones at the Rock of Ages."

"Maybe no one has looked." Trevin pushed a stray dreadlock back under his stocking cap. His honey-brown cheeks were flushed from the strenuous hike. "You could be sitting on a fortune."

"If only," Morgan said.

When Trevin had signed up for the geology class to fulfill a science requirement for his bachelor's degree, Morgan had hesitated to tag along. The handsome young man had assured her he didn't mind having a chaperone to keep coeds at bay. The quip had only been partially sarcastic, and Morgan was only partially effective as a mom-type figure to discourage the interest of the female classmates. Trevin's heart had not yet healed from the murder of his girlfriend four months ago. He was nowhere near ready for college romance.

Rain came down in huge splattering drops for a few minutes. Then just as abruptly, it lightened to a mist. Morgan enjoyed the sensation of walking in a cloud. Ambitious early wildflowers splashed yellow against the pink and gray decomposing granite that passed for soil in this part of Colorado. Professor Esteban consulted his GPS.

"We do not have far to go, as the crow flies," he said. "But there are so many switchbacks, we have three times that to hike." He tucked the GPS into a pocket of his vest. "Now that we are back in the trees, does anyone need to make a rest stop?"

Professor Esteban had reminded them constantly to drink water to avoid dehydration. Frequent trailside bathroom breaks were a necessity. As her classmates stepped off the trail, Morgan could see students through sparse undergrowth between the pines. The men especially did a cursory job of concealing themselves. Some folks seemed to lose all inhibition in the forest.

Trevin stepped back onto the trail. Necessity overrode Morgan's sense of modesty, made easier by the departure of the rest of the class down the trail.

"Go ahead," Morgan told Trevin. "I can catch up."

"No way," Trevin said. "We're supposed to be using the buddy system."

Morgan trudged toward a clump of bushes, weighed down by her heavy daypack. Del Addison, the old cowboy employed by the rock shop, had loaded her pack with what he deemed essential survival gear. Morgan had all she needed for anything from a quick trip to the bushes to a three-day stay in the wilderness.

She could see Trevin standing in the middle of the trail, scanning the pines for birds. Then she saw flashes of red, yellow, and blue as hikers garbed in brightly colored rain gear rounded a switchback. Morgan thrashed through the bushes to a more secluded spot behind a boulder and shrugged out of her daypack.

The call of nature answered, she pulled her pack onto her shoulders and headed for the trail. Morgan wished she could linger in the solitude. The voices of her classmates faded into the forest. Rain dripped off pine needles and plopped onto the rocky soil. A bird chirped a lively spring song. The peace of the forest draped around Morgan like the cloud that hugged Temple Mountain.

I need more moments like this, Morgan thought.

The temptation to linger was tempered by the reality that Trevin was waiting. Although the rain had momentarily stopped, rumbling thunder suggested that more could come. She followed her own boot-prints, the disturbances in the damp leaf mulch and pine needles obvious. Occasionally a perfect print showed in a patch of snow, alongside heart-shaped deer tracks.

A squirrel chattered from a Ponderosa pine tree. Morgan searched the branches for the creature, finally spotting the black fur and tufted ears of an Abert's squirrel. Seeing one of the shy squirrels was a treat. Yanking off her knit gloves, she fumbled for her new cell phone's camera icon, aimed at the squirrel, and tapped the shutter button.

"Darn. Missed."

She circled the trunk of the tall pine, hoping for another chance for a photo. The squirrel climbed higher, scolding her. Morgan backed up a step. Her boot sunk deep into damp mulch. She teetered for an instant, flailing with her arms, but the heavy pack pulled her off balance.

Morgan landed on her side in a narrow gulley stuffed full of rain-slick branches and leaves. As she plummeted headfirst downhill, Morgan clutched her phone with one hand and grabbed with the other at anything to slow her slide. A kaleidoscope of green pine trees and gray sky flashed by until she splashed to a stop in a puddle. Morgan scrambled to her feet, brushing leaves and mud off her wet hiking slacks. Thankfully, the gulley had deposited her at the base of a ten-foot cliff, while the runoff from the rainstorm continued its descent to a swift-moving stream. Much more rain, and she might have been washed halfway down Temple Mountain.

"Trevin!"

Morgan listened. All she heard was water gushing over rocks.

"I'm not lost," she said aloud.

If she was lost, she would do what Del had drilled into her: sit tight and wait for rescue. Morgan wiped off her cell phone. It was undamaged, but there was no signal. Her classmates had attempted several times on the hike to make calls, with no success. They had lost contact with civilization shortly after leaving the trailhead parking lot.

Morgan rested her hands on her hips and forced herself to breathe. Think. Trevin may not be worried right now, but soon he would realize something was wrong.

Morgan cupped her hands around her mouth. "Hello! Trevin!"

No answer.

"Hello!"

The forest muffled her voice, soaking it up like the rocky earth absorbed the rain. Morgan thought a person had to do spectacularly stupid things to get lost in the wilderness, but apparently all it took was losing your footing.

Trevin wouldn't panic and run through the forest looking for Morgan. He had more woods-savvy than that. No, it was more likely that he would return to the parking lot to get help.

For now, the dull light of a cloud-shrouded sun illuminated the pine forest, but soon it would drop behind Temple Mountain. Morgan studied the cliff. Crumbling earth rose above her. Even dry, it would be difficult to climb. Rain saturated, it might be dangerous. The geology class had crossed a bridge during their multi-vehicle caravan up the dirt road, carpooling to the small trailhead parking lot. If she followed the stream, surely it would lead her to the forest service road. Morgan scrambled alongside the cascading water.

When she glimpsed blue through the brush, she dared hope it was a windbreaker worn by one of her classmates. Morgan abandoned the bank of the stream. She trotted across a patch of open ground, where a rock campfire ring corralled rusting tin cans.

"Hello!" She stopped abruptly, her boots skidding on the damp gravel. "Oh."

The blue was the remnant of a tarp, faded by exposure to the elements. The shredded plastic covered a low, narrow door. If Morgan had not noticed the blue contrasting with the greens and browns of the forest, she might have hiked right by the structure.

Prospectors' shelters dotted the Colorado mountains in varied forms, from crude sod huts to finely constructed log cabins. This dugout was somewhere in between, and in better shape than the crumbling ruins Morgan had seen. From the front and both sides, it appeared to be a rough-hewn log cabin, while the rear butted up to the hillside. If she had to spend the night in the forest, the dugout might keep her dry. The wood-shingled flat roof, layered with pine needles and fallen branches, seemed intact.

Flowers in neat mounds framed the doorway. Morgan stooped to squint at them. Rows of tiny elephant heads lined up along the stems. No one would believe her, if she survived the night to tell about them. Maybe fear was making her delusional. Morgan snapped a photo. The flash probably frightened off any woodland creatures in the increasingly dark forest. Either that, or it alerted potential predators.

The clouds released a deluge of cold, stinging rain, ending her botanical study. Morgan pulled the shreds of blue tarp to one side and peeked inside. The shelter was too dark for her comfort, but most likely perfect for spiders and centipedes. She could dig a flashlight out of her pack once inside, but for now she used the flash on her cell phone camera. A half-dozen sturdy pine columns held up the roof. From the mounds of debris and expansive spider webs, she doubted a human had occupied the dugout recently. The shelter might be a disappointment in a dozen ways, but it was dry. She huddled inside the doorway, trying to think of what to do next.

Stay put. Wait for help. When the rain slowed to a drizzle, Morgan fought the urge to continue hunting for the road. Doing nothing was hard, but wandering around the forest would only make things worse. Morgan dropped her pack on the ground and unzipped a pocket, prepared for a long stay in the dugout.

Cracking branches sounded from the far bank of the creek. Morgan pushed the pack aside and peeked through the shredded strips of tarp, hoping to see Search and Rescue.

A dog barked once. A human voice muttered something that seemed to quiet the dog. Morgan strained to see through the gloom, but the sun had dropped behind the mountain, and gently falling rain muted what remained of the light. The noise of movement in the brush stopped. A step crunched in the rocky soil. Not a dog's paw. A boot.

If Trevin or one of her classmates had found the dugout, surely they would call her name, not sneak up from the side. Through the curtain of misty raindrops, she glimpsed a bizarre combination of homeless person and mountain man, dressed in canvas, leather, and fur, creeping closer to the dugout. Definitely not one of her classmates. The dark form of the dog followed.

This had to be how Sasquatch sightings started.

Morgan edged deeper inside the dugout, groping for her pack. Footsteps crunched toward the entrance. Morgan took another step backward. Her heel landed on something hard, twisting her ankle despite her firmly laced hiking boot. She threw her arms out as she stumbled, her hands grasping nothing but spider web as she fell onto the hard packed dirt floor.

The footsteps stopped. Morgan watched the shredded tarp,

knowing Big Foot had to have heard the racket of her tripping and falling. If not that, surely he could hear her raspy, panicked breathing. Silence settled over the forest. Morgan began to wonder whether he was still out there. Maybe the pounding of her heart had drowned out the sound of him leaving.

When she couldn't bear sitting motionless any longer, her body aching with tension, she rolled slowly to her hands and knees. Her right hand planted firmly on the object that had tripped her. A blanket neatly covered the mound. If she had to spend the night here, at least she had a way to keep warm. She pushed herself to her feet. As she tugged the blanket up, a cracked leather hiking boot tipped to one side. Morgan squinted in the dim light. An aspen branch seemed to extend from the bottom of a jeans leg to the boot.

That can't be right, Morgan thought. *Why would someone put clothes on sticks?*

Her mind stumbled through several explanations until the obvious answer slammed home. The rips and holes in the tattered jeans revealed bone.

Chapter Two

Morgan pressed her hands to her mouth, stifling a scream, as gravel crunched under feet just outside the dugout door. She clutched her phone, her fingers trembling as she searched for the camera icon, and the temporary light its flash would give.

A face burst through the tattered strips of blue plastic, the wet, matted whiskers and knotted hair making it seem more animal than human. Morgan tapped her phone. A brief, blinding flash lit up the dugout. The intruder threw an arm across his eyes. Then darkness returned. Morgan blinked, unable to see for an agonizing instant. Spots danced in front of her eyes, obscuring the strips of tarp that swayed from Big Foot's rapid exit.

The interior of the dugout was black as a cave after the camera's flash. When her eyes adjusted to the dark again, Morgan aimed her cell phone at the jeans-clad bones, closed her eyes, and snapped a photo. This time, people would not doubt her when she told them she'd found a dead person. If she made it out alive to tell the tale.

Footsteps crunched in the decomposing granite. The camera flash might not startle him a second time. Morgan found a stick on the hard-packed floor. It was light. Rotten. One blow and it would disintegrate. She would have to make that blow count. Whatever had happened to the skeleton in the dugout, Morgan was not going to join it. Not without a fight.

Big Foot thrust his head through the shredded tarp. The dog

followed. Or maybe it was a wolf, its fur as shaggy and matted as the man's. Morgan shook the stick at them.

"Go away!"

His hand went to his knife scabbard. If he attempted pushing words out past dry, cracked lips, his effort failed. All Morgan heard were guttural animal noises.

He pulled the curtain aside and waved his free hand. He seemed to want the same thing Morgan did—for her to get out. Morgan grabbed her daypack and pushed past him, aware of a smell like wet dog emanating from him, with overtones of sour gym clothes. He made no attempt to stop her.

Morgan bolted down the creek bed, not caring about rain or soaked boots. The skinny wolf-dog ran beside her, prancing playfully until a shrill whistle pierced the forest. He spun around and returned to his master.

Blinded by rain, Morgan nearly ran into a pillar supporting the bridge. She scrambled up the bank and crossed the bridge, then sprinted up the muddy road to the parking lot, the rotten stick still clutched in her hand.

The taillights of a vehicle illuminated the trailhead parking lot. Morgan tossed the stick aside and collapsed against Professor Esteban's lime green van.

"Mrs. Iverson!" Trevin hopped out of the van and raced to her. "I started to look for you, but it's like you just vanished. Are you okay?"

"I'm fine."

Professor Esteban held a cell phone in his hand. "I just called Search and Rescue."

"You can cancel the rescue." Morgan struggled to catch her breath. "It's too late for that. Call the police."

Morgan shivered as she described her encounter with Sasquatch, the words stuttering past her chattering teeth. She doubted she was making any sense.

"Climb inside and warm up," Professor Esteban said.

Trevin joined two other classmates in the back seat of the van. Morgan scrambled into the front passenger seat. Her clothes were soaked, and her muddy boots shed clods of dirt. The heater was on full blast. The windows fogged up, making the interior a warm cocoon. While Trevin asked for details about Morgan's discovery, Professor Esteban spoke into his cell phone, then set it to speaker and placed it on the dashboard.

Police Chief Bill Sharp's gruff voice came from the phone. "If I had to bet on who was going to report finding a body, I'd have placed my money on you, Mrs. Iverson."

"I'm not happy about it, Chief Sharp. I don't find this humorous."

"No, it's never funny when death is involved." Sharp paused. "It's raining here in town. How about there?"

"Raining cats and dogs," Professor Esteban said. "But we have taken refuge in my van."

"How many people you got there with you, Professor?"

"I'm here, sir. Trevin Pike."

"The Wickers." Everett Wicker leaned forward from his seat in the rear and shouted at the cell phone. "Mr. Everett and Mrs. Rose. From Granite Junction. We rode with Professor Esteban, so as you can surely understand, we are not pleased to have been trapped here all afternoon and half the evening."

"I am very sorry, Mr. Wicker," Esteban said. "This situation could not be helped."

Yes it could, Morgan thought. *If I hadn't been so stupid as to fall into a gulley while trying to photograph a black squirrel.*

"Please hold your discussion for a minute, folks." The chief's voice crackled over the cell phone. "Morgan, you said you saw a skeleton?"

"Yes, in an abandoned dugout."

Chief Sharp asked a question here and there, but he mostly listened. Four months ago, the police chief hadn't believed her when she found a body on a hiking trail, then lost it. She had to prove herself to him then. He seemed to take her seriously this time.

"You're sure it wasn't a deer carcass?"

Or maybe not.

"Absolutely not," Morgan said. "I have photographic evidence this time. I got a photo of the mountain man, too. I can see how people imagine they've found Sasquatch if they ran into anyone that looked like him."

"I'd better round up a couple Search and Rescue guys and head out that way."

"Any tracks have already been washed away by this rain," Esteban said.

"But the bones won't be," Chief Sharp said, "unless that mountain man moves them. I'm not taking any chances. Now you folks go on home."

"Don't you want me to show you where I found the dugout?" Morgan asked.

"I'm sure I can find it, from your description of the area," Sharp said. "Frankly, Mrs. Iverson, I'd prefer you keep out of my way this time."

The rain had turned to a frozen slush by the time Professor Esteban dropped Morgan off in Golden Springs. The class had carpooled to save space in the small trailhead parking lot.

"I apologize for inconveniencing everyone," Morgan said, not for the first time.

"The circumstances could not be helped," Professor Esteban said. "There is no need to apologize."

"Seriously," Trevin said, "we're just glad you're okay."

The Wickers did not join in reassuring Morgan. Everett

scowled, and Rose refused to look at Morgan.

It was close to nine by the time Morgan pulled her old Buick into the garage at the Rock of Ages rock shop, a place she now called home. Del sat in his recliner by the woodstove in the shop's attached living quarters, while she shed the heavy daypack, her windbreaker, hat, and gloves, and dropped her muddy boots on the worn linoleum. Morgan's shoulder-length dark curls were plastered flat with rain and sweat. She suspected she smelled nearly as bad as the mountain man.

"I took care of Houdini and Adelaide," Del said.

"Thanks." The rock shop's mascots, two mature donkeys, got cranky when their dinner of oats and hay was late. "How's Adelaide tonight?"

"The vet stopped by," Del said. "Doc McCormick says she and that foal she's carrying are doing fine. I didn't have much to do. Business was slow. Your day wasn't as uneventful, I take it?"

"That's one way of putting it. I told you most of the story on the phone." Morgan knew from past experience that Del would worry about her if she didn't check in when she was running late, especially if she was hiking in the rugged mountains. "I've already been given my full ration, so you don't need to lecture me again. My classmates the Wickers, Mr. Everett and Mrs. Rose, were furious."

"Just imagine," Del said, "if you hadn't found the parking lot, and you were stuck out all night in this weather, you could have died. I'm sure glad you had the survival pack."

The pack would have proved helpful if Morgan had accessed the gear inside instead of panicking. Everything had happened too fast. Morgan steered the discussion away from her lack of survival skills. Del might insist on hand-to-hand combat training if she told him all the details.

"A person has been missing long enough that they've been

reduced to bones." Morgan washed her hands at the sink, then opened the lid of the slow cooker. "I only hope my discovery brings someone closure."

"I've been stirring and adding water," Del said. "Like you told me."

"Did you have dinner yet?" Morgan asked.

"I was waiting for you." Del tugged at his bushy gray mustache.

"Likely story," Morgan said. "I'll bet you just forgot to eat."

The old cowboy was skinny enough without missing meals. A tooled leather belt cinched blue jeans to his lean frame. A thick flannel shirt and fleece vest made him appear heavier than he was, but Morgan knew he'd lost weight recently.

Morgan opened a cupboard door and reached for bowls. There was no dining room. The kitchen and living area were all one room, and not in an open-floor-plan kind of design. The place was just plain tiny.

"I have a theory." Del rose from the recliner. At six foot three, he was taller than Morgan by nearly a foot. "Golden Springs hasn't had many cases of missing people. A few hunters or hikers, the occasional young scout wandering away from their troop during a camping trip."

"You told me when I first moved here." Morgan shuddered, still chilled from her misadventure and the fear of what could have been. "Something about flatlanders' frozen bodies being found in snow banks every spring."

"I may have exaggerated just a bit," Del said. "They've all been found alive. Except for one girl. About sixteen years ago. Gerda's daughter."

"Gerda has a daughter?" Morgan asked. "Gerda the mechanic?"

Gerda Kruger ran the small town's only auto repair garage. She and her two employees kept the citizens of Golden Springs mobile, working on everything from passenger cars to snow mobiles.

"Two daughters," Del said. "One girl moved to somewhere in Kansas. Gerda never talks about her. Rumor at the time was they had a falling out, but maybe the kid just didn't like small town life. Shortly after she left, the other daughter disappeared."

Morgan wondered if that was why Gerda always seemed to have a bottle of booze nearby.

"Tell me about the missing daughter."

Morgan ladled up two bowls of beef stew.

"Back when the West was wilder," Del said, "Golden Springs was populated with prospectors, gamblers, and women of ill repute. Occasionally a person would just disappear. Maybe they left town of their own volition, but some most likely ran afoul of outlaws or claim jumpers. Nowadays we have Pine County Search and Rescue, with all their fancy equipment. Even helicopters. But in this case, nothing helped. The girl was just gone. The one cold case in modern Golden Springs history."

"So did she leave town?" Morgan broke a corn muffin in two and buttered half. "Like the other daughter?"

"Nobody seems to know," Del said. "Maybe she got lost. Like you did today, kid." He nodded at Morgan. To sixty-seven-year-old Del, anyone under the age of fifty qualified as a kid. "The whole town searched the mountains, but that's a lot of territory."

"Do you think Gerda's daughter was murdered?" Morgan hoped not. In January, she had stumbled onto a much more recent body.

"Considering you found her in a dugout on Temple Mountain," Del said, "I think it's more likely she got lost, and wasn't lucky enough to find her way out."

Morgan set her spoon down. "I took photos." She noticed the look Del shot her way, so she explained. "That must seem ghoulish, but after losing the last body I ran across, I wanted to have evidence this one existed. Hopefully the photos turned out."

She pushed back her chair and retrieved her phone from her windbreaker pocket. The new phone had lots of buttons and gadgets. Apps, her friend Bernie called them. Fortunately, they had little icons that mostly matched up to her expectation of what the function of the app was. Morgan worked her way to the photos. Her attempts to photograph the black Abert's squirrel had failed, but she had a pretty good shot of the mountain man. She handed the phone to Del.

"I think you found a dead bear."

Morgan took the phone from him. "No, this is the mountain man. I would have voted for Sasquatch at the time, but when my initial terror faded, he looked more like a homeless man. He had a wild matted beard, his clothes were filthy and torn, and he carried a butcher knife in a leather scabbard at his waist."

Del squinted at the phone's screen. "That's not a butcher knife. It's just a hunting knife."

"What's he hunting? Elephants?" Morgan brushed her finger across the screen to the next photo. "These are the bones."

Blurry and underexposed, the photo did not show much but a dark mound. Morgan enlarged the picture. The subdued colors of faded denim, a red windbreaker, and what seemed to be a yellow knit cap showed against the packed dirt floor.

"The picture of the man looks like a bear, and the picture of the skeleton looks like a pile of laundry. I don't know how these are gonna help any." Del tugged at his mustache. "I sure hope this was due to natural causes. I'd hate to see you caught up in another murder case. The last one nearly killed you."

Chapter Three

In the morning, Morgan braved slick roads. The aging Buick's tires were a few millimeters away from bald, but she had managed to survive the Colorado winter. Now that it was May, she had deluded herself into believing new tires could wait until fall. She was relieved to reach the Golden Springs Community Church without sliding into an irrigation ditch.

The stained-glass windows added visual warmth to the exterior of the stone church. Central heat warmed the interior. Morgan was an unofficial member of the church kitchen ladies, helping brew coffee and set out cookies for the after-service social hour. She walked in and grabbed an apron, wrapping it around her going-to-church wool slacks and pink striped blouse.

"Good morning, Morgan." Beatrice Stonewall clasped her hands together as though she could barely contain her excitement. "So, do you have any news for us?"

The other two ladies looked up from arranging store-bought cookies on trays.

"I do have news." Morgan tied the apron strings behind her back.

If Golden Springs Community Church was the wheel upon which local gossip turned, Beatrice was definitely its hub. The sturdy older woman's short, steel-gray hair seemed to stand at attention as she waited for Morgan's morsel of information. Apparently, Morgan didn't speak quickly enough to suit Beatrice.

"I'll bet I can guess. Morgan, you hit it off with Pete."

Morgan suppressed the urge to cringe.

"I do appreciate you making the arrangements," she said. "But Pete and I don't have much in common."

Morgan wasn't sure why she'd agreed to go to dinner with Pete Melcher, except that Beatrice was a difficult person to refuse. He wasn't interested in any of the things that filled Morgan's world, like hiking, rocks, and donkeys.

"How can you say that?" Beatrice asked. "You have lots of things in common. You both live in Golden Springs. You attend the same church. I'm sure if you get to know Pete better, you'll find you share many of the same experiences."

Perhaps, Morgan thought, but having done some of the same things in life didn't equate with a shared enjoyment of those experiences. Pete did say he had been camping, but his description of a night in a tent had been tinged with horror at the discomforts. In fact, the outdoors seemed to frighten him.

"You can't tell these things after just one date," Beatrice added.

"That's not the news I had," Morgan said, hoping to deflect Beatrice's matchmaking attempt. "I found a skeleton."

"On your date?" Beatrice asked. "Pete didn't tell me anything about skeletons."

"No, not on my date. Yesterday. During my last geology class field trip."

Teruko McCormick shook her head, as though gently scolding Morgan for her penchant for discovering dead people. The woman with a halo of soft white curls had surely never done anything scandalous in her life.

"Del thinks I might have stumbled across Gerda Kruger's missing daughter," Morgan said.

"He could be right." Anna poured a pitcher of water into the industrial-sized coffee pot. The woman's face was lined from years spent hiking and skiing at high altitude. She was tall and lean, and in much better shape than Morgan. "That's the only cold case in recent history."

Beatrice scrunched her face into a thoughtful expression. "How recent was the body?"

"The hiking boots and jeans looked modern," Morgan said. "There wasn't a body, exactly. Just bones. I have a photo on my phone."

Teruko wrung the dishtowel with both frail hands.

"Well, let's see it," Beatrice said.

The ladies erupted with questions. The blurry, poorly exposed photos did not help answer them. Morgan had to tell the tale again of falling in a gulley, stumbling onto the dugout, seeing a skeleton clad in hiking clothes, and having the daylights scared out of her by a smelly man who resembled Sasquatch.

"Del believes she got lost in the forest," Morgan said.

"She might have run away from home," Anna said. "Like the other daughter."

"Impossible," Beatrice said in her no nonsense tone. "Gerda's daughter was twenty-something years old when she went missing. People that old don't run away from home. Besides, she was engaged to Jade Tinsley. Why would she run away?"

"I remember," Teruko said in a quavering voice with a trace of a Japanese accent. "They were very much in love. Carlee would not leave her soul mate."

"Maybe Jade changed his mind," Anna said. "He could have killed her to get out of going through with the marriage."

Beatrice and Teruko spoke at the same time, with the same message. They had known the couple. Jade would never have harmed Carlee.

"Then the most logical answer is that she got lost in the forest." Morgan shrugged. "Del pointed out that if I hadn't found my way back to the parking lot, and I had to spend the night in that sleet storm, I could have died."

"The autopsy will tell the tale," Beatrice said.

"Can a skeleton be autopsied?" Morgan asked.

"Certainly." The heavyset, gray-haired lady who looked like she'd be most at home with a tray of cookies in her hands proceeded to give the grisly details. "There's an old saying that dead men tell no tales, but that's not true. The entire story is written in their remains. Fractures in neck vertebrae mean strangulation. Gouges in the ribs, a knife to the heart. Broken skull bones—"

"Enough, Beatrice." Anna held up a hand to ward off the gushing stream of information. "We understand."

"I'll invite my nephew Roger over for dinner this week," Beatrice said. "He'll have the details."

Beatrice regularly squeezed forensics information from recent cases out her nephew, an employee of the crime lab in the nearby city of Granite Junction.

"If the remains are Carlee Kruger's," Teruko said, "we must treat this as we would any death in the family, even though many years have passed."

"Right," Beatrice said. "We'll take her some casseroles, offer to help arrange a memorial service. People remember her daughter. Carlee was a beautiful girl. Her disappearance left a hole in us all."

"But we don't know if it is her daughter," Morgan said. "You saw the photo. I only caught a glimpse of bone and rotted clothing."

"What did Chief Sharp have to say about the identity of the person?" Beatrice asked.

"Nothing," Morgan said. "He was hoping it was a deer, but I've never seen a deer wear jeans and hiking boots."

The introit music began. The ladies hung up their aprons and hurried into the sanctuary. After hymns, announcements, and a scripture reading by one of the elders, Pastor James Filbury took his place behind the pulpit. He looked the part of a pastor, with thinning silver hair groomed short and neat, and oversized eyeglasses a couple decades out of date.

His sermons were as exciting as a mug of warm milk: soothing, and with a tendency to cure insomnia. The church had a vibrant youth program begun by Morgan's brother Kendall and his wife, Allie, before they left on their mission trip to the Central American jungle. A couple in their late twenties had kept the program going, infusing it with even more energy. When young people graduated from the youth program to the church, they were going to be disappointed.

Pastor Filbury's numbing sermon stopped abruptly, mid-sentence. Expectant silence echoed through the pews. He tugged at the knot of a blue necktie that peeked above his black clerical robe as though it was choking him. The pastor grasped the podium with his free hand, his already pale face losing what little color it had. He slid to the floor.

Congregants rushed from their pews toward the stage, but Pete Melcher and another usher held them back. Elder Thompson knelt beside the pastor.

"Give us some room," Thompson said. "Someone call 9-1-1."

Pete flapped his hands at the congregation. "Will everyone please adjourn to the social hall?" His nasal voice went an octave higher than usual.

Beatrice, Teruko, and Anna jumped into action, coaxing the coffee brewing into high speed and pulling plastic wrap off trays of cookies.

Morgan's part-time employee, Cindy, her husband, Herb, and five red-haired children filed past the kitchen door. Herb held the new baby, number six, in one arm. A shock of fine, pale red hair peeked out from a knitted cap. Cindy leaned into the kitchen.

"Anything I can help with?"

"We've got the kitchen under control," Beatrice said. "You can take these out to the social hall."

She handed Cindy a tray of cookies. Morgan followed, ready to clear space on a long folding table.

"Have you heard anything?" Cindy asked Morgan. "What's going on in there?" She nodded toward the closed sanctuary doors.

"I don't know any more than you do," Morgan said. "Pastor Filbury looked so pale this morning during the sermon."

"The poor man hasn't been the same since that business earlier this year," Cindy said. The kindly old pastor had been falsely accused of a terrible crime. "His reputation was cleared, but I think it broke his heart all the same."

An ambulance pulled up in the parking lot. EMTs rushed into the church. No one seemed anxious to leave, huddling in small clusters in the social hall. After what seemed an eternity, the doors to the sanctuary burst open and the EMTs wheeled out a gurney. Mrs. Filbury hurried alongside, clasping the pastor's hand. Morgan was relieved to see they hadn't covered Pastor Filbury's face with the sheet.

After the ladies had the kitchen clean and in order, Anna pulled Morgan aside.

"Would you mind giving Teruko a ride home? I told Kurt I would help him work on the advertising guide this afternoon."

Morgan smiled. She suspected Anna and her boss, Kurt, owner and editor of the *Golden Springs Gazetteer,* had more than a working relationship. Anna's weathered skin made her appear several years older than Kurt, but Morgan didn't know either's age. She suspected that like her, they were in their forties, when some people still looked youthful while others were already wearing their years on their faces.

"I don't mind at all," Morgan said.

When she and Teruko pulled onto Aspen Street, they saw the police chief's SUV.

"I believe Chief Sharp is driving toward Kruger's Auto Repair," Teruko said.

"Let's see."

Morgan followed as discreetly as she could, considering the street was narrow and traffic was light. The police chief didn't seem to notice. He pulled his SUV into the garage's small asphalt parking lot. Parking spaces were jealously guarded in Golden Springs. A rack of tires marked the division between the self-service laundry and Kruger's Auto Repair. On the right side of the garage, a row of boarded-up cabins hid behind a lot overrun with winter-killed weeds. Morgan's family had stayed in one of the cabins years ago, before the low-budget tourist resort had gone out of business.

"Maybe we should come back later," Morgan said.

"She was a great help to me when my husband passed away." Teruko touched Morgan's arm. "I must return the kindness. Gerda will need her friends."

Morgan hardly considered herself Gerda's friend. A customer, yes, but the squat woman was a difficult person to befriend. When Morgan tried to imagine Gerda doing Teruko a great kindness, an image failed to form. She seemed to hold the world at arm's length. Morgan parked and trotted around the car to give Teruko a hand. Before they were half way across the parking lot, Bill Sharp pushed open the office's scarred glass door.

"Now's not a good time." He spoke through clenched teeth, his cheeks flushed red. Chief Sharp had the rugged looks of a cowboy actor, just shy of handsome, and slightly over-the-hill, with a paunch straining the silver buttons on his leather vest. The star-shaped badge and ever-present cowboy hat completed the look. At the moment, he looked as though he'd just faced down a dangerous outlaw, and come out on the bad end of the deal.

"We are Mrs. Kruger's friends," Teruko said. "She needs us."

"Mrs. Kruger is a tough old bird," the chief said. "She'll be just fine."

"I will let Gerda tell me whether she needs a friend now." Teruko quietly pushed her way past the man who was twice her size, an unquenchable determination propelling the tiny woman in the cream-colored skirt and jacket.

Morgan looked up at the chief. "So the bones I found? They were Gerda's daughter's?"

"We won't know until the dental and medical records check out. Seems likely, though. I wanted Gerda to hear it from me before the news ran through the gossip mill."

"Did she take it hard?" Morgan asked.

"Cool as a cucumber," Chief Sharp said. "But that's Gerda. She doesn't show a lot of emotion. Other than anger."

Chapter Four

Morgan entered the untidy office. Gerda sat behind the gray metal desk, staring at the stained circle where her bottle of bourbon used to reside. She hadn't done much to hide her fondness for drink. She seemed loath to let anyone know she was now attending AA meetings in the basement of the church once a week. Morgan hoped this blow wouldn't push her back to drinking.

While Teruko dragged a metal folding chair next to the desk, Gerda glared at Morgan. Short white hair stuck up from her scalp, and a dark blue jumpsuit splotchy with grease stains covered her stout figure.

"Go away." Her words erupted with a terse German accent. "I wish to be left alone."

"This is not a time to be alone," Teruko said in her soothing, whisper-soft voice. "You need your friends."

"I do not have any friends. I do not need your comfort. Chief Sharp is wrong. That was not my Carlee."

"How do you know?" Morgan hoped Gerda had a definitive reason for doubting the chief's report.

"My daughter ran away from home. She has forgotten all about her mother the drunk. She does not need or want me. That is why I have not heard from her in sixteen years." Gerda stood, pressing her hands against her desk. "You may leave now." In a less harsh voice she added, "Go now. Please."

Teruko stood. Gerda came around the desk and shooed her

toward the office door. Morgan followed. She turned to give a parting dose of ineffective comfort, but Gerda slammed the door in her face.

"That didn't go well," Morgan said.

"The time will come when she needs us," Teruko said, "and she will know we are here for her."

When she returned to the Rock of Ages, a respectable sprinkling of vehicles filled the parking lot. Business had improved since Morgan's arrival in January, due in equal measures to the new sign in town, coupons in the *Golden Springs Gazetteer,* a fledgling website, and the blooming tourist season. The shop was not flourishing, but they were getting by.

Del manned the cash register. Lucy Geary stood beside the display of her handcrafted Native American jewelry. The young woman fussed with the arrangement of necklaces, bracelets, and earrings while two ladies crowded near, asking questions. The jewelry Lucy left on consignment was one of the best sellers in the Rock of Ages. Some were traditional Arapaho beadwork, while the rest had a modern, artistic flair.

When they had a lull in activity, Lucy sat on the aspen wood bench and crossed her long legs. She was dressed in just-came-from-church slacks and a plain blouse that showed her turquoise necklace nicely. Her long, black hair draped down her back nearly to her waist.

"The rumors are all over town," Lucy said. "You found a body and Sasquatch. I'm not sure which one has people more excited."

Del leaned against the checkout counter, a smile lifting the corners of his bushy gray mustache.

"Did you go to Golden Springs High School?" Morgan asked Lucy.

"Home of the fighting eagles," Lucy said. "I'm a graduate.

But what's that got to do with a body and Big Foot?"

Morgan shook her head. "You wouldn't have been in the same class. Sixteen years ago, Carlee Kruger disappeared."

"Right. I was in grade school then, but I remember the searches. The entire town was in an uproar. They never found her."

"Morgan did," Del said.

"Maybe," Morgan said. "As far as I know, the body, or rather, the skeleton, hasn't been identified yet."

Morgan told Lucy the story she had repeated several times in less than a day. Del interjected with running commentary about the proper survival reaction to becoming lost in the mountains.

"When I left church this morning," Morgan said, "Teruko and I saw Chief Sharp stop at Gerda's garage."

"So the bones are Gerda's daughter's," Lucy said.

"The chief seemed to think so," Morgan said. "He wanted to give Gerda a warning before she heard the news through the gossip mill."

"Poor Gerda," Lucy said. "She's had such a tough time. I heard the younger daughter moved away and never talks to her. No wonder she drinks."

"Let's get the gossip straight," Del said. "Gerda's been going to AA meetings." He tugged at his mustache. "She lost her husband, then the younger daughter up and left town. Now you find the remains of the older daughter. I sure hope this doesn't knock her off the wagon."

"She's in denial right now," Morgan said. "Gerda told Teruko and me that the chief is wrong. She said her daughter ran away sixteen years ago, but Beatrice and the church ladies don't believe that."

"What happened to Gerda's husband?" Lucy asked.

"I forget what it was exactly," Del said. "Some kind of cancer."

The same monster that had stolen Morgan's husband, Sam,

over two years ago.

"Gerda's never been one to admit to weakness or ask for help," Del continued. "I imagine dealing with Karl's death, suddenly being a single mom, trying to run the business by herself, it was a lot to handle."

"Neither Teruko nor Beatrice think Carlee would have run away," Morgan said. "She was engaged to some artist."

"Jade Tinsley," Del said. "He's still around. Has an art store off Main Street."

Lucy snorted. "Him."

"What?" Morgan asked.

"I asked once if I could leave some of my jewelry on consignment in his gallery. Jade thought that would be great, but his wife said my beadwork wasn't suitable for a fine art gallery." Lucy's eyes filled with tears. "I can't believe I let it bother me that much. I know my work is good, but she made me feel worthless. She's a witch. Not literally. I don't think. But the less you have to do with Mia Cooper and her entire family, the better."

Morgan smelled a motivation. Jade's wife might have eliminated her romantic rival. "Was Mia around when Carlee disappeared?"

"No," Del said. "She was back east attending college. Swooped in like a hawk on that boy when she did come home. But he's done real well since then. Mia's a Cooper, like Lucy said. Wherever they go, the money follows. And the trouble."

"Maybe Carlee ran away because of her mother's drinking," Lucy said. "Or maybe Jade broke off the engagement and broke her heart."

"After sixteen years, I doubt anyone will find out exactly what happened," Del said. "Stories can change a lot over time."

★ ★ ★ ★ ★

Adelaide snorted, then pawed the straw that padded the packed dirt floor of her stall. The short whiskers that surrounded her mouth seemed drawn into a frown as her large brown eyes followed Morgan. Adelaide was not in a good mood. Houdini wandered around the pasture instead of coming inside the barn for his dinner, perhaps seeking distance from his cranky wife.

"I'm early tonight," Morgan said. "You can't complain."

But Adelaide did, with an impatient stomp of one front hoof. The donkey's sides looked full to bursting with the foal she was carrying, and her spindly legs did not look substantial enough to support her body.

Morgan resisted the urge to give Adelaide extra feed, sticking to the veterinarian's prescription diet. The sturdy little animals did not do well on a rich diet, but Adelaide did need extra vitamins and minerals.

"Anybody here?" a man's voice called.

Morgan turned to the open barn door. Kurt Willard shaded his eyes as he peered inside.

"By the stalls," Morgan said.

Kurt wore sensible walking shoes these days, after filling up his dress shoes with snow while chasing clues in January. He still wore his nineteen forties'–style reporter outfit, covered with a brown trench coat and topped with a fedora, a "press" card tucked into the hatband.

"How's Adelaide doing?" he asked.

"I thought nine months was a long time to carry a baby. Doctor McCormick told me donkeys typically carry their foals for twelve months. The poor thing still has two or three months to go, but she's a tough one."

Kurt reached over the stall to rub Adelaide's forehead. Morgan half-expected the donkey to bite Kurt, but she seemed to like the newspaper editor. Turning to a stack of hay beside the tack room, Morgan tugged at a bale. A mouse emerged from between two of the bottom bales and scurried across her foot. Morgan jumped back and squealed.

Kurt laughed, his cheeks flushing a deeper shade of red. He had the sort of boyish good looks that added years and extra pounds just seemed to mellow. Men were lucky that way.

"You need a cat," Kurt said.

"I'm not afraid of mice," Morgan said.

Kurt raised one eyebrow.

"It startled me, okay?"

Morgan reached again for the bale of hay, dragging it off the top of the stack. She pulled a pink pocketknife out of her jeans pocket and cut the orange plastic baling twine. They had started out adversaries, but when Kurt's quick actions saved Del's life three months ago, she had changed her opinion of the newspaperman.

Morgan broke a flake off the bale and tossed it into the stall, then turned, leaning against the worn wood railings.

"So what brings you out here tonight?" Morgan suspected she already knew.

"You're once again the talk of the town." Kurt pulled his ever-present notepad and pencil from an inside pocket of his trench coat. "Care to make a statement?"

With Kurt, it was better to tell him the story rather than let him find "sources" who made good headlines but got the facts all wrong. Morgan told him about falling down a gulley on the geology class field trip, then stumbling across the dugout. Kurt had questions about the skeletal remains and the smelly mountain man, but Morgan had precious few details. She didn't tell him about the photos. They would end up plastered across the front page of the *Golden Springs Gazetteer.*

"It happened so fast," Morgan said. "And it was rainy and dark."

"I spoke to Chief Sharp. He thinks there's a high probability that the remains are Carlee Kruger's. I asked if there was ID on the body, but he wouldn't say."

"People told me there was a massive search when Carlee disappeared, so I imagine it was in the paper. Do your archives go back sixteen years?"

"Anna has been scanning and filing electronic copies of old newspapers," Kurt said. "They go back to the town's founding in 1876. If the *Gazetteer* ever burned down, so would half the history of Pine County. Or if the mice got into the archives. Maybe I need a cat, too. Long story short, I'm sure we have everything from sixteen years ago."

Houdini finally wandered into his stall. Morgan tossed hay to him, and sprinkled a half a coffee can of oats into the small trough. Kurt seemed in no hurry to leave. When it became clear he was fishing for an invitation, Morgan asked him to stay for stew. If she didn't know him better, she might have thought he wanted to spend time with her socially, but Kurt's motivation was clear. The *Golden Springs Gazetteer* needed headlines. He was hoping for more details about the skeleton and the mountain man.

CHAPTER FIVE

When Cindy showed up Monday morning for work, she carried her baby in a car seat. Both were bundled up against the chilly May morning. Under the layers that Cindy peeled off, she wore her usual ankle-length denim skirt over red cowgirl boots and a loose pioneer-style gingham blouse.

"Good morning, Cowgirl!" It was Cindy's signature greeting. "I hope you don't mind, but I can't leave Hezekiah very long, and it's not worth it for me to drive to work for just a couple hours."

"Not a problem." Morgan peeked inside the blankets covering the car seat. Hezekiah's promising puff of red fuzz matched his mother's hair, although hers was piled on top of her head in a bun. "I understand about nursing babies. And Hezekiah is so quiet."

"You should hear him when he's hungry, or needs a diaper changed. Herb will be happy when the baby sleeps the whole night. Of course he doesn't have to get up to nurse Hezekiah, but it still wakes him when I do."

"Herb must be used to that by now."

"Sure, but he's up for a promotion, and he needs to be to work on time. There's no dragging your behind into work late when you're bucking for the supervisor position."

"That's great," Morgan said. "I hope he gets the job."

"Us too. He'd get a big raise. The problem is, Herb wouldn't have as much flexibility to watch the kids when I go to work.

He'd need to be on site all the time. I'll have to quit."

"Oh." Morgan felt Cindy's words like a knife in the heart. She depended on her part-time employee. Cindy could handle the rock shop by herself, and often did when Morgan needed to run errands. "Should I start looking for someone to replace you? Not that you can be replaced."

"I'll let you know as soon as Herb hears anything. Don't worry. I won't go running off on you without warning."

Morgan's brother Kendall had dumped the Rock of Ages on her without warning. She had not realized at the time how fortunate she was that the staff of two part-time employees knew the rock shop business inside out.

"There's so much I haven't learned yet about running the Rock of Ages," Morgan said. "I've been handling the souvenirs, the advertising, and I have a website up and running. But how do I replenish stock? We're running out of shark's teeth. Where on earth does a person purchase wholesale shark's teeth?"

"Kendall bought things at other shops once in a while, or from local prospectors. But mostly, he'd hit the big wholesalers. That, and he and Allie'd go to three or four gem and mineral shows a year."

With Hezekiah safely tucked away behind the checkout counter, Cindy took her seat on the tall stool by the cash register.

"There are still boxes of stuff in the garage and the barn loft that I haven't gone through," Morgan said. "Kendall and Allie must have been doing more buying than selling."

"Well that's the good news. You might still consider stocking up on more souvenir-type stuff."

"With the summer tourist season coming?" Morgan asked.

"I'm talking about your latest adventure," Cindy said. "People are ready to go hunting Sasquatches in the hills. That might bring in a lot of nosey customers. I'll bet they'd snap up all the Big Foot items you could stock."

Morgan pushed stray curls out of her eyes. "Seriously? Okay, I might have said he resembled Big Foot, but what I saw was a large, smelly mountain man."

"That's all it takes. And whoa!" Cindy waved her arms in the air. "People are off and running. Same thing happened a couple years ago when the Air Force was flying a new fighter jet around, and people thought the aliens were invading. I tried to convince Allie to stock alien stuff in the shop. We missed out on that deal. This might be our second chance."

"I don't know. People might think I made the whole thing up just to make a buck."

Cindy shrugged. "Just trying to help."

"You're right, though. Go ahead and check out the catalogs. See what's out there for Big Foot souvenirs."

Cindy smiled at that, and pulled out the stack of dog-eared souvenir catalogs.

"I'd better take advantage of having you here," Morgan said. "Now that I've got the shop's records straightened out, I need to stay on top of the paperwork."

Morgan closed herself inside the tiny shop office. The files had come a long way from their original chaos, most importantly going from piles scattered over the desk, floor, and on top of the filing cabinet to actually being in the cabinet, in labeled folders. Her friend Bernie, owner of the popular Bibi's Bakery, had suggested Morgan hire her accountant to file the rock shop's taxes, and Morgan was glad she did. He had saved her a bundle. He had also given her a lengthy list of forms and paperwork to keep track of for next year's taxes. Morgan welcomed the interruption of a tap on the door. Cindy opened the door a crack.

"Better pick up this call," she said. "Sounds important."

Morgan lifted the receiver.

"Mrs. Iverson, I actually need your help." There was almost no trace of sarcasm in Chief Sharp's tone. "Can you come down to the police station? The sooner the better."

"Is there a problem?" The classic question people asked authority figures when they weren't certain whether they were in trouble or not.

"I just need you to look at some photos. See if you recognize your mountain man."

The two-man police force occupied an office inside City Hall. The deputy sat at a scarred metal desk, blocking entry into the rest of the room. Cubicle walls divided the back two-thirds of the room into two small offices.

"Good morning, J.B." The deputy looked young enough to be her son. He didn't seem to mind her informality, but Morgan reminded herself to treat him with the deference owed an officer of the law. "Deputy Parker, the chief asked me to come in."

"Yes ma'am." J.B.'s uniform shirt was crisply pressed, and his eagerness to serve was written all over his face. "He wants you to look at mug shots. I mean, photographs. We're not supposed to call them mug shots because it might cause you to be prejudiced and pick the guy that's been arrested before." Deputy Parker glanced over his shoulder, then back at Morgan. He lowered his voice. "Just between you, me, and the fence post, you can tell which are mug shots, even though they tried to trim out the background."

"Deputy." Chief Sharp's voice boomed over a cubicle wall. "Is that Mrs. Iverson?"

"Yes, sir. She's here," he yelled back.

"Well, send her back here, why don't you?"

"Yes, sir." He pointed to a wooden coat rack in the front corner, between two metal folding chairs. "You can put your coat there."

Morgan shrugged out of her lilac-colored fleece jacket and

hung it on a hook. Then she followed Deputy Parker around the desk. At the end of the narrow hallway separating the two cubicles, a calendar from the feed store hung on the wall. Below it was a thigh-high refrigerator supporting a coffeemaker covered with spilled sugar and dried coffee drips. The pot had an opaque sludge coating its bottom, and was in need of a run through a dishwasher. Chief Sharp must have noticed her staring, mistaking her look of horror for desire.

"Help yourself."

"I have water." Morgan lifted her purse, showing him the bottle in a mesh side pocket.

"Why don't you pull up a chair?"

There was no pulling to be done. The folding chair was squished between the cubicle wall and the desk. Morgan squeezed inside the cramped cubicle and perched sidesaddle on the gray metal chair. When she became a Colorado resident, she would vote "yes" to every request for more funds for the police.

"I was thinking about your description of the mountain man you encountered in the dugout." Bill Sharp rested his clasped hands on his desk. With his cowboy hat off, she could see strands of white in his dark hair. "When we went up there, I didn't see any trace of him. Nothing. Of course, all the footprints outside were washed away by the rain and sleet. The ones inside indicated he's one large fella. If he was accustomed to using the dugout for shelter, he was careful not to leave any personal items there."

"Why would he stay in there with a dead person?"

"I've seen stranger things in my career in law enforcement, believe you me."

Chief Sharp pulled out a photo album. Morgan raised one eyebrow at the smiling puppy on the cover.

"Our budget is tight," Sharp said. "This was on sale." He opened the album. "I'd like you to take a look at these photos.

Tell me if any of these fellas look familiar."

He turned the album to face Morgan. The deputy was right. She could tell which were mug shots.

"Before I forget," Morgan said, "I have a photo."

"Of the mountain man?"

"Yes. It's not very good." She pulled her phone out and found her way to the photos. "I also took a photo of the body. Or skeleton. Or whatever you call it."

"Remains." Chief Sharp examined the screen of Morgan's phone. "We took plenty of photos of the scene before the coroner moved the remains. I can barely see anything on this tiny screen."

"I'll email them to you," Morgan said.

"Okay. Might prove helpful. So how about you look at my photos?"

Morgan flipped through the photo album.

"None of these look like the man I saw, and I only got a glimpse of him."

"Any impressions a camera doesn't capture would be helpful."

"Okay." Morgan closed her eyes, trying to relive the terrifying moment. "The impression I got was that he's white, under all that dirt. He was huge, but you already figured that out. He filled the entire dugout entrance, and had to crouch down when he came inside. He had a beard this long." She held a hand halfway to her lap. "His hair was matted. His clothes were kind of Old West in style, but looked like they came from a Dumpster. The thing I noticed the most was his smell. Or stench, I should say."

"Take another look. Maybe something will jump out at you. His eyes, or his nose?"

Morgan held her hands over each photo, blocking out the facial hair, or lack thereof, and the tops of their heads. All she could remember was the tangled beard. She tried to imagine each man with the beard. She held her cell phone, with the blurry photo displayed, next to each of the mug shots. She shook her head.

"He could be one of these guys. I just can't tell."

"If anything comes to mind that you think will help identify the guy, let me know first. Don't discuss this with Beatrice, and especially don't try to run him to ground yourself."

"I'd be happy if I never saw him again. Except for Gerda's sake. Were the bones those of her daughter?"

"The Granite Junction coroner has the remains. I'd say it's more than likely, but remember that I'm just guessing here, based on when Carlee disappeared, and certain other considerations."

"Was there an ID on the, er, remains? Was she murdered?"

"I couldn't tell you even if I knew." Chief Sharp folded his arms across his chest and leaned back in his office chair. "We can't confirm anything until the coroner finishes his job. This being a cold case, it's probably not high on his priority list."

Morgan called the shop. Cindy and her baby were doing fine, so she stopped by the *Golden Springs Gazetteer.* Kurt's newspaper had the feel of a museum, with headlines of local and national historical importance hanging from the walls in rustic frames, and décor reflecting a previous century.

Anna was not at the front desk. The top half of the Dutch door to Kurt's office was open. Morgan peeked inside, but he wasn't around, either. Morgan called out a "hello," then followed the sound of "back here."

Anna crouched over the bottom drawer of a metal filing cabinet. Her power suit was appropriate for working at a major corporation. Morgan still didn't know much of Anna's history, despite the time they spent together in the church kitchen, but it had to be an interesting story. Kurt leaned over a table, sorting folders into stacks.

"The paper's archives go back to the beginning of time," Kurt said. "It took us all morning to locate the correct decade, but we found a considerable amount of information about the Carlee Kruger case."

"I didn't mean to put you through all this trouble," Morgan said.

"Are you kidding?" Kurt came around the table. "Golden Springs's only unsolved case post horse-and-buggy era? You're not the only one who can play amateur sleuth."

Morgan held up her hands. "Oh, no. I learned my lesson back in January. The only reason I got involved in that case was because someone was out to get me. I was investigating out of self-defense." She cradled her left arm against her torso. "My arm has finally healed. I have no desire to risk another cracked bone, or worse, by tangling with a killer again."

"That's good," Anna said. "Kurt doesn't want any competition solving this one." She slapped another folder onto the table. "I've got other work to do."

As she left the room, Trevin Pike entered, carrying a cardboard box. Dark hair hung to his shoulders in matted ropes.

"I found these in the basement," Trevin said. "I think they're negatives."

"Great place for photographic treasures," Kurt muttered. "In the damp basement. I hope they're still good."

Trevin set the box on the floor. "There are lots more. Hi, Mrs. Iverson. And bye."

"Nice to see you, Trevin." Morgan was relieved to see the young man successfully turn his life around. He enjoyed his job at the newspaper, and was doing well in college. He probably aced the geology class.

"What brings you to town?" Kurt smiled.

"Chief Sharp called me in to look at mug shots," Morgan said.

"Did you ID the mountain man?" Kurt asked.

"No. If his picture was in the album, I didn't recognize him. The men in the mug shots were clean and neat, comparatively speaking. The chief thinks there's a good chance the bones might have been Gerda's daughter's, but he wouldn't say anything more than that. Oh, and for me to butt out."

"Did he know whether she died of natural causes?"

"Until the coroner files a report, we won't know."

Morgan reached for a folder on the table.

"Ah, not yet." Kurt threw himself in front of the table. "I want to get everything organized before we start assembling the clues."

"I have no interest in solving the case," Morgan said. "But Gerda needs answers."

Chapter Six

As she pushed open the front door to the Rock of Ages, the cowbell didn't clang. Morgan looked up. A washrag muffled the cowbell's clapper. Cindy sat on the aspen bench in front of the checkout counter, her red cowgirl boots crossed at the ankles. She held a finger to her lips and nodded at her baby, sleeping beside her on the bench. Morgan tiptoed across the creaky pine floor.

"I just got him to sleep," Cindy whispered. "Every time someone opened the door, the cowbell woke him up."

"Did you have customers?"

"Half the time it was Del going in and out. He's working on his trailer. Oops."

The baby scrunched his little red face and pulled his tiny hands into fists. Morgan held her breath until the baby relaxed, still sleeping.

"I can take Hezekiah into the office," Morgan whispered. "It would be quieter."

"Herb's coming to pick me up in a few minutes," Cindy said. "He had an interview for that promotion. I figured he might as well swing by and pick me up on his way home. If you don't mind."

"Not at all," Morgan said. "Where are the rest of the kids?" Morgan couldn't imagine the troop of two girls and three boys accompanying Herb to a job interview.

"He dropped them off at my mom's. She took off work to

watch the kids. He was so nervous."

Morgan couldn't imagine the lumberjack-sized redhead having a case of nerves. He could probably win a wrestling match with a bear.

"You should have let me know," Morgan said. "We could have managed the shop without you for a day."

"Maybe I had a case of the nerves, too. Plus, it's actually relaxing here at the shop."

Coming to work to have a break from the kids. Morgan remembered those days.

"When will he hear about the job?"

Cindy shrugged. "Hopefully soon. I don't want to keep you hanging."

"I don't want you to leave," Morgan admitted. "But you've got to do what's best for your family."

Morgan tiptoed through the quiet shop, dusting shelves of fossils and crystals, and sorting out the wooden bins that held rocks. She quizzed herself on whether they were igneous, sedimentary, or metamorphic, trying to decide whether the time she had spent on the geology class had increased her knowledge. And now she would need to learn more new skills: interviewing, hiring, and training an employee.

When her brother Kendall had abandoned the rock shop, Morgan had considered selling the place. Since then, she had formed an attachment to the land, her new friends, the donkeys, and the community. The people of Golden Springs made her feel at home, but her grown children were in South Dakota.

Gerda's loss had increased Morgan's anxiety about being so far from her pregnant daughter. Sarah was due in June. Tourist season. Morgan might only have one employee by then, and Del couldn't run the place by himself. She had to hire someone and get them trained, or there was no hope she'd be able to head to Sioux Falls for a week or more.

The door opened with a creak and a thunk, not a cowbell clang, and Herb ducked under the low doorframe.

"Ready to go?" he asked Cindy. "Kids are in the van."

After Cindy had been gone for over an hour, and Morgan had settled in for a long, boring afternoon, a new Dodge truck pulled up out front. The black metal-flake paint job gleamed in the spring sunshine. Two men hopped out. The driver was a man a few years younger than Del, while the passenger looked to be in his mid-thirties. There was something about their casual but top-of-the-line outdoors attire and styled hair that said they both had money to spend. Morgan watched through the shop's front windows, hoping they were customers, and not the real estate agents that had been pestering her neighbors the Daltons to sell their ranch. A real estate agent could make a nice commission selling the valuable seventy-five acres the rock shop sat on.

The younger of the two men browsed the ore carts and tables outside, poking around in displays of unopened geodes. Morgan had unstuffed the cowbell when Cindy left, and a loud clang announced the entrance of the older man. After a cursory response to Morgan's greeting, he prowled the shop like he was taking inventory. His skin had weathered poorly from high-altitude sun. Chiseled might have described his face, except for the sagging jowls. The hard face of a man who had spent his career working outdoors, Morgan guessed.

"I see you've got a little topaz in your display case."

"Yes, we do." Morgan hoped he was in the market for the gemstone.

"Local?"

"We know the prospector," Morgan said.

"Where's he get the stuff?"

"I couldn't tell you where his claim is," Morgan said. "Prospectors don't like to give out that kind of information."

"So is this it?"

Morgan didn't have an answer. What did he mean by "it"?

He tried again. "Where do you keep the good stuff?"

"That's all the topaz I have in stock," Morgan said.

The man snorted. "I've got better quality in my junk drawer at home." His sneer revealed teeth so straight and white they had to be dentures.

Morgan squelched the desire to tell him to get out. What was his purpose in coming into her shop? To insult her?

"Do you have any other gemstones?" he asked. "Raw or cut. Don't matter."

Morgan moved to a display case. He followed, leaning close to the glass and frowning.

"Colorado is second only to California in the variety of minerals." Her words were straight from geology class. The man made her nervous. Or angry. Maybe both. So she kept talking. "The Rock of Ages has a nice collection of crystals and gemstones. On display in this case, we have aquamarine, some rhodochrosite, quartz crystals—"

"Naw. Nothing I'm interested in."

"What are you looking for? We have more items in storage that I'm still in the process of sorting through."

"Like in your barn?"

He certainly was nosey. The cowbell sounded as the younger man entered the shop.

"Hey, Dad, I found what I wanted." He eased six geodes out of his arms and onto the scarred glass checkout counter. "You find what you were looking for?"

"Naw, they don't have anything here of interest."

Morgan could see a faint family resemblance now that they stood side by side. Their eyes were the same pale greenish blue, a shade like the turquoise in Lucy's jewelry. That was where the likeness ended. A burn scar ran down the right side of the son's face, but the undamaged left looked nothing like the cranky older man. Where his father's face was coarse, the son's features were refined. Signs of maturity etched gentle lines around his eyes, unlike the father's sun-ravaged skin. His mother had to be a beautiful woman.

The son rolled one of the baseball-sized geodes around on the checkout counter.

"I love these things. You never know what's inside till you bust them open. How much?"

"They're fifteen dollars each."

"I'm buying six." The son aimed a smile at Morgan that told her he was accustomed to using his charm to get his way. "How about a little bulk purchase discount?"

Morgan haggled with him until they agreed on a price. They had just completed the sale when the cowbell clanged. Del stepped inside and stopped in his tracks. He and the older man stared at each other like a couple tomcats ready to unleash claws and send fur flying.

"Well, well, well, if it ain't Delano Addison."

"You know I live here," Del said. "What are you doing on my turf, Cooper?"

Morgan had heard that name before, accompanied by a warning.

"Shopping," Mr. Cooper said. "From the looks of this dump, seems like you'd welcome customers, instead of running them off with your rude manners."

Del took a step toward Cooper, but the other man didn't back up.

"Seems like shopping's what you do best," Del said. "But when it comes time to pay the bill, you're nowhere around."

"As it turns out, I didn't make any purchases here today. My boy did, and he paid in full. I don't see anything here of interest, so if you'll move out of my way, I'll be going."

There was a momentary standoff, Del's mustache bristling and Cooper's calm smirk belied by his clenched jaw, his jowls quivering with tension. Then Del stepped aside. Cooper brushed against Del as he passed.

The son started to follow. He turned in the doorway. The scarred half of his face was expressionless, while the other half seemed to offer an apology.

"You know my dad." He nodded his head toward the doorway as he spoke to Del. "Sorry about the fuss. I should have known better than to let him come with me."

The cowbell clanged as the door closed.

"What was that all about?" Morgan asked.

"It's all in the past. Never mind."

Whatever had happened between Del and Mr. Cooper might have been in the past, but the anger still seemed fresh enough.

"What did he want?" Del asked.

"The son bought geodes. Mr. Cooper didn't find what he wanted, but he wouldn't tell me what he was looking for. Cooper was pretty nosey. I hope they aren't in the same business. He acted like he was checking out the competition."

"The man's done some minor prospecting. Never found anything significant. He mostly buys stuff from miners who don't know what they've got, then sells it to collectors who don't have a proper sense of value. He's a thief."

"Or an astute businessman," Morgan offered. She thought she understood the situation. Mr. Cooper must have ripped off Del in a business deal.

Del tugged thoughtfully at his mustache. "Seems odd. You find Gerda's daughter in a dugout. Probably a prospector's shelter. Might be a mine nearby. Then Cooper shows up."

"You think Mr. Cooper had something to do with Carlee's disappearance?"

Del shook his head. "I know I want to think the worst of the man, but I suppose that is a stretch." He poured himself a cup of coffee from the pot on the checkout counter. "Can I take another look at your photo? I couldn't tell much from it the other night, but maybe something will come to me this time."

"I told Chief Sharp I'd send him a copy. We can look at the photo on my computer."

In a few minutes, Morgan moved the photo from her phone to a file on her desktop. Del watched her every move.

"Man, oh man. Just a few years ago, a person had to shoot up a roll of film, then take it to the drugstore for developing. It could be a week or two before you'd get your pictures."

"It is amazing." Morgan emailed the photos to Bill Sharp, then opened them on the computer screen. "I can enlarge them, make them brighter, whatever we want. But I can't make a blurry photo come into focus."

Like the photo of the flowers with the tiny elephant heads. There was no salvaging the dark, blurry image, and no way to prove she'd seen the impossibly strange flowers. Instead, she demonstrated on the photo of the remains. Adjusting the contrast brought out details.

"It's like she was laid to rest." Del seemed fixed on the idea that the remains were Carlee Kruger's, even though they had yet to be positively identified. "See how she's lying on top of something, like a sleeping bag, and there are blankets, newer blankets, on top. Is that yellow color a hat, or hair?"

"I can't tell, Del."

"A body doesn't stay intact in the forest. The animals drag the bones around."

"Do you think that mountain man was guarding her?"

"Let's see the photo of him again," Del said.

Morgan brought it up. The phone's flash had made his eyes look red. Demonic. Morgan zoomed in on his face.

"Why would he guard her body?" Morgan didn't wait for the

answer she knew Del didn't have. "Did he kill her? Was he hiding the evidence of his crime? Or did he just run across a body, and was too crazy to contact the police about it?" Morgan remembered her terror when he came inside the dugout. The fear that he would kill her, too. Then a less frightening memory came to her. Flowers in neat beds. Almost as though they were being tended. "Del, where's that flower book?"

"In the house, I think."

She rushed out of the office. Morgan unlocked the door at the back of the rock shop with the hand-printed "Private–Do Not Enter" sign thumb-tacked to its center. The door was all that separated the living quarters from the shop.

"What's that smell?"

From the appreciative smile lifting Del's mustache, Morgan could tell he enjoyed the savory odor.

"Chicken soup. The church ladies are taking casseroles to Gerda tomorrow."

Del peered through the glass lid of the slow cooker.

"Looks like a lot of soup for one person."

"I'm going to divide it up into one-serving containers. That way Gerda can freeze what she can't eat right away. We'll have the rest for our dinner."

"Not that I disapprove of being neighborly, but you know that gal's not the type to enjoy being fussed over." Del sat at the kitchen table on a wooden chair. "As long as you and the ladies understand that you're taking Gerda food to ease your own grief, not hers, then go on ahead."

"That's kind of harsh, Del."

He kneaded his forearm where a chainsaw had torn up his arm.

"I'm not saying it's wrong. No, it's the right thing to do. Who knows? Maybe it'll even draw Gerda out of her shell a little. But don't expect her to be grateful for your concern."

Morgan noticed the spine of a book on the bookshelf. "Here it is."

She opened the dog-eared Rocky Mountain flower identification book. Morgan sat beside Del at the table.

"The flowers outside the dugout looked almost like they'd been planted there." She flipped through pages. "Since my phone photo didn't turn out, I was hoping there'd be a picture of it in this book, but I don't know how I'll ever find it."

"Describe it to me."

"This will sound crazy, but they looked like tiny purple elephant heads. Dozens of them, lined up on the stem."

"Sure. There's such a thing as an elephant head flower. But they don't bloom until summertime. They like high meadows with plenty of water. They're not exactly rare, but you only find them certain places."

"Naturally growing, maybe not. But what if somebody planted them?"

Del tugged at his mustache, a sure sign he was either baffled or agitated, or both.

"We won't solve this one easily." Morgan threw her arms in the air. "What am I saying? I don't want to get involved in this case at all."

"Small town," Del said. "You can't help but get involved, whether you want to or not."

Chapter Seven

Monday blended into Tuesday as Morgan enjoyed the rare treat of routine days. In between customers and donkey care, she swept floors in the living quarters and the shop. She was starting a load of laundry when the phone rang.

"Hello?"

"Hi. Mom?"

Morgan felt a flood of relief at the sound of her son, David's, voice. He rarely answered his phone, and ignored her repeated messages for him to return her calls. He seemed to avoid talking to Morgan. Then she felt a tug of panic as another thought occurred, that he or Sarah were in trouble.

"Yes, this is Mom. How are you?"

"Fine. I'm just returning your call."

Calls, Morgan thought.

"Sarah said I should let you know I'm okay," David said.

So his sister had to prod him to call. Morgan's heart sank a little.

"How is school going?"

Here his voice picked up a little vigor as he talked about his classes, and that he was on track to graduate next spring.

"I'm so proud of you." Morgan wanted to add, *after all you went through, losing your father at such a critical age, your sister marrying, your mother frantically trying to hold together the family, a career, and a home, and not doing a very good job at any of them.* Instead, an awkward silence stretched. The elephant in the room, Sam's death, loomed. "I don't know how much Sarah has told you about the rock shop."

"That's all she talks about. That and the baby."

"Cindy's husband applied for a promotion. If he gets it, I'll need to hire someone new. It just won't make sense for Cindy to try to juggle childcare when her husband gets a raise, and his hours are less flexible."

Morgan was explaining too much about a person her son had never met. She was babbling, trying to keep a conversation going, to keep David on the line.

"That's not a bad thing, right?" David asked. "For a mom to stay home with her kids?"

Before Morgan could consider whether David's comment was an indictment of her working full-time as soon as both kids were in elementary school, David dropped a bombshell.

"That's what Sarah's hoping, since the doctor made her quit her job."

"What?"

"Oh, maybe I wasn't supposed to mention that."

"Quit her job? For medical reasons?"

"Working at the library, she was on her feet too much."

In an era when women regularly worked, maintained their physical fitness routines, and in general carried on until their due dates, quitting a job she loved must have meant Sarah's pregnancy was in trouble. She wasn't due for another month and a half.

"It's not that bad, Mom. I know she wouldn't want you to worry."

Telling a mother not to worry was like asking a fish to breathe on dry land.

David was suddenly anxious to end the phone call, and Morgan was anxious to call Sarah. But she hadn't spoken to David in over a month. Every word was precious.

"Are you taking classes this summer?" Morgan asked.

"No, I'm planning to work full-time and save money for fall semester."

"What do you think about spending the summer in Colorado? I'll need help during tourist season, and with Cindy possibly leaving, I have to hire someone. Why not my son?"

There was a pause. Silence.

"You don't have to give me an answer right now," Morgan said. "Think about it. You used to love it here."

"Yeah. I remember." Another pause. "No promises, but I'll keep it under consideration."

As soon as David hung up, Morgan dialed Sarah's number. It went to voice mail. If she was in Sioux Falls, she could drop by Sarah and Russ's house. If she were back home, her son wouldn't have more information about Sarah's pregnancy than her own mother.

Morgan called back and left a message. She attempted patience, waiting for a return call. Unlike her brother, Sarah always retuned Morgan's calls.

She tried to distract herself with work, and to calm herself with a prayer for Sarah's health and safety, but Morgan's heart raced as all the what-ifs forced themselves through her mind. When they all tumbled together in a brain-clogging clot of worry, Morgan dialed her son-in-law's number.

"Hi, Morgan."

It irked her that Russ called her by her first name. Perhaps it was his way of asserting his equality as an adult, along with his refusal to accept financial help or advice from Morgan.

"I'm sorry to bother you at work, but I tried calling Sarah's cell, and she didn't pick up."

"I'm sure she's resting. She'll call you back when she gets up."

"In the middle of the day?"

"That's when people usually take naps," Russ said.

"It's so unlike Sarah—"

"Look, Mrs. Iverson."

The unexpected formality jolted Morgan.

"Sarah's been a little run down lately," Russ continued. "The doctor suggested she take it easy for the rest of the pregnancy. You know how Sarah is. Go, go, go all the time. This is just a precaution."

"I can come home if you need—"

"Everything's okay."

"I just talked to David, and he told me the doctor made Sarah quit her job. That doesn't sound okay to me."

"I know how to take care of my wife."

Morgan noticed the deliberately possessive nature of the statement. My wife, not your daughter.

"Sarah is okay. The baby is okay. We can handle things. I'm sure you have enough to keep you busy in Colorado."

Morgan felt as though she'd been slapped. Russ had probably been waiting for years for the perfect opening to put her completely in her place. Now she wondered whether he was the kind of kid to ship his parents off to the old folks' home the first time they left a kitchen stove burner on. Heaven help the mother-in-law. To be fair, Morgan had been a stereotypical overbearing mother-in-law when Sarah had first married Russ. They had been so young, she was certain they needed her advice. Morgan held her words tightly in check as she spoke.

"I know you're perfectly capable of taking care of my daughter. I was concerned when I got the news from David about her being on bed rest, instead of hearing it from Sarah herself."

There was a brief pause, and maybe Russ was reining in what he really wanted to say.

"David didn't get things quite right. She's not on bed rest, and she took a leave of absence. The library wants her back as soon as she's ready. I'll let her know you called. Morgan, we're not trying to keep you out of the loop. It's just that Sarah knows you're concerned about being so far away. She doesn't want you to worry about every little thing."

There it was again. That impossible directive to not worry. Russ seemed to be trying, though, and so she had to try, too.

"Thank you, Russ. If you and Sarah need me there, just let me know."

"We're looking forward to your visit when the baby arrives," Russ said.

He almost sounded sincere.

The rest of Tuesday passed quickly, with a few customers interrupting Del's project to set up an antique display using pieces of an old wagon he found behind Barton's barn.

The phone rang.

"Beatrice here." Her crisp voice was all business. "Don't forget, we're taking casseroles to Gerda tomorrow."

"I made soup, not a casserole. I hope that's okay."

"Absolutely. Soup is great comfort food. She may finally be willing to accept some support from us. I've never seen Gerda crack, but she came close this morning."

"What happened?"

"She insisted on going to the morgue in Granite Junction. Seemed like she wanted company, so Teruko and I took her. Gerda said she wanted to make sure the bones weren't Carlee's before we ladies made any more fuss over her."

"How could she ID a skeleton? Was it her clothes? Maybe a purse with a driver's license?"

"Nope. Good guesses, Morgan, but it was the hair."

The blur of yellow in Morgan's photo.

"Carlee Kruger had masses of thick, blond hair. If the

mountain man hadn't been taking care of her, the birds and animals might have dragged it all off to line their nests."

"Ick."

"Not many girls in town had hair that long, and nobody had hair that color. Like spun gold. Gerda recognized it at once. I thought the poor woman was going to pass out, but Teruko and I managed to hold her up."

"I don't know which would be worse," Morgan said. "Gerda thinking her daughter ran away, or knowing she's dead, and not knowing why. Did your nephew say anything about how she died?"

"It could be difficult for the coroner to determine cause of death. But there's always the possibility some new information will come out to explain it all."

"For Gerda's sake, I hope so."

Chapter Eight

Between Cindy's announcement, her dust-up with her son-in-law, and encountering Big Foot and his hidden stash of human remains, Morgan decided she'd had enough excitement. At least it was Tuesday, and she could look forward to a relaxing evening with her friend Bernie. Almost every week, they joined the informal running club, O'Reily's Runners, at a pub in Granite Junction. Time to wind down, Morgan told herself.

She parked beside Bernie's late model SUV, a hulking beast designed for rugged mountain roads. Tonight was Morgan's turn to drive to Granite Junction. Bernie exited the back door of the bakery. Her shoulder-length brown hair was pulled into a ponytail, and she wore a bright green windbreaker tailored to flatter her generous figure.

"Hi, Morgan. How has your week been?" Bernie's green eyes sparked with anticipation as she climbed in the Buick. "Any adventures you'd care to share?"

"You've probably heard most of it through the grapevine already." Morgan pulled onto Main Street. "I'd rather decompress first by hearing some good news. I hope you have some."

Bernie did, and chatted about her boyfriend, Rolf, the entire drive down Topaz Pass. The big-and-tall guy seemed delighted with his plus-size gal, and he loved her cooking. Bernie owned Bibi's Bakery, a popular tea and lunch spot in Golden Springs. She and Rolf were a match made in heaven. Just like Morgan and Sam had been.

"We've only been dating three months," Bernie said. "I'm afraid to think about the future. I wish we could fast forward past all this uncertainty, and get to the moment when I know whether we're really meant for each other."

"I haven't seen many people better suited for each other," Morgan said. "Besides, that's how long Sam and I dated before he proposed."

"I'd given up hope I would ever get married." Bernie shivered. "Here I am, so nervous worrying about the future that I can't enjoy finally dating a nice guy."

Bernie stared out the windshield. Maybe she was having visions of her wedding day. Morgan shook off a touch of depression and dash of envy, and let herself feel joy at her friend's happiness.

"So, Morgan." Bernie paused. "It's been over two years now. Have you considered dating?"

"Beatrice strong-armed me into that dinner date with Pete Melcher from church. If that's what dating has in store for me, I'm better off quitting while I'm ahead."

"Pete seems like a nice guy," Bernie said. "It can't have been that bad."

Morgan gave a brief, painful rundown of a dinner date full of long, awkward pauses.

"He's a great guy, for someone," Morgan said. "We just have nothing in common. I rhapsodized about hiking in the mountains, while he told a story about being mugged by a chipmunk. I think he was as relieved as I was when the evening finally ground to an end."

"Okay, so the dating scene's not working out. I haven't seen you since last Tuesday. I've heard the talk around town about the body you found, but I haven't gotten the straight scoop from the eyewitness."

"The last day of geology class was a field trip to Temple

Mountain. Trevin and I carpooled with our professor."

She told the story slowly, hoping something would trigger an explanation for the bones in the dugout, and the mountain man guardian. Or murderer. Bernie asked questions, helping Morgan to fill it out even more. They were pulling into a downtown parking lot before Morgan reached the end.

"Hold that thought," Bernie said. "We'd better get signed in before the run starts."

The pub could have blended in on a Dublin street. Runners crowded their way through heavy wooden doors that remained propped open in spite of the chilly evening air. Lucy waved them over to her station at a chest high table surrounded by three tall stools. Her long black ponytail was threaded through the back of her baseball cap, and she wore sleek black running slacks, yellow and white sneakers, and a thin turquoise windbreaker. Morgan and Bernie had updated their wardrobes with running shoes and fleece lined windbreakers, and Morgan had finally opted for running slacks that weren't very warm, but did prevent chafing. Morgan scribbled her initials beside her name on the clipboard sign-in sheet.

"Two more runs," Lucy said, "and you both get your club shirts."

Bernie bounced on the heels of her running shoes.

"I never thought I'd make it!"

"You can add it to your collection," Morgan said. "Along with your 5K shirts."

She and Bernie had participated in three fund-raising five-kilometer races since January. They walked most of the three point one miles, but the goal was not to win. Besides raising money for a good cause, the 5Ks were part social event and part exercise program.

They lined up outside the pub and listened to the "rules of engagement" announced by a runner standing on a chair.

"Obey the traffic lights and stop signs," he said, "and be careful crossing streets."

Headlamps were no longer required. Even slow walkers could finish the race before the sun went down. The man on the stool yelled "Go!" and runners surged down the sidewalk. After negotiating two stoplights, they ran on the less traveled side streets. Bernie slowed her jog as they reached the park.

"That's enough running for me."

"We go a little farther each time," Morgan said. "I can't say I've lost much weight, but I feel better."

"I've lost eight pounds," Bernie said. "Just from walking. But no one can tell on a girl my size. Oh well, we're doing this for our health, not to become supermodels, right? Now back to your story. How could Gerda be so sure the bones are her daughter's?"

"Her hair—"

"Euw."

"You asked. Carlee had thick, long, golden blond hair. Her natural color. Beatrice said the coroner will look at dental records to be sure."

"What about the mountain man? Have they found him?"

"Not yet."

"Why do we always end up talking about your cases when we're walking though the park by ourselves? At least the sun is still up."

"They're not my cases," Morgan said. "And I'm not involved in this one at all."

"You only found the body that the entire town searched for sixteen years ago."

"And that's all I'm having to do with this cold case. It's up to someone else to solve it. Although not many people think the true story will come out after all these years."

★ ★ ★ ★ ★

They reached the pub after everyone else had been seated for a while, as usual. Morgan was surprised to see Barton at the long wooden table with Lucy, Paul, their two children, and Chuck and Vonne. Barton's long whiskers and shaggy hair made him look more like a mountain man than a dedicated runner, but he participated in nearly every running event in the region, and often placed in his age group. Barton was typically long gone by the end of the run. He wasn't exactly the most social guy.

"Hi, Barton." Bernie slid onto the bench next to him. "You're usually back way before we are. You must have been sitting here a long time."

"I forced him to stay and keep me entertained," Chuck said. "I can't run for the next four to six weeks." He held his foot out from under the bench. His foot was encased in a heavy sock and a low-tech foot boot, but the thirty-something businessman still wore his top-of-the-line running slacks and jacket.

"What happened?" Morgan asked.

"Broken toe," Chuck said. "I tripped over the dog. Didn't hurt him one bit. Vonne made me go to the doctor, but if you've ever had a broken toe, you know what they tell you."

Half the table chimed in with some variation of, "There's nothing we can do about a broken toe."

Danny, Lucy and Paul's black-haired three-year-old, chanted an unintelligible ditty, ending with, "Toes, toes, toes." Then he resumed coloring his kid's menu.

"The doctor wrapped your toe and gave you a boot," said Vonne, Chuck's wife. Her makeup and hair never seemed mussed by running three miles. "It was worth the trip to the emergency room to get you to stop whining."

Barton was typically a man of few words, but he quipped, "For a man with a broken toe, Chuck moved really fast to grab me before I could escape."

"We don't bite," Lucy said.

"But if you're not careful," her husband Paul said, "Lucy will sign you up to volunteer for the next charity race." Paul was a member of the Arapaho tribe, like Lucy. He wore his thick, black hair in braids that reached halfway down his barrel-chest.

Bernie clapped her hands. "Another race? Count me in! What's this one for?"

Paul shook his head. "You never learn."

"You weren't here then, Morgan, but there was a forest fire last summer," Lucy said. "It burned up part of the Golden Springs Homestead Park. We're having a race to raise money for seedlings to replant the damaged area."

"It's on a weekday, though," Paul said, "and just a week away. I don't know how much participation we'll get."

"The city is getting a deal on the seedlings," Lucy said. "We need help planting them."

"So it's not just a race," Bernie said.

"It'll be fun," Lucy said. "There won't be any T-shirts for this race, but you'll have a tree named after you."

"See," Paul said. "That's how she gets you. Lucy promises a fun time for all, then you're knee deep in mud digging holes with a rusty shovel. So can I count on all of you?"

"Sign me up," Bernie said. "How about you, Morgan?"

"If I can get away from the shop. Cindy might quit. Her husband's up for a promotion. Do you know anybody in need of a low-paying part-time job with no opportunity for advancement?"

"Well, when you put it that way," Chuck said, "they'll be knocking down your front door for the chance to work at the Rock of Ages. May I make a suggestion?"

"Sure, Chuck."

"If you're going to run a successful business, you have to learn how to paint things in a spectacularly unrealistic light.

Don't think of how little you can pay a potential employee. Think about how it's a great opportunity for a young person to gain job experience, or for a retired person to earn money to supplement their Social Security."

"There are plenty of reasons a person might want part-time work," Vonne said. "Maybe you can find a college student home for the summer."

Like her son David. Morgan hoped he would consider her offer of a summer job.

"Besides, there must be amateur detectives around who'd jump at the chance to work for the lady who finds bodies," Chuck said.

Vonne punched his shoulder lightly. "Don't give Morgan a hard time." She turned toward Morgan. "We heard all about it. Are you okay? That had to be traumatic."

Morgan glanced at three-year-old Danny and five-year-old Kimmie.

"We have to get the kids home right after we eat," Lucy said. "I've already heard the story. You can fill in the others after we leave."

The topic changed to lighter subjects while they enjoyed fish and chips and Guinness beer. After Lucy and her family left, Morgan described her discovery of the skeleton, and her frightening encounter with the mountain man.

"Does your police chief think the mountain man killed Carlee?" Vonne asked.

"No one is saying she was murdered," Morgan said. "We may never know, unless the cause of death is written in her bones."

Chuck looked at Barton. "You spend a lot of time in the mountains. Have you ever seen this character?"

"I don't run into many people." Barton tugged at his beard, which was neatly combed and trimmed. "Some of those old prospectors can be pretty crusty, but I haven't seen one as rough as the guy you described, Morgan."

"Speaking of prospectors," Morgan said, "Harlan Cooper came in the rock shop yesterday. It seemed like he was hunting for something specific, but he wouldn't say what it was."

Barton had been quiet most of the evening, making little effort to join in the conversation. When the talk turned to prospecting, he took over.

"Cooper's not a pickaxe and shovel prospector. If he files a claim, he'll have a backhoe and a hired crew out there, level the mountain and sift it all through a fine mesh screen to get every last gemstone or flake of gold out of the earth."

"Yikes," Bernie said. "That can't be good."

"Can he do that?" Morgan asked. "Aren't there regulations about mining?"

"Too many," Barton said.

"Not enough," Vonne said at the same moment.

"Cooper might be checking out the rock shop to see if you have gemstones on your land. Don't agree to anything he proposes."

"I'm not going to let anyone dig holes on my land," Morgan said. "Unless it's someone I trust, like you, Barton."

"You should join the Pine County Gemstone Society and Prospecting Club," Barton said. "I'm the vice president."

"That sounds interesting," Morgan said. "I'm surprised Del hasn't mentioned it."

"No surprise," Barton said. "Lorina Dimple is the president."

"Del might be an old-fashioned guy," Bernie said, "but he's not opposed to a woman being in charge, or he wouldn't be working for Morgan."

"It's not that." Barton spun his empty beer glass around in circles in the puddle of condensation on the wooden table. "Del and Lorina had a little history. Things didn't end well."

"What kind of history?" Vonne leaned her forearms on the

table. "Like romantic involvement?"

"That's Del's business," Barton said. "Sorry I mentioned it."

When Morgan got home, Del was already asleep. The old cowboy had confided a while back that he'd tried dating once, after his wife passed away. Morgan might have been tempted to pry out whether the president of the gem club was a former romantic interest, but a person's past could cause him or her a lot of pain. Like Gerda and her family. There might be times when it was better to leave the past alone.

Chapter Nine

Wednesday morning's mail brought a notice from the bank. Morgan had spent more than she had in her checking account. Adding to the pain of embarrassment was a twenty-five-dollar charge, the bank's way of punishing the financially inept.

After a quick review of her account on-line, and shuffling funds around, Morgan had the mess straightened out. She scrolled through her deposits, which were few, and her bills, which seemed to be multiplying like rabbits.

Morgan shoved both hands into her hair, clutching fistfuls of curls in frustration. She knew what she had to do, what she had been avoiding facing. It was time to eliminate the largest drain on her income—her house in Sioux Falls.

The home had been her anchor after Sam's death. She feared cutting that tie might set her adrift. Morgan struggled to be rational. Not having a home in South Dakota didn't mean she could never visit, or even move back.

What was irrational was slipping behind on the mortgage payments to a house that was nearly paid for. It would be foolish to lose all she, Sam, and the kids had put into it.

Morgan went through the door to the living quarters and dug a business card out of her purse. Her friend Dot Borgen ran a realty and property management business in Sioux Falls. Dot had discussed options with Morgan concerning the house, but until now, Morgan hadn't been able to decide anything. She dialed the number.

"How's Nancy Drew doing?" Dot asked. "Dug up any more bodies?"

News had spread quickly among her friends about her misadventure in January. Morgan could not tell the story of her new find, or she would never complete her business call.

"Nothing too exciting," Morgan said, and hoped she could be forgiven for the lie. "I'm calling about my house. Is there any possibility that I could lease it?"

"Of course. But let me warn you, Morgan, that once you rent your home, after strangers live in it, it just won't be the same."

"Are you trying to talk me out of renting?"

"I'm saying that if you're keeping the house as an investment, or renting as a half step to eventually selling, then it might work. But if you're thinking of leasing it out for a while, then moving back in, you might be disappointed."

"That's what I've been doing ever since Sam passed away. Letting go in half steps. Maybe this is one big step."

"As your friend, I'm glad to hear that. Sam would have wanted you to move on. As your real estate agent, I'm happy to tell you that your house could lease for much more than your mortgage payment. After we spoke about your house the first time, I crunched some numbers. You did well, buying when prices were low, and not taking out second or third mortgages like so many people do these days."

"Thank goodness for that."

"How about I do a little market research, and call you back when I have more information?"

"Sounds good."

"Oh, and Morgan, is the house move-in ready?"

Morgan couldn't even remember whether she'd taken the trash out before driving to Golden Springs. She had only expected to be gone for two weeks. Sarah and Russ checked on the house regularly. David had shot down any suggestion that he live there while going to college. Too many memories, he had mumbled. Everyone might be happy to be released of responsibility for the house, but first it would need to be cleaned out.

"I take it by your pause the answer is no?" Dot asked.

"There's a lifetime of possessions, and probably a mountain of junk."

"You could hire someone to clean it for you. I know a company that does good work. But they wouldn't know what you wanted to keep, and what was trash. I'm afraid to tell you, but a trip back to Sioux Falls might be needed before I tackle leasing your house."

"That's not a problem. I've been looking for an excuse."

"Okay, I'll get busy on my end, and you just let me know when you'll be back here. The gang will want to get together with you."

Cindy arrived late to work, her baby in tow. She spent her first half hour getting settled, assembling a crib in the narrow space behind the checkout counter. Morgan had placed the shop mail by the cash register. Cindy flipped through the pile of envelopes and junk mail.

"Oh, good. There's a notice about the Denver gem and mineral show."

A colorful post card announced the event in July. The photo depicted a stunning cluster of one blue amazonite and three smoky quartz crystals jutting from the same base.

"This is the star of the show?" Morgan flipped the card over. "I imagine so, at that price. Thirty grand? Who would pay that much for pretty minerals?"

"Those New Age types are crazy about crystals," Cindy said. "God created them so there can't be anything evil about crystals to begin with, until witches use them in their devil ceremonies."

Morgan had grown accustomed to her employee's hellfire

and brimstone outlook.

"They can't be the only ones who buy crystals," Morgan said, studying the post card.

"Something that nice will go to a collector," Cindy said. "Or a museum. You need to go."

"It's during peak tourist season," Morgan said.

"Kendall and Allie always did good at this show. They sold lots of stuff, and bought new stock. We're getting kind of thin on some things around here."

Morgan's resentment of her brother bubbled up. He had dropped the keys in her hand and taken off for the jungle, without giving her any training in how to run a rock shop.

"If you hire someone now," Cindy said, "you could have them trained by July."

Morgan met Cindy's eyes. "What do you mean hire someone? Did Herb get the job?"

Cindy looked away. "Yes," she said in a small voice.

"That's great." Then Morgan considered Cindy's hesitation. She hoped the seemingly benign Herb hadn't demanded Cindy stay at home, barefoot and pregnant. Although it seemed a little late in the game for him to become an oppressive husband. "It is great, right?"

Cindy finally looked at Morgan, unable to contain a smile. "We're thrilled. This promotion means a lot to our family. We'll be able to take a family vacation, maybe replace our van." The glow of happiness dimmed a notch. "But Morgan, I really hate to leave you in a bind."

"The Rock of Ages will be fine. I'll admit, right now I'm not sure how we'll get along without you. I never would have survived my first months here without your help."

Cindy threw her arms around Morgan in a hug, then stepped back.

"I love this place, and you and Del, but it'll just be too much for my family to handle with Herb's new hours."

"How much longer can you work?" Morgan asked, dreading the answer.

"That's the thing. I need to drop my regular hours right away. But I won't be gone entirely. I can still help out when you really need me, and train my replacement. I can probably even go to the gem show with you in July."

"I'll take whatever help I can get."

The phone rang. Cindy reached for the telephone, then paused, her hand hovering over the receiver.

"This might be my last official phone answering." She held the phone to her ear. "Rock of Ages. Cindy—" She choked on a sob and held the phone toward Morgan. "I can't do it."

Morgan held the phone to her ear. "Rock of A—" She couldn't finish.

"Is everything okay?" Kurt blurted over the phone.

"We're fine. Cindy just told me she's quitting. We're both a little emotional."

"Don't even think about stealing Trevin from me."

The thought had occurred to Morgan, but working for Kurt at the *Golden Springs Gazetteer* was a better opportunity for the young man.

"It's a free country," Morgan teased. "He can work at the Rock of Ages if he prefers low wages and cleaning donkey stalls as part of the deal."

"I'm really afraid now."

"With the semester over, he might be looking for some extra work."

"True. Just don't lure him away permanently. But I didn't call to warn you off from stealing my employees. Anna and I have all the newspaper clippings, public records, and photos of Gerda's daughter we could glean from the files. Her entire life in Golden Springs, at least as depicted in the *Gazetteer.*"

"I can drop by your office tomorrow."

"My schedule is packed through the rest of the week," Kurt said. "I thought we could examine Carlee's life story over dinner Friday night. At my place, so we have room to spread out."

There was room to spread out on the table at the newspaper office. Dinner at Kurt's house sounded like a social invitation. Several scenarios played through Morgan's head. She would feel like an idiot if she made more out of an amateur sleuthing session with Kurt than he intended. Surely Anna would be there, but rather than asking a simple question to clear the entire matter up, she spoke.

"What time?"

Chapter Ten

Beatrice called at closing time to remind Morgan that the church ladies were delivering casseroles to Gerda in half an hour. When Morgan pulled up at Kruger's Auto Repair, the tiny parking area was full. The self-serve laundry would ticket intruders into their parking spaces. To the right, the parking lot for the abandoned cabins was thick with weeds. She found a space on the street, gathered her frozen tubs of soup, and joined the group. Eight ladies from the Golden Springs Community Church climbed out of vehicles, retrieving carefully bundled items. When they trooped toward the office, casseroles in hand, Tom hurried out of the garage to meet them.

"Gerda's home right now." Tom wiped his hands on a red shop rag as he spoke. "She wasn't feeling well."

"Gerda knew we were coming," Teruko said softly.

"I'm sorry." Tom shrugged.

"Then we'll take these to her house." Beatrice started to push past Tom.

"Really, Mrs. Stonewall, this isn't a good time for her."

"And that is why her friends are here," Teruko said. "Gerda once helped me when I needed it most, and I will not turn away from her now."

"Let me give her a heads up," Tom said. "But I'm warning you, she told me she didn't want to be bothered by anyone."

As Tom dialed his cell phone, the church ladies stared at him in silence.

"Gerda?" Pause. "I know, you said not to call unless it's an emergency, but I've got nine ladies here with casserole dishes, and they aren't leaving until they talk to you." He hung up his phone. "She'll be right over. Wait here. If you'll excuse me." He trotted back to the garage with the grace and speed of someone avoiding a nipping Rottweiler.

The ladies stood in a cluster, steam rising from some of the casserole dishes. Others clutched loaves of homemade bread and plates of cookies. After an uncomfortably long wait, Gerda appeared through a gate in the back fence. She stormed forward, her short white hair standing on end as though she'd stuck her finger in a light socket. She wore the blue mechanic's jumpsuit that made her resemble an eggplant. She didn't look sick. Just angry. Gerda stopped a few yards in front of the ladies, placing her hands on her wide hips.

Teruko bravely took a step forward. She held out her casserole dish, nested in a towel.

"We understand that food will not ease the sorrow of your loss," Teruko said, her voice wavering, "but it is a small thing we can do to let you know we care."

"What the hell am I supposed to do with all that food?" Gerda spat out the words, in thickly accented German. "I am alone. You know this."

"You'll need food when your daughter comes for the memorial service," Beatrice said.

Gerda looked utterly lost.

"You will have a memorial service?" Teruko asked. "To honor your daughter's life?"

Gerda's lips trembled, and her eyes filled with tears.

"We'll help," Beatrice said. "Because you're not alone. We're here for you. We'll call your family. Reserve the church. You don't have to do anything if you don't want to."

Silence stretched for an agonizing moment, broken by the

raucous caw of a black and white magpie.

"Perhaps you do not need the memorial service," Teruko said. "Perhaps it is needed by Golden Springs." She turned to look at the ladies. "We need to say goodbye to Carlee."

"There will be no service." Gerda clenched and unclenched her hands, her arms stiff at her sides.

As if to give Gerda's hands something useful to do, Beatrice pushed a casserole dish at the woman. Gerda held it at arm's length.

"Gerda, maybe you don't want to go through this," Beatrice said, "and I can understand that the needs of the town aren't top of your list right now, nor should they be. But what about Camille? Your other daughter? She may need closure."

"I have no family," Gerda said. "And I do not want closure. Closure means an end. Do you not understand? When Carlee was missing, I could imagine she would come home some day. Now there is nothing. Nothing!"

She lifted the casserole dish above her head and slammed it to the parking lot. Ceramic shards splintered across the asphalt as steaming chili spewed out in a reddish-hewed splatter.

Morgan tossed and turned that night, with dozens of issues flashing through her restless mind. Top of the list was Carlee Kruger. After witnessing Gerda's violent outburst, Morgan couldn't rule out that maybe both daughters had run away from home to escape her temper. The fact that they might have left willingly did not answer all the other questions. How had Gerda's eldest daughter ended up dead in a dugout on Temple Mountain? And where was the mountain man?

Even without the unsolved cold case, Morgan had plenty of worries. Would using the excuse of cleaning out the family home in Sioux Falls resolve issues with her son and son-in-law, or exacerbate them? And what about the house? Should she rent or sell?

Kurt's invitation to his house for dinner edged up on her list of worries. What if he and Anna were not involved? Thoughts of her husband Sam intruded. He had passed away over two years ago. Was that long enough? What would her children, with whom her relationship had already been strained by distance, think of their mother living the life of a single woman?

She felt as though she had just dozed off when her cell phone on the nightstand chimed.

"Hello?" Her voice was thick with sleep.

"There's someone behind the bakery." Bernie's voice was a raspy whisper.

"Are you okay?" Morgan asked, suddenly wide awake. "It's only five thirty."

"I'm sorry, but this is an emergency. My day starts early, you know. A bakery and all. I was taking trash to the Dumpster and there was something inside. At first I thought it was a bear. Then I realized it was snoring, not growling. I'm going back inside with Mr. Whiskers."

The enormous gray cat would be no protection from Sasquatch.

"Have you called Chief Sharp?"

"No. This just happened. I screamed, so I'm sure one of my neighbors called him."

"Hang up and call him. I'll be right there."

Morgan climbed out of bed and pulled on her jeans and sweatshirt. She tried to be quiet, but Del must have heard her. He ambled out of the guest bedroom in a red plaid bathrobe covering thick long johns. His fleece-lined moccasins padded across the linoleum.

"You're up kind of early for a Thursday. The shop doesn't open for hours."

"It's Bernie. The mountain man might be inside her Dumpster."

"Where do you think you're going?" Del asked. "Leaping right into danger, as usual?"

"I have to go. Bernie's my friend. And she's calling the police. They'll get there before I arrive."

"You're not going without me." Del headed down the hall.

"Meet me outside," Morgan said. "I'll bring the car around."

As they rolled down Hill Street and onto Main, Morgan saw Chief Sharp's SUV in front of Bibi's Bakery, the lights flashing in pre-dawn darkness.

Morgan parked at a crazy angle across two parking spaces, barely putting the Buick in park before she opened the door. She raced down the narrow walkway between buildings. A dozen people stood behind a boundary of two metal fifty-gallon barrels and Deputy Parker.

"The chief told me not to let anybody by," J.B. said.

"I'm Bernie's best friend," Morgan said. "He won't mind."

Deputy Parker hollered a question at Chief Sharp, who gave his reluctant okay.

"Get on over here, J.B.," the chief said. "I need a hand."

Chief Sharp raised an eyebrow at Morgan, and several paces behind her, Del.

"Do you two always have to be in the middle of the excitement?"

"Just seems to happen that way," Del said.

Sharp turned his attention to his deputy. "Think you can climb in there without disturbing things too much?"

J.B. wrinkled his nose, but accepted the camera and a foot up from Chief Sharp. The expected odors of rotten garbage drifted from the Dumpster, plus the distinctive smell of wet dog and sour human.

"What's the youngster looking for?" Del shoved his hands

inside the deep pockets of his canvas jacket and pulled out leather work gloves.

"Evidence," Sharp said. "And he doesn't need your help. Mrs. Iverson, your friend is in the bakery."

He jabbed a thumb over his shoulder. Bernie stood framed by the window over the sink with Mr. Whiskers cradled in her arms. Her cheeks were flushed as pink as her chef's jacket. Morgan went inside, where the kitchen smelled of fresh coffee and yeasty baked goods.

"Oh, Morgan!" Bernie hugged her, smashing Mr. Whiskers between them. He didn't seem to mind, as his chest rumbled with a purr. "I was so scared! I took a bag of trash to the Dumpster, and I heard noises. Bears come in town, but that's why we have bear-proof Dumpsters. Only someone had left the top unlatched. Or now that I think about it, the mountain man must have unlatched the top and climbed inside."

"Did you see him?"

"Not right away. When I heard the noises, I headed back to the kitchen, hoping whatever was inside didn't notice me sneaking away. After I called you, I heard barking. I thought maybe a dog had fallen inside the Dumpster and was trapped. So I turned around just as a head popped up. Not a dog. A human, more or less, with a long scraggly beard and ratty clothes."

"Smelled bad?"

"I didn't get that close, and it is a Dumpster."

"Right. Did you see the dog?"

"Yes, or was it a wolf? It jumped out and chased me. I got inside and called the chief. That's it. The whole story."

Morgan helped Bernie assemble a tray of to-go coffees and pastries, then went outside to help her distribute them. When Chief Sharp sipped real coffee, he smiled. The deputy rustled around inside the Dumpster. Morgan heard the click of the camera's shutter.

"Shouldn't you tell your partner about the coffee?" Del asked.

"He's busy," Chief Sharp said.

"Holy moly!" echoed from inside the Dumpster. The deputy's arm shot out, his hand clad in a disposable glove. "Look at this!"

They all leaned toward the Dumpster, then pulled back in unison, with expressions of disgust at the smell. Pinched between J.B.'s thumb and forefinger was a diamond engagement ring.

"I haven't had any reports of a missing or stolen ring," the deputy said.

Chief Sharp pulled on a glove and took the ring from the deputy. "No one's been missing this ring for a long time."

"Is it Carlee Kruger's?" Morgan asked.

The chief ignored her. "Deputy Parker, get the evidence bagged up, then we'd better look for that guy."

"I'd be happy to make some calls," Del said. "Get some of the boys helping you search."

"We don't need a bunch of vigilantes and wannabe cops running around town," the chief said. "I just want to ask this guy some questions."

"Then how about letting people know to be watching for the guy?" Del asked. "Surely that couldn't hurt."

Bernie looked anxiously from Del to the chief.

"I need to take a statement from Miss Belmont," Chief Sharp said. "I don't need for any citizens to go off half-cocked. There's been no crime committed here, as far as we know. Why don't you just go home and take it easy, Mr. Addison?"

The crowd dispersed, and people got back to minding their own business. Morgan and Del opened the shop early. They had settled into dull routine when Beatrice pulled up.

"I just came from the bakery. Bernie told me about her run-in with the mountain man. Awfully strange. Why is he in Golden Springs now, when no one ever saw him in town before?"

"I have a theory," Del said. "The police took Carlee's bones away, and the mountain man is searching for her."

"He might have been just looking for food," Morgan said. "Bernie's Dumpster must contain some real treats."

Del ignored her comment. "Did Bernie tell you about the ring?" he asked.

"No," Beatrice said.

"Deputy Parker found a diamond ring in the Dumpster," Del said, "mixed in with the mountain man's gear."

"Carlee had an engagement ring, as I recall," Beatrice said. "Jade Tinsley gave it to her."

"Then Gerda might remember if it's Carlee's," Morgan said.

Del tugged at his mustache. "Or it could have been dropped in there by some woman who's now frantic. And for that matter, it might not even be real. Could have been a kid's toy."

"It looked real to me," Morgan said.

Del nodded. "Me, too. I'm just sayin'."

"Hopefully we'll find out soon." Beatrice sat on the aspen bench. She obviously had more to say. "There was an emergency meeting of the church elders last night."

"I heard your pastor had a heart attack," Del said. "How's he doing?"

"He resigned."

Morgan grimaced, remembering with guilt her uncharitable thoughts about Pastor Filbury's dull sermons.

"He told the elders he's been contemplating retirement for some time now," Beatrice said. "When his doctor suggested he retire, Mrs. Filbury jumped on the idea. She's wanted to move closer to their children for years now, or so I hear. It's a disaster for the church."

Morgan considered a new pastor might draw a larger, younger

crowd. But she couldn't say that to one of Pastor Filbury's biggest fans.

"They'll find a suitable replacement."

"I'm not just worried about the church," Beatrice said. "If Pastor Filbury leaves Golden Springs, his seat on City Council will be open. If Piers Townsend or somebody like that wins the seat, power will go to the wrong crowd."

Piers and his faction had already tried once to rezone the Rock of Ages, a move that could have caused Morgan to lose the property to developers.

"There'll be an election to replace him, right?"

"Yes. Of course."

"Seems to me," Del drawled, "you need to decide on a candidate now, and convince him or her to start campaigning."

The previous night had been anything but restful. As Morgan crawled under her comforter, she relished the feel of clean sheets and a soft bed. She dropped off to a deep, dreamless sleep almost instantly.

A sound intruded. Not the sighing of wind through the pines, or the scratching of an aspen branch against the side of the house. Those she could ignore.

Braying.

Morgan was out of bed and half dressed before she was fully awake. She ran into the narrow hallway, and nearly into Del, who was hopping on one foot while he pulled a cowboy boot onto the other.

"The donkeys," Morgan said. "Something's wrong."

Chapter Eleven

Morgan grabbed her jacket off a peg. She threw open the kitchen door, panicked by the insistent braying of the donkey.

"Bring your cell phone," Del said, "in case we need to call the vet."

Adelaide, a donkey of advanced years, was with foal for the first time in her life. Morgan and Del raced toward the barn, following the hoarse, raucous braying.

"Over there."

Del aimed his flashlight. Morgan followed with her own shaky beam. A man and a dog loped across the pasture, followed closely by Houdini. The female donkey waddled several yards behind him. Del pulled his handgun out of the holster strapped under his left arm. Morgan placed a hand on his arm.

"You might hit Houdini."

"He's too far away." Del replaced his gun in the holster. "Did you get a good look?"

"In the dark?"

"The moon's pretty bright."

"Even from this distance," Morgan said, "I'm sure it was Big Foot. Ratty clothes. Wild hair. Wolf dog."

The donkeys abandoned the chase at the rear pasture fence. Beyond loomed the dark form of a mountain, part of which Morgan and her brother owned. The donkeys walked purposefully toward Morgan and Del.

"Yet again," Morgan said, "I wish those two could talk."

"You don't call that braying talking?"

Morgan rubbed Adelaide's forehead. "Good girl."

Houdini demanded attention. Del wrapped an arm around the donkey's neck and gave him a squeeze.

"You earned your feed again, boy."

Del looked toward his trailer, perched behind the barn. Years ago, Kendall and Allie had let the old cowboy park his single-wide trailer on Rock of Ages land. Del had been a fixture ever since, although after his accident with the chainsaw, he had moved into the rock shop living quarters.

"Hey, my door's open." Del strode across the pasture toward the trailer. The door swung in the breeze, knocking against the side of the trailer. "Must have been that guy Houdini chased off." Del peered inside, shining his flashlight around. "Looks like he's been in here."

Del set a foot on a wooden step to the trailer door. The board sagged.

"Del, be careful."

He grasped the doorframe and clambered inside. Morgan followed. Everything looked intact, as far as she could tell. A threadbare sofa, a television with a coat hanger and aluminum foil antenna, a tiny kitchen. Del disappeared down a narrow hallway.

Morgan waited in the living room, scanning the small room with her flashlight. Water stains on the ceiling matched spots on the shag carpet.

"He stole my jacket!" Del yelled.

Chief Sharp bounced up the rutted drive to Del's trailer in his SUV, the lights flashing red and blue against the side of the trailer, the barn, and the donkeys.

"First Miss Belmont wakes me up at o-dark-thirty with her Sasquatch in a Dumpster," Chief Sharp said, "then you two drag me out of bed in the middle of the night for a thief in a trailer house. I need to catch this guy before I suffer any more sleep deprivation."

"He took off across the pasture when Houdini chased him," Del said. "He might of left tracks."

Del led the chief in the general direction the mountain man had run, their flashlights dancing back and forth across the pasture. Morgan held onto Houdini's halter. He seemed eager to join the investigation. The men disappeared beyond the back fence and into the pine trees covering the mountain.

Morgan waited, listening. A breeze kicked up. May in the mountains alternated chilly weather with intensely beautiful spring days. They had enjoyed a stretch of sunny days in the fifties and sixties, but cold was moving in again. Morgan shivered.

"How about we go inside?" she asked the donkeys.

Not waiting for a reply, she headed into the barn through the open stalls. Houdini and Adelaide followed, perhaps hoping for seconds on dinner. Morgan obliged them with a handful of oats each.

Hay rustled in the loft. Mice. Maybe she did need a cat. But not one like Bernie's pampered Mr. Whiskers. No, Morgan needed a hungry mouser.

Del and Bill Sharp finally came back.

"Couldn't track him in the dark," Chief Sharp said. "I doubt I'll have much more luck in the morning, but J.B. and I will drop by and give it a shot."

Friday morning Morgan ran to the hardware store to pick up a lock and hasp for Del's trailer. He stayed behind to stand guard, convinced that his trailer was at risk of another break-in. Morgan avoided the temptation to stop at Bernie's for coffee and conversation. As she drove up Hill Street, her cell phone rang. Morgan pulled to the side of the narrow dirt road. There wasn't much traffic, so it wasn't like blocking half of the uphill lane would bother anyone. The caller ID showed her daughter's name. Morgan pawed through her purse for the headset that had come with her phone, gave up, and held the phone to her ear.

"Sarah?"

"Mom, I'm sorry I haven't returned your calls. The doctor told me to slow down, and I guess I did. I slept most of the last few days. Russ told me you talked to him, and he gave you the updates, so I wasn't in a hurry to call back."

"Yes, Russ let me know he had things well in hand."

"I'm sorry if he was abrupt with you, but Russ was really scared. There's not anything wrong with me or the baby that rest wouldn't cure. I feel better already. If Russ overreacted—"

"Don't apologize for your husband. I understand Russ's viewpoint. I need to trust him more."

"Has Uncle Kendall called you yet?"

Morgan caught a glimpse of movement through the cottonwood trees. They had only begun to leaf out, a blush of green on the bare branches, but the trees were thick along the irrigation ditch.

"Mom?"

"Sorry. I thought I saw something. It was probably one of my neighbor's cows. No, I haven't heard from Kendall. Not recently. If you don't want me to tell him about your situation, let me know. With all the troubles Allie had, they would worry about you even more than I do."

Her brother Kendall and his wife Allie had been unable to have children, enduring several miscarriages.

"He called earlier today," Sarah said. "I didn't mention anything about doctor's orders and all that. There's nothing they can do from that far away. I couldn't understand him really well. The line was full of static. But it sounded like he and Allie are coming home. I was hoping he called you so I'd know if it was true."

Morgan's heart skipped a beat. That's what she had wanted, three months ago. Now that she was settled in, Kendall could stay in the Central American jungle forever, as far as she was concerned.

"Coming home for good," Morgan asked, "or for a visit?"

"I'm not even sure I heard the 'coming home' part correctly."

"It would be nice if he'd let me know."

Another flash of movement caught Morgan's eye. Vernon Dalton raised a small herd of cattle. He and his wife Sherry sold beef quarters and halves, and homemade jerky.

"I'm sure Uncle Kendall will catch up with you soon. I talked to David, too."

Family communication was certainly healthy these days. Except that Morgan was excluded from the loop. She felt obsolete.

"I did finally have a conversation with him," Morgan said.

"He said he wasn't interested at first in spending the summer at the rock shop, but then he talked to some friends who were envious of all the outdoors stuff he could do, so now he's considering the idea. He told me he knew he wouldn't make as much money working for you, but then he wouldn't be paying rent, so he could still save for fall semester."

If Kendall and Allie did come home, and David showed up, the tiny living quarters would be cramped. Morgan envisioned the Rock of Ages becoming like the little old woman in the nursery rhyme who lived in an overpopulated shoe. Two beds. The current tally was now five people. Something had to give. She would just have to hope Sarah had misunderstood her uncle's phone call.

They chatted another couple of minutes. Long distance and her imagination had made mountains out of molehills. Still,

Morgan looked forward to seeing them in person. She placed her phone back in her purse and put the car in gear.

There it was again. Something moving in the field. Then she heard the familiar raspy bray of a donkey.

"Houdini!"

The escape artist donkey had managed to leave his home pasture, cross Hill Street, and find a way onto the Dalton ranch. Morgan turned off the Buick's engine and climbed out. She zipped up her lilac fleece jacket and pulled a knit cap over her dark curls. The door of her late model car made a ridiculous amount of noise, creaking, then closing with a loud bang. Houdini glanced her way, his ears showing above the tall grass like a shark fin in the ocean, but he was a donkey on a mission.

Ancient cottonwood trees hugged the banks of the three-foot-deep irrigation ditch. Morgan dashed across the gravel road and slid down the side of the ditch. She waded through knee-high weeds, hopped over water rushing with spring snow-melt, then clambered up the other side.

Houdini ignored Morgan's pleading. She followed the stubborn donkey across the pasture and along a barbed wire fence. He seemed to know exactly where he was going. Morgan plodded along behind him, knowing she could not catch him unless he let her. But she couldn't leave him on another person's property.

A dozen cattle moved toward an open gate. Houdini trotted ahead of the herd and stood his ground, blocking them. Morgan hadn't known that herding cattle was in the donkey's repertoire. The reddish-brown bovines moved slowly, grabbing mouthfuls of grass as they plodded along. One finally came nose to nose with Houdini. The small gray donkey nipped the heifer's nose. If the cattle wanted through that gate badly enough, they might trample him.

"Houdini!" Morgan called. "Come here, boy!"

He ignored her, preoccupied with herding angry cattle.

"Ho! What's going on?"

The man's voice called from behind Morgan. She turned, and through the trees saw a person dressed in what could have been Del's stolen clothes. Dull colors. Thickly padded for cool weather. The kind of garb worn by ranchers and outdoors people in Colorado. And by thieving Sasquatches.

Then Morgan saw the beard. Her heart missed a beat or two, until she realized these whiskers were neatly groomed. Vernon Dalton was probably wondering what her meddling donkey was doing in his pasture.

"I'm so sorry," Morgan said. "Houdini must have gotten a gate open."

"Impossible."

Vernon's cheeks were ruddy above long whiskers, and his brown hair was close-cropped under a hand-knit wool stocking cap. He carried a .22 rifle in the crook of his arm.

"My gates are all donkey-proof," Vernon said. "This isn't the first time someone's trespassed on my property and left gates open."

An inviolable law of the West was to leave gates the way you found them. Morgan followed Vernon across the pasture. He shooed his herd away from the gate. Houdini waited patiently. When Vernon raised a hand to rub the donkey's forehead, Houdini leaned into him, closing his big brown eyes.

"You know you done good, little fella." Vernon turned to Morgan. "This gate opens to Golden Springs Homestead Park. My herd would've been running around downtown." Vernon gave Houdini another pat. "We operate the ranch on a tight margin. If I lose one animal to theft, or to injury because some fool leaves a gate open, it could really hurt us." Vernon pulled off his stocking cap. "This is the kind of thing that makes me consider selling."

"You can't do that!" Morgan said. "The ranch has been in your family for generations."

"The land's worth too much for its own good. I've had some awfully tempting offers lately that made me think hard about selling this place and buying land farther east. I love these mountains, but a man has to be able to feed his family."

With the cattle safely out of the way, Morgan grabbed Houdini's halter and led him into the pasture. Vernon hooked the gate closed. He reached into the grass and held up a short length of chain.

"Someone cut the padlock off."

"We had a break-in last night," Morgan said. "I wonder if they're related."

Vernon shook his head, causing his long whiskers to brush back and forth across his Carhartt jacket.

"What's this world coming to? I started carrying my varmint rifle, hoping people would think twice about messing with my cattle. They didn't get the triceratops horn, did they?"

The most valuable fossil in the Rock of Ages was a seventy million-year-old triceratops brow horn. They kept it locked in a glass display case, in a shop with no more security than an armed old cowboy and two watch-donkeys.

"He didn't break into the shop," she said. "He hit Del's trailer house, and stole a jacket. Chief Sharp is looking for this guy in connection with a cold case."

"Carlee Kruger," Vernon said. "I've been hearing the rumors around town. So what's the story on this guy? Is there a killer on the loose?"

"Chief Sharp wants to question him about Carlee Kruger. And he seems to be avoiding the police. He's not a suspect. Yet. The first time I saw him, he looked like Sasquatch, but with Del's stolen clothes, he might blend in better now."

"My wife was in the same high school class as Carlee. That

was a sad deal. We talk about her from time to time. Always wondered what happened to her. Now we know."

"Not quite," Morgan said. "There are a lot of unanswered questions yet."

"I'll keep an eye out for a strange mountain man in Del's clothing. I'd better tend to my animals. And get a new lock." Vernon shook his head again. "What's this world coming to?"

Chapter Twelve

The only gate on the Dalton property facing Hill Street was the one to their driveway. The ranch was an uneven rectangle of land encompassing most of the good pasture between Golden Springs and the base of the mountains. Morgan and Houdini had to hike a quarter mile on a path studded with cattle hoof prints that paralleled the barbed wire fence. When they reached the gate, Sherry Dalton stepped out on the wrap-around porch of the log ranch house. She held up her cell phone.

"Vernon told me to expect you." She trotted down the steps. "And that your donkey prevented our herd from escaping."

While Sherry held open the driveway gate, Morgan gave her a brief rundown on Houdini's adventure.

"I don't understand how he got inside your pasture," Morgan said. "All the gates are closed. Unless he snuck into town this morning, and came back through the historical park."

"Your donkeys have been known to visit downtown Golden Springs." Sherry patted Houdini's neck. "I shudder to think what could have happened if he hadn't blocked that gate. You're a good donkey."

Houdini melted under Sherry's affectionate neck rub.

"Did Vernon tell you to watch out for a mountain man?" Morgan asked.

"We weren't on the phone long enough, but he told me to arm myself." Sherry pressed a hand to the pocket of her canvas slacks. "He said there might be a thief in the area."

Morgan's rural neighbors, like Del, often carried guns. The police couldn't be expected to get up the hill fast enough to save them from trouble. Ranchers had to rely on their own resources. Sherry was petite, with a pixie's face and raven black hair falling past her shoulders. She looked vulnerable, but Morgan had heard she was an excellent shot.

"The mountain man stole Del's jacket." The Daltons had already heard about her discovery of Carlee's remains. She skipped a repetition of details. "He was the same guy who scared the wits out of me at the dugout on Temple Mountain. Vernon said you went to high school with Carlee."

"I helped search for her. After all those hours on foot and in the saddle, we didn't find a single clue. That's when people latched onto the alternate theory, that she left town. Car, bus, whatever. But not through the hills. Guess we were wrong."

"Any ideas about what could have happened to her?" Morgan asked.

Sherry shrugged. "She seemed happy enough, but I wasn't in her circle. I ran with the 4H crowd, and then she went off to college in Granite Junction, and I went to Ag school. I know her mom had some problems, and Camille, her younger sister, ran away right after she graduated high school. But Carlee seemed to have her act together."

Houdini shook himself, sending a cloud of dust and shedding hair into the air.

"I'd better get my runaway home," Morgan said. "Sorry for the trouble."

"Not at all," Sherry said. "Your donkeys can visit us any time."

Morgan led Houdini through the gate and down Hill Street to the Rock of Ages, watching the fence line for breaks or donkey-sized gaps, and seeing none. She delivered Houdini to the pasture, then she walked back down Hill Street to her car.

Finally, she parked inside the converted carriage house garage. The doors stood open, and the ATVs were gone. Morgan hiked behind the barn to Del's trailer. Chief Sharp's SUV sat in front, but there was no one around. Then she heard ATV engines. They were out tracking the mountain man, no doubt. And Del was in the thick of the hunt.

They could have accidentally left a gate open, allowing Houdini to escape the rock shop property. Yet every gate Morgan checked seemed secure. The donkeys hadn't been named after famous magicians on a whim. Maybe new gate latches should go on her shopping list.

The Rock of Ages parking lot was empty. Morgan reminded herself that the pace of life was slower in the small mountain town of Golden Springs, unlike her former home in the big city of Sioux Falls, South Dakota. Instead of inventing work to keep her busy indoors, she headed for the barn. Adelaide dozed in her stall. Morgan opened the tack room and retrieved a rubber bucket full of grooming tools.

"Hey, old girl. You need to keep a better eye on your husband. He went on another adventure this morning."

Morgan slipped inside Adelaide's stall and brushed her gray coat. Wads of shedding winter hair clogged the currycomb. Morgan combed out Adelaide's bristle brush of a mane, and a tail that lacked long hair until halfway down its length, where it began to resemble a horse's tail. Adelaide seemed to relish the attention, her large brown eyes drooping to half-mast.

Everyone was having babies. Adelaide and her summer foal, Sarah and Russ, Cindy and her recent birth. Morgan, in her mid-forties, was past that stage of life. Yet she wasn't old yet. She hoped she had a couple more decades before that designation fit. She knew women in their seventies for whom the label "elderly" would be absurd.

Morgan was free to live life for herself, if only she could

figure out what that meant.

Adelaide's gray coat glistened, and Morgan wasn't any closer to an answer. She cleaned the stalls and straightened the tack room. Del and Bill Sharp showed no signs of returning from their manhunt. Morgan had nothing left to do but return to the real world.

A lime green van sat in front of the rock shop. As she approached, Professor Esteban hopped out. Under a thick fleece jacket that matched the color of the van, he wore khaki dress slacks. Morgan guessed he had come straight from the classroom.

"I was about to give up." He flashed a generous smile.

"Sorry, Professor. I was up at the barn. I guess no one put out the be-back-in sign." Shop owners in Golden Springs placed signs with clock faces in their windows when they were gone during business hours. They set the hands of the clocks to the time they expected to return. Morgan unlocked the door. The cowbell clanged. "Welcome to the Rock of Ages."

Professor Esteban pulled his knit wool cap off thick black hair and clutched it between his hands, almost as though he were entering a church. Maybe a rock shop was akin to sacred ground, for a geologist.

"I've been meaning to drop by since I learned of your store." He nodded. "Quite the interesting collection."

"Are you looking for something in particular?" Morgan asked. "Or just window shopping?"

"I'm always on the hunt for the rare. The unusual. But you could call my visit today window shopping. Do you mind if I look around?"

"Please. Make yourself at home."

Morgan wondered if he would find any errors in the classification of the rocks, minerals, and fossils. Would the Rock of Ages make a passing grade?

Professor Esteban strolled up and down the aisles, his hands clasped behind his back. He paused in front of Del's antique display, peered inside locked display cases, and collected odds and ends in a battered handheld shopping basket.

Morgan straightened out the narrow tables in the center of the shop. Customers were constantly mixing up the contents of the rough-hewn wooden cases. Pyrite, also known as Fool's Gold, glittered among the polished agate, and arrowheads had spilled into the fossilized shark teeth. When she looked up, Professor Esteban stood at the checkout counter.

"I'm sorry," Morgan said. "I didn't know you were ready."

"I was admiring your triceratops horn. I'm afraid I don't have that kind of cash, but believe me, it is tempting. Although I don't see how you could possibly give up such a treasure."

"For the right price, I could find a way," Morgan said. "We have bills to pay."

Professor Esteban held his hands out, palms up, and looked around the cluttered shop.

"Your store is brimming with treasures. Surely there are many more items of high value besides this triceratops brow horn."

Morgan remembered Mr. Cooper's visit to the rock shop just days ago. He had asked nearly the same question, in an entirely different way.

"Was there something in particular you wanted?" Morgan asked. "Maybe it's tucked away somewhere."

"Ah." He smiled and shook his head. "What I am searching for would certainly be under lock and key."

Just get to the point, Morgan wanted to tell him.

"We keep our gemstones and the more valuable fossils in the locked display cases," she said. "I can pull some things out, if you want a closer look."

A line creased between his eyes.

"While I saw many lovely fossils and minerals, I have samples of everything in your store in my own collection. No, I am looking for that special item I do not have."

Morgan looked at his shopping basket. "And these?"

"Gifts for a colleague's birthday."

"Ah, yes. Coprolite is very popular."

Professor Esteban wasn't the first person to buy petrified dinosaur dung as a birthday gift.

"And the fossilized fish will look nice on his desk," he said.

Morgan rang up the sale, then wrapped the items in newspaper. He had his own canvas shopping bag.

"Do you have business cards?" Professor Esteban asked. "I would be happy to refer my students to your shop."

"I recently had some printed." Morgan handed Esteban a stack of cards. "If you tell me that special item you're looking for, I can keep an eye out for it, and give you a call if I run across it."

The professor paused in the doorway. "You will know it when you see it."

The cowbell clanged as he left.

Morgan was cleaning shelves when Del, Chief Sharp, and Deputy Parker returned. Del led them into the living quarters and started a pot of coffee, his typical gesture of hospitality.

"Big Foot left lots of tracks in the mud." Del set out mugs, sugar, and cream.

"Then we lost him," J.B. said. "He headed for the rocks where he wouldn't leave tracks."

Chief Sharp pulled off his brown cowboy hat and brushed back his silver-streaked dark hair. "The guy has lived in these hills for—who knows—decades? His entire life? Usually we know who's wandering around out here, but this guy is an unknown."

"He'll turn back up," Del said. "I have this theory that he's looking for Carlee's bones. He was her caretaker these sixteen years, and now we took her away from him."

Bill Sharp shrugged. "Who knows, Mr. Addison? You might be right. But how do we smoke this guy out?"

"Do you think he killed Carlee?" Morgan asked.

"You're friends with Beatrice," Sharp said. "I'm sure she's already told you. There's no clue to how Miss Kruger died. So it's not a murder case at this point. But I sure would like to know how she came to be in a dugout, guarded by a mountain man nobody knows."

The shadow of the mountain crept across the rock shop before Morgan and Del started closing up. The shop's hours were flexible. Customers had trickled in for the past hour and a half, so they stayed open late.

"Days like this make me realize how much we need to replace Cindy," Morgan said. "Not that she can be replaced. But it's not even peak tourist season. We'll never have a break."

"Remember, kid, you're running your own business. You don't get breaks."

"While you were hunting Sasquatch, my geology professor dropped by."

"What'd he think of our shop?"

"The man makes his living teaching students about rocks, minerals, and fossils. He seemed right at home. But I felt like he was snooping around for something."

"He's a typical rock hound," Del said. "You're lucky he didn't break out a pick ax and a shovel."

"No, Del. This was different. He even said he was looking for something special. Kept hinting around that I might have it locked away, like I was holding out on him."

Del tugged at his mustache. "Maybe that was his way of sweet-talking you. He's a nice looking fella. One of those dashing Latin types."

"He's happily married. He talked about his wife all the time during our class. That wasn't it. His questions reminded me of our visit from Harlan Cooper, but Professor Esteban was polite."

Del pulled on a string, turning on one of the overhead fluorescent lights. "Hey, it's getting late. I can finish closing up. Don't you need to get ready?"

"I'm just going to Kurt's for dinner," Morgan said. "I don't need to dress up."

"I seem to recall how much time you spent primping for your date with Piers a few months ago. And then there was that fellow from church."

"Piers was different. I was having dinner with a potential murderer. I had to figure out what to wear to hide the gun you insisted I carry. And as for Pete Melcher, that was just unfortunate all the way around. He's a nice guy, but not the one for me."

"And Kurt is."

"This isn't a date."

"Really?" Del's mustache lifted on one side in a smirk.

"We're going over all the newspaper articles he and Anna dug up about Gerda's daughter. Anna will be there. I think."

"Well, then, that's different."

"Del, you're interested in the case. Do you want to go? I'm sure Kurt wouldn't mind."

"I'll stay here. That mountain man might make a return appearance." He pulled the handgun out of his shoulder holster and checked the ammo. "You know, kid, it's okay if you decide to live your life again."

"What do you mean? I am living life. I'm so busy, I barely have time to sit down."

"No, I mean your romantic life."

"Speak for yourself."

"I'm a geezer. My time for romance has come and gone. You've got a lot of years ahead of you, and it would be a shame to see you spend them alone."

"Del, it's not too late for you, either. There are plenty of eligible ladies your age."

Del shook his head. "I've got a nice life, kid. I don't want to mess it up going down that dead-end trail again."

Morgan hadn't known there were modern townhomes in Golden Springs, but on the outskirts of town sat two small developments. One had the look of a Swiss chalet while the other, across the narrow street, had a southwest look with red tile roofs, sandstone-colored stucco, and strings of dried peppers called *ristras* hanging in the entryways. Kurt had opted for the southwest style.

When he opened the door, Morgan felt woefully underdressed. She had changed due to her time spent in the barn and cleaning the shop, but her jeans and turquoise blouse were casual compared to his shirt and tie. Nineteen forties' vintage, as usual.

"Come in." Kurt opened the door wide and waved her inside. "Welcome to my home."

The outside might look southwest, but the living room was straight from a movie set. In spite of the open floor plan, the combined living and dining area felt cluttered with antique loveseats and chairs, curio shelves crammed with toys and dishes and books, and an oak table buried under folders and newspapers.

"As you can see, we won't be dining in here."

Morgan followed Kurt into the kitchen. Flickering candles, a bottle of wine, and service for two made Kurt's intentions obvious.

CHAPTER THIRTEEN

Morgan stared at the romantic table setting for perhaps a bit longer than she should have. When she turned to Kurt, a blush flamed across his cheeks.

"I thought—" Morgan began. "Well, I assumed Anna would be here. Since she helped you with the research."

"Oh. Well, I thought it was understood. I should have been more clear."

They stood beside the table, neither speaking for a long minute. Then they both spoke at once.

"Of course it's okay—"

"If you want to cancel—"

Both laughed.

"I'd be happy to stay for dinner," Morgan said.

"This does seem a bit much for dinner between friends," Kurt said, probably attempting to ease his own discomfort.

"It looks just fine," Morgan said. "Smells delicious."

Kurt confessed that the main course and dessert were carry-out from an Italian restaurant in Granite Junction, near his business meeting earlier in the day. The salad and garlic bread were his own inventions. After a half glass of merlot, Morgan admitted to herself that a visit to Kurt's world had its charms. The appliances and cabinets were modern, but the mismatched china was antique, as was the silverware. An embroidered cloth decorated a table with metal legs. The chairs had vinyl seats and backrests.

"This dinette set looks suspiciously nineteen fifties," Morgan said.

"I assure you, it is from the forties, and it is authentic." Kurt lifted the wine bottle. "Need a refill?"

"Not yet."

She felt comfortable with Kurt in a way that had been totally lacking with Pete Melcher. Besides, she and Kurt had already shared one adventure, and now had a cold case to solve. No, Morgan reminded herself, Kurt had a case to solve. She was not getting involved in this one. They sailed right past the implications of the candle-lit dinner and plunged into work.

"Let's move to the dining room," Kurt said.

A timeline ran down the center of the table, hand written on a long narrow sheet of newsprint. Strings ran from the timeline to folders and photos.

"You must have spent hours putting this together."

"This made the most sense to me. Start with a timeline of Carlee Kruger's life, then fill in the events that were made public in some way."

"You're taking the cold case quite seriously."

"I came late to the party for your last case, and you were nearly killed. I don't want that to happen again." Kurt's expression was a little more tender than Morgan was prepared to handle, but he changed the subject quickly. "Besides, if the *Golden Springs Gazetteer* solves the case first, think of the publicity for my paper."

That was the Kurt Willard Morgan knew—the self-serving newspaperman.

"Have you discovered anything that explains Carlee's disappearance?" she asked.

"I don't want to prejudice your take on her life. Let's start at the beginning."

Kurt and Anna had amassed an incredible amount of

information about a small-town girl who disappeared at the age of twenty-three. The timeline began with her birth announcement in the *Gazetteer.* She had been born in Doctor Drewmoore's clinic in Golden Springs. Four years later, her sister Camille was born in a Granite Junction hospital.

The *Gazetteer* reported nearly every school event imaginable, especially athletics. The timeline had a surprising number of strings leading to newspaper articles with Carlee's name.

"Carlee was a busy girl," Morgan said.

"An overachiever?" Kurt asked. "Or were academics and athletics the only outlet for a bright kid in a small town?"

Carlee's name appeared on lists of students going to regional debates, soccer and swim meets. She had even participated in beauty pageants, going as far as state. Morgan would have been incredulous, but there was photographic evidence of her beauty, and of her proud parents. Carlee's father had been a looker, and Gerda was lovely before age, anger, and alcohol had soured her expression.

A string led from the timeline to an obituary. Karl Kruger died after a brief illness.

"He seemed awfully young," Kurt said.

"Beatrice told me he died of cancer. That's what took my husband, Sam. Way too young and way too quickly."

"I'm sorry."

"Me, too." Morgan pointed to the timeline, eager to move past the memory of the most difficult time of her life. "So Carlee graduated, class valedictorian and senior prom queen."

A black and white photo showed beautiful Carlee with the prom king. Morgan picked up the photo, holding it closer. The prom king had a military-style haircut, cut close to the scalp, nothing frivolous like an attempt at style. He stood ramrod straight. His slacks had a crease that would slice through butter. Kurt moved closer to look over her shoulder. Morgan could smell his aftershave and a hint of garlic.

"Carlee must have been tiny. This Evan guy towers over her."

"You'll notice the important point. The king is not Jade Tinsley," Kurt said. "Of course, the prom king and queen aren't necessarily an item, but I'm not sure when Tinsley came onto the scene."

"From what I heard, they were high-school sweethearts," Morgan said. "But I don't see Jade's name on the timeline. You didn't notice him on the honor roll, or listed on the baseball or football team?"

"No. Nothing. They seem like a mismatched couple."

"Do you have any information about this guy?" Morgan set the photo on the table.

Kurt shuffled through the newspaper clippings. "Joined the military straight out of high school."

"No surprise there."

"He suffered head trauma when an IED blew up his transport truck near Fallujah."

"How bad was his injury?" Morgan asked. "Did he move back to Golden Springs?"

"I haven't investigated secondary figures in this story yet." Kurt grinned. "Investigate. I like the sound of that."

"I don't," Morgan said. "You remember what happened to me when I tried my hand at detective work."

"I'll take it as a good sign that you're worried about me." Kurt tapped the timeline with one finger. "But there's more to Carlee's story."

After Carlee graduated from high school, her appearances in the *Gazetteer* thinned out. For several years, any mention of Carlee was brief, and brought tidbits of good news. Jade started to appear in news stories, too. He won a ribbon at the state fair for a painting, had showings in local art galleries, and a few months later was awarded a scholarship to an art school. Both attended college.

When Camille entered high school, the newspaper virtually ignored the younger sister. There were no beauty pageants or athletic trophies. She leaned more toward academic accomplishments, making the honor roll and winning a prize in a regional science fair. Those moments of acclaim seemed to fizzle out midway through high school.

"About the time Gerda falls apart," Morgan said. "At least in public."

Gerda appeared in an article about an assault case in a local bar in which she was the aggressor. A few months later, she totaled her car when she rolled in a ditch.

"Sound like she might have been drinking?" Morgan asked. "I can't imagine Gerda having an accident. She's kind of a car expert."

"Knowing how to repair cars doesn't mean you know how to drive them. What caught my attention was that she doesn't start having problems, at least in public, until several years after Karl's death."

"It could have taken time for all the consequences of her husband's death to really hit the family." Morgan and her grown children seemed to be going through a long, drawn out mourning process for Sam. The delayed reaction made sense to Morgan. "Maybe Gerda and her daughters held things together for the first few years, but they just couldn't keep it going."

"Maybe Carlee was the one holding them together. Gerda and Camille seem to fall apart after she goes away to college."

A notice announced that Camille and three other students had graduated from high school in December. The former honor student had hobbled through to her diploma a semester late. Then she vanished, as far as the *Gazetteer* was concerned.

A string led from the timeline to a society page article.

"Carlee and Jade Tinsley became engaged," Morgan said.

"I've heard that from a dozen people already, but this makes it seem more real."

The youthful faces smiling at them from the newspaper were attractive and full of life.

"And they all should have lived happily ever after," Morgan said. "The kids make it through high school, the oldest daughter is engaged. Gerda seems to be staying out of trouble."

"Until three months before Carlee disappears."

Kurt followed a string from the timeline to a newspaper. Gerda made front-page news for her drunk-driving arrest.

"That seems cruel," Morgan said.

"Driving while intoxicated?"

"No. Smearing Gerda's name all over the front page," Morgan said. "Couldn't they have tucked it inside somewhere? Wouldn't you have?"

Kurt had acquired the newspaper four years ago. In an era when papers large and small were folding, the *Gazetteer* hung on with its gossipy coverage of local news.

"She could have been one of those drunk drivers who hit a car head on," he said, "taking out an entire family. There's no reason to cut a person any slack for endangering others."

"You're right," Morgan said. "If I only read about her in the newspaper, and didn't know her personally, I'd feel the same. But she is trying to change. She's going to AA meetings."

"Let's hope reopening her daughter's cold case doesn't push Gerda off the wagon."

Kurt pressed his beefy hands onto the oak table. His brown hair was breaking free from whatever gel he used to plaster it into place, and curled at the edges. He wasn't a small man, but then, Morgan hadn't worn size six jeans in over a decade. He was a nice looking man, with a solid jaw that hinted at a stubborn streak. His gold-flecked hazel eyes seemed to take in everything. Morgan realized, with a twinge of guilt, that she was glad Anna Heiden hadn't come to dinner.

Startled by the attraction she felt, Morgan moved back a step on the pretense of needing a sip of merlot, and focused on the case. As she studied the oak table, an organized mess of folders, newspapers, and photographs, it hit her that this was the sum of a young woman's life.

"We're getting near the end." Kurt watched Morgan for a moment. "Shall we keep going?"

Morgan shook her head. "I don't know if I'm ready for this." Tears filled her eyes.

"Are you okay?" Kurt asked.

"The whole story is so incredibly tragic." Morgan wiped a hand across her eyes. "I didn't even know Carlee. Well, I didn't know her before. Now she seems like a real person. Of course she was real." Morgan looked up at Kurt. "I feel like I know her now."

"Maybe that's the key to finding out what happened to her. We have to know her. Know what she would have done. Where she went, and why."

Now the stacks of folders became thicker, the strings leading from the timeline forming a spider's web. News of Carlee going missing dominated the *Gazetteer* for weeks. The search parties, a reward offer, interviews, clues.

"How could they have missed finding her?" Morgan asked.

"You're assuming she was dead when the search began," Kurt said. "We don't know when she died, or where. If she did run away, like some people think, maybe she came back after the searchers gave up. A month, six months, a year later. But there's another problem." Kurt rolled out a map of the area, with the search parameters highlighted with a dark border and hash lines. "This is the area they searched. And here is where you found her."

Kurt tapped his finger on a spot outside the search area.

"Why did they search here?" Morgan traced the boundary line.

"Trails from Golden Springs lead to this side of Temple Mountain. The searchers must have assumed Carlee left town on foot."

"Maybe they were wrong about that." Morgan pushed her hand through her hair, her fingers twining through her wild curls. "How will we ever know what really happened?"

"Someone talks. And the way to get them talking is to find the key people who knew her at the time. People who saw her last. The fiancée, her schoolmates, Gerda."

"Good luck with that," Morgan said. "Gerda is angry with anyone who tries to talk to her. So why are you investigating this case? If it's just to drum up new headlines for the *Gazetteer*, you might end up with a lot of upset readers."

"I'm not as opportunistic as you think," Kurt said. "As bristly as Gerda can be, I feel sorry for her. She lost both her husband and a child. Two children, really."

"Chief Sharp thinks the mountain man is the key," Morgan said. "I'm inclined to agree. At first, I just wanted answers for Gerda's sake, but after Bernie's run-in with him behind the bakery, and then breaking into Del's trailer to steal clothes, it's getting too close to home."

"The story's out there," Kurt said. "Someone might have gotten away with murder. I'm determined to find the answer."

Morgan picked up the prom photo. "I just moved away from my children, but I still feel the pain of loss. I can't imagine what Gerda's been through."

"My sons are in California," Kurt said.

"I didn't know you had a family."

"Had is right. Past tense. When I first bought the paper, I imagined I'd convince my ex to patch things up and move here with me. In hindsight, I realize how lucky I am that didn't happen. The boys visit me every summer, and with computers and phones, we're not ever really apart, but it's not the same as being there physically, as you know."

Morgan nodded. She knew. Kurt kept talking.

"I'm sure the boys resent me for moving to Colorado, but it was a once in a lifetime opportunity. I'm trying to convince them to apply to Colorado colleges so they'll be closer to me. Their mother may not appreciate that, but they're young men now. Eighteen years old. They can make their own decisions."

"They're both eighteen?" Morgan asked. "Twins?"

"That's an entire story in itself," Kurt said. "For another time. But for now suffice it to say they're stepbrothers."

"You must be younger than me," Morgan said.

"I'm pretty sure I started my family later in life than you did. I'm forty-eight."

"Only two years older than me."

"What about your kids? How old are they?"

"Sarah is twenty-three, married, and about to have a baby. David is twenty-one, but has been living on his own since shortly after his father passed away. He's putting himself through college. I suppose I should be proud, but I wish they both needed me a little more."

"I know how you feel. I haven't been a part of my sons' lives the way I imagined I would."

Kids. And not middle-aged children who might be grateful their parents were finally getting involved with someone. No, Kurt's boys and Morgan's children were young enough to be resentful of a romantic interest in their parents' lives. Especially Morgan's son, David, who had yet to start healing from the loss of his father. The conversation was getting uncomfortable. She steered it back to the cold case.

"But at least our children are alive."

Kurt turned the map around. "I'd like to see where you found

Carlee. Can you take me there?"

Del could handle the shop for a few hours. Morgan could lead Kurt to the dugout tomorrow if she wanted to, but the thought of a walk through the forest alone with Kurt was a bit much to contemplate after their evening together.

"Saturdays are busy at the shop. And I need to run it by Del, since he'll be managing the shop by himself."

"I'd like to go soon. I'll call Chief Sharp to make sure the dugout's not off limits." Kurt scribbled a note on a pad of paper.

Morgan glanced at the clock on the mantle, an antique, of course. The hands had a utilitarian grace as they pointed to numbers in an art-deco font.

"It's later than I thought," Morgan said.

"Only ten o'clock. Early for a Friday night. Can I interest you in another glass of wine?"

"I need to get home. I'm a rancher, according to my tax accountant. I have to get up early to take care of my herd of donkeys."

"Do two donkeys constitute a herd?"

"Soon to be three," Morgan said.

Kurt helped her into her coat and walked her to the Buick. He opened the driver's door.

"I enjoyed tonight," Kurt said.

"Me, too." Morgan shrugged. "Dealing with Carlee's case isn't exactly fun. But the dinner and conversation were nice."

Kurt beamed a smile, his cheeks flushed red in the chill night air.

"Maybe we can do this again some time. The dinner, I mean."

Morgan surprised herself with her swift and sincere reply. "I'd like that."

Chapter Fourteen

Saturday morning Morgan woke on time to feed Adelaide and Houdini, then allowed herself the luxury of crawling back into bed. It was a shame to waste a beautiful morning in the Rockies sleeping, but Morgan was exhausted. She ignored the sun peeking through the southwest-patterned curtains in the bedroom window, until she heard the shop's cowbell clang. Disoriented, Morgan rolled out of bed and yanked on yesterday's jeans and sweatshirt.

A man's voice called from the shop. "Hello!"

Del wasn't in the living quarters, and if a customer had to holler for help, he wasn't in the shop, either. Morgan shoved her feet into slippers and opened the door dividing the living quarters from the shop. Barton Potts stood at the checkout counter. Perhaps he had brought more topaz.

"Good morning," Morgan said.

"I'm looking for Del."

"So am I."

The old cowboy opened the front door and leaned in.

"About time everyone showed up" he said. "I'm not getting any younger, you know."

"What's going on?" Morgan felt she had missed out on something vital by sleeping in.

"After that old boy broke in and stole from me," Del said, "I decided I'd better do some fixing up to make sure nobody can get inside my home again."

Morgan hoped that meant boarding up the windows and doors of the broken down old trailer house.

"It's time I moved back in my own place," Del continued. "Come on. I'll show you what I've got planned."

Morgan squeezed into the cab of Barton's truck for the short, bumpy ride to the trailer.

"I understand you want to protect your belongings," Morgan said, "but with a potential killer running around, I'd rather you stayed in the shop living quarters."

"I will. Until that fella's captured. But after that I think it's time for me to get out of your hair."

The trailer looked worse in the light of day. Hail had left dents in the siding, the roof sagged, and the skirting had peeled back in places. Dry rot had eaten up the steps leading to the front door.

"What's the plan?" Morgan asked. Hers would have been demolition.

"New steps first," Barton said. "Then we can haul Del's collection out safely."

"Collection?" Morgan asked.

"You probably didn't notice the other night in all the excitement," Del said. "Come on in."

He clambered inside the trailer without placing his feet on the rotten steps, then held out a hand to Morgan, helping her through the door. She remembered the living room, with its low ceiling and ratty sofa. The place had a few touches of femininity, leftover from the deceased Mrs. Addison. Doilies on the furniture, knickknacks that included cherubic children in Germanic lederhosen and dirndls, a hand-crocheted afghan thrown over the back of an aspen-wood rocking chair, and framed family photos.

"The thief didn't touch your collection." Barton flipped on a light, illuminating a china cabinet. "Probably didn't know what you have here."

A china cabinet full of rocks, Morgan thought.

She had learned enough about geology and gemstones to recognize the excellent specimens of crystals, including one with three perfect crystals in black, white, and blue rising from the same base. It reminded her of the amazing crystal on the Denver gem show postcard, and had to be worth as much.

"You could sell that one and buy you a new trailer." Barton squinted into the cabinet.

"Not a bad idea," Morgan muttered.

"That cabinet contains my retirement fund," Del said. "I can't touch it except in an emergency."

Morgan glanced around at the interior of the trailer, and wondered what constituted an emergency in Del's book. Another thought intruded. The trailer's exterior might be a wreck, but inside it was neat and tidy. It would do just fine for summer quarters. Barton bent over to peer up inside the cabinet.

"I think that leak is about to break through."

Above the particleboard cabinet, Morgan saw a dark stain on the ceiling.

"Dripping water will reduce the cabinet to wood pulp in no time," Morgan said.

"Maybe I should move it out of here until I get the roof redone."

"The roof?" Barton asked. "Del, I really think you should consider whether your place is salvageable." Barton glanced at Morgan and shrugged. "I told him he could move in with me. At least until he decides what to do."

"I don't know," Morgan said. "Maybe the trailer is worth fixing up. For now, he could move the valuable items into the shop."

"I'm standing right here." Del placed his fists on his narrow hips and frowned. "Somebody could ask me what I want to do."

"Okay," Barton said. "What do you want to do?"

Del flapped his arms. "I want my house back. This is where me and the missus spent some very fine years together. A little patching up, and I'll move back in."

This wasn't about fixing up a place. Not if Del had the means to replace the trailer. He stomped down the hallway to the bedroom. Morgan heard drawers slamming.

She spoke in a low voice to Barton. "I'm getting out of the line of fire. I'll walk back to the shop."

Morgan was juggling customer questions, ringing up sales, and wishing Del would give up on the trailer and come to work, when the phone rang.

"Rock of Ages," Morgan said. "How may I help you?"

"This is Vernon." He took a couple breaths. "Sorry. I've been running. Chasing after a couple guys. Might have been the ones that cut the lock off my gate. I tried to get the registration numbers on their ATVs, but they were too fast for me. They must have been up to no good, or they wouldn't have run off."

"Were they rustling cattle?"

"No, they were digging. Prospecting on private property. I'm reporting this to Chief Sharp, but I wanted to warn you. If they were digging on my place, they might hit yours next."

"With Houdini chasing after intruders? I don't think a person would take the risk."

"That might be true if he was home," Vernon said, "but your donkey's over here."

"Again?"

"You know, I could swear he was heading for the digging site."

"I'll send Del over to get him."

With two donkeys who were escape artists, the Rock of Ages gates were checked and double-checked constantly. Morgan chided herself for not looking into replacing latches with something more ingenious than a determined donkey. She called Barton's cell phone and told him about the intruders. He sounded as disgusted as Vernon.

"People think they're just having fun digging for buried treasure," Barton said, "but they're stealing just the same as some guy hotwiring a car or robbing a bank."

"Houdini is on Vernon and Sherry's place again. I'm swamped with customers. Can you ask Del to round up the donkey?"

"I'll go with him," Barton said.

A steady stream of rock hounds and tourists out to enjoy the spring day found their way to the Rock of Ages. The ringing cash register drowned out worries about claim jumpers and cold cases. Close to closing, Bernie called.

"Do you have plans tonight?" Bernie's words sounded like they were spoken through clenched teeth.

"No," Morgan said, "but I thought you were going out with Rolf."

"Meet me at the Hot Tomato at six thirty."

"Is there something you want to talk about?"

"Just be there."

As Morgan hung up the phone, she decided to check the phase of the moon. Everyone was acting crazy today. Thankfully, Del did agree to let Barton haul a load of his possessions to his place for safekeeping, while he decided what to do about the trailer. Del's most valuable mineral and crystal samples went into locked display cases in the Rock of Ages.

Morgan closed shop for the day and was heading through the door to the living quarters when the phone rang. She almost let it go to voice mail, but decided to pick it up.

"Hello, Rock of Ages, how may I help you?"

The line was silent for a moment, then Gerda's gruff voice

came through the receiver.

"You found my daughter."

She already knew that, Morgan thought, so it must not be a question. "Yes. I did."

"You know the place."

Gerda's voice was strained, but her words were not slurred. She sounded sober.

"I know where it is," Morgan said. "Yes."

"I need to see where you found her. Will you take me?"

In a day that just got stranger by the minute, Morgan made plans to pick up Gerda after church the next day and take her to the dugout. Then she called Kurt. Morgan wasn't sure whether she wanted Gerda to chaperone her walk through the mountains with Kurt, or vice versa, but either way, three were company while two felt dangerous.

Morgan looked forward to dinner. Bernie had been too busy lately to spend time with her. She anticipated a relaxing evening of girl-time, until she entered the Hot Tomato. Bernie typically dressed in clothes to flatter her plus-size figure, and wore just enough makeup to enhance her naturally pretty face. Tonight she wore baggy sweats. Her eyes were puffy and red, and her shoulder length brown hair hung in limp disarray. Morgan slid onto a chair across from her friend.

"Bernie, what's wrong?"

The baker pressed a paper napkin to her eyes. "It's Rolf. He lied to me."

Morgan's blood pressure spiked. Bernie had confided that she thought Rolf might be The One, and he'd already reduced her to tears.

"What happened?"

"He has a daughter." She sniffed. "He's been married."

The waitress drifted by, no doubt attempting to be discreet

and attentive at the same time. Morgan nodded to her, and she hurried to their table. When Bernie's lips quivered and her eyes filled with tears, Morgan ordered for her. Comfort food. Macaroni and cheese gourmet style, and a side salad. That sounded good, so Morgan ordered the same. The brief respite over and the waitress gone, she turned her full attention to a fragile Bernie.

"What did Rolf lie about? Is he married now?"

Bernie gave a vigorous shake of her head. "No. It's worse. He has a daughter."

"You mentioned that. So he was married, but he's not married now. And he has a daughter. By the failed marriage?"

Bernie nodded. The waitress brought a pot of hot water and a basket of tea bags to the table. Morgan started a cup brewing for her friend. Bernie definitely needed calming chamomile.

"We've been dating for three months," Bernie said. "And he just now remembers to mention, oh, by the way, Bernie, I have a thirteen-year-old daughter?"

"I wouldn't have guessed Rolf was old enough to have a child that age."

"High-school romance." Bernie squeezed a lemon wedge into her tea and added a dollop of honey from a clear plastic bear. "They had to get married. They were too young to understand what they were getting into. Things fell apart almost immediately, according to Rolf." Bernie sounded like she had her doubts.

Morgan was burning to ask whether Rolf attended the same high school as Carlee, but now was not the time.

"They divorced?" Morgan asked instead.

"When Stacie was just a baby. Rolf claims he wanted to make it work, but don't men always say it wasn't their fault when a marriage fails?"

"Not necessarily," Morgan said. "When do we get to the part

about Rolf lying to you?"

"That's it. He didn't tell me he'd been married. He didn't tell me he has a kid who's practically grown. How does a person forget to mention something that huge?"

"Did he ever imply he had never been married?"

"I know what you're getting at, Morgan, but it was the sin of omission. Not bringing it up was like lying. Wasn't it?"

Morgan saw the waitress approaching. She held her hand up slightly to signal Bernie to hit pause on her rant. With the salads and mac and cheese placed before them, and assurances that they had everything they needed, the waitress left them.

"I'm scared, Morgan." Bernie speared a pasta shell with her fork. "He wants me to meet her. This weekend."

"You were supposed to meet her tonight, weren't you?" When Bernie didn't answer, Morgan added, "You chickened out."

Bernie set her fork down. "What if she hates me? What if she likes me, and Rolf and I don't work out, and she gets her heart broken? I'm not ready to be a mother. Not this way. I imagined it all different."

"It's always different from the fantasy," Morgan said. "Believe me."

"I'm thinking of calling the whole thing off."

"This weekend? Or forever?"

Bernie's lip trembled again. "It's not supposed to be this hard."

"What isn't?"

"Love." The word was a whisper.

Morgan ate a few bites, giving the conversation space to settle. Bernie seemed to breathe a little easier as she sipped the calming tea.

"Okay," Morgan said. "Here are your options, as I see them. You can let your fear of failure destroy what you told me might be your last chance to find love. Of course, I don't think it's your last chance, because you're younger than me by over a decade, so if you're ready to throw in the towel on romance, that pretty well means I'll be spending the rest of my life alone."

Bernie's mouth quirked up at the corners in a weak grin.

"Or you can take a chance that this will work out, understanding that stepparenting can be a tough job, but also realizing that Rolf's daughter is thirteen, so it's unlikely that you'll be blamed if she turns into a train wreck."

Bernie almost giggled. "I get your point." She took a deep breath and exhaled slowly. "I need to calm down and give this a chance. It's scary, you know?"

Morgan thought of her own recent fumbling attempts at romance.

"I know."

Chapter Fifteen

Sunday a pastor from the regional pool gave an especially bland sermon. Maybe that was what drove Morgan's brother, Kendall, to Central America. His faith was deep and passionate, a ship with wind-whipped sails riding the rolling swells of a stormy sea, while the Golden Springs Community Church preferred sailing paper boats on a duck pond.

As the service concluded and people moved into the social area, Beatrice, Teruko, and Anna hurried to the kitchen. Morgan rinsed coffee cups and loaded the dishwasher. She considered telling the ladies about her planned excursion with Gerda, but however well-intentioned, Gerda's pain might become grist for the gossip mill once again. And if Morgan mentioned Kurt Willard, she would never hear the end of it.

Morgan picked up Kurt first. He had exchanged his 1940s' reporter costume for standard Colorado hiking gear of khaki slacks with plenty of pockets, boots with waffled soles, and a fleece-lined windbreaker. With his apple-red cheeks and the breeze rumpling his short brown hair, he almost looked like a rugged outdoorsman. Or maybe an over-the-hill boy scout.

"Gerda wasn't happy when I told her you were coming," Morgan said, "but I explained about the mountain man, and that we needed a bodyguard."

"I'll be as unobtrusive as I can," Kurt said. "I even left my notepad and pencil at home."

Gerda requested that Morgan pick her up at the auto repair

shop, which made Morgan more curious about her mysterious house behind the gate. As Morgan pulled up in front of Kruger's Auto Repair, Gerda emerged from one of the bays. She was dressed for a hike in stretch jeans and hiking boots, her short white hair covered with a floppy hat.

"So," Gerda said, looking at Kurt, "you did come."

"I'm just here to help," Kurt said. "I'm not here in my capacity as editor of the *Gazetteer.*"

"Let us keep it that way," Gerda said as she climbed in. "This is a private moment. I do not wish to see it splashed across the front page of your little rag."

Kurt's face flushed a deeper red, but he kept his mouth shut.

Morgan couldn't think of anything to say that didn't sound inane, and Gerda didn't help her out with any small talk. They all knew where they were going, and why. After driving several miles up the highway, Morgan pulled off on a forest service road, then into the Temple Mountain trailhead parking lot. She turned off the engine, and they sat in silence.

"Let us get this over with then," Gerda finally said.

Kurt hopped out to open her door, and offered his hand. Gerda ignored him, hoisting herself onto her feet.

Morgan took the lead, Gerda followed, and Kurt took up the rear. The mountainside was green and glorious for a few precious weeks before the dry summer would set in. The wind sighed through the trees, a rushing sound as though the earth itself was breathing. Their boots crunched across rock, and padded across pine needles. Gerda paused several times, her breathing labored. They were at high elevation, in oxygen-thin air.

Morgan feared it would be difficult to find the dugout, but the police chief, deputy, coroner, Pine County Search and Rescue, and Granite Junction law enforcement personnel had stomped a fresh trail through the sparse grass. She followed the deep imprint of boots. Most of the moisture from the recent rain and sleet had already been sucked into the rocky soil.

Morgan stopped. The creek widened. The water slowed its downhill rush over moss-covered boulders. Sunlight cast a mottled golden pattern through the trees. Yellow crime scene tape flapped from tree trunks, forming a loose fence around the dugout.

"So they think it was a crime," Gerda said.

Morgan was afraid to speak. All she had heard was conjecture.

"The police still don't know whether Carlee's death was a crime, or an accident." Kurt tugged a strip of yellow tape away from a tree. "Chief Sharp said the scene has been cleared. We can go as close as we want."

As Gerda approached the dugout, Morgan felt as though she had accompanied the older woman to a funeral home viewing.

"Those flowers." Gerda pointed to the spikes of elephant heads sprouting in neat mounds, surrounded by polished river rocks. "They were my Carlee's favorite."

Morgan hoped this was the moment when Gerda found healing. Perhaps she would wax sentimental, maybe even shed a few tears, as she recalled poignant memories of her daughter.

"What the hell are they doing here?" A frown deepened the crease between Gerda's eyes.

"They're wildflowers," Kurt said.

"Not here." Gerda turned and frowned up at Kurt. "They are high-altitude flowers. They do not grow naturally at this elevation. I know. Carlee made a study of them for her high-school biology class."

She turned to face the dugout. Morgan glanced at Kurt. He shrugged. Flowers out of place. Del had said the same thing. Elephant-head flowers grew at higher elevation, and he had added that they did not bloom this early. Morgan wondered whether the mountain man had planted them as a memorial. To what? The stranger he found dead in a snowdrift? The girl he murdered?

Gerda threw her arms in the air and jumped back a step. "Ahh!"

An Abert's squirrel popped out from behind the flowers, clutching something in its little paws. Morgan fumbled for her camera, but she was too late. The squirrel's shimmering black fur and tufted ears disappeared up a Ponderosa pine.

"What did that rodent have?" Gerda knelt in front of the ring of stones and brushed her hands through the elephant-head flowers.

"Maybe someone dropped a granola bar," Morgan said. "There's a wrapper over here." She picked up the foil wrapper and stuffed it in her jacket pocket.

Gerda plucked something from the dirt, then stood. "This is not food."

She held out the small object pinched between her forefinger and thumb. Sunlight refracted off an oval the size of Morgan's pinky fingernail. Yellow, green, and orange swirled through the opalescent stone.

"There is more." Gerda jerked her head toward the spot.

Brilliant stones sprinkled the ground near the entrance to the dugout. Morgan crawled on hands and knees beside the older woman until they had each collected a palm full of bright stones. Or maybe it was shell. Morgan wasn't sure which. They looked like shattered bits of rainbow, each containing different combinations of color.

"Look at this." She held out her hand to Kurt. "It almost doesn't look natural." Morgan studied the chips in her palm, twisting her wrist to make the sun play off them. "I take that back. This does look natural. Like opal. Is opal found around here?"

"You're the rock expert," Kurt said.

Unfortunately, Morgan wasn't an expert. She placed the chips in her jacket pocket to show to Del later. Kurt placed a hand on her shoulder and nodded toward Gerda.

The stout woman faced the dugout entrance. Someone had blocked the doorway with a barrier of pine branches. Gerda touched the branches tentatively, then pulled them apart, opening a gap. She peered through, her head swiveling as she looked from side to side. Several long minutes passed, then Gerda bowed her head. Morgan looked away, toward a mound of elephant-head flowers.

"I am done." Gerda marched back to them, some of her old take-charge attitude firmly back in place. She glared at Kurt. "You may now take your photos."

"Gerda, I'm going to take some pictures," Kurt said, "but I won't publish them in the paper. I'll keep them in case Chief Sharp needs them, although I'm sure he had someone with a camera on the—" Kurt paused. "Recovery crew. If I print them in the paper, curiosity seekers might find the dugout. I don't want to be responsible for it being disturbed."

Gerda reached out to squeeze his arm briefly. "You are a better man than I thought."

They hiked back to the trailhead parking lot in silence. When they were headed to Golden Springs, Morgan worked up the courage to ask the question she knew the church ladies would want answered.

"Do you think you're ready to have a memorial service for Carlee?"

Gerda stared out the window at the walls of rock on either side of the highway.

"Yes," Gerda said. "A memorial service. Not for me. I have said my good-bye. For Golden Springs. I remember how everyone came out to look. Day after day they searched the wrong part of the mountain. There were dogs." Gerda snorted.

"Those animals could not smell their own backsides."

A silence filled the car that was just a bit more comfortable than the awful quiet they'd had on the ride up. Then Gerda spoke again.

"I fear what happened will never be known. Morgan? Kurt? Do you believe Carlee lost her way?" The stern woman teared up, her voice quavering. "That she wandered these hills, cold and frightened, until she died, all alone?"

Neither had an answer.

"I would like to know, did she suffer?"

"If we learn anything," Kurt said, "we'll let you know."

"Please. Keep looking." The steel returned to Gerda's words. "And if someone hurt my baby, there will be hell to pay."

Gerda's words sent a chill crawling up Morgan's back that didn't thaw by the time they reached the auto repair shop.

"Can you join us for an early dinner?" Kurt asked.

"You shouldn't be alone," Morgan said.

"You are wrong. I prefer to be alone." Gerda climbed out and waved her hand, shooing them away. "Do not worry. I will not hit the bottle."

Morgan was worried, though. Gerda seemed tough as nails, but today surely opened old wounds.

"How about you?" Kurt asked. "Can I entice you with dinner at the Hot Tomato?"

"I just had dinner there last night with Bernie," Morgan said. "How about someplace else?"

It wasn't just repetition that steered Morgan away from the restaurant. The large windows facing Main Street afforded passersby a view of the entire dining room. She wasn't ready for her afternoon with Kurt to end, but she also didn't want to be on display for every nosey gossip in town. They settled on a place down the pass, between Golden Springs and Granite Junction. The chain sandwich shop could not be mistaken for the location of a hot date.

"I'd better let Del know where I am." Morgan pulled her cell phone out and called the old cowboy. She promised to give him all the details later. "I'll be home soon."

"No rush," Del said. "I just closed the shop. I've got my feet up, watching a fishing program on the television and enjoying a lazy Sunday afternoon."

Morgan put her phone away.

"I'm glad you have him around," Kurt said. "I didn't mention it when we were there, but I saw fresh boot prints near the dugout."

"The mountain man was huge," Morgan said. "Well, he seemed huge when I was trapped inside the dugout with him. Were the prints big?"

"No. I placed my foot beside a print and took a photo. It was about the same size as mine." Kurt shrugged. "The prints could have been made by the police, or a curious hiker. Whether they were Big Foot's or not, until Chief Sharp catches up to the mountain man, I'll worry about you."

Del was dozing in front of the television when Morgan got home. She felt guilty for leaving him alone at the shop all day. Soon it would be tourist season, and she wouldn't be able to traipse off whenever she wanted. Before Morgan removed her lilac-colored jacket, she emptied the pockets onto the kitchen table. The iridescent chips spilled across the wood.

"You're home." Del yawned. "What you got there?"

"I was hoping you could tell me."

Del pushed himself up out of his recliner. He picked up a chip, held it to the light, and whistled.

"Where did you get this?"

"When Kurt and I took Gerda to see where I found Carlee,

these colored rocks, or shells, or whatever they are, were scattered in front of the dugout."

Del looked from the chip to Morgan. "Who knows about this?"

"Kurt, Gerda, and me."

"That's two too many people." Del tugged at his moustache.

"Is it opal?"

"Let's find out. Can you please hand me a gem and mineral book? That one from your class will do."

Morgan retrieved a book from the small table beside her rocking chair and handed it to Del. He thumbed through the pages, then set the book aside.

"Nope. There's a book on fossils on the bookcase. The little one, with all the pictures."

Morgan retrieved the well-worn book. Del consulted the index, then flipped to a page.

"Ammonite."

He handed the book to Morgan. She studied the photos of ammonite fossils. The dull spirals of shell were not a particularly exciting fossil.

"That's not what Gerda found."

"Turn back a page," Del said.

Morgan did as instructed, then pressed the book open on the kitchen table. One page detailed the science and location of ammolite, while the facing page displayed photos of multiple samples of the gem.

Morgan held one of her larger pieces next to the photos. "That's it."

"Ammolite is an organic gem."

"I thought all rocks were organic."

"People call everything organic nowadays," Del said. "They throw the word around to make things sound healthy. I mean organic in the sense that it was alive once. Rocks are minerals, but ammonites are fossils. Shells, specifically. And when just the right minerals happen along during the fossilization process, it turns into this." He picked up a dazzling blue, green, and gold gem. "Ammolite."

Morgan skimmed the paragraph in the book on how ammolite forms. "So there are only three gemstones produced by living organisms. This stuff, pearls, and amber. Wow."

"If there's ammolite in the hills around here, all heck will break loose."

"So ammolite is valuable?"

"Very rare." Del picked up a chip and studied it. "If you had ammolite on your property, you'd have no money problems."

"That would be nice," Morgan said, "but unfortunately this came from the dugout where I found Carlee."

"It would be a crying shame if some prospector staked a claim before we got to it." Del tugged at his mustache. "And Mr. Newspaper knows." Del sighed. "I suppose we'll have to cut him in on the deal. If he makes a headline out of this find, it'll be the Gold Rush all over again."

The urgency with which Del spoke made Morgan panicky. "I can call Kurt."

"I wish you would."

Morgan went into her bedroom to unplug her cell phone from its charger, then decided to stay in her room to call Kurt. As soon as she dialed his number, Morgan felt silly. But if Del was right, she needed to let Kurt know that the shell-gem needed to be kept quiet. Kurt picked up.

"Sorry to bother you so soon," Morgan said.

"Call any time." Morgan could hear the smile in Kurt's voice.

"You remember the rocks, or shells, Gerda and I found at the dugout?"

"Yes. You said they were like opal. I'd have to agree."

"Did you take any?"

"I did."

"Don't show them to anyone. Del thinks they're ammolite. Apparently, ammolite's a very rare fossilized gem, and that makes it valuable. He's afraid if word gets out, he might miss the chance to stake a claim."

"And Del was afraid I'd plaster the news, complete with photos and a map to the dugout, across the front page of the *Gazetteer.*"

Morgan laughed. "Something like that."

"You can let him know I'll keep it on the down low."

"Thanks. Del also said that he figured he'd have to let you in on the deal if he stakes a claim."

"I'll take him up on it, if he strikes it rich. And Morgan?"

"Yes?"

"I enjoyed spending time with you today."

Morgan felt a blush creeping up her cheeks. She was glad she'd taken the call in her room. Del would be sure to notice, and tease her about it.

"Other than the part about taking Gerda to her daughter's final resting place, I enjoyed today, too."

When Morgan returned to the kitchen, Del had spread a topographical map across the kitchen table. The lines designating elevation squiggled across the thick paper like fingerprints.

"So where exactly is that dugout?"

Morgan studied the map.

"It's not far from the Temple Mountain hiking trail." She traced a fingertip along the line designating the trail. "I came down the creek to the road. Here's the bridge. The parking lot." She drew an invisible circle on the map. "So somewhere in here. In the National Forest. Chief Sharp, the coroner, and Pine County Search and Rescue were all there."

Del shook his head. "Not good. Okay, first we need to know if this area is open to mineral entry." Del scribbled an "x" on the map with a pencil, making it look like a pirate's treasure map. "Then find out if that old dugout is on a valid claim, or better yet, was abandoned years ago." Del tugged at his moustache. "I can't believe anybody'd let an ammolite deposit revert back to the government. But people mostly looked for gold and silver way back when. Nowadays they're after aquamarine and topaz and such. I'll ask Barton to look up the records for this area."

"Hey, you told me I had to keep this under wraps. Now you're telling Barton?"

"He's got expertise at filing a mining claim. If we're gonna claim that site—"

"Gerda's the one who found the ammolite."

"So now we got you and me, Kurt and Gerda, and add Barton if he wants in on the deal." Del grabbed the landline phone. "This is getting too complicated for my tired old noggin. I'm calling Barton."

Chapter Sixteen

At first light, Barton arrived at the Rock of Ages, parking his battered pickup truck behind the living quarters. Morgan poured coffee in a thermos while Del opened the kitchen door. If Carlee's guardian, or killer, resembled a Sasquatch version of a mountain man, Barton looked like a mountain man turned long-distance runner. He wore a fox fur hat, probably made from animals he had trapped himself. His full beard and fringed leather coat added to the look, but from the waist down he was thoroughly modern, with water repellant hiking slacks in a synthetic fabric, and lightweight hiking boots protected with nylon gaiters. Barton shook himself, sending a shower of snowflakes onto the kitchen linoleum.

"It's snowing?" Morgan asked. "It's the middle of May!"

"It's May in Colorado." Del peeked out the curtain on the back door. "Won't last long. How're the roads?"

"Clear enough." Barton studied the rainbow-colored bits of ammolite on the kitchen table. "If anyone knew about this, weather wouldn't matter. There'd be a stampede."

Del pulled on his insulated Carhartt coat and grabbed the thermos and a bag of bagels.

"Did you take your blood pressure medicine?" Morgan asked.

"Yes, ma'am." Del flicked his fingers across the brim of his cowboy hat in a mock salute. "In case you hadn't noticed, I'm old enough to take care of myself."

After the men left and Morgan tended to the donkeys, the

shop phone rang.

"Morgan, this is Cindy. My mom's off work today, and asked to take the kids to the zoo. Do you need help today?"

"That's generous of your mother," Morgan said. "Taking six kids to the zoo can't be easy."

"The older ones help with the younger ones," Cindy said. "You'd be surprised. And I'll have Hezekiah with me, so it's just the five."

"But it's snowing!"

"Won't last long," Cindy said, echoing Del's weather forecast.

"And you don't want to take advantage of having a day to yourself?"

"Honestly, Morgan, I can use the money. Herb won't get a paycheck with his raise for two weeks. If you can use me for a couple hours, Hezekiah and I will come on over."

"I do need to run some errands. You know we won't get much business today. But I have to warn you, the mountain man is in the area. He was in Bernie's Dumpster behind the bakery, and he stole a jacket out of Del's trailer."

"The fella sure gets around. I'll be okay. I'll bring my friend."

"Who is that?" Morgan asked.

"Mr. Smith and Wesson."

Morgan began to ask more questions, but decided she didn't want to know if Cindy had been packing her "friend" in her diaper bag. After Cindy showed up in a small truck, Morgan headed to town. The snow had already melted off the gravel road, but she couldn't take chances with her nearly bald tires. She drove slowly down Hill Street. Morgan parked in front of the *Golden Springs Gazetteer* and crunched across ice melting crystals spread on the wooden walk.

Anna sat at the receptionist desk, wearing her typical power suit and designer heels. A pair of snow boots rested on damp newsprint beside her desk.

"Hi, Anna. I came to check on my ad layout for the business directory."

Anna pushed her chair back and stood. She was taller than Morgan, even without heels. Anna led Morgan to the room with the big wood table. Where the cold case folders had been, there were now pages spread out for the directory.

"We're a little old fashioned here," Anna said. "We could do this all on the computer, but Kurt likes to work with hardcopy for the final layout. Here's your ad."

The Rock of Ages had used the same graphics for ads since she and Kendall inherited the shop from their great-uncle Caleb. Morgan hired local graphic artists, also owners of a T-shirt shop, and gave them carte blanche to develop a new look.

Dinosaurs, bones, and rocks formed the frame for a concisely worded ad giving the rock shop's hours of operation and brief directions. The graphics were eye-catching, with enough white space to stand out among more cluttered appeals for customer attention.

"Very nice," Morgan said.

She glanced up. Morgan still wasn't clear whether she was competing with Anna for Kurt's attention. The woman was all business at the newspaper, and even at church she rarely talked about her personal life. Morgan realized she knew very little about Anna Heiden.

"Is Kurt around?" Morgan watched her face.

"Yes, but he's heading out in a few minutes." No reaction. Nothing. "You might be able to catch him if you hurry."

"There's no rush," Morgan said. "Just dropping by."

Anna smiled and placed a hand on Morgan's arm. "I think Kurt would like to see you." She propelled Morgan toward his office.

The top half of the Dutch door sat open, while the bottom half was closed. Kurt pulled on his brown trench coat. When he saw Morgan, his smile was welcoming, so Morgan leaned on the door and watched while he gathered his notepad and camera.

"I'm heading out to interview candidates for the City Council position," Kurt said. "Running a two-page spread."

"Are you going to throw your hat into the race?"

"With Jade Tinsley running?" Kurt snorted. "I don't stand a chance against him."

"Jade Tinsley? He's the guy who was engaged to Gerda's daughter, right? How could you not have a chance against him? I think you'd be great on City Council. Nobody knows more about Golden Springs than you."

"I'm an outsider."

"After four years?" Morgan asked.

"I've settled in, sure, but Tinsley is a born and bred local, plus he's charismatic and good-looking. Local kid makes good. He'll win it, hands down."

"Doesn't finding Carlee's remains cast a negative light on him? Or at least arouse suspicion?"

"Everything I've heard on the street is that he was devastated when she disappeared. Accusing him of killing Carlee would be a hard sell in this town without smoking-gun evidence."

"They could have had a fight gone wrong. Or he changed his mind about marrying her after Gerda's drunk-driving arrest, or she wanted out for whatever reason. Lots of scenarios for a moment-of-passion murder."

Kurt smiled. "You have a suspicious mind. You'd make a great private investigator."

"Oh, no. Not interested."

Kurt put a pen in his shirt pocket and placed a fedora on his head. He looked like he had stepped out of the newsroom in a black and white 1940s'-era movie.

"Tinsley was never a suspect. Sorry. I've got to go."

Kurt tipped his hat and rushed from the office. After Kurt

left, Morgan focused on Anna.

"Are you a Golden Springs native?" she asked.

Anna looked up from her computer screen. "My parents moved here when I was a child. I'm nearly a native."

"Do you remember Jade Tinsley?"

"I was forty when Carlee Kruger disappeared."

Morgan must have made a face as she attempted the math, because Anna saved her the trouble.

"I'm fifty-six, Morgan."

"Oh. I didn't realize. I mean, I thought you were closer to my age."

"I will take that as a compliment," Anna said. "Obviously, I am not interested in dating Mr. Willard, nor is he interested in me."

Morgan wanted to protest that she hadn't been prying for information of that sort when clearly she had been, but she already felt silly enough. She felt her face go hot with a flush of embarrassment.

"Now that we understand each other," Anna said, "let's get back to the cold case. I did not know Carlee and Jade personally, although as small as Golden Springs is, I naturally heard the gossip. Jade was inconsolable when Carlee disappeared. He left for several years, then came back and opened a gallery off Main Street."

"I've walked by it," Morgan said. "I haven't been inside."

"In my opinion, he's wasting his talent hawking derivative commercial art to tourists and the unsophisticated." Anna shrugged. "But who knows? Maybe that's all he can do."

Despite Kurt's suggestion that she'd make a great investigator, Morgan resisted the temptation to go straight to Jade's gallery. Instead, she dropped by Bibi's Bakery to grab soup to go.

"Oh, good!" Bernie said when she saw Morgan. "I'm glad

you stopped in. Business is slow. I can take a quick lunch break."

Bernie had apparently recovered from the shock of Rolf's revelation. She seemed her usual cheerful self again, her pink chef's hat balanced at a jaunty angle on her neat brown hair. She disappeared into the kitchen, returning with a tray. Steam rose from two bowls of minestrone soup, and a mini loaf of wheat bread.

Bernie cut the mini loaf into slices and spread butter on a piece. "Any developments in your case?"

"It's not my case. If anything, it's Kurt's case."

"And you just happen to be helping?" Bernie studied her soup. "A lot?"

"Oh, all right. The gossip will get around soon enough. I went to dinner at his place Friday night to discuss the cold case."

Bernie's green eyes sparkled with mischief. "I knew it was true. Although I don't know what's more intriguing. Your involvement in the Carlee Kruger case, or your involvement with Kurt Willard."

"All over town already, huh?" Morgan shook her head. "I hope we don't disappoint people. One dinner does not exactly make for a scandalous romance."

"That depends on what happened at dinner. Or after." Bernie wiggled her eyebrows.

"Nothing," Morgan said. "Not even a goodnight kiss. But I have more interesting things to talk about than my nonexistent love life."

Morgan told Bernie about the church committee's attempt to deliver home-cooked meals to a grieving Gerda.

"Seriously?" Bernie asked. "She really did smash the casserole dish."

"You heard that through the grapevine, too?" The speed at

which gossip travelled through the small mountain town amazed Morgan.

"I actually heard that one straight from Beatrice when she was in to buy bread."

"It was frightening," Morgan said. "We all put a lot of love into those meals. To see her throw the dish on the ground was like seeing her visibly rejecting our outreach to her."

"Do you think she started drinking again?"

"Teruko and Beatrice were on the front line of that battle. Teruko would never speak ill of a person, but Beatrice agreed that she didn't smell any liquor on Gerda. She was just upset."

"Angry sounds more like it."

"Gerda's coming around. In her own way." Morgan told Bernie about the trip to the dugout.

"I'm glad she finally agreed to a memorial service." Bernie glanced at the clock above the bay windows. "I've got some dough rising. I'll have to end my break soon."

"I've got to enjoy moments like this while I can," Morgan said. "Once Cindy quits for good, I won't be able to run errands during the day."

"You can use your be-back-in sign."

"We have just enough business that I hate to leave the shop unattended," Morgan said. "If David spends the summer here, I won't need to hire a replacement. Not yet."

"When the time comes to hire someone," Bernie said, "I can give you my insider tips on who would make a good sales clerk. Speaking of tips, I need some advice of the maternal variety. I'd appreciate anything you can tell me about teenagers. After dinner with you, I decided to face my fears. I spent Sunday with Rolf and his daughter."

"How did it go?"

"I was a quivering mass of shredded nerves by the end of the day."

"She can't be that bad. Did you try to find out what she likes?"

"All I learned is what she doesn't like, which was pretty much any subject I brought up. She hates me." Bernie's face crumpled into a pained expression. "What should I do?"

"You can't fool teenagers," Morgan said. "Don't try to be her mother, and don't try to be her friend."

"Where does that leave me?"

"Just be you." Morgan admitted to herself that her words sounded not the least bit helpful.

Bernie gathered the dishes and set them on the tray.

"How did you know Sam was Mr. Right?"

Morgan reached into her memories. It seemed so long ago, almost as though those times belonged to a different person.

"I can't explain it. I just knew."

"No doubts?" Bernie asked. "No cold feet?"

Morgan shook her head. "I guess you could say it was love at first sight."

Sam was supposed to have been the man she spent the rest of her life with, while Bernie's romantic fantasies hadn't imagined a ready-made family.

"Bernie, however it turns out with Rolf, enjoy the moment."

"Seize the day, and all that?"

"Right. Because you don't know how many days you'll have."

Chapter Seventeen

When Morgan returned to the rock shop, Del was by himself. He sat in his recliner, thumbing through a *Field and Stream* magazine. He told Morgan that after Barton dropped him off, Cindy had left. The door connecting the shop to the living quarters stood open so he could hear the cowbell.

"Hope you don't mind," Del said. "Business slacked off."

"No problem. I'm sorry I missed Cindy," Morgan said. "I brought her soup from Bibi's. There's plenty here. And cookies, too. Are you hungry?"

"Is it lunchtime already?" Del asked.

"Way past." Morgan retrieved a bowl from the cupboard. "No wonder you're so skinny, Del. I have to remind you to eat." She filled a bowl with soup and placed it on the kitchen table with a package of crackers. "Did you find the source of the ammolite?"

"Funny thing. Barton doesn't think the ammolite came from that area. He's already given up on the idea of staking a claim. Too bad. Could have made us rich."

"So how did the chips get there?" Morgan asked.

"I have a theory." Del moved from the recliner to the table. He slurped down a couple spoonfuls of soup, then wiped his mustache with a paper napkin. "Big Foot might have been collecting bits of gemstone he found somewhere else to decorate Carlee's grave."

The cowbell above the shop door clanged, the sound reaching all the way back into the living quarters. Morgan leaned through the doorway to look into the shop. Beatrice stepped through the front door of the shop and stomped mud off her fleece-lined vinyl ankle boots.

Morgan waved to her. "Come on back."

"Hello, Morgan," Beatrice said, her no-nonsense voice unusually cheery. "Del, how are you?" Not waiting for a reply, she continued. "I have news."

"I would expect nothing less," Del said.

"I had my nephew Roger and his fiancée over for dinner."

"Let me guess," Del said. "He's the one who works in the crime lab in Granite Junction?"

"The same." Beatrice pulled a chair out from the table, hung her puffy winter coat over the back, and sat. "Oh, I hope I didn't interrupt your meal."

"I'm just having a bowl of soup," Del said. "You hungry?"

"No, I had lunch already."

Morgan grew tired of the chitchat, and interrupted. "What's your news? Have they learned how Carlee died?"

"When there's no tissue to examine," Beatrice said, "just bone, it's much more difficult to determine cause of death. Damage to the bones was consistent with decay in a natural setting. Her skull was intact, there were no nicks from a knife or a bullet, and no damage to the neck vertebrae from strangulation. Roger told me the coroner hasn't absolutely ruled out murder, but unless some other evidence turns up, Carlee's death may remain a mystery."

"That doesn't give Gerda much chance for closure," Morgan said. "She wants to know whether Carlee died of natural causes, or if there's someone out there who got away with murder."

"Sad deal." Del shook his head.

"I have other news," Beatrice said. "The selection committee is nearing a decision on our new pastor."

"That was fast," Morgan said.

"Not considering that all the candidates had delivered at least one sermon during Pastor Filbury's brief absence earlier this year. The good news is that Pastor Filbury expects to be well enough to speak at Carlee's memorial service."

"Gerda told me Sunday she was ready to have a service," Morgan said. "I kind of doubted she'd go through with it."

"When will it be?" Del asked.

"First we have to contact Gerda's daughter, Camille," Beatrice said in her take-charge tone. "They haven't spoken in years. Teruko is trying to track her down. Once we know the dates she's available, we'll reserve the church and get things rolling. Finally, Golden Springs will get to say good-bye to Carlee Kruger."

The phone rang early Tuesday morning. Caller ID showed a South Dakota area code, but it wasn't David or Sarah's number.

"Hello?"

"People are clamoring for good rentals," Dot Borgen said. "Give me the word, and I can have your house rented out within a couple weeks. Do you have a fax machine? I need to send you some papers."

"No, I don't." Morgan's brain processed Dot's words. "A renter? Already?"

"You sound disappointed. That's what you wanted, right? Lease out the house until you decide whether to move back or sell it?"

"Yes. I just didn't think it would be this quick."

"The rent will be higher than your mortgage payment. Plus, didn't you tell me you only have a few more years to pay off the house?"

"Yes." Morgan felt a mixture of dread and elation. "I do want to lease it, but the house isn't ready."

"Did you decide whether you want to hire a service to clean the house? They can even put things in storage for you, if you tell them what you want to keep."

"That's the problem." Morgan pressed her free hand to her forehead. "I don't know what I want to keep." Then it hit Morgan that this was the perfect excuse to dash home for a quick visit with her children. "I have to go through it myself."

"The sooner the better. The market is in your favor at the moment. So you don't have a fax? I can email you the papers."

"This feels so sudden." Morgan recited her email address for Dot. "I'd better call David and Sarah and let them know."

Her children had grown up in the house. Morgan thought it only fair that she warn them about her plans, but they both seemed remarkably detached when she called. Perhaps the sad memories of their father's passing overrode any attachment to their childhood home. They both encouraged her to fly to Sioux Falls as soon as she could to clean the house.

Everything was falling into place. Morgan should have been pleased, but cutting ties to the past seemed too easy. She wondered whether it was better for family ties to snap under the pressure of tragedy, as Gerda's apparently had, or for them to slowly deteriorate from disuse.

Morgan threw a load of jeans and sweatshirts into the washing machine. She needed to stock up on more jeans. In Sioux Falls, she had worked at a desk, until the engineering firm downsized. Her job was one of those cut. Managing the Rock of Ages required outdoors attire. One day soon she promised herself a trip to an outfitter's store.

Until then, she was stuck doing laundry frequently. She tossed a few pairs of socks on top of the jeans, then opened the plastic tub of laundry detergent. A few lemony-scented grains of detergent dotted the bottom of the tub. Not enough for a load.

She found Del in the rock shop, ringing up a customer's purchase of a necklace from Lucy's display.

After the customer exited the shop, Morgan rattled her car key. "I need to run to town. We're out of laundry soap, and I'm out of clean jeans."

Del tugged at his mustache. "Darn. That's my fault. I thought I told you we were out."

Morgan might have been irritated, but at least the old cowboy did his own wash. He added a few more items to her shopping list, and insisted on giving her cash to help out. Morgan typically protested his generosity, but now that she knew about his mineral collection, worth tens of thousands of dollars, she figured he could spare a few bucks for soap and groceries.

Hill Street was dry as she drove into town. Groceries were a little more expensive in Golden Springs than they would be at a big box store in Granite Junction, but it was worth it to save a trip down Topaz Pass. Morgan loaded her cart with laundry soap, coffee, a roasted chicken, fresh broccoli, and deli potato salad. She would be having dinner at O'Reily's tonight. She suspected Del didn't eat unless she left him something. Too many times, that had meant a hastily prepared sandwich. The old cowboy needed more substantial fare if he was going to gain back any of the weight he'd lost.

The smell of the chicken filled the car and made Morgan's mouth water. She started to drive back toward Hill Street when a large, colorful sandwich-style sign on Main Street caught her eye. Propped up on a wooden walkway, an arrow directed customers to Jade's Aspen Gold Art Gallery, tucked away at the end of a half-block pedestrian mall.

None of her groceries were frozen. A slight delay wouldn't ruin anything. She parked the old Buick. A gentle bell tinkled when she opened the door, unlike the clanging cowbell at her shop.

"May I help you?" The salesgirl pushed her magazine aside and climbed off a stool behind the checkout counter. She wore jeans and a tight polo shirt with the store logo embroidered above the left breast pocket. Casual, and yet slick, at the same time.

"I'm just looking," Morgan said.

"I'd be happy to help if you're looking for something in particular. A birthday gift? Graduation?" As though mentioning gift-giving events would spur Morgan to make a fine art purchase. "We offer lay away and payment plans."

"Just looking," Morgan repeated.

She wandered to the far side of a display wall. Native American flute music added to the Rocky Mountain atmosphere, clearly an attempt to appeal to tourists. Not a bad idea. Even setting a radio to a country-western station might improve the rock shop ambiance. She strolled past artwork, half looking, half listening to the music.

The uniformity of the paintings struck Morgan as dull, considering the prices. She studied the jewelry displayed in a locked glass case. The "authentic Rocky Mountain gemstones" were high quality, and so were the prices. There was no ammolite.

Tucked in an alcove in the back, neglected by the spot lighting that was pervasive in the rest of the shop, a half dozen unframed canvases hung. They depicted the same mountains, waterfalls, and flowers on display in the rest of the gallery, but with wild colors, and in a style somewhere beyond Impressionist but shy of Abstract.

Morgan heard voices from behind a thick curtain hanging in the doorway next to the alcove. A woman spoke in anger, but she couldn't make out the words.

"I need more time for my art," a male voice answered. "Being on City Council would mean giving up what little time I do have."

"We haven't sold one of your artsy paintings in over a year," the female said. "Tourists want something to hang on their wall that reminds them of Colorado. Not those weird orange and purple streams, or blurry deer with green antlers."

"If City Council is so important to you, why don't you run for office?"

"Everyone loves you." The woman's words were tinged with bitterness. "They'd never vote for me."

"We'll just waste time and money on my campaign." The man had to be Jade Tinsley, the charismatic artist Kurt believed would win the Council election. "There are half a dozen people running for Filbury's seat."

"Yes. And there's no reason you couldn't be the one to get it."

There was a pause. Morgan considered leaving before the people behind the curtain realized she had been listening in on their domestic dispute. She peeked around the corner toward the front. The salesgirl had her nose stuck in her magazine, oblivious to the backroom drama. The woman behind the curtain spoke again.

"You can run for City Council or you can help me with the real-estate business."

"I'm not a politician or a salesman. I'm an artist. You knew that when you married me."

"That was the deal. I did the selling. You did the art. It's not enough now."

"We have all we need and more," the man said. "What's changed?"

"It's not enough. That's all."

Heels clipping across wood alerted Morgan a moment too

late. She tucked herself further inside the alcove as a woman stormed through the curtain. Her build was angular as opposed to athletic, and she wore her auburn hair short. The perfectly applied makeup wouldn't have been necessary if frown lines hadn't etched furrows between her turquoise eyes and around her downturned lips. She wore a black jacket and skirt that did not match the rugged mountain feel of the shop. She gave Morgan a brief glance, assessing and dismissing her in an instant.

After the curtain had settled back into place, a man peeked out. He wore a Native American–style ribbon shirt and stonewashed jeans tucked into knee high moccasins. His luxurious blond hair hung down his back in a long ponytail. The look, like the art in the majority of the gallery, was a bit predictable and forced.

"Excuse me," he said. "I didn't mean to startle you."

Morgan tried to appear as though she hadn't heard a word of the earlier conversation, glancing up at Jade Tinsley with what she hoped was a calm expression.

"I was admiring these paintings. They're a different style from those in the rest of the gallery."

"These are from my heart." He pressed one hand to the front of his shirt. "The rest of the gallery, it's what supports this." He waved a hand at the paintings, hidden away in the corner of the gallery as though they were an embarrassment.

"Your nature scenes are lovely, and certainly skilled, but I like these better."

A broad smile creased his handsome face.

"Thank you." He extended a hand. "I'm Jade Tinsley. But then, you probably already figured that out."

Morgan clasped his hand for a vigorous handshake.

"I'm Morgan Iverson. I manage the Rock of Ages."

Jade dropped her hand. He glanced toward the counter,

where the young lady was still engrossed in her magazine. Jade pulled Morgan deeper into the alcove.

"You're the one who found Carlee." He spoke in a husky whisper.

Morgan shouldn't have been surprised. News traveled fast in Golden Springs.

"Yes, I did."

"She and I—" He seemed unable to continue.

"I heard you were engaged when she disappeared."

"I had almost reached the point of not wondering anymore about what might have been. Wondering what happened to her. Where she was."

Almost, Morgan thought. *After sixteen years.*

"I'm sorry," Morgan said. "It must be a blow. But at least now you know."

She watched his face for any sign that maybe he had known, or had something to do with her disappearance. All she saw was grief.

"You've got to understand," he said. "My wife, Mia, she doesn't appreciate your discovery."

He seemed to run out of steam, his shoulders slumping.

"I imagine it's stirred up some painful memories for you," Morgan said.

"Yes, but like you said, at least now I know. Mia doesn't see it that way. She thinks I'm mourning for lost love. Maybe have been our entire marriage." He shoved his hands deep into his jeans pockets and leaned back against a wall, as though he needed something to hold him up. "Was she—was Carlee—you just found bones, right?"

Was he seeking closure, or wondering whether he'd left any evidence behind? Jade's grief seemed real, but maybe Morgan was reading him wrong.

"Just bones. Well, and clothing."

If he wanted to know more, he didn't ask. Morgan wasn't about to volunteer information to a potential killer about the condition of a crime scene.

Tears welled in Jade's eyes. He glanced around as though fearful of being caught in a state of emotion.

"I have to go." His brow creased.

"It's your gallery," Morgan said. "I should go."

His broad shoulders, bunched up with tension, relaxed a notch.

"Right." He offered a weak grin. "Really, though, I don't mean to run you off. You're welcome here any time."

"Thanks, Jade. I need to get home. I have groceries in my car. It was nice meeting you."

Morgan walked past the salesgirl and her magazine, ignoring her curious stare. As she pulled open the front door, movement in the window display caught her eye. A delicate mobile of icicles in shades of cold, pale blue twisted in the faint breeze. Morgan stepped outside the gallery, but stood on the brick walkway in front. The display of glass vases, nightlights, and sculptures captured light and transformed it into molten motion.

Several plaques of glass hung directly behind the window. They seemed to contain pressed flowers, but Morgan could tell they were formed by different colors of glass. The Colorado state flower, the blue columbine. Purple wild irises. Orange and red Indian paintbrushes.

Purple elephant heads. Just like the ones outside Carlee's dugout.

A small easel held a foam board describing the art and artist. The photo of Chase Cooper had been shot at a slight angle, perhaps so that the scarred half of his face would not dominate the portrait. The unscarred half closely resembled Jade's wife, Mia. They were obviously brother and sister. Morgan recognized him. He had been in the rock shop last week with his father, Harlan Cooper.

Chapter Eighteen

Cars filled the parking lot when Morgan returned to the shop. She felt guilty for leaving Del alone so long, spending fruitless time chasing clues to Carlee's death. After unloading the groceries, Morgan waded into the fray, answering questions with a little more knowledge after taking the geology class.

A high-school student needed an intact geode to break open for a science project. Chase had bought several the other day, and had managed to clean out most of the good ones. Del disappeared for a long time, hunting in the garage for a box containing more geodes.

Sales ringing up on the cash register were a welcome sound, but Morgan realized her stock was depleted. Even Lucy's display of Arapahoe jewelry needed replenishment. Finally the crowd thinned, then the shop was empty. The cowbell clanged one last time as Del closed and locked the front door.

"We're running out of geodes, quartz crystals, and the smaller fossils and gemstones," Morgan said.

"That reminds me," Del said. "Cindy left this for you."

Inside a binder was a neat compilation of information about the gem and mineral show: what Morgan would need to take, the hotel where Kendall and Allie stayed, how they loaded the van and rented a lockable utility trailer. They had given away the van when they moved to Central America, and Morgan couldn't tow a trailer with her Buick.

"This looks like an expensive venture," Morgan said. "Are

you sure it's worth it?"

"Was every time Kendall and Allie went," Del said. "They at least broke even, and they always came back with something interesting. You rent a booth or a table, and then you can buy, sell, and trade with all the other dealers there, as well as hundreds of customers. Hey, you could take the triceratops horn. Even if it didn't sell, you'd get lots of people stopping at your table."

"Did Kendall and Allie just close up shop when they went to one of these shows?" Morgan asked.

"They used to, until I moved my trailer onto the property. Then I could run the shop while they were gone. Of course, we weren't so busy back then."

Morgan opened the refrigerator and pulled out the roasted chicken. While it re-heated in the oven, she steamed the broccoli.

"Del, remember the two men who came in the shop last week?"

"The Coopers?" he asked.

"You didn't tell me Chase Cooper is an artist, too."

"I didn't know. How did you come by that bit of information?"

"After getting groceries, I went by the art gallery."

Del tugged at his mustache. "I thought you weren't investigating."

"I'm not," Morgan said. "I saw a display in the window of beautiful glasswork. It was made by that guy who was in here last week with Harlan Cooper. His son, Chase. The interesting thing was, some of the glass pieces were in the form of elephant-head flowers."

"Like the ones you saw at the dugout?"

"Exactly. Did you and Barton notice them?"

"We weren't paying attention to flowers. Maybe you should tell Bill Sharp about this."

"And say what? That a local artist makes elephant-head glass-work? If I looked around, I might find them in every shop window in town."

"Or not," Del said. "When anything bad happens in Golden Springs, a Cooper is sure to be nearby."

"Chase is Mia's brother, right?" Morgan asked.

"Yep."

"It is interesting that Carlee Kruger's fiancé married into the Cooper family."

"I'm tellin' ya," Del said.

Morgan made sure Del sat down to dinner. Then she got dressed for O'Reily's Running Club. Bernie picked her up at the rock shop, driving her oversized SUV to Granite Junction.

Before the run started, Lucy announced the fundraiser for the Golden Springs Homestead Park the next day. Even with such short notice, plenty of runners signed up.

Once they were walking, back of the pack as usual, Morgan asked Bernie about Rolf.

"I've calmed down," Bernie said. "Or maybe it's just knowing I have a week of Rolf all to myself. Stacie will be back this weekend. I can see having her around makes Rolf happy, but he doesn't seem to know what to do with her, so I end up stuck— No. I refuse to have that attitude. I'm not stuck."

"That's the spirit."

"Whether things work out long-term for Rolf and me, I'm glad I'm dating him now. I guess I have you and Lucy to thank for coercing me into going to that first fundraising run."

"He might have gotten up the courage to ask you out while he was buying zucchini bread."

"Banana bread," Bernie corrected. "That's his favorite."

They passed a footbridge arching over the creek.

"I might have to go to Sioux Falls soon," Morgan said.

"Is your daughter okay? She's not due for another month or so, right?"

"Everyone is fine. I have to clean out my house." Morgan explained her decision to lease her home in Sioux Falls.

"That's better than letting it sit empty," Bernie said. "Does this mean you're ready to move on with your life? And do your plans include Kurt Willard?" As Bernie smiled, a mischievous twinkle lit up her green eyes.

"Too soon to tell," Morgan said. "I enjoy Kurt's company, but I'm nowhere near getting serious. With Sam, I knew right away."

Bernie stopped at an intersection and waited for a car to pass. Then she and Morgan stepped off the curb and trotted across the street.

"I wonder why Gerda never remarried," Morgan said.

"She's got the personality of a porcupine."

"There's someone for everyone," Morgan said. "Isn't there? Gerda did decide to have a memorial service for Carlee, so the church ladies have forgiven her for the casserole smashing incident."

"I wonder if Sasquatch will attend the memorial." Bernie shuddered.

"Maybe Chief Sharp can stake out the church," Morgan said.

"I wish he'd solve this soon. I get the heebie-jeebies every time I go to my Dumpster."

"I met someone else who would like to attend the memorial, but probably won't."

"Who?" Bernie asked.

"I went to Jade Tinsley's gallery today."

"You said you weren't going to investigate."

"I just wanted to see the place. Then I overheard Jade and Mia, his wife, fighting. She wants him to run for City Council, but he just wants to paint. He realized who I was, and I thought he was going to cry when he started talking about Carlee."

They sped up as they neared the pub, walking quickly down the crowded sidewalk. Loud music spilled out of a cowboy bar a half block ahead. A couple strolled out of the open door. Morgan jerked to a halt. She pulled her friend into the wide entryway of an expensive dress shop. The door was inset deeply between two large glass window displays of summer fashions.

"What is it?" Bernie asked.

"I know that guy."

Bernie leaned around the window display and looked. "I don't see any mountain men."

"No. Harlan Cooper."

"Who?"

"The guy who upset Del with his mere presence."

People downtown in the evening were headed to restaurants, the theater, or the clubs. Nobody seemed to notice two women spying on the older couple outside Ruby's Two Step.

"Want to fill me in, Sherlock?" Bernie asked.

"That's Harlan Cooper, Jade's father-in-law."

"Who's the woman?"

"I don't know."

Morgan's guess was that she couldn't possibly be the mother of Mia and Chase, unless they were adopted. Not that she wasn't pretty for an older lady, but she looked nothing like the Cooper siblings.

The woman with Cooper was dressed to kill, in a cowgirl kind of way. Tight jeans hugged her size-three hips, a western-style blouse emphasized her top-heavy figure, and pink and black boots with heels taller than anyone needed for riding a horse pushed her tiny frame into altitudes well over her actual five feet. Her helmet of short hair was a shade of pinkish-orange that only an older woman with attitude could wear.

"They're coming this way!"

"Act natural," Morgan whispered.

Morgan pretended to study the dresses in the window, discovering as she did so that the mirrored backdrop allowed her to see the street scene perfectly.

The woman's cowgirl boots clip-clopped on the sidewalk. Morgan could hear the couple's voices, see their lips moving in the mirror, but their words mingled with other conversations. They walked arm in arm, Cooper's head tilted toward the woman attentively. As they passed the dress shop, the woman stopped, pulling her arm from his. Morgan cringed, fearing she had noticed the two women staring at her in the mirror's reflection.

"You know good and well I don't know," the cowgirl said. "And frankly, even if I did, you're the last person I'd tell."

"You don't have to," Harlan Cooper said. "I'm zeroing in on it just fine without your help. But I have a feeling you could save me some time and effort. I have the resources, and if you want in on it—"

"Like you let me in on that last deal?" the woman snapped. "That didn't work out so well for me."

"It'll be different this time," Harlan said. "We'll be partners."

The cowgirl snorted. "Like I believe that."

"I could use the advice of an expert." Harlan brushed a stray hair off her forehead in an intimate gesture.

Bernie leaned close to Morgan and whispered. "She must have missed one with the can of hairspray."

"You know more about prospecting in these hills than anyone," Harlan continued. "Don't shut me out. If you help me, I'll cut you in on it, and you can have that in writing."

"If we make a deal this time, you can bet your sweet tush I'll get it in writing."

"Great." Harlan spoke as though whatever it was they were

discussing was a done deal. "Then I'll see you Wednesday."

"The gem society is my territory." The cowgirl jabbed a long fingernail at Harlan's chest. "Just don't you forget that."

They started walking again. Morgan tugged on Bernie's sleeve.

"Come on."

"They're going to catch on," Bernie said. "You have to be more subtle."

Morgan tried to hang back, pretending to have a conversation with Bernie. When the couple disappeared, she ran up the sidewalk, then pressed her back to the brick bank building and peeked around the corner.

"Darn. They're leaving."

Morgan took a step toward the pay parking lot, but Bernie grabbed her arm.

"What are you going to do? Chase their truck?"

"I suppose not."

"Let's get to the pub, Morgan. I could use a Guinness."

"Sorry. They were talking about a deal. Arguing. And it sounded like she mentioned the gem society Barton told us about. I'm just curious."

"Does this have something to do with your—excuse me, Kurt's—cold case?"

"Probably not, but it might have something to do with Del."

Barton didn't join their table this time. Morgan wished he had. She was bursting with questions.

When she pulled into the Rock of Ages parking lot, the place was dark. She parked in the old carriage house that had been converted into a garage. Walking as quietly as she could, she listened for any sound of Sasquatch skulking about. She trotted the last feet to the back door of the living quarters. The door was unlocked, and Del sat on his recliner by the wood-burning stove.

"Have a good run?" he asked.

"Bernie and I did run, for three blocks. But we were still back of the pack."

"Nothing wrong with that. At least you're out doing something."

Del had placed his stash of ammolite chips in an antique tea saucer. Morgan fished out a chip and studied it in the light. She debated asking him point-blank about his history with the Pine County Gemstone Society and Prospecting Club, but she had a feeling if she started prying, he would walk out of the room like he had the last time. She decided on a more subtle approach.

"Del, I'm trying to learn more about minerals. Barton told me about a gemstone and prospecting club. Maybe I should go. I was wondering if you'd go with me."

"No can do. I put in my time. Even went so far as to serve as vice president of the group."

"Then it might be fun for you to see your old friends."

Del pushed himself up from the chair. "I won't tell you not to go, Morgan, but the world of gemstones and prospecting is dog-eat-dog. Just watch out for yourself, and don't breathe a word about ammolite."

Barton arrived at the rock shop early Wednesday morning, ready to take Del to his physical therapy session in Granite Junction. Morgan wondered how Barton managed to take so much time off from his GPS map software company. Maybe he had trained minions to do his bidding while he was absent. Morgan needed to acquire some minions of her own.

"I'm heading out," Del said.

"Remember your key," Morgan said, "just in case I'm not here when you get back. I'll be running a 5K with Bernie this afternoon."

"Be sure to plant a tree for me."

The cowbell jangled as he closed the door. Morgan was stuck at the shop. She opened the folder Cindy had created and studied the list of items she should take to the mineral show.

plastic storage bins in barn

Del had retrieved geodes from a box in the garage. Her brother and sister-in-law had apparently used both buildings to store rock shop inventory. Now was as good a time as any to see what was where. Morgan would keep an eye on the parking lot this time in case customers arrived. She grabbed her fleece jacket. There was the promise of summer in the air at moments, followed by reminders of winter.

With only two donkeys who liked to spend most of their time outdoors, there was plenty of empty space in the barn. Morgan opened the smaller door to the right of the tractor-sized double doors and inhaled deeply. Under the odor of old wood and hay was the mild scent of manure and leather.

The barn might be part of the solution to how her family would fit into the Rock of Ages. She had seen magazine spreads of barns converted into luxury homes. She needed the barn to remain a barn, but the loft could house her son, David, and maybe Del wouldn't mind sharing the trailer with Kendall and Allie. That would be just the place for her brother. He would no doubt try to move back into the shop's living quarters, if he actually showed up, but he'd handed Morgan the keys when he left the country. As far as she was concerned, Kendall had given up possession of the place.

She climbed the wooden ladder to the loft and peered around. Dusty blue, beige, and green plastic tubs sat in untidy stacks against one wall. Morgan climbed the rest of the way into the loft. The floor was solid. Two small donkeys did not eat a lot, and so only half of the loft was occupied with rectangular hay bales.

Morgan grabbed a plastic tub and moved it near the ladder.

She wrestled it down to the ground, then climbed back up, repeating her trip a dozen times. Some bins were light, possibly empty, while others were obviously full of rocks. She started to climb down the ladder with one last bin when she noticed cloth sticking out from under some tousled hay.

Morgan crawled back into the loft and tiptoed toward it, wondering if she should call Chief Sharp, but afraid if she did, the cloth would turn out to be an old burlap feed bag. Besides, her cell phone was in the living quarters. Morgan reached for the cloth.

Please, no more bodies, Morgan thought.

A mouse scurried out. Morgan screamed and jumped. Once her heartbeat and breathing returned to a near normal rate, she grabbed a handful of hay and lifted it away from the cloth. No body. Instead she saw a bundle of ratty clothing, a blanket, a water bottle, and a couple of plastic grocery bags, one with a mouse-sized hole chewed in the corner next to a pile of cookie crumbs.

Sasquatch was living in her barn.

Chapter Nineteen

Morgan scrambled down the ladder, her heart thudding in her chest. Once at the bottom, it occurred to her that if the mountain man wasn't in the loft, he might be hiding in one of the stalls. Or the tack room. She escaped the barn and dashed across the empty parking lot.

She had left the rock shop unlocked, figuring that she could hear cars pull into the parking lot. She hadn't thought about intruders on foot. The mountain man could have been watching her from the barn loft when she left the shop earlier. He might have circled around out of her line of sight, and could be in the shop right now. Morgan picked up a weathered axe handle from an ore cart and crept toward the front door.

Ducking beneath the windows, she reached up and turned the door handle. Morgan froze. If she pushed the door open, the cowbell would clang, and she would lose the element of surprise.

She gripped the rough axe handle and shouldered the door open, jumping up, raising the handle above her head, and yelling. No one answered. She made a quick survey of the shop, then the living quarters. All was quiet and undisturbed.

Morgan sat at the cash register and dialed the police, her fingers trembling. Deputy Parker answered.

"Golden Springs Police Department."

"It's Morgan Iverson. The mountain man was here again."

"Oh, wow. Are you okay, ma'am?"

"I didn't run into him, but there's a stash of clothing and food in my barn loft." Morgan's voice shook. "I think he's living in my barn."

"Okay, ma'am. The chief is out right now. Seems like everyone in Golden Springs has spotted the mountain man. He was sighted near the cemetery when Mrs. McCormick was putting flowers on her husband's grave. Then Abe saw someone hanging around the back of the auto shop. It's like everyone is seeing Elvis. Oh, or I guess in this case, Big Foot."

"I'm here by myself today," Morgan said. "I'd really appreciate it if you or the chief could drop by soon. The mountain man might come back for his stuff."

"Well, stay away from the barn. I'll call the chief and try to get him over there right away. I can't leave the office with all these calls coming in."

Morgan thought her evidence was more important than hysterical sightings by an alarmed citizenry. While she waited, she considered returning to the barn to take photos. But the mountain man might decide to retrieve his gear, trapping her in the loft.

The phone rang. Morgan snatched it up without checking the caller ID.

"Hello?"

"Is this the Rock of Ages?" a familiar voice asked. "Morgan?"

"Oh, Dot, I'm sorry. I was expecting a call."

She didn't tell Dot the call she was expecting was from the police chief, who she hoped would drop by before a deranged mountain man broke in and did to her whatever he had done to Carlee Kruger.

"I have renters ready to sign a lease. A nice couple. Both teach at the university. They want to move in immediately, but I told them the house won't be ready for a week and a half."

"That soon?"

"They are very anxious, Morgan. They're currently residing in the wife's mother's small apartment. With two kids and a cat."

"A cat?"

"Morgan, you had three cats in that house at one time. The Madsens are willing to pay a pet deposit. They'd move today if I gave them the key. So what do you say?"

"I don't know. It's so sudden."

"If you're not ready . . ." Dot let her words hang.

The house was Morgan's last tie to Sioux Falls. Her backup plan if things didn't work out in Colorado. The house was sitting empty, like her heart after Sam died. She wondered what sort of people the Madsens were, and if they would fill the house with as much love and laughter as her family had. She was a few months away from losing the house entirely. If it was her emotional safety net, it was full of holes. There was only one rational option.

"I'm ready, Dot. I'll book a flight, right after I call Sarah and David. I'll need their help."

"The old gang will be happy to pitch in," Dot said. "Everyone is anxious to see you."

Morgan called Sarah first, who answered on the first ring.

"Sarah, Dot leased the house."

"Really?" Sarah didn't sound happy. "That's a good thing, right? Financially?"

"Absolutely. Otherwise I'll lose the house."

"You know I'd love to take on the mortgage," Sarah said. "But our place has the land both Russ and I wanted. We can raise livestock eventually, once we get the fence built. And I'm sure David would take the house, if he were finished with school. But the memories . . . I don't think it would be good for him. You're right, Mom. Renting it out is the way to go."

"I'm checking flights as we speak." Morgan tapped on her

laptop keyboard. "I can fly out this Friday."

"So soon?"

There was a pause, during which Morgan wondered whether her daughter just didn't want to see her. Tears filled her eyes. She tried to keep her voice steady, but her words trembled.

"I have to clean it out this weekend. The renters—"

Sarah broke into sobs. "I'm sorry, Mom. It's the hormones. I cry all the time for no reason."

Morgan's own tears spilled down her cheeks.

"The thought of a stranger living in our house," Sarah said. "*Our* house."

"I know, honey. We've been blessed to not have to make a decision for all these months."

"You're right. But it doesn't make it any easier." Sarah blew her nose. "How long can you stay?"

"Just the weekend, I'm afraid."

"I wish you could stay longer."

Sarah's words brought tears to Morgan's eyes again, but happy ones this time.

"Me, too. We can talk this weekend. I have a dozen things to do before I can leave town."

"You can stay with us," Sarah said. "We have a futon in our guest room now."

"You know, Sarah," Morgan said, thinking of her strained relationship with her son-in-law, "I think it would be better if I stayed in a hotel."

"You can't sleep in the old house?" Sarah asked.

"That would make more sense," Morgan said, "but I just don't think I can handle it."

Sarah sniffled. Morgan feared another outburst of tears, but her daughter's words were calm.

"If you change your mind, you can stay here."

"This is going to be an emotional weekend," Morgan said. "I think we'll all want our space."

When she realized how much a last-minute flight would cost, plus her rash decision to take a hotel room, Morgan nearly changed her mind. The house had to be cleaned out before it could be leased. This was a case where she would have to spend money to make money.

Her car would not make the trip, and her next idea of renting a van would cost as much as a plane ticket, once she calculated the gas. And take two extra days. She hit the keys on her laptop to confirm her reservation.

"There goes my tire fund."

Chief Sharp arrived after Morgan booked her flight to Sioux Falls. He didn't find anything noteworthy in the loft stash, except for the fact that someone, presumably the mountain man, had been staying there. They stood outside the barn. Morgan felt safe in the company of an armed officer of the law. She was in no hurry to end their conversation.

"I'll see if Deputy Parker can stake out your barn tonight." The chief picked straw off his jeans. "I really want to catch this guy and ask him some questions."

"The sooner, the better," Morgan said. "I was planning a trip to Sioux Falls this weekend. Should I cancel?"

"It might be better for you to be out of the way a few days. Maybe he'll lose interest."

"You think so?"

Chief Sharp shrugged. He didn't seem optimistic.

"I'm a little nervous about leaving Del here alone," Morgan said. "And then there are the donkeys." Morgan glanced back through the open barn doors. "Speaking of donkeys, they're usually good at alerting us to intruders. They chased the mountain man and his wolf away just a few nights ago. Why would they let him move in?"

"Maybe he bribed them with carrots." Chief Sharp tilted his cowboy hat back. "How about if Deputy Parker stayed a couple nights at the shop? I guarantee he can't be bribed with carrots."

"Do you think he would?"

"He lives with his parents," Chief Sharp said. "Claims he's looking for a place of his own, but he's been working for me for eight months, and he's still there. It would do him good. He might consider it a vacation."

That's what Morgan had thought when she first arrived in Golden Springs. She was just going to manage the shop for two weeks. It would be like a vacation. Over three months had passed now, and she had no intention of leaving.

Morgan picked up Bernie at the bakery. Parking in the tiny lot at the Golden Springs Homestead Park was impossible. They found a space a quarter mile down the road and hiked in.

"I've only been here once," Bernie said. "The old homestead is interesting. I haven't hiked any of the trails."

"This will be my first time," Morgan said.

For a last minute event on a weekday, a surprising number of runners milled around in front of the 1850s' era farmhouse.

"Over here!"

Lucy waved at them from the registration table. Chuck sat beside her.

"Let this be a warning to you," Chuck said. "This is what happens when you break your toe and can't go running. You get stuck at the registration table."

"And we really appreciate the help," Lucy said.

Chuck pushed forms across the folding table to Bernie and Morgan. "No T-shirts this time, but here's what your registration bought."

He held his hands out like a game show host, indicating a

pine seedling, roots wrapped in burlap, decorating the registration table.

"Paul and some other runners marked the route with chalk so no one can get lost," Lucy said, "but here's a map, just in case."

Morgan studied the photocopied paper. "I just learned a few days ago that the park runs along the edge of the Dalton ranch. I had no idea their place was so huge."

They spent a few minutes chatting with friends while the serious runners stretched and jogged around to warm up for the race. Pockets of snow hid in the shade of the historic homestead farmhouse and beneath trees, but fine dry gravel covered the trail. Clouds clung to the tops of the hills, brilliant white against the blue sky. Although the air was crisp, Morgan knew she'd be unzipping her windbreaker after they started walking.

The announcer's voice crackled through a loudspeaker. The report from the starter's pistol echoed off the hills briefly, and the runners took off. Morgan and Bernie were not at the very back of the pack. Several walkers strolled behind them. When they reached an orange cone with "half mile" painted on it in white, one of the walkers expressed relief that they were halfway already.

"We've only gone a half mile," another walker responded. "We're less than a sixth of the way."

"Seriously? I must be in worse shape than I thought."

Bernie nudged Morgan with her elbow.

"That was me, a few months ago," Bernie said. "Remember our first race?"

"We've definitely made progress."

"Let's run!"

As Morgan jogged after her friend, her shoes crunched into the gravel in a steady rhythm. They splashed through slushy puddles, sending up sprays of melt water. A startled gray bunny leapt out of their way as they careened down a hill.

Bernie stopped as abruptly as she'd begun. Placing her hands on her knees, she bent over and wheezed a few breaths.

"Woo, that was fun!"

They started walking again.

"Rolf must have been here." Bernie pointed to a trail that cut across the chalk-marked runner's route. ATV tracks dug deep into the soil.

Bernie's boyfriend volunteered with Pine County Search and Rescue. He assisted at charity runs by riding around on an ATV packed with first aid and rescue gear.

"Why would he go uphill?" Morgan checked the map Lucy had given her. "That doesn't intersect the trail we're on again. It leads to the Dalton ranch. Hang on."

She clambered up the slope to the top of a hill. Bernie caught up with Morgan.

"What's wrong?"

"Friday the Daltons' cattle almost escaped through that gate. Houdini stopped them. The very next day, Houdini was over there again, and Vernon chased ATVers off his place. I'm sure Vernon replaced that lock, but look. It's been cut again." Morgan unzipped her windbreaker pocket and pulled out her cell phone. "I've got to warn the Daltons. These tracks look fresh. The trespassers might be on their land again."

Sherry answered the phone. "Yes, Vernon heard the ATVs. He's out there right now, looking for them."

"If someone sneaked onto your ranch, they can't get past us," Morgan said. "There are fifty or more runners in the park."

"Be careful. We don't know what these folks are up to."

"They cut the lock on the same gate."

"I'd better call Vernon, let him know which way to look." Sherry hung up.

"What do we do now?" Bernie asked.

"I'm staying here in case Vernon scares the ATVers off his place. Maybe I can get their registration numbers."

"I hear one now." Bernie pointed back the way they had come. "But from the park."

Morgan watched the trail, wondering what she would do if the ATVers tried to roll past her and onto the Dalton ranch. Surely they wouldn't be that bold. But they'd been bold enough to cut a lock off a gate twice. They had to be up to no good.

"It's Rolf." Bernie waved her arms and yelled, although he surely couldn't hear through his helmet and above the roar of his engine. "Rolf! Up here!"

He must have glimpsed Bernie's fluorescent green windbreaker, because he turned his ATV onto the cross trail and gunned the engine. The machine lunged uphill until he pulled alongside Bernie. He cut the engine and pulled off his helmet. His sandy hair stuck to his scalp.

"Are you okay?" he asked.

"Some people broke into the Dalton ranch," Bernie said.

Morgan pointed at the gate. "They cut the lock. Vernon heard ATVs on his place. He's looking for the intruders. If Vernon runs into them, they might head back this way."

Rolf detached a walkie-talkie from the holster on his hip.

"I'll call Lonnie. You girls should head back to the homestead, in case things get serious."

"We'll be okay," Bernie said.

Rolf shook his head. "I don't want anything to happen to you, Bernie. Besides, someone should let Paul and Lucy know what's going on."

Reluctantly, Morgan and Bernie headed back to the main trail. Morgan studied the map.

"We might as well finish the race. There's no shortcut back to the homestead."

Bernie glanced over her shoulder a dozen times in the next half mile.

"He'll be okay," Morgan said.

"I sure hope so. I'd hate if anything—" Bernie stopped. "I hear ATVs."

Morgan listened. Her brain told her the noise had to come from behind them, back at the gate Rolf and Lonnie guarded. Her ears told her differently. Morgan unfolded the map again.

"There's another gate." She looked up, then pointed.

This part of the park had been burned in the forest fire. Charred stumps jutted from bare earth. The fence was new. The metal posts and barbed wire gleamed in the sunlight. The wide gate looked like it came fresh from the hardware store, without the dings, dents, and rust typical of a well-used ranch gate. The sound of ATVs grew closer.

"Quick! Hide!"

The options were limited. Blackened debris had been bulldozed into a pile after the fire. Wearing their brightly colored windbreakers was a definite handicap, but Morgan and Bernie ducked behind the sooty pile. Bernie called her boyfriend. Then they waited. The sound of ATV engines grew louder, then faded, then grew louder again.

"They're definitely coming this way," Morgan said.

"I see them!"

Two machines, gray with mud, rolled to a stop. They were on the Dalton ranch side of the locked gate. The riders wore heavy jackets and helmets with face shields, making it impossible to identify them. One hopped off an ATV and rummaged in a plastic crate bungee-corded to the back of the machine. The rider pulled out chain cutters and cut off the lock. Then he, or she, pushed open the gate, hopped on the ATV and drove through.

Rolf roared up the trail in an attempt to block the gate, but he was too late. The ATVers were already in the park. When their helmets turned to face Rolf, they seemed to panic, gunning their machines and spraying mud as they headed cross-country. Rolf followed, zigzagging around charred stumps and blackened rocks. He closed the gap, nearing the trespassers. The driver in the rear stopped, pulled a pistol out of a jacket pocket, and aimed.

A shot sounded. Rolf lurched to one side and fell off his ATV. The machine halted the moment his hand slipped from the accelerator, sputtering riderless beside Rolf.

Bernie screamed. She burst from their hiding place and ran toward Rolf. The shooter's helmet turned her direction. The gun aimed at Bernie. The other driver hit the shooter's arm and pointed. Morgan could hear an ATV behind her. Lonnie. The two drivers revved their engines, spewing mud and gravel in high arcs as they raced through the park.

Lonnie started to follow, but Bernie waved her arms.

"Lonnie! They shot Rolf!"

She dropped to her knees beside her boyfriend. Lonnie jumped off his ATV and grabbed a medical kit. Morgan ran to them.

"Can I help?"

"Call 9-1-1," Lonnie said.

Bernie had her phone out before Morgan.

There must be something I can do, Morgan thought. But Lonnie was an EMT, and Bernie was talking to the dispatcher, pacing in tight circles around Rolf.

Vernon galloped toward the gate on a tall palomino gelding. Mud splattered the horse's white legs and golden belly. Vernon handled the reins with one hand, and in the other he held his .22 rifle. He nudged the horse with his heels and headed toward Morgan.

"They went that way." Morgan pointed. "But one has a handgun."

"Did you see their registration numbers?"

"I looked, but any identification on the ATVs was covered with mud. It looked like they deliberately covered them. Vernon, they're headed for a park full of people!"

Vernon raised his rifle, and for a moment, Morgan thought he was going to take a shot. He was just using the gun's scope like a telescope, though.

"There's another exit. They're headed for National Forest, not the park."

"Thank God."

"I'd say so." Vernon glanced heavenward for an instant, his eyes closed. Then he looked at Morgan. "Neither one of them looked like your Sasquatch."

"I couldn't see faces, but you're right. They were average sized. I'd say they were both men, but I suppose they could have been women. In those heavy jackets and helmets, it was hard to tell, but the mountain man's beard would have been obvious."

Vernon slid his rifle into a scabbard attached to the saddle. He swung down and led his horse toward Rolf.

"He gonna make it?" Vernon asked Lonnie.

"Dislocated shoulder from the fall," Lonnie said. "The bullet missed him."

"Praise the Lord," Vernon said.

Tears spilled down Bernie's cheeks, but her voice was steady as she spoke to the dispatcher. "They want to talk to you." She handed the phone to Lonnie, then knelt beside Rolf again. "The ambulance is coming," Bernie said.

"I'm going to be out of commission for weeks." Rolf struggled to sit, wincing with pain. Bernie helped him up. "A bullet wound might have healed faster than this," he complained.

"Not a bullet to the head," Vernon said.

Rolf met Morgan's eyes. "Did you see who it was?"

Morgan shook her head. "They had on helmets. They covered anything that would have identified them with mud."

"They tried to kill me."

"Kids horsing around where they've got no right to be," Vernon said, "that's one thing. Shooting a man, that's serious business." Vernon lifted his rifle. "This little .22 wouldn't have done much damage at that distance. If they come back, you can bet I'll have something more serious to greet them. We'll get them, Rolf."

"Don't play vigilante on my account," Rolf said to Vernon. He looked at Morgan again. "Or detective. I don't want anyone else hurt."

Lonnie interrupted. "Rolf, you think you can ride down to the homestead?"

"Sure, but I can't drive."

Bernie hopped onto Rolf's ATV while Lonnie and Morgan helped him climb on behind her. Morgan rode with Lonnie. They met Chief Sharp at the homestead. Morgan finally felt useful helping Paul and Lucy with crowd control. When Kurt arrived with two cameras dangling around his neck, he trotted up to Morgan and gave her a brief hug.

"Are you okay?" he asked.

"I'm fine."

"I'd rather stay with you," Kurt said, "but . . ."

"Hot story," Morgan said. "I understand."

Planting trees was out of the question with the police investigating a shooting. Lucy announced that the event would be rescheduled for Saturday. The crowd milled around until the sun dropped behind the mountains. As Morgan drove up Hill Street, she kept glancing across the fence at the Dalton ranch. The ATVers were long gone. They'd be stupid to come back, but they'd already trespassed at least twice. And now they'd tried to kill Rolf.

What did they want on the Dalton ranch that was worth a man's life?

Chapter Twenty

Several times Thursday Morgan reminded herself that she was not responsible for Life On This Planet. Now didn't feel like the right time to leave. Adelaide was in a delicate condition. Del had to be reminded to eat. A mountain man who might be a killer had been living in her barn.

And her best friend's boyfriend had been targeted by a masked assassin.

But Morgan couldn't afford to throw away her most valuable asset, no matter how bad the timing was for her trip.

Trevin called to ask whether Del needed help while she was gone. Spring semester was over, and he could use the extra money. Morgan welcomed any hours he could put in at the shop, and they agreed on the pay per hour.

Del lugged an enormous hard-sided suitcase to her room.

"You can use this. It'll hold up to any abuse by the airlines."

"Del, I'm only going for a weekend. I'd have to check that bag."

"It's for the return trip," he said. "You'll be bringing back pictures. Your kids' school trophies. That kind of stuff."

"Of course." Morgan tugged the comforter off her bed. "You're two steps ahead of me. Thanks. Can you help me change the bedding?"

Deputy Parker would watch the barn Friday and Saturday night for the return of the mountain man, and sleep in the rock shop living quarters during the day.

Del tugged at his mustache. "You sure you want that kid staying here?"

"It's not just me, Del. Chief Sharp assigned Deputy Parker to stake out the barn. We're performing a public service by letting the police use our place to catch a potential murderer."

"You sure it isn't to keep an eye on me? I'm perfectly capable of dealing with intruders."

"I know, Del. But we don't know who the mountain man is, or what he wants. And after the people on the ATVs shot at Rolf? Frankly, I'd rather you stayed at Barton's."

"Neither Trevin or Deputy Parker know how to take care of the donkeys. I wouldn't feel right leaving Adelaide for a weekend with strangers. Besides, I'm getting tired of you conspiring with Barton to get rid of me."

"That's not true. Barton invited you over. I'm not trying to kick you out. I need you here. I just hate dumping the shop on you. We've been busy lately."

Del shook his head. "You just take care of your family's business this weekend, and don't worry about a thing on this end. I've got everything under control."

Morgan wished she could say the same.

David met her at the airport Friday afternoon in the pickup truck that had been his father's. Morgan wasn't the only one having trouble letting go.

"It's a good thing I have the truck," David said. "That suitcase wouldn't fit in a car."

"This was Del's idea. He thought I might need a big suitcase to bring things home—" Morgan paused. "Back to Colorado."

Morgan gave David the address of her hotel.

"You're not staying at Sarah and Russ's?" David asked. "Or at the house?"

"No," Morgan said. "I thought neutral ground might be more

comfortable."

David nodded in understanding. "Have a good flight?"

Morgan attempted small talk, but they slipped into silence. Perhaps David was holding back his emotions, or maybe he was just a quiet guy, like his father. Morgan stole a glance at David's profile as he studied the road through the pickup's windshield. He had gotten his brown eyes and dark, curly hair from Morgan, but there the resemblance ended. Working construction to earn college tuition, his lean body had become solidly muscled. Just twenty-one, his features held a trace of boy, while his jaw had a determined set to it. He looked so much like Sam, it made Morgan's heart ache.

"I'm meeting some of the old gang for dinner tonight," Morgan said. "You're welcome to come."

"Just my idea of fun. Dinner with a bunch of old ladies." His words were spoken with a smile. He was being funny, in his own way. "I'll pass, Mom. Have a good time with your friends. I'll pick you up early tomorrow." The smile was gone.

Morgan tried to rest in her hotel room, but she felt like she was wasting time. She dressed in the one nice outfit she'd brought and attempted to tame her dark curls. Then she paced the small room until Dot picked her up for dinner.

"I feel silly staying at a hotel when I have a house here," Morgan confessed. "But I couldn't bear the thought of staying in my old bedroom."

"That was wise," Dot said. "You don't want to get attached to the place all over again."

"You look great."

Dot Borgen had received her height and her blue eyes from her Scandinavian ancestors. Since Morgan last saw her, Dot had sacrificed her blond hair to a severe modern hairstyle.

Dot patted her head. "I'm still shocked when I look in the mirror. I guess it's the age. Time to whack off the girlish locks."

"You have the face for short hair. It makes you look younger." Morgan wasn't ready to chop off her hair just because she was over forty. Anyway, she doubted she could pull off a look like Dot's. The woman was a natural beauty.

"You've lost weight," Dot said. "Are you on a diet?"

"No. Just walking a lot. And taking care of livestock."

The conversation felt awkward, as though their years of friendship had evaporated in the short space of a few months. Maybe it had become strained even before Morgan left Sioux Falls, during the long dark days after Sam's passing, when she had withdrawn from life. Dot pulled up to the restaurant. She parked, and sat for a moment before turning to Morgan.

"So how are you doing?"

The question cut through all the chatter to something real. Morgan smiled.

"I'm good. For the first time in a long time."

Dot seemed to relax. "I was afraid, you know? After Sam. And then when you moved away and didn't come back. Well, I didn't know." Dot reached for Morgan's hand and gave it a squeeze. "Good to have you back."

Dot had reserved a table for eight. The wait staff had to push another table together when several more people showed up.

Half the dinner was spent catching up. In the less than four months since she had left Sioux Falls, there was plenty of news. Morgan had not done a good job staying in touch with her friends. There had been too much happening in Golden Springs. Then it came time for her news. Everyone wanted to know about her involvement in the Dawn Smith murder case. Morgan didn't mention the new one, Carlee Kruger's cold case. They were already dubbing her Miss Marple. Morgan retold the story with as little drama and as much respect for Dawn as she could. Then it was on to other news.

"Are you dating any Colorado cowboys?" A mischievous grin

creased Franny Gundersen's plump cheeks. The middle-aged housewife, a perpetual volunteer, could ask intrusive questions with an air of innocence that often caused victims to spill their every secret.

Morgan felt a blush creep up her face, and was glad for the dim lighting. "No." It wasn't a lie. Granted, she and Kurt spent a lot of time together, but not on dates. Not really. And besides, he wasn't a cowboy. "I'm not ready."

"Sam has been gone three years," Franny said.

"Not three," Morgan said.

"Well over two," Dot said. "Sam was a special guy."

Morgan suddenly felt guilty for even thinking Kurt Willard could take Sam's place in her heart. She was determined not to tear up. The ladies fell silent.

"I'm sure Sam wouldn't have wanted you to spend the rest of your life alone," Dot said.

"I knew at first sight that Sam was The One," Morgan said. "I don't expect anyone to be able to top that."

Joan Sundheim snorted. "Please, honey. I was there. We very nearly couldn't convince you to walk down the aisle."

"That's not true," Morgan said.

" 'Fraid so," Franny said. "You had a case of cold feet so huge we couldn't have squeezed you into a size-twelve pump."

Morgan looked to Dot for support, but the Nordic blonde nodded.

"You were terrified, right up until the 'I do' part."

"That's not how I remember it," Morgan muttered.

The ladies giggled.

"Ah, memory," Joan said. "We often paint it in the colors of our own choosing."

"You're quite the philosopher these days," Franny said. "Must be that college professor rubbing off on you. Oops! I didn't mean it that way."

The others laughed. Joan flipped her long gray hair over one shoulder. Her purple batik tunic and dangling crystal earrings would have caused Morgan's employee Cindy to brand Joan as a witch.

"My divorce is final." Joan lifted her wine glass. "I can do what I want without causing a scandal." Joan's smile was that of the cat who ate the canary.

The gossip felt alien to Morgan, like she was a layer removed. Or maybe it was the physical distance, being almost a thousand miles away from her friends. After another hour of chatter, some serious and some silly, the party began to break up.

"What time should we come over to help?" Dot asked.

Morgan shook her head. "I think the kids and I will need all day to sort through the house. Sunday we should know what goes in storage, and what goes to charity."

"I'll be happy to arrange for the church to send around a truck," Franny said. "We can use anything you've got for the yard sale. And I can give you a donation receipt to use for your taxes."

"That would be great," Morgan said.

"We'll see you Sunday, then," Dot said.

Morgan sat up in the hotel bed. She wished she had consumed more than the one glass of white wine at dinner. Then she might have been able to sleep. But maybe that's how Gerda got started. Just another glass to let her sleep, and then another, and another. Morgan might as well have stayed at her house. She could have gotten a head start on sorting through papers and closets, rather than tossing and turning, and pacing the hotel room.

Her cell phone rang at dawn.

"Ready, Mom?" David asked.

"As ready as I can be."

On the silent drive to their old home, Morgan remembered that she had not gone through any of Sam's things. She had intended to start, right after she returned from her two-week Colorado stay. That had turned into more than three months. Now it looked like she was never moving back. She rubbed her temples, agonizing about what they were about to go through, and wondering if David was strong enough for the task.

"Wild night, Mom?"

"No. I couldn't sleep."

"Me neither."

The house looked just like she'd left it in January, except that the lawn was green, not blanketed in snow. The iris beds Morgan had spent so much time cultivating were covered with buds. Someone else would be here to enjoy the fragrant blooms. The Madsen family. She hoped they appreciated the flowers.

"You okay, Mom?"

Morgan swiped a sleeve across her eyes.

"I knew this was going to be hard. And we're not even inside yet."

David reached for her hand. "We'll get through it."

They were outside, loading David's truck with Sam's woodworking tools from the garage when Sarah and Russ arrived in a rented moving truck. Sarah had tied her long, strawberry-blond hair into a ponytail. She had a lean, athletic build, even pregnant. Morgan would have said her daughter was too thin, but she had decided to keep her good advice to herself this trip.

Russ was a big guy, tall and broad-shouldered. He came from such a large family, they could have staffed their own Viking longboat. Russ looked perfectly capable of caring for an entire village, much less one wife and child.

Morgan and Sarah exchanged teary hugs.

They went inside together and started cleaning, filling packing boxes marked "storage" or "yard sale" with a thick black marker, and tossing the hopeless items into plastic trash bags. David and Sarah each made their own piles for items they wanted to take. It was all very businesslike the entire morning, with swift decisions and an amicable division of pots and pans, furniture, linens, and artwork. Their church would have an abundance of nice goods for the annual yard sale to raise money for the food pantry.

Russ and David both watched to make sure Sarah didn't do too much lifting or standing. They assigned her the task of running a shredder, making confetti out of mountains of papers, including hopelessly outdated receipts, paystubs from the days before electronic payrolls, and warranties for appliances that had been discarded over a decade ago. By late afternoon, Morgan dared feel optimistic that they would finish by a reasonable hour, when David and Russ climbed into the attic. They handed down boxes and bags, an old trunk, lamps and furniture and rugs.

"I don't remember putting all this in the attic," Morgan said. "I'm guessing most of this should have gone to the church yard sale years ago."

"I think we're done." Russ emerged from the attic, mopping his forehead with a bandana.

"Wait." David's feet scuffed across the beams and Morgan heard rustling. "What's this?"

He climbed down the attic ladder. David carried a bright orange canvas shopping bag with a hardware store's name and logo printed in black.

"I didn't see that," Russ said.

"It was hidden," David said. "My flashlight reflected off the orange color, or I might not have noticed it."

"What do you think's inside?" Sarah asked.

David shrugged. "Nails? Caulking? Dad probably fixed

something in the attic, and left the bag up there."

They took seats on the kitchen chairs. David emptied the bag onto the table. Colorful paper wrapped four objects.

"Christmas presents," Sarah said

"They're not mine," David said. "I always hid my presents in my closet."

"Me, too." Sarah looked at Morgan.

Morgan shrugged. "They must have been your dad's." She felt a catch in her throat as she added, "Before he got sick."

Sam, in his usual utilitarian style, had printed names on each package with a marker. David handed the small packages across the kitchen table.

"Should we save them for Christmas?" Sarah asked.

"These were for Christmas at least two years ago," David said. "Or more."

The trio looked at Morgan.

"We open them now."

There was no earth-shattering revelation in Sam's handmade stocking stuffers. Just the knowledge that he had thought of each of them. They had discovered his one last gesture of affection as they cleaned out the family home.

Sarah burst into hormonal tears as she held up her gift, a wooden manger scene Sam had carved in his garage shop. Russ threw an arm around her and pulled her into a comforting hug as he pushed his gift into the center of the table: a stack of numbers, their street address, ready to nail to the front of Sarah and Russ's home. David opened a package containing a whittling knife and a donkey, obviously carved with that knife. Maybe it was one of the rock shop donkeys David had loved as a child, or perhaps it was meant to represent the animal the Savior had ridden into Jerusalem.

"Open yours, Mom." Sarah sniffled and wiped her nose with Russ's bandana.

Morgan's fingers trembled as she tore open the green and red paper. The eight- by ten-inch wooden plaque was a picture of a mountain scene. Each element in the picture—mountains, pine trees, and a cabin—was formed from thin layers of wood. Different types of wood made the elements distinct. Lighter mountains, darker trees, and the cabin a shade in between.

"It's Golden Springs," David said. "That cabin we stayed in one summer."

"Dad always wanted to stay there again," Sarah said. "We never did."

Russ grasped her hand. "Your family had that time. Focus on that."

"I remember that cabin." Morgan wiped her eyes with a paper napkin. "We couldn't figure out how to light the heater that first night, and it was so cold."

Sarah smiled. "David and I had bunk beds in the next room, but we piled into bed with you and Dad."

Soon they were all in tears, sharing reminiscences of Sam, and Morgan realized that they had never truly mourned him as a family. Each had immersed themselves in their own sorrow, perhaps trying to withhold their pain from the others. Morgan sent a silent prayer of thanks to Sam for giving them this moment.

It seemed the work went faster with their hearts unburdened. By sunset of a day entirely too long and wearying, loads had been delivered to a storage locker, Sarah and Russ had packed furniture and boxes to take to their house, and David had stuffed what he didn't put in storage into his truck. Morgan filled her enormous suitcase with framed photos and photo albums, shoes and clothes, and some of Sam's old clothes that looked about the right size for Del. The house was not empty by any means, but the important things had been dealt with.

Dinner at Sarah and Russ's house was wonderfully relaxing.

Everyone seemed relieved of emotional burdens they'd been carrying for over two years. David took Morgan back to her hotel room, despite Russ's insistence that she stay with them. As her son dropped her off, Morgan repeated her invitation for David to spend the summer in Golden Springs.

"I need help at the shop," Morgan said. "I can't pay much, but you'll have free room and board."

"Mom, the place is tiny. Where would I stay?"

"We'll make room." Morgan smiled as she thought of Del's trailer and the barn loft. "You'd be surprised."

Chapter Twenty-One

The next morning, Morgan's back ached and her muscles were sore, but she was ready when Sarah and Russ picked her up. They met David for breakfast, then went to church services. Even a day ago, being fussed over by her old congregation would have been unbearable. Instead, it felt like a family reunion.

Then it was back to work, emptying out the rest of the house. Morgan's friends came to help, and a considerable number of Russ's family, too. They loaded three trucks with the church yard-sale donations, hauled a load of trash to the dump, and vacuumed, scrubbed, and dusted.

As she handed the keys to Dot, Morgan thought she might start crying again, but it seemed her tears had finally all been shed.

That night they attended a Sons of Norway dance with Russ's family. David seemed quite interested in one blond-haired Nordic miss, dressed in traditional costume. The evening ended early. Most folks had to work the next day. Saying her good-byes was more painful than Morgan anticipated.

The next morning, she took a cab to the Sioux Falls Regional Airport. She would be back soon enough, when Sarah had the baby. The plane lifted off. As she watched the South Dakota farmland below, Morgan accepted that there was no going back now. Not to the life she had known.

★ ★ ★ ★ ★

Del and Barton picked her up from the Granite Junction airport. Morgan settled into the seat between the two men and watched the scenery up the pass. Del seemed to understand Morgan's silence, and Barton just didn't talk much anyway.

"Whoa!" Barton slammed on the brakes. The tires squealed.

Morgan gripped the dashboard as Barton swerved to miss a car in the opposite lane. The driver had misjudged the curve. The narrow canyon didn't offer much shoulder, but Barton managed to miss both the oncoming car and the rock wall towering on their right.

"Man, oh man," Del muttered. "That was some good driving, Barton. You saved all our necks, including that numb-brain driver."

Topaz Pass had more than its fair share of accidents. The two-lane road twisted down the narrow canyon, giving drivers plenty of blind spots.

"It's easy to miscalculate that curve," Barton said, "especially if you're not familiar with the pass. I'm just glad we avoided an accident."

Del tugged at his bushy mustache. "Can you call it an accident when someone's driving too fast?"

An accident that was someone's fault reminded Morgan of Rolf, and how he'd thrown himself off an ATV to avoid being shot. The gunman, or woman, had caused his accident, but in this case the result was far better than what they'd intended.

"How is Rolf?" Morgan asked. "Have you heard anything?"

"He's back at work already," Barton said.

"Rolf's a tough guy," Del said. "A dislocated shoulder is no fun. Lucky thing that's all he's dealing with, though. The chief recovered the bullet that missed Rolf. It was a hollow point. If it had hit him, it would have torn him up pretty bad."

"It would have killed him," Barton said.

"Did Chief Sharp find the ATV people yet?" Morgan suspected it was too much to ask that the bad guys be in custody just because she was home now.

"Not yet," Barton said. "Lonnie and some other Pine County Search and Rescue folks are keeping an eye out for ATVs and helmets matching what he saw."

"Under that coating of mud," Morgan added.

"Unlikely the guy who took a shot at Rolf will be out riding trails any time soon," Barton said.

They reached Golden Springs, and then took the turn up Hill Street. Trevin must have heard them pull up. The young man, his honey-brown skin framed by dark hair in shoulder-length dreadlocks, met them at the back door to the living quarters. Trevin helped Barton drag the suitcase through the back door and into the kitchen.

"We've got customers," Trevin said. "I have to get back to work."

Morgan liked the sound of that, then reminded herself Trevin was on temporary loan. She kicked off her pumps, even though the worn linoleum was chilly under her stocking feet.

The kitchen looked and smelled like home, with a wood fire going in the stove and coffee scenting the air. A vase with a rustic arrangement of wildflowers sat in the center of the table. Morgan leaned close to smell the perfume of springtime in the mountains. Then she noticed the delicate lavender spikes of elephant head in the bouquet. Morgan felt dizzy as her heart jumped into panic mode.

"Where did the flowers come from?" she asked Del.

"They weren't here when I left."

Morgan rushed through the door separating the living quarters from the shop. A startled customer nearly dropped a fossilized fish. Morgan padded across the pine floor in her stocking feet, giving them fatal runs.

"Trevin, where did you get the flowers?"

"Big Foot gave them to me, after I fed him lunch."

"Flowers and lunch? Trevin, he's wanted by the police for questioning. Deputy Parker stayed here hoping to catch the guy. Is he still here?" Morgan scanned the shop, but there were no Sasquatches. Just tourists and rock hounds.

"No. I tried to get him to hang around, but he and his wolf bolted."

Morgan shook her head. "You fed him lunch? You'd better start at the beginning."

A customer approached the checkout counter, glancing at Morgan's shredded stockings. Trevin rang up a sale, then joined Morgan on the aspen bench.

"I heard a noise outside," Trevin said. "I thought it might be raccoons. But it was this old guy, digging through the trash. He was really scruffy. He reeked." Trevin pinched his nostrils to indicate how intense the odor had been. "I figured he was your Sasquatch. I mean, he was a big guy, huge, and he had a long beard that could have had birds living in it, it was so knotted up. Not like my hair." Trevin pulled at one of his dreadlocks, the matted ropes of dark hair hanging in orderly fashion. "It looked really bad. There can't be more than one guy like that around here."

"Did Deputy Parker see him?"

"That's the bad part. I called his cell phone, but he was gone on a call. Some biker was busting up the bar in town. He'll be back as soon as he can."

"But the flowers, Trevin?"

"I took a plate of food out to him. I hope you don't mind. I sorta raided your fridge. I told him to stick around, but then I got busy with customers. When I had a chance to check on him, I noticed there was this bouquet of flowers on the windowsill alongside the empty plate. I put them in water."

"Did he say anything?" Morgan asked.

"He never said a word. It's like he was mute."

Great, Morgan thought. *If Bill Sharp ever does catch up with the mountain man to question him, the guy won't be able to tell him anything.*

Trevin waved his cell phone. "I got some pics of him."

Morgan hoped his photos proved more helpful than hers.

Police Chief Sharp arrived with the deputy close to closing. A dark bruise circled his left eye.

"What happened to you?" Del asked.

"Drunk biker," Sharp said. "I was sure glad J.B. showed up. I don't know what they're teaching in the military these days, but it worked."

A blush spread up Parker's neck and his cheeks flamed. Morgan noticed the young deputy didn't have a black eye.

Sharp questioned Trevin while Parker and Del checked the barn loft and the trailer. There was no sign that the mountain man had been in either again. Morgan wished the deputy could extend his stay at the shop, but only two men policed Golden Springs, and Sharp couldn't spare his deputy another night.

After they closed the shop, and Trevin went home, Morgan unpacked her suitcase. Del was fixing his specialty for dinner: canned chicken-noodle soup and saltine crackers.

"Del, I don't know if these will fit, but I thought you could use something to replace what the mountain man stole."

She handed him a stack of flannel shirts, a fleece vest, and an insulated winter coat.

"They were Sam's," she said. "David and Russ took what they could use."

Del accepted the stack of clothing, placed it on the table, and held up a shirt.

"This still has the tags. You sure?"

Morgan nodded. "I couldn't bear to give these to the church yard sale. Some are brand new, and the rest Sam barely wore."

"I meant, will it bother you to see me wear Sam's clothes?"

"It's not like those were his old favorites. Even if they were, I have to let go sometime."

"Yeah," Del said. "It took me a while, but I finally cleaned out Harriet's closet a couple years ago. Funny thing, but I guess I kept hoping she'd show back up, and she'd need her old things. Beatrice said she knew some ladies around town who could use a warm coat or a new outfit. New to them, anyway."

"We donated three pickup loads of items for our church yard sale," Morgan said. "It felt good knowing pieces of our old life will be sold to fill the shelves of the food pantry. It wasn't fun, but I'm glad we finally cleaned out the house. The trip back was good for all of us."

Over a steaming bowl of soup, she told Del about finding the stash of Christmas presents. How it had been just the thing to tip them all over the edge, and let the tears flow. Now she felt like healing was finally happening for her children.

"And what about you?" Del asked.

"Somehow Sam leaving those presents helped me realize he wouldn't want his family living in sorrow the rest of their days. If it had been me to go first, I'd feel the same way."

Morgan retired early, exhausted from travel and the busy day at the shop, but the moon shone bright through the southwest-patterned fabric of the bedroom curtains. The mountain man might be out there, or in the barn, or prying boards off windows to get inside Del's trailer.

Why here? Morgan wondered. *Is it because I found Carlee? That I'm the one who caused people to take her away?*

She shuddered and huddled deeper under the quilt at the thought of the mountain man watching Carlee's body slowly decay to bone. If that's what happened. He might have stumbled across her body long after she died. But scavenging animals usually dragged body parts around.

What was with the flowers?

Had the mountain man planted them for Carlee? And had he brought the ammolite from somewhere else, or was there treasure buried in local mountains?

When Morgan finally fell asleep, she dreamed about finding a pile of opalescent ammolite in a rainbow of colors on the hill behind the rock shop. But when she tried to excavate the gems, she discovered they were attached, not to shells, but to human bones.

Chapter Twenty-Two

Tuesday morning, Del hitched a ride with Beatrice to his doctor's appointment in Granite Junction. Morgan was stuck at the shop by herself. When the veterinarian showed up, Morgan was glad he knew the donkeys and the property well enough to let himself in the barn. He returned in between customers to give Morgan the report.

"Temple Mountain Feed and Seed carries this equine supplement." Doctor Alvin McCormick scribbled on a prescription pad. He was one of Teruko's grown children, and had inherited an exotic blend of her delicate Japanese features and his hearty Irish-American father's red hair and freckles. "Give Adelaide a dose of the pellets with her oats once a day. A measuring scoop comes with the bucket of supplements."

"Is she okay?"

"Just a precaution, to make sure she and her foal are getting enough vitamins and minerals. I don't think Adelaide is as far along as I estimated."

"The poor thing," Morgan said. "She already looks about to explode."

"Donkeys carry their foals for as long as a year. She's doing fine, and so is the foal."

The cowbell clanged as a customer entered. Business was steady, and Adelaide's health hadn't been affected by the excitement of chasing intruders. Morgan hoped the rest of the day would be as good.

★ ★ ★ ★ ★

During a lull in business, Morgan registered for the Denver gem show. The deadline to reserve a vendor's table was approaching, and she didn't want to miss out. Morgan hit the send button. She was committed now.

Del seemed energized when Beatrice brought him home. Maybe he was finally on the mend. He volunteered to watch the shop so the women could visit. Morgan invited Beatrice into the living quarters for a pot of tea.

"I heard Sasquatch returned," Beatrice said. "Del told me Trevin fed him lunch."

"And his dog, too. I have this creepy feeling the mountain man's hanging around. He never left. I don't know what he wants."

"The return of Carlee's bones?"

Beatrice dropped a sugar cube into her herb tea. Her grandmotherly look of short, steel-gray hair and navy-blue polyester pantsuit combined with her take-charge attitude was comforting. Beatrice was a woman determined to ensure that all was right in her world.

"All this time," Morgan said, "I've been assuming Chief Sharp will squeeze the story out of the mountain man when he catches him, but Trevin told us the guy couldn't speak."

"It's all very strange, isn't it?" Beatrice said. "And Gerda hasn't been forthcoming. I think she feels guilty. Maybe something happened between her and Carlee before the girl disappeared, but if so, she isn't saying anything about it."

"Did you contact her other daughter?" Morgan asked. "Maybe she can tell us something."

"Camille doesn't want to come," Beatrice said. "Too many painful memories, she told Teruko. The Kruger family is on my prayer group's list, along with Pastor Filbury and a dozen other souls in need of healing."

"I don't know how the Krugers will ever find healing when they don't know how Carlee died," Morgan said.

"Reuniting with her estranged daughter and having a memorial service for Carlee would help them all. That is, if we can convince Camille to come to Golden Springs." Beatrice stood and pulled on her jacket. "I have a meeting at church. We're reviewing the final three candidates for the position as our new pastor."

"Who did you narrow it down to?" Morgan asked.

"Charles Quinton and Tip Zander."

Morgan tried not to let her face fall. Neither had exhibited the fire she thought the Golden Springs Community Church needed to revive its flagging membership numbers. Solid, dependable, but nothing flashy. And yet maybe that was the kind of preacher the church wanted.

"That was only two. You said there were three candidates."

"We'd like to invite your brother, Kendall, to apply. I heard he's coming back to town."

"Where did you hear that?" Morgan had only heard the rumor secondhand, through her daughter. Kendall had yet to talk to Morgan about his plans.

"Through the grapevine." As though anxious to change the subject, Beatrice pointed to the wooden mountain scene Sam had created. "That's new."

"David found it in the attic when we were cleaning out the Sioux Falls house." Morgan was already thinking of it as "the" house, not "my" house. "Sam made it."

Beatrice stood and walked closer to the plaque, the crepe soles of her sensible shoes squeaking on the worn linoleum. "Beautiful. He was a talented man."

Morgan told Beatrice about that intensely emotional time with her children. "We hadn't mourned Sam's passing as a family. We were all trying to stay strong for each other."

"I have to apologize," Beatrice said.

"For what?"

"For pushing you into going to dinner with Pete Melcher. You weren't ready. But maybe now that you've had this time of healing with your children—"

Morgan held up a hand. "Beatrice, I appreciate your concern. Pete's a very nice man, but we have nothing in common."

"You have your faith in common, and that is no small thing." Beatrice squinted at Morgan, as though she were trying to peer inside her head. Or maybe her heart. "I've heard you've been seen around town with that newspaperman. Let me warn you, Morgan, it is no fun being in a marriage with a non-believer."

"Marriage? Kurt and I haven't even been on a real date."

"Thank goodness. Remember the scripture about being equally yoked. Kurt Willard is an atheist."

Morgan shook her head vigorously, then brushed a stray curl out of her eyes. "I don't think so. He's just not a church kind of guy."

In truth, they hadn't engaged in any theological discussions. How well did she know Kurt? And how important was it to her that they share the same faith? Beatrice certainly had a way of stirring things up.

"Just be careful, dear." Beatrice patted her hand. "I've got to go, but feel free to call me if you need to talk. Or if you want me to set up another dinner with Pete."

Morgan relieved Del, who admitted he would like to put his feet up for a few minutes. Then business slowed down, and Morgan brought her laptop to the front counter. She tinkered with the very basic website she had set up, striving for slick and professional, but pretty sure she was presenting a small business with no IT budget.

Then she searched for the Pine County Gemstone Society

and Prospecting Club. They had an equally basic website, with even fewer bells and whistles than her own, but that conveyed the information about the club adequately. Their next monthly meeting was Wednesday night. Tomorrow.

An adrenaline rush shot through Morgan when she saw the title for the meeting. Amazonite. For an instant, she thought it read ammolite. Once she got that straight in her mind, she relaxed. Of all the rumors racing through the gossip grapevine, the rare gemstone was not one of them.

The speaker was her geology class instructor, Dr. Tony Esteban.

"I'm definitely going," she said aloud. The talk would be informative and entertaining, if it was anything like his geology class lectures.

Del shuffled into the shop two hours later, from a nap, judging by the rumpled remnants of his thin gray hair and the sleepy look on his face. A moment later, the cowbell clanged, and in walked Chase Cooper.

"Hi, Morgan. I came back for more geodes."

How many geodes did one man need? Morgan thought. From Chase's muddy boots and the mud-stained knees of his canvas pants, he might have been digging somewhere trying to locate the minerals himself.

"We're fresh out." All the drowsiness evaporated from Del's face. He was on full alert.

"A sale is a sale," Morgan whispered to Del. To Chase, she said, "I restocked the unopened geodes. They're outside in the ore cart."

"Right. I'll take a look around inside first, to see if there's anything else I need."

Chase stood in front of Lucy's display of jewelry for several minutes. Morgan wondered whether he was checking out the competition.

"Do you have any other jewelry?" Chase asked. "Handcrafted, like this?"

"No," Morgan said. "That's all we have, other than some plastic beads for children."

After making a loop through the shop, studying tables, shelves, and display cases, he slouched down onto the aspen bench in front of the checkout counter. Chase flashed a smile. At least, one side of his face smiled. The puckered skin on the burned side pulled up in more of a grimace. He carried himself with a confidence that caused a person to look past the disfigurement.

"I like your topaz," he said.

"You should," Del said. "They're top-quality stones."

A dozen topaz gemstones were locked in a display case. Despite the elder Cooper's poor assessment of their value during his visit, Morgan knew they were worth a lot. When Morgan first saw topaz in its natural state, she had been unimpressed. She had since learned that the rough little fingertip-sized nuggets cleaned up and cut in gemstone fashion could be worth hundreds of dollars.

"I could take a few off your hands," Chase said, "for the right price."

"I thought you worked with glass," Del said. "What do you want with topaz?"

"It's for our jeweler," Chase said. "She doesn't have time to hunt down raw gems."

He and Del haggled, until Chase finally agreed on a price for three topaz nuggets. He rolled them around in the palm of his hand, an admiring look in his turquoise-colored eyes.

"Do you have any other gemstones this nice?"

"You looking for anything in particular?" Del seemed to have softened his opinion of Harlan Cooper's son. Perhaps it was the pocket full of cash Chase flashed.

Chase shrugged. "Whatever's local. Aquamarine, jasper, tourmaline. Ammolite?"

In the ensuing silence, Morgan felt as though the oxygen had been sucked out of the room.

"You must mean ammonite," Del said, emphasizing the "n" in the word. He waved a hand toward a wooden bin. "We have plenty of ammonite fossils."

"No, I mean the gem." Chase pulled a folded paper out of one of the many pockets on his mud-stained slacks. "Look, I don't know feldspar from quartz. I'm going off a list our jeweler gave me. She told me to buy all the ammolite I could find. Doesn't matter whether it's raw or recycled from old jewelry."

"Then your jeweler doesn't know diddly about gems." Del tugged at his mustache. "Gem quality ammolite isn't found in this area, and if we did have any in stock, I doubt even a Cooper would have enough money to buy it all."

Chase wheedled and pried for several more minutes before finally giving up. He paid for the topaz and left.

"Really strange," Del said, after the door closed behind Chase. "Word must have gotten out about the ammolite. Could be the Coopers have got it in their heads that we know where it is, and they want in on it. Maybe they caught wind of me and Barton nosing around about staking a claim."

The phone rang, and caller ID told Morgan it was her real estate agent in Sioux Falls. She felt a twinge of dread. The rental deal had probably fallen through. Or maybe the prospective renters had turned the house into a meth lab already.

"Hi, Dot."

"Morgan, good news."

Morgan sat on the aspen bench, a wave of relief washing over her.

"The renters' first check came through. You should see a bump in your account."

They had set up a direct deposit for Dot to send Morgan the rental money.

"For the first few months, every penny is going to the mortgage," Morgan said. "Thank goodness for that. The bank has been patient, but they do want their money."

"And after you're caught up, you'll be making an income off the house."

Once she caught up on mortgage payments, there would be money to use toward restocking the shelves of the Rock of Ages. Or putting new tires on her car. There would be routine house maintenance, both on the rock shop living quarters and the Sioux Falls house. If the renters didn't flake out, or lose their jobs. Morgan chided herself. When had she become such a pessimist? Everything would work out.

Chapter Twenty-Three

Bernie picked Morgan up for their weekly run with the O'Reily's Running Club. Her huge late model SUV handled dirt roads and the highway with equal confidence.

"How's Rolf?" Morgan asked. "I thought he was coming with us tonight."

"He did want to walk tonight, but I convinced him to give himself another week to heal. He has a dislocated shoulder, for goodness sakes."

"He's so lucky the bullet missed him."

Bernie shuddered. "I could have lost him, Morgan." She released her grip on the steering wheel with one hand to wipe away tears. "Here I was, ready to give up on a relationship because he has a daughter. This really put things in perspective." She glanced at Morgan. "I imagine that sounds pretty lame considering you did lose the love of your life."

"I'm glad you've decided to make things work with Rolf. And I owe you an apology."

"For what?"

"I've been telling tales about love at first sight. My Sioux Falls friends reminded me that I nearly didn't walk down the aisle with Sam."

"How could you forget something like that?" Bernie asked.

"I suppose I painted the past the way I wanted to remember it," Morgan said. "When I lost Sam, I put him, and our marriage, on a pedestal. The old gang reminded me that I did have cold feet. Obviously, I got over it, and you know the rest."

"Happily ever after." Bernie bit her lower lip. "Oops. Sorry. I really stuck my foot in my mouth."

"It was happy," Morgan said. "Just not 'ever after.' "

"Tell me about your trip."

Morgan described to Bernie her reunion with old friends, and then told about David finding Sam's wrapped gifts in the attic, and how they brought healing. The conversation came full circle when she told Bernie about returning home to learn that Trevin had fed Big Foot lunch, and received the elephant-head bouquet as thanks.

"Weird. But if the elephant-head flowers are a clue to a murder, why would the mountain man put them in a bouquet for Trevin? He's either guilty and crazy, or he's innocent, or maybe he's trying to out a killer."

"Gee, that really narrows down the options," Morgan said. "If Carlee was murdered, the mountain man seems the most likely suspect, so I'd vote for guilty and crazy. Del thinks that if something bad happens, a Cooper must be involved, and I have to admit, it does seem awfully coincidental that Jade ended up married to Mia Cooper. I can't remember whether there were elephant-head flowers in his paintings, but they're definitely a theme in Chase Cooper's glasswork. He came snooping around the shop today. He's up to something."

"Here you go again with a suspect list." Bernie pulled into a downtown Granite Junction parking lot. "Let's see. Who have you got on it so far? Jade Tinsley, Chase Cooper, and Sasquatch."

"I'm not counting out Chase's sister, Mia, yet."

The 5K walk was a nice distraction, and the beer and fish and chips afterwards were the best in town. Lucy and Paul told her about the seedling planting party she had missed while she was in Sioux Falls. Morgan felt herself unwind from the tension of the past two weeks.

On the drive home, traffic backed up on the narrow highway. Bernie stopped her SUV. Red and blue lights flashed on the downhill side of Topaz Pass.

An ambulance screamed up behind them. Bernie edged to the side of the road. There was not much of a shoulder. Rock cliffs rose on both sides of the highway. The ambulance whizzed by, then pulled a U-turn in the middle of the road.

"Morgan, that looks like Gerda's car."

Bernie climbed out. Morgan scooted across the seat and followed. As they waited for a string of cars to pass, Morgan stared at the remains of Gerda's car. The passenger side crumpled against the canyon wall. A long streak of white paint on the red rocks marked the point of first contact, leading to the car's resting place. Steam seeped from the hood, forming a cloud of fog in the chilly night air.

Deputy Parker held up a hand to stop cars as Bernie and Morgan dashed across the road. The ambulance came to an abrupt halt behind Gerda's car, and paramedics jumped out. Chief Sharp pointed at Bernie and Morgan.

"You two need to leave. You're in the way."

"Gerda needs a friend," Bernie told Sharp.

Morgan followed the paramedics while Bernie had the chief occupied. After assessing her injuries, they eased Gerda out of the vehicle and loaded her on a gurney. Morgan trotted to keep up. Alcohol fumes burned her sinuses.

"Gerda." Morgan wanted to scream at the white-haired mechanic. If she wanted to kill herself, then do it in the privacy of her own home, not driving drunk, where she risked the lives of innocent people.

Gerda's hand reached out from under a blanket, gripping Morgan's arm.

"I was not drinking." Gerda's words, thick with her German

accent, sounded labored. "Tell them. I lose control of my car. The brakes failed."

"Do you want me to come with you?" Morgan asked.

"Teruko." Tears squeezed out of Gerda's eyes as she grimaced with pain. "Please send Teruko."

The paramedics began to load her into the ambulance.

"Wait. I demand the police give me the breath test." She tried to sit up. "Morgan, bring Sharp here!"

"They'll do that at the hospital, ma'am," an attendant said.

"I want no questions," Gerda said. "I take the test now."

On the drive to the hospital, Morgan called Beatrice. That call set in motion the ever-ready church ladies. Beatrice assured Morgan she would bring Teruko. Morgan hung up her cell phone and filled Bernie in on the details as they followed the ambulance.

"I am so mad, I'm shaking." Bernie lifted one hand off the steering wheel and held out her trembling hand. "Someone messes with her brakes, and then tries to make it look like Gerda was driving drunk. As if she doesn't have enough to deal with right now."

The Breathalyzer results proved any alcohol was *on* Gerda, not in her. She had no liquor in her system.

"Why? What is the motivation?" Morgan shook her head. "The only reason I can think of is her daughter's body being found. Maybe Carlee's killer thinks Gerda knows something?"

"But even the coroner hasn't figured out how Carlee died," Bernie said. "No one is talking about murder. And that was sixteen years ago. Would a killer even stick around?"

"If he or she thought there was no evidence, they might."

"You'd think they'd keep quiet, not try to kill someone else all these years later."

"Unless the killer was crazy," Morgan said. "And that leads

us right back to Big Foot."

The hospital emergency room was the usual combination of chaos interwoven with tedious waiting. After the church ladies arrived, it was obvious Morgan and Bernie weren't needed. Gerda was banged up, but would be okay after an as-yet undefined stay in the hospital.

By the time Bernie pulled into the Rock of Ages parking lot, the lights were still on and Del was pacing new holes in the worn kitchen linoleum.

"How is Gerda?" Del asked when the women walked in.

They filled Del in on the wreck, and brainstormed reasons for anyone to frame Gerda for drunk driving, at the least, and at the worst, attempt to kill her. There seemed to be only one explanation. Finding Carlee's body had stirred up a hornets' nest.

When Del yawned, Bernie glanced at the clock.

"Is it really that late? I need to get home."

"Maybe you should spend the night here," Morgan said. "There might be a killer out there."

"I have to open the bakery early. And then there's Mr. Whiskers. Besides, where would I sleep? I'll call you when I'm safe inside."

Morgan made Bernie stay on her cell phone until she was locked inside her apartment above the bakery.

"You'd think this was the big city," Morgan said to Del. "Finding a body, being stalked by a homeless man, and now a suspicious car wreck."

"Just another day in the Wild West."

Chapter Twenty-Four

Wednesday morning, Morgan had trouble waking up. Business carried on, though, regardless of personal drama. Morgan perched on the tall stool behind the checkout counter and poured herself another cup of coffee. The phone rang.

"Rock of Ages. Morgan speaking. How may I help you?"

"I don't have long, so please forgive me, and just listen."

"Kendall? Finally! I only know you're alive because Sarah tells me—"

"I need you to wire money."

"How much?"

"Three thousand dollars." His straight-from-the-pulpit voice boomed through the receiver with authority.

Morgan's heart skipped several beats. "Is something wrong? Has Allie been kidnapped? Are you in trouble?"

"I can't talk about it right now. Take this down."

"Hang on."

Morgan grabbed a pen and notepad. The last time she had seen her brother, his wild hair was a gray-streaked tangle of curls, and a beard covered his face. He and Allie had worn psychedelic T-shirts and jeans. Hardly the look of a respectable lay-preacher and his wife. Morgan could imagine a dozen scenarios placing them in danger.

"Ready."

Kendall gave her instructions for wiring money via Western Union. It seemed like a shockingly simple procedure.

"I realize you may not have that kind of cash lying around—"

"No kidding."

"But if you can get it to me within the next week—"

"Kendall. A week? Three thousand dollars? You absconded with all the cash from the rock shop, and I don't have that kind of money."

"Can you call Pastor Filbury?"

"The man just had a heart attack."

"What? Heart attack? Is he going to be okay?"

"Yes, but I really don't want to call him asking for money right now. He has enough going on." Morgan decided not to mention Beatrice's announcement that the Golden Springs Community Church had placed Kendall in the running for the pastor's job.

"There should be cash in a coffee can at the bottom of the grain barrel."

"Seriously? In the barn?"

"Yes. I can't remember how much is there, but it should be a start."

"Kendall, what is going on?"

"I can't say just yet. Please, do what you can. It's life or death, almost. Not mine or Allie's exactly. We need plane tickets."

"You're coming home?"

"With a little luck and three thousand dollars, yes. I'll explain later."

"It's going to be a tight squeeze. Del is living at the rock shop. David might spend the summer here, too. I don't know where we're going to fit everyone."

"I thought you didn't want to stay in Colorado. You said you wanted us to come home, so you could go back to South Dakota."

"Maybe three months ago. A lot has changed."

"A lot has changed here, too. Look, we'll figure it out when I get there. If I get there."

Kendall sounded stressed, and maybe a little scared. Coming from her take-charge brother, the situation had to be bad. Very bad.

"Call this number when you send the money." Kendall recited a phone number.

Her brother had once again thrown complications into Morgan's life, with no apology or explanation. And yet the urgency in his voice frightened her. Kendall and Allie had gotten themselves into big trouble in the jungles of Central America. And somehow it had fallen on Morgan to bail them out.

Before she could demand he give her the specifics, the cowbell above the door clanged, announcing the entrance of Beatrice and Teruko. If anyone could pry information out of an unwilling soul, it was Beatrice.

"Kendall, someone just came in who will want to say hi to you."

"No time," he said. "Say hi and give our love etcetera."

Click. Morgan glared at the receiver in her hand.

"Did I hear you say Kendall?" Beatrice's short gray hair was flattened to one side of her head.

"He and Allie say hi," Morgan said. "They send their love." *Along with a hasty and insincere etcetera.*

Morgan entertained the brief thought that maybe she should let Kendall rot in the Third World predicament he'd gotten himself into.

"Are they well?" Teruko asked.

The tiny Japanese lady was stylish, as usual, but her mid-calf skirt was rumpled, and her halo of white hair mussed. Both women must have spent the night at the hospital.

"They want to come home." Morgan decided the best way to

unburden herself of the worry and guilt Kendall had just dumped on her was to share a little of it with the church ladies, excluding her suspicions that their situation was somewhere beyond dire. "They don't have money for plane tickets."

"Then we'll raise it for them." Beatrice kicked into high gear. "We do quite well with bake sales. When do they need the money?"

"Within a week," Morgan said. "Talk about short notice. But we can discuss Kendall later. How is Gerda?"

"We came from the hospital," Teruko said in her soft, wavering voice. "Gerda is resting."

"Teruko convinced Gerda's daughter Camille to come to Golden Springs. She used words to the effect that Gerda is on her deathbed."

Teruko smiled innocently. "Perhaps I did."

"I didn't know she had it in her," Beatrice said. "It was quite the show. Fortunately, Gerda was out cold, so she didn't hear any of it."

"When I came to America with my Neil, I did not see many of my family ever again." Tears welled in Teruko's eyes. "My grandparents and parents passed away many years before international telephone calls became less expensive, and before computers allowed conversations. You do not abandon family, if you have a choice."

"So Gerda's daughter Camille and her two kids are coming this weekend," Beatrice said. "The memorial service for Carlee will be in a week and a half. Saturday after next."

"Will Gerda be mobile by then?" Morgan asked.

"She's bruised and battered, but she'll be out of the hospital well before the memorial service. Thank goodness for airbags."

"Gerda likes being in charge," Morgan said. "I can't imagine her lying helpless in a hospital bed."

"As it turns out, this accident was a lifesaver," Beatrice said.

"Well, she didn't die," Morgan agreed.

"Not that," Beatrice said. "Cancer."

"The nurse noticed spots on Gerda's face," Teruko said. "They are running tests."

"Gerda avoided doctors like the plague for over a decade," Beatrice said. "My guess would be she was scared they'd make her do something about her alcohol problem."

"Poor Gerda," Morgan said.

"Lucky Gerda," Beatrice said. "If she hadn't ended up in the hospital, no one would have noticed the melanoma. That's one of those cancers you have to catch early if you want a chance of beating it."

Morgan knew too well. Her Sam had passed from colon cancer.

"Gerda reeked of alcohol when I saw her," Morgan said. "But the Breathalyzer test proved she was sober. Do the police know what caused her wreck?"

"She insists there was something wrong with her brakes," Beatrice said. "But what are the chances of that?"

The precise German lady was unlikely to let something like auto maintenance slip.

"There's only one explanation that makes sense," Morgan said. "Gerda's brakes were tampered with."

"But why?" Teruko asked. "Who would want to hurt Gerda?"

Beatrice's eyes glittered. "Someone who didn't want Carlee to be found. Someone who doesn't want Gerda digging into this. The person who killed Carlee."

When the ladies left, Morgan turned around the be-back-in sign. She grabbed the small canister of pepper spray Del had given her and walked to the barn. Adelaide saw her, and waddled along the other side of the fence.

"It's not dinnertime yet," Morgan told the donkey.

When she entered the front of the barn, Adelaide was already waiting in her stall.

"Doctor McCormick told me not to overfeed you. But I suppose a little hay wouldn't hurt."

Morgan peeled a thin flake of hay off a bale and tossed it into Adelaide's stall. While the donkey munched, Morgan entered the tack room and unfastened the band on the metal fifty-gallon drum of oats. The barrel was only a third full. Morgan plunged her hand inside. She couldn't feel anything, but then she could not reach the bottom. Not anywhere close.

She climbed the ladder to the loft, pepper spray in hand, and paused at the top. The loft appeared empty. Perhaps the mountain man had decided not to come back. She found an empty plastic bin and climbed back down the ladder. The barrel of oats was heavy, but Morgan managed to tip it up. The oats rattled and echoed off the metal barrel as she poured them into the plastic bin. Adelaide huffed a brief donkey bray.

"I told you, it's not dinnertime."

As she upended the barrel, a red plastic coffee tub tumbled into the bin.

"That was a lot of trouble," Morgan said to an attentive Adelaide. "I hope there's money inside."

She peeled back the black plastic lid on the tub. Inside were several envelopes.

"Unpaid bills?" Morgan asked.

But the envelopes had all been opened, the top edges torn and ragged. Kendall and Allie were remarkably frugal, recycling envelopes to use in organizing their secret money stash. The first, a former utility bill envelope, contained twenty-five dollars. A used telephone bill envelope contained forty-two.

"This is going to take too long."

Morgan poured the oats back into the metal barrel. She took Adelaide a handful, depositing them in the wooden trough inside the stall. Then she resealed the barrel, locked the tack room, and headed for the shop with the coffee tub.

Only two customers and a man in a suit needing directions to the Dalton ranch interrupted her counting. Morgan sorted the bills into stacks, wrapping them together with rubber bands. When she finished, her tally came to five hundred and thirty three dollars.

Morgan couldn't imagine a bake sale netting the rest of the three thousand Kendall needed. She hoped he could escape whatever situation he was in with a lot less.

After closing the shop for the day, Morgan heated up a store-bought lasagna casserole for dinner.

"I'm going to the gem society meeting tonight," Morgan said. "Are you sure you don't want to go with me?"

"No, thanks," Del said. "Don't mention the ammolite, or you'll have a dozen new best friends, all wanting to follow you home."

Chapter Twenty-Five

The Pine County Gemstone Society and Prospecting Club met in City Hall. The building was modeled after the Denver capitol, but instead of a gold dome, Golden Springs's was wood shingle. The public meeting room shared the lower level of the two-story building with city offices and the police department.

Morgan had attended a very different function in City Hall several months ago. That group had been free-thinking New Age types. She suspected that prospectors were equally independent-minded, but quite possibly poised on the opposite end of the political spectrum.

As Morgan walked into the room, she was happy to see a familiar face. Barton Potts carried a cardboard banker's box to the wooden table at the head of the room. Before she reached him, a skinny cowgirl intercepted her.

"Hello. I don't believe I've seen you here before."

Morgan had seen her. Last week, outside Rudy's Two Step in Granite Junction. Tonight she wore a different blouse, but the tight jeans and pink and black cowgirl boots looked the same. She extended a hand tipped with polished pink nails.

"I'm Lorina Dimple, president of the Gemstone Society."

Not Cooper. Morgan hadn't thought she was Harlan's wife. Lorina's grip was strong for a skinny old broad. Seeing her up close, and not reflected in a dress shop mirror, Morgan could see the age in her face. Gray roots struggled against the pinkish-orange dye job in her short hair.

"Morgan Iverson, manager of the Rock of Ages."

Lorina dropped her hand. "Kendall's sister?"

Morgan had given up trying to separate her identity from her brother's. "Yes."

"How is that crazy son-of-a-gun?" Lorina's manicured fingers flew to cover her lips. "Oh, I didn't mean to say it quite that way."

"He and Allie are fine." Morgan wasn't about to share family gossip. She changed the subject. "Since I'm managing the rock shop, I thought I'd better come to a meeting and try to learn more about rocks and minerals."

"You came to the right place." Lorina wrapped her arm through Morgan's and dragged her along. "This here is our vice president, Barton Potts."

Barton turned from unpacking a box.

"We know each other," Morgan said. "Hi, Barton."

"From the Rock of Ages," Barton said. "You know." He looked uncomfortable. "Del lives there."

Lorina punched Barton's arm. "We already made our introductions. You mean to tell me that old geezer Delano is still alive?"

"He's nearly healed up from his chainsaw accident," Morgan said.

"I did read about that in the paper. A man his age shouldn't be playing around with power tools. Does he still hang out in that broke-down old trailer?"

Morgan was willing to bet Miss Lorina had seen the interior of that trailer more than once. Before she had to answer, Dr. Tony Esteban walked in the door, struggling to balance a bulky leather briefcase on top of a plastic storage tub.

"Professor," Morgan said. "Need a hand?"

"Mrs. Iverson, so glad to see you are still cultivating your interest in geology."

Lorina scrunched her face up to one side. "And here I thought you'd need introductions all around. You already seem to know everyone."

Her flashy boots clopped across the pine floor as Lorina sought less attached newcomers to ride herd on.

The room didn't exactly fill up, but a few more prospectors and rock hounds wandered in. When Harlan and Chase Cooper made their entrance, Morgan expected Lorina to react, but she ignored the man she'd been arm-in-arm with just a week ago. By the time the meeting started, two dozen people sat on the metal folding chairs. Lorina called the meeting to order.

"Myra, will you please read the minutes from our April meeting?"

The young woman stood, turning to face the attendees. Morgan was certain none of the men listened to a word she read as she rattled off the dry meeting minutes, but she had their full attention. Myra was a stunning red-haired twenty-something. Although dressed like a prospector, no gold miner ever filled out a pair of jeans or tight safari-style shirt the way Myra did. The men probably didn't notice her hesitant reading either, or how she stumbled over the big words.

Barton seemed as affected as the rest. As Myra handed him a copy of the minutes, he fumbled the paper to the floor, bent over to pick it up, and hit his head on the podium.

"If I could have everyone's attention," Lorina said, obviously annoyed by her much younger competition, "let's move on to new business."

A heated discussion began about why their April fundraiser had been a bust.

"Cate was supposed to get us some free advertising from the *Gazetteer,*" a man said. "We would have had plenty of people there for our event, if Cate had done her job."

"Since Cate isn't here to defend herself," Lorina said, "how about we move on to the next issue?"

One of the Society's numerous subcommittees gave a report on their annual mineral show to be held mid-summer.

"We can't take chances this time that tourists will just happen to wander into City Hall and find us," Lorina said. "Last year we barely raised enough money to print our Society brochures."

Morgan wasn't about to offer her assistance getting free advertising from Kurt, but decided she would mention it to him later. More new business, involving more mutual blame and arguing, filled another fifteen minutes. It was a contentious bunch. Maybe prospectors were too independent to form a cohesive group.

"Now we're finally to the good part," Lorina said. "Tonight we're honored to have with us Professor Tony Esteban from the University of Colorado at Granite Junction to talk on amazonite."

Morgan didn't think one mineral could possibly entertain for forty-five minutes, but Professor Esteban had a slideshow presentation, samples, and an engaging style. He put Morgan on the spot by asking her a couple of questions mid-lecture, but they were easy ones, and she passed with flying colors.

Then Chase waved his hand, like a kid in a grade-school class.

"Professor, you mentioned several other local gemstones in your amazonite talk, but can you tell us if there's any ammolite around here?"

Tony Esteban's deeply tanned face went pale. When Chase had asked about ammolite at the rock shop, he had made it sound like he was asking on behalf of a jeweler, as though he was not aware of the organic gem's rarity and value. Playing dumb. Morgan wondered what else he was covering up.

Dr. Esteban recovered his composure, shaking his head.

"There are wild rumors circulating about ammolite in the hills around Golden Springs. Fossilized ammonite is typically found in sandstone deposits in this area, but I have yet to see ammolite," he pronounced the "l" in the word carefully. "That would be a significant find."

"So it is possible?" Chase asked.

"Let us just say, I will believe it when I see it."

When the Q and A portion of the lecture ended, and people gathered around the front table to examine Professor Esteban's mineral specimens, Morgan managed to get Barton's attention away from Myra. She tugged on his arm to draw him closer.

"Maybe we should show the professor a piece of the ammolite," she whispered.

Barton shook his head. "Not until we figure out where it came from."

Then Barton noticed that Chase had moved in on Myra. The young woman stared at his scarred face, but Chase didn't seem to notice. As Barton attempted to break into the conversation, Lorina took his place at Morgan's elbow.

"How about that?" Lorina asked. "Chase Cooper thinking there's ammolite around here. What an amateur!"

"Colorado has almost every other gemstone in existence," Morgan said. "I might have asked the same question, if I didn't know better."

"Do you know better?" Lorina asked.

The skinny cowgirl was trolling for information. Del had warned her about the club. Morgan considered an answer.

"Professor Esteban is an expert. If he says there's no ammolite, I'd take his word for it."

Lorina shook her head. "He didn't say it's impossible. People make incredible discoveries all the time, like record-setting aquamarine deposits worth a king's ransom. If a person were to run across something big like ammolite, they might need an expert to make sure some slick operator didn't swindle them. You catch my drift, missy?"

A voice sounded behind Morgan, startling her.

"That would be something, now wouldn't it?"

Morgan turned. Harlan Cooper stood so close, if she'd taken a backward step she would have tripped over his alligator cowboy boots. Morgan felt like a fish at the center of a shark-feeding frenzy.

"I suppose the first question is, does anyone have a claim on ammolite?" Harlan lifted one eyebrow above a turquoise-colored eye as he smiled at Morgan. The geezer with the bulldog jowls was turning his charm on full blast. "That would settle the whole issue, if the person holding the claim would just make it public. There's a fortune to be made, for a person smart enough to call on the right resources."

"No true prospector blabs about their claims or mines." Lorina glared at Harlan. "Just like a good poker player knows to hold her cards close."

Lorina pressed one hand to the top of her blouse like she was hiding a royal flush in her cleavage. There was no flirtation in the gesture. Her reply was delivered with such a cool air, Morgan couldn't believe they had recently been holding hands in downtown Granite Junction.

"Miss Lorina, you of all people know that mining is an expensive venture." Harlan shrugged. "It's one thing to own a claim. It's a whole 'nother thing to have the wherewithal to dig. Some minerals can't be harvested with a pick axe and shovel. They require heavy equipment. But for something like ammolite, a delicate hand might be needed. An amateur could damage a good portion of their find. Chop it all to bits."

Cooper was digging now, for information.

"You worry about your own resources," Lorina said, "which may be considerable, but money won't pull gems out of thin air, or unproductive dirt. You can keep your heavy equipment and leave us little people to our puny pick axes. We'll do just fine, thank you, Mr. Cooper."

Lorina flounced off to rescue Myra from the competing attention of Barton and Chase. Morgan wondered if a dozen or more years ago a similar scene had played out between Lorina, Harlan, and Del.

When she got home, Del studiously avoided asking her about the meeting. Morgan wanted to discuss the conversation she'd had with Lorina and Harlan. They both suspected Morgan knew where the ammolite was, but neither had come right out and asked. She ventured one comment.

"The rumors about ammolite have reached the prospecting club."

"And you didn't confirm any of them?"

"I'd rather climb in a shark tank. In fact, I felt a little like I was in one."

"I'm tellin' you, those people are dog-eat-dog."

Morgan had a feeling "those people" included Lorina Dimple. Whatever had happened between Del and Lorina, it must have cut deep. Morgan couldn't imagine Del being the one to wrong the skinny cowgirl, but she might never learn that bit of history. In any event, it was a good lesson to observe. In a small town, a romantic involvement that went wrong could have long-lasting consequences.

When Morgan went to the barn Thursday morning to feed the donkeys and check their water trough, she heard hammering. After tending to Houdini and the ever-expanding Adelaide's needs, Morgan followed the construction sounds to Del's trailer.

"A little to the left," Del said. "A little more."

While Barton held the board to the new porch steps, Del hammered a nail into it.

"Good morning."

Both men glanced up at Morgan, each muttering a hasty "morning" between hammer blows.

"How is the repair project going?" Morgan asked.

"After I put my foot through a board," Del said, "we decided fixing the steps took priority over the roof."

"Let me know if there's anything I can do to help," Morgan said. "We're going to need all the space we can find soon."

"Why's that?" Del asked.

"Kendall and Allie are coming back, if they can cobble together money for air fare," Morgan said. "I was thinking about trying to convert part of the barn loft into an apartment."

"You'd consider putting them in the loft?" Del asked. "They might not like that idea, after living in the shop all those years."

"My brother gave me no warning about leaving Golden Springs, and he certainly didn't ask my permission to move back home." Teruko's story reminded Morgan of how fragile family relationships were. She bit back more harsh words about being inconvenienced by her brother, and released a frustrated sigh. "We'll just have to find a way to squeeze everyone in. I don't think David would mind living in the loft."

In her imagination, she could see David happily taking the loft, while Kendall arm-wrestled her for who got to stay in the rock shop living quarters, and who had to move into Del's trailer. The guest room, well, that might actually be used by guests again.

"Oh, is your son coming to Colorado?" A smile lifted the corners of Del's mustache.

"I'm trying to talk him into working here this summer," Morgan said.

The logistics of Morgan's announcement seemed to sink in.

"If David's going to be here, and Kendall and Allie, then it's a good thing I decided to fix up my place." Del turned toward the trailer. "I'd better get busy."

Del whacked another nail into the steps. Barton crooked a finger at Morgan. She followed him a few paces away from the trailer. Since Del's accident with the chain saw in January, Barton spent more time with the old cowboy. The relationship seemed good for them both, drawing Barton out of his hermit lifestyle, and giving Del a buddy who could play the role of caretaker without Del suspecting he was being taken care of.

"I'm trying to talk Del into moving to my ranch," Barton said. "I have plenty of space, but I can't get him to budge."

"He's pretty attached to the trailer," Morgan said. "I think it's because of the time he spent here with his wife. Memories, you know?"

Barton lowered his voice. "The trailer is falling apart. It isn't worth fixing up."

The weight that had been lifting off Morgan's shoulders settled firmly back into place.

Chapter Twenty-Six

Morgan used her be-back-in sign and made a trip to the Temple Mountain Feed and Seed. The pasture was greening up with warmer spring days. Donkeys normally didn't need much more than that, but Adelaide and her additional cargo needed the equine supplements Dr. McCormick had prescribed, along with the oats they both loved.

The smell of grains and hay mingled with poultry feed and a hint of leather. She paid for her order while a shop employee loaded three bags of oats into her trunk. Shop owners Fern and Snowy Bahr listened attentively to Morgan's update on Adelaide's condition.

"When's your brother coming back?" Fern Bahr asked.

Everyone in Golden Springs must have heard the news by now.

"As soon as he gets money for plane tickets."

"That reminds me," Fern said. "Can you ask Beatrice to put me down for a dozen of her pecan cinnamon rolls? They're the first to go at the church bake sales."

The people of Golden Springs were anxious for Kendall and Allie to return. Morgan was more worried about where to put everyone. Especially now that Del's trailer was out of the picture.

Instead of heading home, Morgan drove up Main Street to the pedestrian mall where Jade's Aspen Gold Art Gallery resided. She had found both the elephant-head flowers and ammolite at the dugout. Surely one of them provided a clue to

Carlee's demise. Jade painted the flowers, and Chase sculpted them in glass. Add in Jade's past relationship with Carlee, and Chase's interest in ammolite, and Morgan was certain there were answers to be found in the gallery. Now, if she could just be certain of what the questions were . . .

The over-eager clerk in the black polo shirt greeted her, then seemed to remember Morgan was the deadbeat looky-loo from the other day, not a potential customer. Her attention shifted back to her magazine.

Elephant-head flowers were the central theme of several pieces of glasswork, two miniature paintings, and as part of the scenery in a dozen paintings. Chase claimed he wanted ammolite for a gallery jeweler. Three different artists displayed necklaces, bracelets, and earrings. Lucy's jewelry was every bit as good as anything in the glass cases. None of it used ammolite. Of course, Chase claimed he was hunting for the fossil gem on behalf of a jeweler. There would be no ammolite jewelry until he found the raw material. So much for that theory.

On the other hand, his interest might be due to a desire to stake a claim on an ammolite find, with his father financially backing the mining enterprise. With Jade sure to win the City Council seat, they could push through re-zoning if the ammolite was in an area currently off limits to mining.

The curtain to the back room pulled aside. Jade shouldered his way through as he wiped paint-stained hands on a cloth. Morgan caught a chemical whiff of paint and thinner, and the organic scent of wood.

"Lynn, did those new brushes arrive yet?"

She dropped her magazine with a guilty look. "UPS hasn't been by."

"You did order them next day?"

She gave him a blank look.

"Well, let me know when they get here." He headed back,

then noticed Morgan. “Oh. Hello. Mary, right?”

“Morgan. I was in here last week.” Lynn’s attention was on her magazine. Morgan lowered her voice to a whisper. “There will be a memorial service for Carlee Kruger the Saturday after next. June sixth, at Golden Springs Community Church.”

Jade wrung the rag in his hands. His glorious mane of blond hair was drawn back in a ponytail. “I wish I could.” He glanced over his shoulder. “If I can get away . . .”

“I understand.” Morgan gestured at a painting. “I noticed you use elephant-head flowers in several of your paintings.”

His face didn’t betray any reaction to Morgan’s question.

“The reason I ask,” Morgan continued, “is because it looks like someone planted elephant-head flowers near the location of Carlee’s remains.”

The color left Jade’s face. He leaned against the wall, seeming to forget the expensive artwork behind him until his shoulder bumped a frame. He glanced toward the checkout counter. The clerk was enthralled with her magazine.

“Do they know,” he began, then stopped. “How did—how did Carlee die?”

“The coroner hasn’t said. Why? Do you know something about her death?”

“No!”

Jade glanced at the front again. The girl looked up from her magazine briefly, but seemed spectacularly uninterested in her employer. Or maybe she was just good at listening in. Morgan wondered whether part of her job responsibilities included reporting Jade’s activities to his wife.

“Why are you so jumpy,” Morgan whispered, “unless you do know something?”

“It’s not that. If Mia sees me chatting with a pretty woman, she’ll be upset for days.”

Jade’s statement startled Morgan on several levels. She hadn’t been called pretty by a man not related to her by blood or marriage in many years. But Mia's jealousy was troubling. Was she possessive enough of Jade to knock off her competition?

"Jade, was Mia around when you were dating Carlee?"

"Mia is six years younger than me, so dating wasn't an option back then. After high school, Mia moved on to bigger and better things than a life in Golden Springs."

"But she came back, obviously," Morgan said.

"Funny how things turn out. When Carlee disappeared, I was really broken up for a long time. Mia came back to visit her parents one winter. She had graduated and gotten a job with some high-powered marketing firm back East, but her family is very close. We ran into each other, and, well, things just worked out."

"You married her on the rebound."

Jade shook his head. "It wasn't like that. Mia drew me out of my depression, encouraged my painting. In a way, she saved my life. With her marketing skills, and my painting, we've made a good life."

A miserable life, from what Morgan could see, but perhaps it hadn't always been like that. She started to ask another question when she heard a man's voice.

"Mia made you rich."

Morgan turned to see Chase Cooper step through the curtain. He was shorter than Jade by several inches, and his black hair contrasted with the artist's golden locks. If not for the burn scar on the right side of his face, Chase would have been every bit as handsome as Jade.

"I'm glad you dropped by."

He extended a hand to Morgan. She clasped his hand briefly, feeling an unexpected strength, and rough calluses. Perhaps glasswork was more strenuous than she realized. She wondered how long he'd been listening, and decided to head the conversation in a different direction.

"I can't believe those aren't real flowers." Morgan pointed at one of the glass rectangles in the window.

"Early in my career, I actually tried creating the pieces with real flowers." He laughed. "Obviously, molten glass and flowers do not interact well. Then I experimented with dried flowers, but they lost their vibrancy."

Chase reached into the window and retrieved a three dimensional columbine, handling it with loving care. He rattled on about his artistic process, but Morgan hadn't heard much past his first sentence. He had tried creating art glass using real flowers. She wondered whether he had used elephant heads from Carlee's final resting place.

"Glasswork is not a forgiving art," Chase said. "In an artistic sense, or," he swiped a hand down his scar, "technically."

He seemed to invite the question, so Morgan asked.

"You burned yourself creating art glass?"

"The furnace is twenty-one hundred degrees," Chase said. "A blob of molten glass hit me. Mother wanted to send me to a plastic surgeon, but I think the scar gives me character."

Morgan wanted to ask more questions, but Chase turned to Jade.

"Dad says we can't miss the deadline. Or were you hoping?"

Jade grinned, but there was a measure of pain in his smile. "Maybe I was hoping." He glanced at Morgan. "The deadline to register to campaign for the City Council seat isn't until next week."

"And we'll have hell to pay if we miss it. Let's go."

Chase gripped Jade's arm and steered him through the curtain to the back. Morgan made her exit through the front door, past the bored clerk. Instead of heading to the rock shop, she drove the two blocks to the *Gazetteer.* Morgan needed to report the results of her recent snooping. At least, that was her excuse. Harder to admit to herself was that she just wanted to see Kurt Willard.

Morgan stopped at the front desk to tell Anna a little about her trip to Sioux Falls. She would deliver the full report Sunday in the church kitchen. Trevin took a break from researching Founding Father's quotes for Kurt's editorial about the importance of City Council.

"So the police haven't caught that dude yet?" Trevin asked.

"No. Big Foot is still on the loose," Morgan said.

"I should have kept him at the rock shop," Trevin said. "The whole town could rest easy now if I'd just tied him up."

"Trevin, the guy is huge," Morgan said. "And he carries a machete for a pocket knife."

"I know you're just trying to make me feel better."

"Morgan is right," Anna said. "If you had confronted him, tried to detain him, you might have endangered customers at the shop as well as yourself."

Trevin looked half convinced. "I had fun working at the shop, other than the close encounter with Sasquatch. Let me know if you need help again. When I'm not working here, of course."

"That's why we like you, Trevin," Anna said. "You have your priorities straight."

"Morgan, I thought I heard your voice." Kurt pushed open the top of the Dutch door to his office. "Come on back."

As Morgan entered Kurt's office, she wondered whether he would give her a hug, and how she should react if he did. Instead, he turned to his desk.

"I haven't seen you since last week," Kurt said over his shoulder. "How did your trip go?"

"I needed to go, for reasons I didn't even know. On the bright side, I leased my house."

"Congratulations." Kurt glanced at his watch. "I didn't realize it was so late. I need to get to City Hall to shoot some photos."

"Catching one of the candidates registering to run for office?" Morgan wondered if Kurt was giving her the brush-off. She attempted a smile.

"You must have a nose for news," Kurt said.

"I was in Jade Tinsley's art gallery before I came here. He's being dragged to City Hall by his brother-in-law."

Morgan relayed her suspicions about Chase Cooper while Kurt loaded his camera bag.

"I'll be rubbing elbows with him in a few minutes. Maybe he'll crack under the scrutiny of my *Gazetteer* lens and confess everything."

"That would be convenient," Morgan said. "But unlikely. I'd better get back to the shop and give Del a break."

"Did you hear about the Prairie Rockhound show this weekend?" Kurt asked.

"No, I didn't."

"Would you like to go with me Saturday?"

Just when she'd convinced herself that Kurt had lost interest in her.

"If Trevin can help Del with the shop. It sounds fun."

Friday was a blessedly routine day. Del spent most of his time in his recliner, snoozing or reading magazines. In between customers, Morgan studied books about fossils. Barton, vice president of the gemstone and prospecting club, didn't think the ammolite came from near the dugout where she had found Carlee. He wasn't the only expert. Morgan reached for the telephone to call Tony Esteban, then reminded herself she had promised not to show the ammolite to anyone.

Maybe the rock show would give her the opportunity to quiz an expert anonymously. If she had a chance to have the chips examined, Morgan didn't want to appear to have a large amount. She divided her stash into two sandwich bags. She tucked the larger quantity in the drawer of her bedside table, and slipped the other inside a zippered pocket of her purse.

When Beatrice called, it was a welcome interruption to a slow day. The church ladies had kicked into high gear to raise funds for Kendall and Allie's plane tickets.

"The first bake sale will be this Saturday," Beatrice said. "We managed to claim a spot at a mall in Granite Junction. Amazing, on such short notice."

"Do I need to be there?" Morgan hoped she wouldn't have to cancel her day at the Rockhound show with Kurt.

"Heavens, no. We have too many volunteers as it is, and you have a business to run."

Beatrice would have a fit if she knew Morgan was skipping bake sale duty to go on a date with Kurt Willard.

"We can use baked goods, though," Beatrice continued. "Especially things that can be sold as single servings."

"I found cash Kendall set aside before they left the country," Morgan said. "Not all he needs, but it's a start. Five hundred dollars."

"We typically make that much with a well-organized bake sale. Having it at the big mall will be even better."

Morgan couldn't imagine anything Beatrice was involved with being unorganized.

"Next we'll have a bake sale at the church after the service," Beatrice continued, her voice on the phone sounding confident. "We can count on a crowd, since Gerda's daughter Camille will be attending with her children."

Morgan hoped Kendall and Allie weren't in such dire straits that they couldn't wait a few months for rescue. It might be a long, slow haul to buy those plane tickets.

"Someone will step up with a big donation," Beatrice said.

"The Lord has a way of providing."

After Beatrice hung up, Morgan called Bernie to let her know about the bake sale. The baker volunteered three dozen cookies and two dozen cupcakes.

After selling one of Lucy's bead necklaces to the last customer of the day, the phone rang.

"Hey, cowgirl."

"Hi, Cindy. How is Herb's new job going?"

"His new schedule takes some getting used to, but we really enjoy the extra money."

They chatted about the baby, Morgan's trip to Sioux Falls, and Adelaide's condition.

"So I didn't just call to yak," Cindy said. "Remember I said I'd be available to work here and there?"

"I didn't want to bother you," Morgan said.

"I appreciate it, but I could use a little pin money for Herb's birthday next month. Could you use some help?"

"Any time! Today was slow, but we've had too much business on weekends for one person to manage, and I wanted to go to the Prairie Rockhound show Saturday."

"Good idea. That'll give you an idea of what to expect when we go to Denver in July, even though it's tiny in comparison."

"Trevin is going to work Saturday and Sunday morning. You can have whatever other hours you want."

Morgan and Del had dinner in the kitchen, then settled in for a quiet evening. Instead of focusing on the television program about Alaska, Morgan found herself distracted with worry. She hoped they made enough in sales this weekend to justify paying two extra employees. A little tremor of terror seized her at the thought of being caught by Beatrice at the rock show with Kurt.

Guilt propelled her to bake an additional pan of bake sale brownies. They were cooling on the counter, and Morgan was washing dishes, when she heard braying. Morgan turned off the faucet and listened. The donkey repeated its hoarse alarm.

Del heard it, too. He clambered out of his recliner and pulled his jacket on.

"Del, wait. I'm coming with you."

Chapter Twenty-Seven

Del loaded the shotgun while Morgan pulled on her boots. They exited the rear door to the back pasture. The wind whistled around the building. A blast of needle-like snow pellets stung Morgan's face. Snow in May. Colorado weather was full of surprises. Del leaned against the wall and peeked around the corner, the muzzle of the shotgun aimed at the ground.

"I don't see anything," he whispered. "No lights in the barn."

"The donkeys don't give false alarms," Morgan said.

"There's a cold front moving in fast. Good night to seek shelter in a barn."

The clouds covered any potential light from the stars and moon. Del didn't want to alert an intruder with the beam of a flashlight. They followed the fence line to the barn in darkness. A donkey brayed again, its raspy voice echoing off the mountain behind the back pasture. Del lifted the muzzle of the shotgun as they neared the barn.

"Better to go through a stall," he whispered. "An intruder will expect us to come through the front door."

Morgan crept along behind Del, mindful of every crunching pebble under her boots, certain her breathing could be heard all the way to Golden Springs. They crouched down and entered Adelaide's stall. She turned to look, the whites of her eyes showing. Morgan hoped she wouldn't go into donkey attack mode, but she seemed to relax when she saw her people.

Del squeezed around her. Morgan followed. They tiptoed

through the narrow gate to Adelaide's stall and into the barn's wide center. A scuffling sound came from the loft, too loud and heavy to be mice in the hay. Del aimed his shotgun up the ladder.

"Hey! You up there!"

The scuffling stopped. Morgan held her breath.

"I'm going up," Del whispered.

He grasped the ladder with one hand, the shotgun in the other, and placed a foot on the bottom rung. A bulky shadow appeared at the top of the ladder, half climbing and half falling, knocking the old cowboy to the ground. Del dropped the shotgun as he landed.

The intruder scrambled to his feet before Del. He was every bit as huge and menacing as Morgan remembered. The stolen jacket didn't soften his wild appearance. The mountain man glanced at the gun, then at Morgan. He was closer to the weapon. He only needed to bend over and close his enormous hand around it, but he didn't make a move to pick it up. Morgan lunged forward and grabbed the shotgun. She aimed it at the mountain man and wondered how to turn off the safety.

"Hold it right there." She hoped bluffing would work.

The mountain man grunted something.

"I don't understand."

He grunted again, and took a step toward Morgan. Del rose slowly.

"You gonna use that gun?" Del asked.

Morgan hefted the shotgun to her shoulder and aimed. The mountain man backed away.

"Stop!" Morgan yelled. "Stay where you are!"

The mountain man watched her as he continued stepping backward. He bumped up against the barn wall, reached behind himself to tug at a board, then squeezed through the gap. Morgan and Del nearly ran over each other as they raced to the loose board. Del pulled it aside and they stepped outside.

"Where'd he go?" Morgan asked.

Del took the gun from Morgan. "You check the donkeys. Make sure they're okay. And call the police."

Morgan went back through the loose board. That explained how Houdini was escaping. The donkey brayed again, and kicked the side of his stall.

"It's okay, boy," Morgan said. "He's gone."

She clicked on the overhead light. Adelaide seemed to be okay. Then she checked on Houdini. His ears were flattened and his teeth bared, his attention focused on a corner of his stall. Morgan leaned over the top rail.

A dog with matted fur huddled in the corner. The dog resembled a wolf, but it lacked wolf attitude. His eyes were wide with fear.

"I lost him," Del said. "What's all the ruckus in here?"

"Houdini has the mountain man's wolf-dog trapped."

Morgan began to unlatch the stall door, but Del grabbed the sleeve of her coat.

"A scared dog's a dangerous dog."

"I'm afraid Houdini's going to kill it."

"That might not be a bad thing," Del said.

Houdini backed up, seemingly ready for the humans to handle the intruder. The dog lowered itself to the ground with its front paws extended in a submissive gesture. It crawled forward a step, its belly scraping the ground.

"Does that look dangerous?" Morgan opened the stall door and reached toward the dog, but Del stopped her.

"I have leather gloves," he said. "Won't hurt me much if he does bite."

Del lowered one hand, letting the dog sniff. The dog wagged its matted tail, thumping it against the ground. Del patted the dog's head, then rubbed his hand down its side.

"He doesn't seem vicious, but be careful."

Morgan reached for the dog. It flinched away.

"Slowly," Del said. "He's skittish."

She took a step closer. The dog sniffed her knit glove. Morgan touched her fingers to the top of its head, then patted gently.

"Were you giving Houdini a hard time?" Morgan asked.

The donkey had backed off, but was still watching closely.

"The dog was probably trying to follow the mountain man into the barn," Del said. "It's gonna be a cold night. Come to think of it, maybe that's why Houdini didn't sound the alarm other times the mountain man slept in the loft."

"But he did tonight."

"Right. Maybe the other times, the dog stayed outside and kept Houdini distracted while the mountain man got in the loft. Tonight, the dog had enough of the outdoors, and tried to come inside."

"Setting off the donkey alarm system."

Chief Sharp and Deputy Parker both arrived in the official Golden Springs Police SUV. After a search of the area around the barn, they joined Morgan and Del in the kitchen.

"Vanished." Sharp held his hands up in a frustrated gesture. "The guy knows these mountains better than anyone. I suspect he won't be found unless he wants to be."

"From what you told us," the deputy said, "he had a chance to grab the shotgun and didn't. He hasn't shown any signs of being dangerous."

"Other than hanging around with a dead girl's remains?" Morgan asked.

Chief Sharp shook his head. "We don't know the full story there." He gulped down coffee and set his mug on the table. "Treat him like he's a threat. Don't take any chances. But I think it's a good sign he just ran away tonight."

After the police department, all two of them, left the rock

shop, Morgan filled a pail with water, and a bowl with leftovers for the skinny wolf-dog. Del suspected a trap. At the very least, he said, the mountain man had to be nearby. He insisted on walking with Morgan back to the barn, fully armed, of course. Driving sleet pelted them.

Springtime in the Rockies, Morgan thought. *What a treat.*

The dog jumped up from his nest in a pile of straw. He smiled at them, his tongue hanging out one side of his mouth and his tail wagging furiously.

"What are we going to do with him?" Morgan asked.

Del shook his head. "First, I doubt this mutt, or wolf, or whatever it is, has had his shots. Second, if we let it stick around, that'll just encourage his master to bed down in the loft again."

"He's so skinny, he'll freeze outside."

The dog inhaled the leftovers, then jumped onto the pile of straw he had claimed as his own. He circled twice, curled into a ball, and stuck his nose under a foreleg.

When the animals were settled for the night, they returned to the living quarters. By the time they reached the warm kitchen again, sleet coated Morgan's hair and Del's mustache.

"Looks like you might not make that hot date with Kurt," Del said. "The roads will be treacherous tomorrow morning."

"We're just going to a mineral show." Morgan shrugged out of her coat and washed her hands. "Not exactly a romantic date."

"I don't know." Del kicked off his boots and slipped his feet into fleece-lined moccasins. "I always thought gemstones could win a fella a little romance, if he played his cards right."

"If you keep teasing me about Kurt," Morgan said, "I might start asking questions about a certain cowgirl prospector."

The smile pulling up the corners of Del's mustache vanished.

"I didn't realize I was upsetting you." He grabbed a shop rag and wiped down the shotgun.

"I'm sorry, Del."

He ignored Morgan.

"She's the one, isn't she?" Morgan asked. "You dated Lorina after Harriet passed?"

Del settled the shotgun against the wall by his recliner. He flipped open his *Field and Stream* magazine to a trout fishing article. Morgan thought the conversation was over, and regretted bringing up Lorina when she had caused Del so much pain. She settled into her rocking chair on the other side of the wood-burning stove and opened the romance novel she'd been trying to finish for the last month. Popping sap and crackling flames punctuated the silence, while pine-scented wood smoke gave the living quarters the odor of a cozy cabin. Morgan was nearing the happy conclusion of the story when Del spoke again.

"Harriet was my rock, and after she was gone, I let a lot of money slip through my hands pretty fast. Guess I didn't figure I'd be around to need it. Or maybe I hoped I wouldn't be around. Lorina's not a bad gal. She's just more interested in what's in a man's wallet than what's in his heart. I had a lot in one, and not much in the other. And as it turned out, Lorina ended up not getting either."

He leaned back in his chair to read his magazine. Del was done talking.

Del seemed to be over it by morning, and Morgan was careful not to revive the topic of Lorina Dimple. In return, Del didn't tease Morgan about her "date." She began loading her purse with everything she needed for an all-day outing. When the purse developed an unsightly bulge, she switched the contents to a canvas southwest-print bag. If there was ammolite at the Prairie Rockhound show, Morgan could compare her sample against the real deal. She stuffed the baggie of ammolite deep inside the canvas bag.

"Trevin will be here before nine," Morgan reminded Del. "If business is slow, he can straighten out that mineral display. I think he learned more in the geology class than I did."

"He can help me give that dog a bath," Del said.

"I forgot about him. Hey, last night you were going to let Houdini kill the dog."

"Guess I changed my mind." Under Del's bushy gray mustache was the hint of a smile.

"I'd better fix the pooch something to eat. If he's still here."

"From the looks of his ribs, I'd say its last few meals consisted of road kill and old boots. He'll be here."

Morgan scrambled eggs and tore up bread, mixing it together in an aluminum pie plate. She pulled on a coat and gloves, and draped the strap of her canvas bag across one shoulder.

"You should take this." Del placed his handgun on the kitchen table. "Big Foot might be stalking you."

Morgan shook her head. "I'm not comfortable carrying a gun. Not yet. Maybe after I take a class."

"Then I'm going with you." Del picked up his handgun.

When Morgan stepped outside with the pan full of food, she nearly lost her footing on the icy paving stones.

"You sure you don't want to reconsider your trip?" Del pulled on his boots and jacket.

"Kurt is driving to the rock and mineral show. All I have to do is make it to town."

The dog squeezed through the barn door before Del got it all the way open. The dog bounded around on the frozen ground, slipping and sliding.

"Don't make me drop your breakfast," Morgan said.

Del gripped his shotgun so tight his knuckles were white. He wasn't going to drop it again. The only other occupants of the barn were Houdini and Adelaide. Morgan emptied the pie plate into the dog's bowl. He inhaled it, then looked at her expectantly.

"I'll get you some real food in town today."

"That's how it starts," Del said. "You feed a stray a meal or two, and pretty soon he's running the place."

After feeding the donkeys and checking their water, they worked up the courage to climb the ladder to the loft. There was no sign of the mountain man.

"In my experience," Morgan said, "dogs don't switch allegiance easily. The mountain man has to be around here somewhere."

"Maybe the dog didn't follow Big Foot out into a sleet storm because it's smart."

The driveway and rock shop parking lot were slick. Morgan turned onto Hill Street.

"Not bad. Easy. Easy."

She rolled slowly downhill. Gravity increased her momentum. Unsure of how slippery the road was, Morgan tapped the brakes. The car didn't slow. Morgan tapped again, not wanting to go into a slide, but when the brakes didn't respond, she mashed on the pedal. Nothing.

Main Street appeared through her windshield at the bottom of the hill, busy with Saturday morning traffic. The heavy Buick gained speed while Morgan pumped the brake pedal with her foot. She turned the steering wheel, hoping that zigzagging would slow her down. Instead, the Buick slid across the ice toward the irrigation ditch.

Morgan straightened out. The car rolled faster. She grabbed her parking brake and pulled. The tires seemed to grab hold for a moment. The road was too icy. The car went into a slide.

Almost to Main Street. She had seconds to make a choice. A wooden fence surrounded a parking lot on the right, a brick building loomed to the left, and Main Street was straight ahead. Morgan jerked the steering wheel to the right.

She screamed. Wood splintered and cracked as the aging Buick plowed through the fence, sounding like fingernails scratching across a blackboard. The car launched upward briefly, then slammed down. Metal screeched and wood cracked as the Buick jerked to a halt, crushing the weathered fence like balsa wood. The airbag inflated, smacking Morgan in the face, then deflated like a popped balloon.

The details of the wreck scrambled in her mind with Del's warning to cancel her date. If only she'd listened. Or been sensible when she realized how slick the ground was in the barnyard. What-ifs couldn't take back what was done.

The heater blasted in her face. Morgan turned off the ignition. Her left shoulder ached where she'd slammed against the door. Her right knee must have hit something, too. Morgan didn't feel any serious pain. She had felt like she was flying down the hill, but maybe the lumbering Buick hadn't gained all that much speed.

Piers ran out the back door to his Faerie Tales metaphysical shop. The last person Morgan wanted to deal with in Golden Springs was Piers Townsend, but his fence had been the safest option.

Piers's usual uniform of yoga slacks and a loose tunic looked ineffective against the Colorado cold. He stared at the tangle of fence and Buick with his mouth gaped open, but made no move to help.

Typical, Morgan thought.

A different citizen tapped on her window. Morgan had seen the woman around town, but had not yet met her. This was definitely the way to make a lasting impression.

"Are you okay?"

Morgan reached for the door handle. Blood dripped from her

left hand. Her stomach went queasy for an instant, until she realized it was just a cut. No bone or tendons hanging out. She would probably live.

"I'm better than the fence, right?" Morgan attempted a laugh.

She jerked on the handle and pushed the door open. The slender woman held the door and offered her a hand.

"I don't want to get blood on you," Morgan said in a shaky voice.

"I called 9-1-1. Help is on the way. Is there anyone I can call for you?"

Morgan wrapped her neck scarf around her hand.

"I have a cell phone." She crawled across the seat and reached for her canvas bag. She dug the cell phone out and dropped the bag onto the driver's seat. Who to call? Del would just worry. He had no way of driving down the hill, unless he hitched the donkeys to their cart, and even then, Adelaide's harness might not fit. Bernie would be busy with her morning rush at the bakery. Morgan punched in Kurt's number. He was waiting for her, after all. And he had a car.

He answered on the first ring. "Are you almost here?"

She imagined him looking out the front window of his townhouse.

"No, I'm not going anywhere at the moment."

"Is something wrong?"

"My car. The brakes didn't work." Morgan tried to hold back a sob, and failed. "My car. It's destroyed."

"Where are you?"

"Behind Faerie Tales. On top of the fence."

"I'll be right there."

Shop owners, customers, and local folks curious about the commotion stepped cautiously across ice-coated pavement and wooden walkways. News travelled fast, and soon it seemed half the town was crowded around Morgan and her car. Hannah and Mike from the T-shirt shop, Lorina Dimple in pink and black cowgirl boots, Fern Bahr from the feed store, Bernie from the bakery, and a dozen more people milled around, trying to be helpful but just adding to the chaos.

Kurt hopped out of his vintage Plymouth and ran toward Morgan. He slid to a stop, waving his arms to keep his balance. Bernie rushed down from the bakery at the same moment that Chief Sharp pulled up, the lights on his SUV flashing.

Auto accidents had a way of bringing a person's plans to a grinding halt. Deputy Parker scribbled in a notebook. Bernie retrieved Morgan's canvas bag and dug out her insurance card and driver's license. Piers teetered on the edge of despair, until one of his customers pointed out how nice a new fence would look. After Jason, the younger of Gerda's two mechanics, towed the Buick to Gerda's shop, there was nothing to distract Morgan from her injuries.

"It's time for you to see a doctor," Kurt said.

Deputy Parker tucked his notebook into a jacket pocket. "We should call an ambulance."

"My hand is okay." Morgan held up her left hand. The scarf she had wound around it several times was seeping blood. "Just scrapes and bruises. Nothing urgent enough for an ambulance ride."

"You never know what's really damaged until later," Kurt said. "After everything swells up, it's too late. It's better to get a professional evaluation now. I'll call Doc Drewmoore."

"Kurt is right," Bernie said. "I'll go with you."

Bernie had obviously been in the middle of a Saturday morning breakfast rush, her pink striped chef's hat perched on her brown hair and her matching apron tied snug around her waist.

"You have customers," Morgan said.

"And I'm not working today," Kurt told Bernie. "We'll check

in with you after the doctor has a look at Morgan."

Morgan tried to relax on the drive up Main Street in Kurt's 1947 Plymouth Coupe. When the car slid on a curving side street, she mashed her foot on an imaginary passenger side brake pedal.

"You don't have to hurry," Morgan said.

Kurt eased his foot up on the accelerator. "Sorry. I imagine riding in a car isn't your favorite thing right now. But the ice is melting. It'll be gone by noon."

"I know the chief and everybody else thinks I wiped out on an icy street," Morgan said. "Just dumb luck. Happens all the time. But Kurt, I hit my brakes and nothing happened. I lived in South Dakota for most of my life. I know how to drive on ice and snow."

"It hasn't been cold enough to freeze your brake line. If that sort of thing can happen. I'm not a mechanic. But your car is old."

"Not as old as yours," Morgan said.

"Almost everything in this vehicle has been replaced. It was a bucket of rust when I found it abandoned in a rancher's pasture. The man nearly paid me to haul it off. But back to your car. Have you had trouble with your brakes before?"

"Gerda's mechanics went over my whole car not long ago. As I recall, there was brake fluid involved, so I assume they checked my brakes."

"And she said her brakes went out, too. What are the chances her mechanics suddenly forgot how to maintain brakes?"

"Slim to none. Why did anyone want to hurt Gerda? And why me? The same way?" Morgan didn't wait for Kurt to answer. She was still riding an adrenaline rush, chattering a mile a minute. "That shows a serious lack of imagination. What's the connection between Gerda and me? There is none. Other than her daughter. Maybe Gerda knows something about Carlee's death that she's not telling us, but I'm a newcomer. I didn't even know Carlee."

"You found her remains," Kurt said. "That might have been enough."

"If I had helped Beatrice with the bake sale today, instead of trying to sneak off to the rock show, I wouldn't have wrecked my car."

"No matter what, those brakes were going to fail," Kurt said. "Someone made sure of that."

Chapter Twenty-Eight

Morgan was happy to avoid the hospital emergency room, which typically turned into an all-day event. Doctor Henry Drewmoore ran what amounted to an urgent care clinic from the ground floor of his Victorian style home. He and his wife Patty were semi-retired. Patients needing anything more than routine care were sent to Granite Junction, or in extreme cases, the ambulance came up Topaz Pass while the doctor kept the patient stable. If Morgan's injuries were serious, he would send her to the hospital in the city.

She gave the doctor the details of her wreck and told him what hurt. He cleaned up her cuts and scrapes. No stitches, thank goodness. And no X-rays, unless she experienced an increase in pain, or swelling. Patty insisted they have a slice of homemade coffee cake before leaving. Morgan had lost some blood, and needed to replenish her strength. Morgan suspected it was a pretense to learn firsthand about the on-going recent drama she had been involved in: the mountain man, Carlee's remains, Bernie's Big Foot in a Dumpster, Rolf's close call, and now her own wreck, which was suspiciously similar to Gerda's. She hadn't told Kurt about last night's visit from the mountain man yet, and he listened intently. He didn't pull out his reporter's notebook and pencil as he asked lots of questions. Maybe this story wouldn't end up in the *Gazetteer.*

When they finally left the Drewmoores, Morgan asked Kurt to make a stop at the feed store. He carried the bag of dog food out to his trunk, then insisted on picking up lunch at the Hot Tomato, including turkey sandwiches for Del and Trevin. The restaurant staff who knew Morgan expressed concern about the accident, and asked about her injuries. After the communal curiosity had subsided, she and Kurt sat on a bench to wait for their carryout.

"The Prairie Rockhound show runs tomorrow, too," Kurt said. "I'll pick you up this time. I doubt your car will be repaired any time soon."

"I promised to drop off more brownies at church in the morning for the bake sale," Morgan said. "I have to go. They're having the bake sale for my brother and his wife."

Morgan described Kendall's sudden need for plane tickets.

"Three thousand dollars?" Kurt asked. "Those are expensive tickets."

"I thought so, too, so I checked on line. Maybe they have to pay off a kidnapper or a drug overlord before they'll be allowed to leave the country. Kendall and Allie are not the types to get involved in illegal activities, but they could have run afoul of a drug cartel."

"If it was a ransom situation," Kurt said, "or someone was in jail, I hardly think he'd be willing to wait so long for the money. He'd head to a US embassy."

"I thought that was kind of odd, too. If it's so urgent, why wouldn't he want to get out of the country immediately?"

"He'll have to tell you eventually. So are they going to move back into the rock shop?"

"I haven't figured that one out yet. I just know I'm not leaving."

Kurt smiled. "Glad to hear that. I'd be happy to give you a ride to church. You could drop off the brownies, and then we could go to the Rockhound show."

"I do want to go to the rock show, but Gerda's daughter will be at church."

Kurt's eyebrows lifted in surprise.

"I didn't know that," Kurt said. "I must not be as in-the-loop as I thought. I'd like to meet her. She may have answers to some of our questions. Giving you a ride will be a good excuse to get my foot in the door."

Kurt's motivation might be merely predatory, in a reporter-after-a-story kind of way, but the church ladies wouldn't understand the arrangement wasn't something more meaningful.

"I don't know if that's a good idea, Kurt. I can just imagine the looks on the kitchen ladies' faces if we walk in together tomorrow." Morgan laughed. "You know how they like their gossip."

Kurt apparently didn't see the humor in Morgan's comment. "I can let you out up front," he said, "then hide in a back pew. Don't worry. I won't embarrass you."

He didn't speak again until they left the restaurant with their to-go bags and drove up Main Street.

"Maybe I've been a little pushy," he finally said, "but I do like you, Morgan. And I am fully aware that this is a small town. There is no such thing as casual dating in Golden Springs. I wouldn't be pursuing this if my feelings were casual."

The intensity of his words stung Morgan.

"My son David might be spending the summer here." The words stumbled awkwardly off her tongue. "He didn't handle his father's death well. I just don't know if I can complicate things by starting a relationship right before David shows up."

As they turned the corner at Piers's metaphysical store, Morgan could see the splintered remains of the fence stacked in a heap. When they were halfway up Hill Street, Kurt spoke again.

"Let me ask one question. Is this a very polite brush-off?"

Morgan thought for a moment, choosing her words carefully this time.

"A week ago, it might have been. When I went back to Sioux Falls, my family had a healing moment. I let go of a lot of baggage while cleaning out our home, but the feelings are still raw. Maybe what I'm trying to say is I need a little time."

The Plymouth passed the dinosaur sign and nosed into a parking space in front of the rock shop. Kurt left the engine running.

"Slowing down is an option," he said. "I'd rather do that than drop our relationship before it has a chance to develop. I haven't felt this comfortable with a woman in a very long time."

Comfortable wasn't a word to sweep a girl off her feet, but then taking it slow probably wasn't the surest route to a man's heart. Maybe they were just friends after all. She tugged on the door handle and began to climb out.

"You're welcome to come in," Morgan said.

Kurt turned off the engine. "I can't eat all this carryout food single-handedly."

Morgan held up her bandaged left hand. "That's the only way I'll get to eat."

She almost didn't recognize the dog when it bounded up to her. His matted fur had been shaved off. What was left of his mottled coat was several shades lighter. The white patches glistened, and the reds, browns, and blacks were distinct. His pink and black speckled nose went straight for the carryout bags in Kurt's hands.

"Knock it off, boy," Morgan said. "You have to eat dog food from now on."

"This doesn't look like the dog you described," Kurt said.

"I wasn't expecting him to be cleaned up."

They entered through the shop door, sending the cowbell clanging.

"You're back early," Del said.

Morgan held up her bandaged hand. "We never made it to the rock show."

"Hi, boss," Trevin said to Kurt. "Other boss, I mean."

Kurt lifted the to-go bag. "I brought you lunch. Don't say I never gave you anything."

"I deserve something after cleaning up that dog." Trevin pointed at his T-shirt, which was damp and bore several paw prints.

The cowbell clanged again as a customer entered the shop.

"We'd better eat in shifts," Trevin said. "Mr. Addison first."

Del remembered he was hungry when Kurt opened the white paper bags. Morgan and Kurt gave Del the details of the wreck and Doctor Drewmoore's assessment of Morgan's injuries while they ate.

Del shook his head. "I warned you the roads were slick, but it sounds like your wreck was due to mechanical failure, not weather."

"I agree," Kurt said. "Morgan told me the mountain man was here again last night. Do you think he could have damaged the brakes?"

Del tugged on his mustache. "I hadn't thought of that."

Kurt frowned. "Why not? It seems obvious to me."

Morgan and Del exchanged a glance.

"He seemed—" Morgan hesitated. "Benign. He could have grabbed the shotgun and wasted the both of us, but he didn't. I don't think he means to harm anyone."

"Except maybe Carlee Kruger?" Kurt asked.

Morgan had to sort through her impressions of last night.

"It doesn't make any sense, I know. He might be a crazed killer."

"Until he's captured," Kurt said, "can you promise me you won't go to the barn alone?" He turned to Del. "Either of you?"

"Not a bad idea," Del said.

Kurt wadded up his sandwich wrapper and tossed it in the trash. "I'd better be going. What time should I pick you up for church?"

"Eight thirty," Morgan said. "Send Trevin in. I'll spell him for lunch. If I'm going to the rock show with you, we'll need him again tomorrow."

Del managed to keep his mouth shut until Kurt was out the door.

"Church services?" Del asked. "I knew you two were getting friendly, but man, oh man, I never expected this."

"Kurt insisted on driving me to church tomorrow because I don't have a car."

"Well, there is that."

"I thought you liked Kurt," Morgan said.

"He did grow on me some after saving my life back in January. Still, I guess I was kind of hoping you and Barton would hit it off."

"Not a chance," Morgan said. "Barton is infatuated with Myra. She's the secretary for the Pine County Gemstone Society and Prospecting Club, and she's a knock-out."

Del chuckled. "I know Myra. The thought of a brainiac like Barton falling for Myra. Now that's an odd couple." Del raised one eyebrow and studied Morgan.

"What?"

"Now that I think about it, maybe you and Kurt aren't a bad match after all."

Morgan might have agreed with Del, but she had the sinking feeling she might have missed the chance to escalate her friendship with Kurt to something more.

The morning chores at the Rock of Ages had grown. After helping Del feed and water the donkeys, Morgan filled the dog's dishes. Both of them worked one-handed, with Del holding his pistol in his right hand, and Morgan's left hand wrapped in bandages. At least her fingertips were free, peeking out from the white gauze.

Morgan rubbed the animal's speckled head. With his new haircut, he looked more like a dog than a wolf.

"We're going to need a name for you," she said. "What did the mountain man call you?"

"I wouldn't get too attached to him," Del said. "He's liable to run off to the hills again if the mountain man comes back for him."

The dog wagged his tail and rolled on his side for a belly rub. Morgan obliged his unspoken request, then headed to the living quarters with Del, refusing the dog entry indoors. Morgan showered and re-bandaged her hand. She tried to dress nice enough for church, but casually enough for an afternoon at the gem and mineral show. Khaki slacks and a long-sleeved sage top seemed to fit the bill. Her outfit could be dressed up with pumps for church, and dressed down with walking shoes and a fleece vest for the show.

Being gone all day meant she needed to have everything with her. The southwest-print canvas bag she had used yesterday held as much gear as her hiking daypack, but looked nice enough for church. Morgan added bandages and hand sanitizer. She took a quick inventory, ensuring she still had the small canister of pepper spray, then pawing through the rest of the bag's content.

"Huh. Where is it?"

She emptied the bag, shaking it upside down over her bed. The baggie with the ammolite chips was gone. Maybe it had spilled out during the wreck. She didn't remember seeing any items strewn on the floor before her Buick was towed away, but a lot had happened fast. She remembered Bernie placing the bag on the driver's seat after handing Morgan her insurance card and driver's license. A dozen people had been milling around. Who could have access to the car, and not be questioned for digging through her bag? Police Chief Bill Sharp. His deputy. Bernie. None of them seemed likely. The mountain man hadn't been there. Kurt? He didn't need to pilfer the gemstone from her bag when he could collect his own samples.

Morgan opened the drawer on her nightstand and shook ammolite chips from that baggie into a new baggie. This time, she slid it into the pocket of her slacks.

The shop wouldn't open for another hour, so Del was sleeping in. When Kurt called her cell phone, she grabbed her brownies and met him at the front door.

"You look nice," he said.

"Thank you," Morgan said. "You, too."

Kurt could have stepped out of a Newsreel in his dashing 1940s'-era suit.

"If I spend much more time with you," Morgan said, "I'm going to need to raid Greta Garbo's closet. Wait. Make that Katharine Hepburn. That's more my style."

"I'll take you to the vintage clothing store where I find my wardrobe one of these days. How are you today?"

"Just sore," she said. "It could have been a lot worse."

"If your car is totaled, maybe you should consider an SUV like Bernie's."

Morgan's friend drove the equivalent of a tank.

The streets were wet this morning, making a shushing sound as Kurt drove. As promised, he dropped Morgan off in front of the church. She carried her brownies to the kitchen.

"Morgan, I heard about your accident." Beatrice pointed at the bandage on Morgan's hand. "Anything broken?"

"No, just scraped up a little." Morgan wiggled her fingertips, extending from the mass of cotton gauze.

"The streets were slick yesterday morning," Beatrice said.

"Thank goodness they thawed out quickly."

Morgan wanted to tell the ladies that it wasn't the weather or her driving that had caused the wreck, but there was a stranger in the kitchen.

"Morgan, this is Camille Folsom," Teruko said. "Mrs. Kruger's daughter."

Morgan had expected someone younger. All the talk had been of people in their late teens and early twenties, but of course that had been sixteen years ago. She clasped hands with the frumpy thirty-something woman.

"Nice to meet you. I wish it was under happier circumstances."

"That's my family for you." Camille brushed a lock of dishwater-blond hair out of her eyes. "We Krugers have never been accused of being short on drama."

A freckle-faced boy leaned through the doorway. His wavy brown hair needed combing, and half his shirttail was untucked. Morgan guessed him to be no older than ten or eleven. "Mom, the service is starting. Gayle saved us seats."

Morgan heard the introit music. As Camille joined her son, Beatrice hooked an arm through Morgan's and began whispering.

"Camille resembles her sister, but wait until you see her daughter, Gayle. Spitting image of Carlee."

As they headed to the church ladies' accustomed pew, Morgan risked a sideways glance at Kurt. He smiled and winked. Beatrice didn't seem to notice him, which was amazing considering her general nosiness and his vintage suit. Camille's son joined a teenage girl on the pew in front of theirs. She looked about five years older than the boy. She glared at him as he bumbled his way past seated people. The resemblance to the photos Kurt and Anna had dug up of Carlee Kruger was striking, except for the streaks of orange and purple in her long, golden-blond hair. A thin, cream-colored sweater hugged her shoulders.

Pastor Charles Quinton was several years younger than Pastor Filbury. He wore his thin reddish brown hair neatly styled, and his eyeglasses were the modern version of horn rims, but there the differences ended. Quinton preached with the same bland style as Pastor Filbury. Morgan didn't think this was the sermon that would make a convert out of Kurt Willard. Still, as she followed the ladies back to the kitchen to ready the coffee and cookies, he was engaged in conversation with a group of men. Morgan attempted a subtle hand motion to indicate she would be in the kitchen. This time, Beatrice noticed Kurt, her eyes opening wide in alarm. When Beatrice glared at her, Morgan caved.

"He gave me a ride this morning." Morgan shrugged. "My car is in the shop after my wreck."

"We'll talk about that later," Beatrice said.

Morgan felt like her mother had scolded her for hanging around with the wrong crowd.

Camille's son trotted to her side with the grace of a spring colt and hung on her arm. Gayle followed, wobbling on the platform soles of slinky pink sandals. The sweater covering her torso was tight, and her skirt too short for church.

"Mom, they have a youth group here," the boy said. "It's supposed to be intense. Can I go?"

Camille looked to Beatrice, who had swiftly established herself as the leader of the kitchen ladies.

"The youth group activity is an hour long," Beatrice said. "We can go to the hospital afterward."

"Come back here when you're done," Camille told her son.

"What am I supposed to do for an hour?" Gayle asked in a whining tone.

"It's either youth group," Camille said, "or you can help us wash dishes."

Gayle vanished.

The ladies chatted amiably as they cleaned up. Morgan was off dishwashing duty, with her bandaged hand, so she helped with the bake sale in the social hall. When the sale ended, Morgan joined the ladies in the kitchen as they waited for Camille's children. Anna brewed a pot of tea. Morgan got clean mugs from the cabinet.

"Isn't your ride waiting?" Beatrice asked Morgan, raising one eyebrow.

"Ride?" Anna asked.

The ladies froze in the middle of tea preparation to stare at Morgan. She willed her face not to flush, and failed.

"Kurt Willard gave me a ride."

"You didn't see him?" Beatrice asked the other ladies. "He sat in the back row. Hiding. Probably taking notes for some tell-all story in that scandal rag he calls a newspaper."

"Beatrice," Anna said, smiling, "calm down. It could be that Kurt is genuinely interested in finding a church home."

Teruko remained, as usual, politely neutral.

"He's more likely to be interested in a certain member of the congregation than in the sermon," Beatrice said. "You watch yourself, Morgan Iverson."

"Oh, Beatrice," Anna said, "you don't have to worry about Morgan. She's old enough to know what she wants."

Teruko seemed to be the only one to remember they had a guest in their midst who had no clue what they were talking about.

"Morgan is a widow," Teruko told Camille. "Her husband has been gone for over two years now."

"After my trip to Sioux Falls, the kids and I finally had some closure." Morgan realized she was on the verge of giving a justification for her association with Kurt. Part of her felt indignant that Beatrice thought her life was any of her business, but another part realized she was a member of an extended family now. Morgan's life was their business, with all the best and the worst that entailed.

"Two years," Camille said. "It's been sixteen since Carlee disappeared. My family still hasn't had closure."

"Perhaps they will now," Teruko patted Camille's plump hand. "How long has it been since you have seen your mother?"

"In person, sixteen years," Camille said. "And I'm not looking forward to seeing her now. The last time we talked on the phone, she was so drunk I don't think she even realized when I hung up on her."

Camille's eyes shimmered with unshed tears.

"Gerda's been sober for months," Beatrice said. "Give her a chance."

"She wasn't there when Carlee and I needed her. After Dad died."

Morgan touched Camille's arm with her unbandaged hand. "When his father died, my son withdrew from the rest of us. But last weekend, I felt like he finally accepted his father's death. Not that he'll ever get over it. But maybe now he can move past it. The same healing will happen for your family."

Some of the tears in Camille's eyes spilled over. She mopped them up with the cuff of her loose-fitting sweater. "I'm guessing you weren't a drunk."

"No," Morgan said. "But I did fall apart. I wasn't there for my kids when they most needed me. We get caught up in our own grief, and get blinded to the needs of others."

"That sounds all neat and clinical," Camille said. "What about when you live every day not knowing whether you've suffered a loss or not? For all we knew, Carlee ran away. She could have been living the high life somewhere, never thinking about us."

"Would it help to know what happened?" Anna asked.

Teruko handed Camille a napkin. Camille wiped her eyes again. She nodded.

"My boss, Kurt, the newspaper editor, he's trying to piece together what happened."

"I knew it," Beatrice said. "He's here scoping out a story."

The commotion of energetic teens filled the community room.

Beatrice stood. "We should head to the hospital."

"Are you ready to see your mother?" Teruko asked Camille.

Blotchy spots of color erupted on the woman's face, and she grabbed for the back of a chair. She was scared. With Gerda as a mother, that wasn't an irrational emotion. Morgan had a thought.

"Maybe it would be better if you went alone," Morgan said.

"What would the kids do?" Camille asked.

"I'm going to a gem and mineral show," Morgan said. "I could take your children with me."

"Morgan's safe," Beatrice said. "Her brother and sister-in-law used to run the youth group."

The arrangement was settled remarkably fast. After introductions to eleven-year-old Farley and fifteen-year-old Gayle, Morgan found Kurt engaged in conversation with Pastor Quentin and Herb Lyons.

"Kurt, we're taking Gayle and Farley with us to the Prairie Rockhound show."

"Oh. Change of plans." Kurt didn't exactly look happy, but he played along.

"Rock and roll?" Farley looked suspicious.

"No," Kurt said. "Rocks and minerals. I think you'll have fun."

"A rock show," Gayle said, her words dripping with a sarcasm reserved for teenage girls. "I'm sure it'll be thrilling."

Chapter Twenty-Nine

The sun shone in a cloudless sky as the temperature neared sixty degrees.

"Cool car," Farley said. "What kind is it?"

Kurt rattled off details about his vintage Plymouth. Farley climbed in the front seat without being invited. Considering the trauma their mother was reliving, good manners could be suspended for the day. Morgan sat in the back with Gayle.

Steam rose off damp streets. Green buds on aspens poised on the edge of unfurling while the cottonwood trees had already leafed out. Both children ignored the scenery as Kurt drove down Topaz Pass. The gem and mineral show was in a small town on the prairie a half hour's drive east of Granite Junction. Morgan was saved attempting conversation with Gayle by the teen's ear buds and pink smart phone, as she simultaneously listened to music and texted a friend. Farley's interest in the car faded. Soon he was asleep, his brown curls mashed against the window.

Morgan caught Kurt's eye in the rearview mirror and silently mouthed the words "I'm sorry." He shrugged and smiled.

The small community center was jam-packed. Tables lined the outer walls, and canvas canopies marked out the vendors in the center. There were rocks, as promised, but Morgan felt she had stepped into an 1850s' shopping mall. Leather wares in the form of purses, moccasins, and boots were displayed on tables. Mountain man, pioneer, and Old West clothing hung from racks.

Hides and furs lay in heaps in one booth. Antique guns, modern knives, prospecting tools, arts and crafts, wind chimes, beeswax candles, and jewelry filled out the rest.

"It's not just rocks." Gayle pulled one ear bud out to listen to Native American drumming and flute music. "Cool."

The kids trailed behind Morgan and Kurt as they slowly perused the mineral tables. This was going to complicate her search for ammolite. When she felt a hand on her shoulder, she spun around. Bernie bounced on her toes, a big smile on her face.

"Morgan, I didn't know you were coming to this. But I should have known. Who are your friends?"

"This is Gayle, and her brother Farley. Gerda's grand-children."

Gayle rolled her eyes at the word "children," but Farley extended his hand to Bernie.

"Pleased to meet you." Perhaps he did have manners after all.

"You need to meet Rolf's daughter." Bernie waved a hand toward a jewelry display, where Rolf and a young lady were examining strings of beads.

Rolf ambled over. His arm was in a sling. "Hi, Kurt. Morgan. This is my daughter, Stacie."

The girl looked a couple of years younger than Gayle, but she had her father's height. She was taller than Gayle. Stacie wore her sandy hair cut in a bob, and had the lean build of an athlete. She dressed in blue jeans and a long-sleeved T-shirt, which looked warm and modest compared to Gayle's revealing skirt and tight sweater.

"Hi, Stacie. I'm Gayle. Did you get those earrings here?"

"No," Stacie said, "but I saw some just like these." She tugged at a concoction of tiny amethyst crystals dangling from her ear-lobe. "I'll show you."

Gayle started to follow, then waved her cell phone at Morgan. "You know how to reach me."

"Just don't leave the building," Rolf called to Stacie's back. She ignored him. "How's your hand?"

Morgan held up her bandaged hand. "It looks worse than it feels. How are you?"

"I'd say the same, but that would be a lie. Ha."

"Has Chief Sharp made any progress finding the gunman?" Kurt asked. "Or gun woman?"

"If so, he hasn't told me," Rolf said.

A gravelly speaker announced an arrowhead-making demonstration. The men took Farley to watch.

"Well, this worked out nicely." Bernie looked like she'd just come from church, dressed in a mid-calf wool skirt and a bright sweater that flattered her generous figure. "So how did you and Kurt acquire Gerda's grandchildren?"

Morgan explained the situation, including the embarrassing grilling at church by an unexpectedly hostile Beatrice.

"You understand why she's giving you a hard time about Kurt, don't you?"

Morgan shrugged. "Beatrice suspects he's just after a story."

"No, Morgan. She tried to set you up with her pick, that guy you had dinner with."

"Pete Melcher."

"Yeah. So then you show up at church with Kurt Willard. That's serious."

"It just happened that way. My car—"

"Don't kid yourself. You upset Beatrice's matchmaking attempt. But I'm sure she'll get over it eventually."

"Gee, thanks. I feel so much better."

Morgan and Bernie wandered through the maze of booths, doing more talking than looking.

"I'm glad you showed up," Bernie said. "I get a little break. I feel like I'm on all the time when Stacie is around."

"Relax. She seems like a typical kid." Morgan shoved a hand in her pocket and felt the baggie of ammolite chips. "Bernie, yesterday when I wrecked my car, do you remember any of the people who came to watch?"

"Half of Golden Springs, it seemed like."

"Did anyone go near my car?"

"Oh, that's a tough one. Let's see." Bernie scrunched up her face and tapped a finger against her cheek. "Chief Sharp and Deputy Parker, of course. Me. Kurt. Um, the couple from the T-shirt shop."

"Mike and Hannah?"

"Yeah. Deputy Parker did run off a few looky-loos, but I don't think I can tell you specifically who. You said near, right?"

"Close enough to reach my bag."

Bernie's mouth dropped open. "Someone robbed you while you were going through that trauma?"

"They only took a bag of mineral samples. No money. Not that I carry much cash. Did you notice whether anything fell out of my bag? Maybe onto the seat or the floor?"

"I wasn't paying much attention to the car or the crowd. Just you. Sorry."

"That's okay," Morgan said. "You don't know how much better I felt knowing you were there." Morgan moved out of the way of a woman in a pioneer style dress who seemed anxious to reach a booth with bolts of calico fabric and old-fashioned sewing notions. "This crowd certainly seems to be spending money."

"It looks like some of the same stuff you carry in your shop," Bernie said.

"Cindy has been trying to talk me into having a table at gem and mineral shows," Morgan said. "I can see now that's a good idea."

"Hello, Mrs. Iverson."

Morgan looked around. Professor Tony Esteban sat behind a table along a wall. A banner hanging across the front read "University of Colorado at Granite Junction Geology Club."

"We seem to be running in the same circles," Dr. Esteban said.

"I guess the world of geology is a small one," Morgan said.

"Even though it is the entire planet." Bernie laughed.

Morgan introduced Bernie to the professor. He wore prospecting clothes of a canvas vest with a half-dozen pockets over a flannel shirt. His black hair was neatly combed.

"Are you recruiting students for the university?" Bernie asked.

"That is a side benefit," Professor Esteban said. "I am really here because I enjoy showing off the geology department's collection."

There were some impressive fossils on display in clear plastic cases. Del seemed to think it would be a bad idea to show Professor Esteban the ammolite, but Morgan wanted an answer.

"Is there a way to tell where a particular gemstone comes from? I know diamonds are strictly documented for their provenance."

"You mean blood diamonds." Bernie shuddered. "How could you think your jewelry was beautiful if it came from someone else's suffering?"

"That is true for some valuable minerals, too," Professor Esteban said. "American legislation is catching on globally to regulate the sources of minerals used in cell phones, like tantalum and tungsten. They call them conflict minerals."

"Excuse me," Bernie said. "This is very interesting, but Rolf is waving for me."

Morgan waited until Bernie was out of hearing. Not that she didn't trust her friend, but knowing about the ammolite only seemed to cause people trouble.

"I'm more interested in a type of gem," Morgan said. "I'm

pretty sure this came from America. Or maybe Canada."

From the encouraging look on his face, it almost seemed Professor Esteban knew what she was going to ask. Morgan dug in her khakis pocket. She opened the plastic bag and emptied the chips onto a pad on top of the table. Professor Esteban pulled out a magnifying glass. At the meeting Wednesday night, he said he'd heard rumors about local ammolite. There was no shock on his face as he studied the chips.

"This is the real thing." Professor Esteban looked up at Morgan. "I am reasonably certain it came from jewelry settings. There are dabs of adhesive on the back. The sign of an amateur jeweler who does not know how to set stones properly. The two questions I cannot answer are why someone would destroy valuable ammolite jewelry, or where the ammolite originated."

Morgan remembered Kurt's observation of boot prints when they took Gerda to the dugout. He had placed his foot next to one and taken a photograph. She guessed it would match the soles of the boots the professor was wearing.

"I think you know the answer to one question," Morgan said. "You went to the dugout to look. Kurt Willard saw your boot prints."

Dr. Esteban smiled and leaned back in his folding chair. "When I cleaned out my van after the geology class hike that ended so disastrously, I noticed ammolite on the floor beneath your seat. I assumed you did not know what you had stepped in. I did go to the dugout to have a look-see. I found a few chips myself."

"Why didn't you ask me about it?" Morgan asked. "Or tell the Coopers? Chase asked you point blank about ammolite."

"With a find this dramatic, it is best that the fewer people who know, the better. Especially the Coopers."

"We're a little late for damage control," Morgan said. "Word has leaked out to half of Golden Springs already."

"These broken chips are not worth much." He lifted the pad and tapped it to slide the chips back into the baggie. "What is valuable is knowing the source of the ammolite. It is possible it came from Canada." He held the bag out to Morgan. "But if it was mined locally, well, that would be very exciting."

"Is there any way you can find out?" she asked. "Barton knows a lot about gemstones, and he thinks it might have come from a Canadian mine, too. He looked around, like you did, but he didn't find the source near the dugout, either."

"Unfortunately, this is not the same situation as diamonds, which are tracked and marked to ensure their provenance." Professor Esteban thought for a moment. "The only way this mystery may be solved is if someone files a claim and starts bringing the gems into the market."

"If the source is on land that can be mined," Morgan said. "Even if Barton had found an ammolite mine, he said the dugout where I found this is closed to claims."

"This sample appears to be from a piece of poorly made jewelry." Professor Esteban shrugged. "I will certainly be watching for ammolite, but I am not hopeful."

The ammolite might not be the key to a treasure chest, but it was a clue to Carlee's death. A clue that too many people knew about.

Bernie headed back from a hallway. An overprotective Rolf had asked her to accompany his daughter to the restroom, she told Morgan. When Stacie joined Farley at a gold panning demonstration, Morgan and Bernie made the rounds of the show again. Morgan was about to suggest they had done all there was to do when Bernie grabbed her arm and pointed.

"That woman who just came in the door," Bernie whispered. "She was there yesterday at the scene of your wreck. One of the looky-loos."

Lorina Dimple's pinkish-orange hair looked shellacked into place, her makeup did a thorough job of dragging a few years off her face, and her tight jeans and low-cut western blouse showed off a figure that didn't look natural on a woman her age.

"She's the same woman we saw downtown Tuesday night," Bernie said. "The one you were spying on. Deputy Parker had to tell her to move away from your wrecked car twice."

"Interesting. She's president of the Pine County mineral club. If anyone at the scene of my accident would steal a mineral sample, it would be her. I need to talk to her."

"The guys are headed our way. They must have run out of manly things to see. I'll keep them busy."

"I'll only be a minute."

Morgan tried to catch Lorina alone. The skinny old cowgirl greeted nearly every vendor and shook more hands than a politician, making her way slowly to a small folding table tucked in a far corner of the community center. Morgan hadn't noticed the Pine County Gemstone Society and Prospecting Club had a presence at the show. She followed Lorina across the crowded community center and watched as she relieved an annoyed volunteer.

"You said you'd be here an hour ago." The short, brown-haired man sitting behind the folding table had been at the meeting Wednesday night. "Other people have lives, too, you know."

"I'm sorry, Larry." Her tone was anything but apologetic. "One of my horses got out. I had a heck of a time catching her."

Larry gathered a small cooler, a canvas shopping bag, and several plastic bags. He huffed past Lorina. Morgan gave her a moment to settle her tooled leather purse under the table.

"Hi, Lorina."

She looked up from straightening out the poorly photocopied club brochures. Lorina snapped her fingers.

"I remember." Lorina resumed organizing the small folding table, avoiding Morgan's eyes. "New member. Joined a couple nights ago."

"Morgan Iverson."

Morgan held out her hand. Lorina gave her a brief, limp handshake.

"I didn't hear the club had a booth at this show when I was at the meeting," Morgan said.

"That knucklehead Myra left it off the minutes. We could have used another couple volunteers. So you got a booth here?"

"No. I'm still learning the business. I can see it's a good idea to attend these events. Is the gem society drumming up new members?"

Lorina picked up a clipboard. "Not hard enough. There's only a half-dozen names on here, and we've had a table up all weekend."

Morgan could see lots of opportunity to increase club visibility, but she suspected if she gave her thoughts, she'd be recruited to implement them. She wasn't ready to volunteer. Not when the club president might be a thief.

"You remember at the meeting," Morgan asked, "when Chase Cooper asked Professor Esteban about ammolite?"

"That was a shocker, huh?" Lorina said.

"He came around my shop one day asking if we had any."

"Ha. I knew it."

"We don't," Morgan said.

"That's what you told him?"

"Of course. I carry the usual fossil ammonite, but who around here has gem quality ammolite?" Morgan leaned forward, resting her hands on the table. She decided to go for a bluff. "I know you got into my bag yesterday."

Lorina reared back, pressing a hand to her mostly exposed chest. "I did no such thing."

"Someone saw you. Give me back what you took."

The cowgirl thought about it for a long minute.

"You don't even know what you have." Lorina tried to stare Morgan down, then shook her head. "You're as stubborn as that brother of yours." She hefted her heavy tooled leather purse onto the table, extracted the baggie of ammolite chips, and tossed them at Morgan.

"You stole from me while I was dealing with the aftermath of a car wreck."

"I had to know."

"Know what?"

"What you know."

"I don't know anything." Morgan shook the baggie. "If you know something about this ammolite, you'd better talk to Chief Sharp."

Lorina's mascara coated eyes opened wide. "I gave it back." She jabbed a manicured fingernail at the baggie. "What more do you want, missy?"

Morgan leaned close enough to whisper. "I found this with Carlee Kruger's remains."

"Lord have mercy." Wheels seemed to be turning inside Lorina's pinkish-orange head. Everyone in town had heard about Carlee, but maybe word about the ammolite being found with her hadn't. "Her remains. I figured the girl ran away to Hollywood and became a movie star. Or married some rich man. She was pretty enough."

"All her dreams ended sixteen years ago," Morgan said. "And it might have had something to do with ammolite. So I'll ask the same question Chase did. Is there any around this area?"

"If there was," Lorina said, "I would have found it."

"You've been prospecting for ammolite?"

"It was a wild goose chase," Lorina said. "Nothing came of it but blistered hands and broken hearts. Still, it would be something if someone found ammolite. You done any digging on your land?"

"No."

"I could take a look around—"

"No," Morgan said. "I can't trust you after you stole from me. At the scene of an accident. Yeesh."

"I hope you understand." Lorina's cheeks flushed red under her makeup. "Whatever you know, do not tell the Coopers. Those folks'll steal everything you have, up to and including your very soul. If you stake a claim, they'll find a way to take it from you by means legal or otherwise."

"Then why were you sweet-talking Harlan Cooper outside Ruby's Two Step?"

Lorina scowled at Morgan, deep lines creasing in a weathered face that had once been beautiful. "Have you been following me around?"

Morgan didn't answer.

"Harlan thinks I know where the ammolite is. Somebody knew, once upon a time, but it ain't me. I don't need to get mixed up in any Cooper family monkeyshines again." Lorina looked over Morgan's shoulder. "Heads up. Here comes that newspaperman. You don't want this blabbed all over the front page of the *Gazetteer.*"

"He's with me," Morgan said.

"Holy crap."

"You can trust Kurt," Morgan said. "He doesn't care about rocks or gems. He just wants to know what happened to Carlee."

Morgan turned to Kurt. "Is everyone ready to go?"

"The natives are restless." He stuck a hand out. "Kurt Willard, editor of the *Golden Springs Gazetteer.*"

Lorina reluctantly shook his hand. "I know who you are."

"Then you know that Kurt saved Del's life," Morgan said.

Again Lorina's face flushed. "How is that cantankerous old cowboy?"

"Fit as a fiddle," Kurt said.

"He's had a little trouble with his heart." Morgan stared at Lorina, trying to impress upon her the meaning behind her words. "But he has friends looking out for him."

"Del's a good man." Morgan thought she detected a catch in the tough old cowgirl's words. "You take good care of him."

Chapter Thirty

Kurt turned his wrist and glanced at his vintage watch. "No wonder I'm hungry. It's nearly dinnertime. The show will be closing soon."

"I had a hotdog," Rolf said. "I'm ready for some real food."

The Prairie Rockhound show might seem set in the 1850s, but the vendors offered strictly modern junk food.

"I have an idea," Bernie said. "I blew my budget here." She glanced around at everyone's bulging shopping bags. "Darlene called me to let me know business was slow today. We have a lot of soup left from lunch. Let's have dinner at my bakery."

"Let me check with Camille," Morgan said. "She may want her children back."

Beatrice picked up Morgan's call.

"It took all afternoon," Beatrice whispered into the phone, "but they're finally talking. Can you keep the kids a little longer?"

Morgan was torn between relief and annoyance, as the presence of Camille's children kept her time with Kurt from qualifying as an actual date. "Call me when you're ready for them."

The kids had scattered. They found Stacie and Farley panning for gold at a wooden trough.

"I found a nugget!" Farley said.

Rolf was attentive as Stacie showed him the traces of black sandy residue in the bottom of her plastic panning plate. Chances were good it was real gold. The panning material came from the tailings of a working gold mine.

"Where's Gayle?" Morgan asked.

Farley glanced around. "She was here a minute ago."

"We told the kids not to leave the building," Bernie said. "She's got to be close by."

Morgan pulled out her cell phone. "No problem. I have her number."

The phone rang several times before going to voice mail. Now it was a problem. Rolf, Stacie, and Bernie headed down one side of the community center, and Morgan, Kurt, and Farley went down the other. Gayle wasn't in the restroom, the snack bar, or the hallway. Morgan had nearly worked herself into a panic, and was going to dial 9-1-1, when Farley yelled.

"There she is!"

All Morgan saw was a waterfall of golden hair, streaked with purple and orange, at a workbench behind a folding table. Chase Cooper hovered over Gayle. He reached for her hair and brushed it back from her face in a gesture far too intimate for a man in his thirties to use with a teenage girl. Gayle probably hadn't heard her cell phone due to the loud rattling of a rock tumbler in the booth next to them.

"Hey," Morgan yelled. "Gayle!" Of course it was just that moment when the rock tumbler stopped, making Morgan's voice loud and harsh. The girl looked up, startled.

"I called your cell phone," Morgan said in a more civil tone.

Gayle reached for her little purse and checked her phone. "Oh. I didn't hear it."

Chase seemed to catch Morgan's concern. "I was showing Gayle glass blowing techniques."

Gayle lifted the tube clutched in her hands, showing off a misshapen vase.

"We have to go," Morgan said.

"But I'm not finished. Just a few more minutes?"

"We just need to detach the vase from the blowing tube," Chase said. "It'll only take a minute."

"I'll wait," Morgan said. "Right here."

Chase kept his proper distance from Gayle as he finished off the vase, reforming it a bit, Morgan noticed. The operation was scaled down from real glass blowing, using a propane torch instead of a furnace. The glass had pretty pink streaks through it. Chase wrapped it in tissue paper and put it in a box.

"This should keep it safe for your trip back to Topeka," Chase said.

"Thanks, Mr. Cooper. How much is it?"

"I can't charge you," Chase said. "You're practically family."

Gayle gave Chase a hug. Morgan could see the effect her innocent embrace caused him from the blissful look on his scarred face.

"Thank you! I hope we get to come to your art store before I have to go home."

"Jade's Aspen Gold Art Gallery," Chase said. "Mrs. Iverson knows where it is."

A pink and white striped awning shaded the front bay window of the bakery. Silk banners decorated with bright appliquéd flowers flapped from flagpoles on either side of the glass-paned front door. Under "Bibi's Bakery," in loopy pink script, a sign in the window read "closed." Bernie unlocked the door.

"We have the place all to ourselves," she said.

Gayle ran to the bay window and sat at a bistro table covered with a pink and white striped tablecloth. Stacie followed.

"How cute!" Gayle said. "I wish we had a place like this in Topeka."

Morgan noticed how Stacie absorbed the older teen's comment, her eyes seeming to survey the pink stripes and ruffles that dominated the décor with renewed respect.

"Thank you, Gayle," Bernie said. "But if we sit out here, people will think the bakery is open. We'll have to sit in the kitchen."

Morgan knew Bernie's upstairs apartment was too small to accommodate seven people. Plus Mr. Whiskers, her enormous fluffy cat, might take offense at the invasion of his domain. The men grabbed chairs and carried them to the kitchen, where Bernie cleared off an island work station. She heated three different soups, and warmed mini loaves of bread.

"This is delicious." Rolf slid his arm out of the sling so he could attack the soup and bread more efficiently.

"Your mom is a great cook," Farley told Stacie.

"She's not my mother," Stacie snapped. Then her tone softened. "But she is a great cook."

Morgan noticed Bernie wince as she turned away. She seemed deafened to Stacie's little nuggets of positive comments.

After the dishes were in the industrial dishwasher, Bernie turned everyone loose on the day's leftover pastries and desserts. What they didn't consume, Bernie would donate to her church's soup kitchen. While the men and kids sampled the baked goods, Morgan had a chance to talk to Bernie. They moved to the far side of the kitchen. Bernie perched on a tall stool, while Morgan leaned against a stainless steel counter.

"I didn't like how Chase latched onto Gayle," Morgan said. "Her aunt Carlee was older when she disappeared, but it's amazing how much Gayle resembles her."

"From what you told me," Bernie said, "Chase was never involved with Carlee. She and Jade were inseparable practically from birth."

"All we know is what we read in the newspapers from that time, and what we've heard from people who were there. People's memories can have gaps, or repaint the picture entirely." She thought of Jade's commercial paintings, and how he freely mingled flowers that rarely shared space in the natural world. "Should I warn Gayle? Or her mother?"

"I think Camille has enough to handle right now, and they're not going to be in town much longer. Besides, your church ladies aren't going to let that family out of their sight."

"It only takes a moment," Morgan said. "For heaven's sakes, I turned her loose in a crowd of strangers!"

"And she happened to find Chase, and nothing happened. I think you're stressing out, Morgan. Lighten up a little."

Morgan's cell phone rang.

"We're almost back to Golden Springs," Beatrice said. "Can you bring the kids to my house?"

"Camille doesn't want her children to meet their grandmother?" Morgan asked.

"Today was a good day." Beatrice had to be sitting right next to Camille in her rental car, so perhaps her words were more positive than the situation warranted. "But Gerda is worn out. There'll be plenty of time in the next few days for the kids to meet her."

When Morgan dropped the kids off, Beatrice glared at Kurt, but invited him inside. Gayle unwrapped her blown glass vase to show her mother and Beatrice.

"Look what I made at the rock show."

Farley pulled a baggie of damp rubble out of his jeans pocket. "I panned for gold! Can we come back this summer, so I can really pan for gold? Like in a creek?"

"We'll have to talk to your father about that." Camille glanced at Morgan. "He's on a business trip. He travels a lot."

Dark half-moons of exhaustion shadowed beneath Camille's red-rimmed eyes. She looked older than her thirty-four years. Morgan tried to see past the slouched shoulders and added pounds to find any resemblance to the beauty her older sister had been, but Camille had obviously struggled with a lot of stress in the past sixteen years. With an alcoholic mother, perhaps her entire life had been a struggle. When Beatrice offered coffee and cookies, in true kitchen-lady style, Morgan and Kurt declined.

"It's been a long day," Morgan said, "and we both have to work in the morning."

"It was kind of you to help Morgan out by driving her around," Beatrice told Kurt, her words not exactly brimming with sincerity.

"Thank you so much for taking the kids with you," Camille said. "I'm sorry to have imposed on your day off."

"My sons are both in California," Kurt said. "I miss them. It was a pleasure to spend time with Farley and Gayle."

Beatrice walked them to Kurt's car, parked at the curb of the narrow, sloping street.

"Thanks again. Both of you. Camille and Gerda couldn't have had the conversation they needed with the children around."

"The kids seemed to enjoy the rock show," Morgan said. "And we ran into Rolf and Bernie. He has a daughter a little younger than Gayle. They hit it off."

"I'm glad they had a good day," Beatrice said. "The rest of the week might not be as pleasant."

"It has to be difficult for the kids," Kurt said, "dealing with all the adult drama over an aunt they never knew."

"Speaking of drama," Morgan said, "I ran into Lorina Dimple at the rock show. She asked about Del, but I don't get the impression he's interested in her."

Beatrice placed her hands on her hips. "I sincerely hope she's not trying to get her hooks into Del again. That woman—Well, I know a lot about Lorina Dimple, but the things I have to say wouldn't be fitting coming from a Christian lady's lips."

Beatrice pressed her lips together, attempting unsuccessfully to stem the tide of juicy gossip.

"I'll just say this," Beatrice continued. "Lorina got her comeuppance. She left Del to play Jezebel with a married man, expecting him to leave his wife for her. She was just his plaything for a season. I wouldn't wish evil on anyone, but there is some satisfaction in thinking she might have been hurt as bad as she hurt Del. People play with fire when they toy with others' hearts."

Beatrice raised an eyebrow and glared at Kurt briefly. He returned her singeing look with a smile.

Morgan discussed clues and hunches with Kurt on the short drive up Hill Street, including Professor Esteban's confession that he had discovered ammolite on his van's floorboards. Kurt shared her concern about Chase's interest in Gayle.

"If Chase killed Carlee," Morgan said, "then some of the clues make sense. He knows where to find elephant-head flowers. He could have given the ammolite necklace to Carlee. Professor Esteban said the ammolite had an adhesive, the sign of an amateur. Chase makes art glass now, but he might have tried his hand at making jewelry sixteen years ago."

"We're missing something," Kurt said. "Motivation. And the means. What have we learned? Mia's relationship with Jade didn't start until a few years after Carlee disappeared. Chase wasn't in high school at the same time as Jade and Carlee. How would Chase have come into contact with her?"

"I'll invoke the principle of small towns. They had to move in some of the same social circles, participating in local events or bumping into each other on the sidewalk."

"Okay. You have a point." Kurt pulled into the Rock of Ages parking lot. "You have company."

"Del has company. That's Barton's truck."

"Oh?"

Morgan thought she detected a trace of jealousy in that one short word, combined with Kurt's raised eyebrows.

"I think Barton wants to adopt Del. He hangs around him a lot."

When they stepped out of Kurt's vintage car, the dog raced up to Morgan and jumped on her, smearing muddy paws down her khaki slacks.

"Dog! Down!"

Dog lowered himself to the ground, cowering from her loud words.

"Now you've scared him." Kurt rubbed the dog's head. "You might consider taking him to obedience school."

"Big Foot might take him back," Morgan said.

"When he gets real dog food here," Kurt asked, "and not the dredges of the local Dumpsters? I think you're stuck with him."

Morgan looked down at her ruined slacks. "Now that I'm all dirty, I might as well check on the donkeys. Would you like to come with me? You did request Del and I use the buddy system."

"Sure. I'll be your buddy."

They hiked across the parking lot to the barn. Houdini and Adelaide munched contentedly in their stalls.

"Del must have beat me to it," Morgan said.

"So is that the ladder to the loft?" Kurt asked.

"Yes. The infamous home of Sasquatch. I think I can make it livable for my son David this summer. Want to see it? I won't even charge you admission."

"Sure."

Morgan motioned for Kurt to precede her up the wooden ladder. She followed, her climb awkward with one bandaged hand. Kurt reached the loft, then helped Morgan up. Late afternoon sun filtered through gaps around the loft hay-loading door, making ordinary dust motes dance like flecks of gold. The loft smelled strongly of hay and mildly of donkey.

"What college kid wouldn't enjoy living in a barn loft apartment?" Kurt asked. "If your son doesn't take you up on it, maybe one of mine will."

Morgan laughed.

"What?" Kurt asked.

"It just seems funny, talking about our grown children. When Sam and I met, our conversations were entirely different."

"Hopes and dreams and all that heady stuff?" Bitterness tainted his words.

"I think our marriages must have been very different," Morgan said.

"Oh, I think most start in the same place. But I don't want to ruin the moment dredging up the past." Kurt looked around. "Were you thinking of making the entire loft an apartment?"

"I still need space to store hay. I was thinking half the loft would easily work for a summer apartment."

"No heat that way?"

"Colorado summer nights can be cold. We'd have to arrange for some kind of heat. Something really safe, with all these combustibles around."

"What about plumbing?"

Morgan pushed her fingers through her dark curls. "I hadn't even thought about that."

"Planning's overrated." Kurt reached for Morgan's hand. "Sometimes you just have to go with the flow."

Kurt pulled Morgan closer.

Chapter Thirty-One

Morgan hadn't decided whether she wanted to resist or not when it was obvious Kurt was going in for a kiss. She didn't find out. The sound of boots clomping across gravel alerted them. Morgan stepped away from Kurt as Del and Barton came inside the barn.

"There you are," Del said. "I saw the car out front of the shop."

"I was telling Kurt about our idea to make an apartment up here."

"Barton has some other thoughts on that topic," Del said. "But we can talk about that over some elk stew."

"I hope you don't mind," Barton said. "I used your slow cooker. There's plenty for everyone."

Morgan didn't mind at all that Barton had cooked dinner for Del.

"We already had dinner," she said.

"I could make room for elk stew," Kurt said.

Dog accepted the dinner invitation with much less grace than Kurt. He leapt and danced, nearly tripping Morgan, until he was invited inside. Dog lay beside Del at the kitchen table, snuffling the linoleum politely when crumbs or bits of elk hit the floor.

After the dishes were cleared, Del tapped a spoon against his water glass.

"As you know, I've been concerned about how we're going to

fit all these people in here when Kendall and Allie come home, and then David and who knows who else shows up this summer. Then Barton came up with an idea, right after he put a foot through my trailer roof."

A sheepish look was visible through the forest of Barton's whiskers. "That trailer's a total loss. Think I finally convinced Del of that fact."

"What's your idea?" Kurt asked.

"Those old cabins next to Gerda's garage," Barton said. "They've been sitting empty for a decade. I heard talk they're planning to level that lot and build condos. The owner might let those cabins go for a reasonable price."

"You think they'd survive the move?" Kurt asked. "There must be a reason the place closed down."

"I don't know what condition they're in," Barton said.

Morgan envisioned a row of cabins sitting in the space Del's trailer currently occupied. Gingham curtains hung in every window, and half-barrels of flowers sat by every door.

"We can find out," she said. "Kurt and I have news, too, but it's not good."

Morgan told about their trip to the rock show, and learning that Professor Esteban had not only found ammolite in his van, but had gone to the dugout to search for more.

"He had already figured it out," Morgan said, fudging the facts a bit, "so I showed him a sample of what we found."

"What did he have to say?" Barton asked.

"It's from jewelry. But he couldn't say for certain what the source was. Canadian or local."

"That is bad news." Del tugged at his mustache. "Half of Pine County must know about the ammolite."

"There's more," Morgan said. "Lorina Dimple knows about it, too. She stole a baggie of ammolite chips from my bag when I had my wreck."

"I'd expect nothing less," Del muttered.

"She gave it back, with a warning. The Coopers will try to jump any ammolite claim."

"There's no point," Barton said. "No claim can be made. That's an off-limits area."

"That's good," Morgan said. "Then there should be no danger of fortune hunters tearing up the Temple Mountain trail."

Barton shrugged. "Or thieves and amateurs will invade who'll do lots more damage than a commercial operation."

"Unless the area is rezoned," Kurt said. "The government might make exceptions if enough pressure is exerted. There's a lot of tax money to be made off a producing gem mine."

"And Jade Tinsley is running for City Council," Morgan said.

The rest of the evening involved speculation about the Cooper family's malevolent plans to monopolize ammolite mining, the Kruger family's ongoing tragedy, the cabins, and the location of the mountain man. Morgan was glad Del and Barton were around to ward off any more attempts at a romantic moment from Kurt. Not because she didn't want the attention. Because she suspected she did, and wasn't ready to face the consequences a romance would have in the small mountain town.

Monday morning, Chief Sharp called.

"I got a report from Kruger's Auto Shop. I owe you an apology, Mrs. Iverson. Your driving was not at fault. The bleeder valve was open just enough to let the brake fluid leak out slowly. When enough fluid was lost, the brakes failed."

"Is that what happened to Gerda's brakes?"

"Yep. Same thing."

Morgan closed her eyes, gripping the checkout counter for support as her head spun.

"Why?" Morgan asked, even though she knew the chiefwouldn't have an answer.

"I'll have to make some amendments to that accident report. I'd like you to drop by when you have a few minutes. Maybe around two?"

Being vindicated never felt so bad as when the explanation made things so much worse.

"No sign of the mountain man?" she asked.

"He hasn't shown his face, or should I say his beard, since you caught him in your barn Friday night. Of course, he might not be the one who opened your bleeder valve. I just hope he hasn't left the area."

Or worse, Morgan thought, been killed by the person who did tamper with her brakes.

Morgan stayed busy enough the rest of the day to keep her mind off her troubles, until she left Del in charge to walk to town and talk to the chief. Next she went to the car rental shop and picked up a vehicle to use until her Buick was either repaired or relegated to the junkyard. When she came back, Del went to work packing up his trailer. Beatrice dropped by just before closing time.

"I'll start with the good news," Beatrice said.

"Uh-oh," Morgan said. "Which means there's bad news?"

"First, the bake sales were a success. We raised seven hundred and fifty dollars for Kendall and Allie's plane tickets at the mall, and another three hundred at the church."

It would take a few more bake sales to bail them out of whatever trouble it was they'd gotten into.

"That's great." Morgan hoped she sounded grateful.

"Don't worry," Beatrice said. "Five anonymous donors kicked in the rest."

Beatrice handed Morgan an envelope thick with cash.

"I'm guessing you know who they are."

"If I told you, then they wouldn't be anonymous."

"So what's the bad news?"

"I'll have to start at the beginning."

Beatrice launched into a tale with plenty of extraneous details about taking Camille, Gayle, and Farley to the hospital. This was the first face-to-face meeting of the children and their grandmother, so there was plenty of high drama. Then Beatrice left Camille and brought the children home with her. They walked to Bibi's Bakery for a late afternoon snack. Morgan was growing weary of the story until Beatrice finally got to the point.

"We were walking back to my house to get the car so we could go pick up Camille from the hospital when the mountain man burst out of the alley. He grabbed Gayle's arms. I was afraid he was going to kidnap her, so I pulled out my pepper spray, but the wind was blowing the wrong direction, so I didn't spray him."

Beatrice paused to breathe.

"What happened?" Morgan asked.

"Farley is quite the little hero. He pushed the mountain man away from Gayle. I started to pepper spray him then, but he repeated something over and over. We tried, but none of us could understand him."

"Did the police catch him?"

"Several people heard Gayle screaming and Farley shouting. I dare say my voice carried some distance. They all gave chase, but he just evaporated, like a spirit."

Coming from no-nonsense Beatrice, that was quite an admission.

With the mountain man being so elusive, the solution to the cold case seemed to hinge on the ammolite and the elephant-head flowers.

"Del, I'd like to go back to the dugout."

"Barton and I've been over that area a few times. Didn't see anything."

"I want to look again." She repeated a condensed version of Beatrice's story about Gayle being grabbed on the street by the mountain man. "Someone tried to shoot Rolf, and Chief Sharp confirmed both my and Gerda's brakes were deliberately tampered with to make them fail. Sitting back to see what's going to happen next isn't working."

Del checked his handgun and grabbed his shotgun. When they reached the trailhead parking lot, he tried to hand the shotgun to Morgan.

"I can't carry a gun," Morgan said.

"This is national forest. It's legal to open carry, and I insist on having backup. There could be more people out there than just the mountain man. Like illegal prospectors."

Morgan pulled on a heavy daypack. Del helped her sling the shotgun across her chest. The trail to the dugout was much more well-defined than Del liked seeing.

"Been some traffic." He pulled his pistol out of his shoulder holster and held it in his hand. "Keep your eyes open."

A sign was posted near the dugout, warning that mining was not permitted in the area, and trespassers would be violating federal law. That had not stopped people from digging numerous test holes.

"See that?" Del asked, pointed to a place where dirt had recently been turned. "And that? People are digging down a few feet to see what they can find. If they don't hit anything interesting, they move on."

"And leave the ground disturbed," Morgan said. "Nice."

"So now that we're out here, what exactly do you intend to do?"

"Professor Esteban thinks the ammolite came from a piece of jewelry," Morgan said. "The police could have missed something."

An Abert's squirrel chattered at them as they pawed through

the stone ring full of elephant-head flowers, where Gerda had first found ammolite chips. They crawled on hands and knees in front of the dugout. All they found were more chips of the opalescent gem. Morgan stood and pushed away branches covering the dugout entrance. She pulled aside the strips of tattered blue tarp and peered through the doorway.

"Maybe it's inside, where Carlee was."

"You know there's most likely a hundred spiders in there. Not to mention snakes."

"Thanks, Del." Morgan pulled a knit wool hat over her hair and stuffed the long curls inside. The bandage on her left hand was already filthy. She pulled a flashlight out of her daypack and flicked it on. "Will you pull me out if I get stuck in a giant spider's web?"

"I'll think hard about it."

Morgan stepped into the doorway. The ceiling was so low, she had to stoop over. Her flashlight didn't help much. The sun was behind the mountain, but the sky was bright. The flashlight only seemed to intensify the shadows. There were spider webs in the corners where the police and forensics investigators hadn't disturbed them. Suspended in midair from one ancient web was the skeleton of a small bird. Carlee's resting place was all but obliterated, the pallet of blankets on which she had rested gone.

"I could be wrong, Del."

"How's that?"

"If there was any jewelry here, the coroner probably took it with the bedding."

"Then we can go?"

"Hang on. Let me look around a little more."

Morgan pushed the toe of her hiking boot into the dirt floor. It was hard packed and unyielding. She scanned the walls of the dugout. The front and the sides were rough-hewn log cabin.

Dried mud and gravel filled the gaps between the logs. Different shades of gray indicated that some of the filler might be original, but the rest looked newer. Someone, presumably the mountain man, was maintaining the dugout.

The back wall was dug into the side of the hill. The original occupant had built a fire ring on the floor of the dugout, vented to the outside through a hole in the roof. In recent decades, someone had placed a legless barbecue grill under an old stovepipe that had rusted through in places. The grill was so packed with pine needles, dried grasses, and leaves, that it was nearly unrecognizable as human-made. The shelter had never been intended to be permanent, but had held up remarkably well for a hundred years or more. Morgan picked up a stick and walked close to the walls, brushing away spider webs and shining the flashlight into crevices.

"Finding anything?" Del asked.

"No," Morgan said.

Del crouched down and shuffled through the door. He grasped his own flashlight, which had a much stronger light. He scanned the walls, too, but turned up nothing.

"I'm afraid this was a wasted trip," Morgan said.

"You had to satisfy your curiosity," Del said. "We'd better head back before it gets too dark to hike that trail safely."

Morgan exited, then turned to watch. Del took small steps, keeping his head bowed.

"Ahhh!" Del waved his hands around his head. "Spider!" He hopped back a step. Morgan heard the crack of skull meeting log. "Ow." A shower of dirt came down on his shoulders. "Well, that's just great."

"What is it, Del?"

"I stepped on that rusty old grill. Put my foot right through a packrat nest. I hope I don't get the hanta virus or the bubonic plague."

"I'm sorry. Are you okay?"

"Nothing damaged but my pride."

He hobbled toward the doorway, shaking his foot. Morgan looked around him into the darkening gloom of the sod house.

"Don't rodents collect things in their nests?"

"I didn't see anything but dried grass and droppings." Del shuddered and brushed his hands down his sleeves. "I would really prefer not to go in there again."

The entire trip was a bust, and now Del's head was busted, too. Morgan shone her flashlight inside, hoping to glimpse something shiny.

"Just one last look," she said.

The flashlight was more effective in the deepening gloom. Del had overturned the packrat's nest, scattering nesting material across the dugout floor. Morgan kicked at a clump of leaves, and a millipede ran out.

"Euw."

"I tried to warn you," Del said.

"I don't think a rat's lived in here for a while."

"Too accessible for snakes and foxes, I'd think," Del said.

Morgan spread the litter around with her boot. There were a few metal objects. Beer bottle caps, a dime, and bits of blackened foil from some ancient campfire meal. Her light reflected off an iridescent bit of shell.

"Del, I think I found it."

He grudgingly reentered the dugout, aiming his intense light at the toe of Morgan's boot.

"Well, looky here." Del picked up a fistful of debris and backed out of the dugout.

Morgan joined him, aiming her light at the palm of his gloved hand. Shells the size and shape of garden snails reflected the flashlight in opalescent colors.

"It's raw ammolite," she said. "Professor Esteban and Barton were both wrong. They said the ammolite was from jewelry."

"Maybe the stuff you and Gerda found had been cut." Del held a shell between his thumb and forefinger. "If this ammolite is local, man, oh man."

Tuesday Morgan was on her own. Barton picked up Del at first light to search for the source of the ammolite again, this time armed with gadgets from Barton's company. Morgan packed them lunch, knowing Del would forget to eat, and Barton might, too, in his excitement to make an historic find.

Business was light but steady. Hardcore tourists had not yet flocked to Golden Springs, so many of the customers were rock hounds, Sasquatch enthusiasts, and some homeschool kids looking for fossils for a diorama.

Three calls broke up the day. Morgan's insurance company assured her that her policy covered Piers's damaged fence and the rental car. After the deductible, her car repairs would be covered, too. Morgan doubted the car was worth it, but she wasn't in the position to shop for a new vehicle.

The second call came from Kruger's Auto Repair. Gerda's senior mechanic, Tom, could patch together the old Buick. Since the insurance would cover it, she gave Tom the go-ahead.

Toward the end of the business day, Kurt called.

"Jade Tinsley is announcing his candidacy for City Council early Wednesday evening," Kurt said. "His in-laws, the Coopers, are hosting the fete. It should be the social event of the year, by Golden Springs standards."

"A press conference? That seems a bit much for a City Council campaign."

"Small town politics are deadly serious. As a member of the press, I'm invited. I wondered if you'd like to go as my date."

Morgan considered the investigative possibilities. She would be inside Jade's world, or at least a part of his world. Maybe she would learn whether the Coopers were trying to get the inside track on rezoning national forest land for a commercial ammolite mine. She might even run across a clue to Carlee's death.

"Absolutely."

"No overt investigating," Kurt said. "I don't want to be banned from future events because I bring a date in a Sherlock Holmes trench coat and deer-hunter's hat."

"I promise to dress appropriately."

But Morgan had no idea what that was, in Golden Springs. She could ask Bernie tonight.

As they signed in for the O'Reily's 5K that evening, Bernie squealed.

"This is our tenth time!"

They had missed a couple of runs since joining in January, due to bad weather.

"You'll get your shirts tonight." Lucy held one up. A bear dressed like a leprechaun was in the act of stealing a beer from a picnic basket. "We're having a special ceremony, since so many people hit their tenth run tonight."

That evening, Bernie and Morgan jogged farther than they ever had, making it halfway around the three-mile course.

"Just think," Bernie said. "When we first signed up for O'Reily's Runners, you weren't even sure you'd be here long enough to earn your shirt."

"A lot has changed. You hadn't met Rolf yet."

"Which reminds me, if you don't mind, he's finally going to come with us next week."

"His shoulder must be healing."

"He's feeling much better. How is your hand?"

"Good as new." Morgan flexed her left hand, the gauze bandage several layers thinner. "Don't feel you and Rolf have to walk with me."

"It's our tradition." Bernie was silent while they walked past the bridge. Then she spoke, hesitantly. "You could invite Kurt."

"I don't know, Bernie. I'm not sure my heart is keeping up with the gossip."

"Be careful. Kurt is smitten. I think his heart is all in."

"I've just accepted the idea that Sam is really gone. That it's okay to live my life without him. I'm scared to jump right into a relationship."

"Me, too," Bernie said. "I'm terrified of being a stepmom. Stacie hates me. I don't know if I can cope with that the rest of my life."

"You didn't catch it, did you?" Morgan asked.

"What?"

"Stacie's chink-in-the-armor moment when we had dinner at your bakery."

Bernie shook her head. "I obviously missed something. What do you mean?"

"When Farley told Stacie her mom, meaning you, was a great cook."

"And Stacie snapped at him."

"And then Stacie said . . ." Morgan paused, waiting.

"Okay, I must have stopped listening after her 'she's not my mom' crack."

"Stacie said, 'but she is a great cook.' "

Bernie walked in silence for half a block. The Granite Junction park was in full bloom. Beds of red tulips and yellow daffodils provided splashes of color against a lush green lawn.

"I'm underwhelmed," Bernie said.

"You shouldn't be. That was huge, for Stacie to admit you were not only good, but great at something."

"I suppose so." Bernie didn't sound convinced. "How is your cold case going?"

Morgan didn't correct Bernie this time. She did have a lot to fill Bernie in on, from Del's find of the raw ammolite, to the confirmation of tampered brakes, to Jade's planned announcement of his candidacy for City Council.

"Kurt invited me to go with him to the press conference."

"You're going, right?"

"It's a great opportunity to snoop for clues to Carlee's past, but if Kurt and I show up together, that pretty much seals it as far as us being a couple."

"I wouldn't have thought so three months ago," Bernie said, "but you two are ideal for each other. He's got the newspaper, and you keep running into bodies. You'll keep each other occupied solving murders for years to come. Like Nick and Nora."

"Oh, great. Their heyday was smack in the middle of Kurt's favorite decade."

"The forties? See, it's meant to be. Anyway, I think you're reacting too much to your fear of small-town gossip. Just because you date a guy in Golden Springs doesn't mean you're doomed to spend the rest of your life with him. Lighten up, Morgan. Have some fun."

"I'll try. Maybe life has been serious for so long now, I've forgotten how to have fun."

"You need a plan," Bernie said. "For when you get inside the Cooper mansion. What are you going to snoop for?"

"Ammolite, obviously. Elephant-head flowers. I can't question the guests about Carlee in front of Jade's in-laws. I'm sure they'd rather forget that chapter of his past."

"You never know. Maybe someone will be there who knows something about Jade's history with Carlee. Like a political rival trying to thwart his run for City Council."

"Now to the really important question," Morgan said. "What do I wear to this shindig?"

"If you really want to impress people, wear your O'Reily's Runners T-shirt."

Chapter Thirty-Two

By Wednesday afternoon, Morgan had changed her mind a half dozen times about her outfit, finally settling on a blouse with a subdued floral print, black slacks, and ankle boots with a slight heel. She replaced the gauze wrapped around her hand with a beige bandage. When she attempted styling her curly hair, everything she did seemed to make her look like a flower child from the sixties instead of a serious businesswoman and amateur detective.

After a short drive across the highway and up a steep road into wooded hills, Kurt pulled his Plymouth onto the Coopers' curved driveway. A teenager she'd seen around town ran up to them. He wore a valet jacket with his jeans and sneakers. Formal only went so far in Golden Springs. Kurt gave the kid instructions about how to drive his vintage automobile. He bit his lower lip as the car pulled away.

"Your baby will be okay," Morgan said.

"Welcome!"

Harlan Cooper waved them up wide stone steps and through double doors opening to a spacious foyer. His black slacks, long-sleeved white western-style shirt, and bolo tie made him appear casual, but Morgan could tell by the cut and the fabric that the clothes were expensive. The clasp of the bolo tie was a chunk of turquoise worth more than anything in the Rock of Ages, except for the triceratops horn. The greenish blue stone matched the color of Harlan's eyes, and was almost as cold. The woman at his side looked a decade younger, and from the resemblance, was most certainly Mia and Chase's mother.

"Honey," Cooper said to his wife, "you know Kurt Willard, editor of the *Golden Springs Gazetteer.*"

She murmured something innocuous in a breathy tone and clasped hands briefly with Kurt.

"And this is . . ." Cooper snapped his fingers and scrunched his craggy face. As though he didn't remember stalking Morgan's shop for ammolite three weeks ago, and speaking to her at the prospecting club just days ago.

"Morgan Iverson," Kurt said. "Manager of the Rock of Ages rock shop. Morgan, you know Harlan Cooper, I believe?"

"And this is my blushing bride, Marlene."

Morgan held out her unbandaged hand. Marlene gave her a limp handshake. Morgan could almost see the mental calculations going on behind Marlene's swimming-pool blue eyes, pegging Morgan at the low end of the Golden Springs business spectrum. Unlike Morgan's department store attire, Marlene wore a silk tunic in an abstract pattern that managed to be both bright and subdued, over sage slacks and heeled sandals that looked too cold for the weather. Her toenails glittered with gold-flake polish.

"Kurt," Cooper said, "other members of the press are in the den. Come with me and I'll introduce you. What am I saying? I'm sure you already know your competition."

"Everyone else is gathered in the garden," Marlene said to Morgan, her words barely louder than a whisper. "Follow me."

She herded Morgan away, but not before Morgan got a glimpse of the den as Kurt entered the room. The décor was not what she expected from Harlan Cooper. There were no animal heads on the walls, no heavy leather furniture. Marlene must have demanded the English countryside look.

Mrs. Cooper led her down the hallway. Her sandals clacked

as she walked slowly, deliberately, taking the careful steps of someone who was perhaps dosed with prescription drugs. Morgan might have enjoyed the brief tour of the house, except that all the doors were closed. She did catch a glimpse of a spacious kitchen so neat and tidy, it was difficult to imagine meals had actually ever been prepared on the state-of-the-art appliances. Trays covered with plastic wrap sat on marble counters.

Out the back door, Morgan followed Marlene onto a redwood deck larger than the rock shop's living quarters. A gas grill big enough to barbeque a buffalo dominated one end of the deck. The rest was filled with outdoor furniture and umbrellas. Kurt's 1940s' vintage reporter outfit did not seem out of place among the varied costumes on display in the expansive flower garden. All the usual Golden Springs types paraded around the graveled pathways or clustered near outdoor heaters. Piers had gathered a group of sandaled and tie-dyed types around him. They smelled of patchouli oil and maybe something else that had recently been legalized. Western shirts and cowboy hats mingled with the perennial Colorado fleece vests and hiking boots, and a few, like Anna, wore New York boardroom power suits.

Jade was the center of attention, and someone had dressed him for the part. Probably Mia, who was at his elbow. She was stunning in an Asian-inspired black dress covered with large red flowers. With her lean build, the dress worked. Spike heels lifted her to the lofty heights of Jade's shoulder. Her short auburn hair was in a softer style, rising from her scalp in gentle waves. Jade wore a Nehru-collared jacket in a black that matched Mia's dress. His long golden hair was swept back in a ponytail and tied with a narrow red ribbon.

The crowd around the beautiful couple was three-deep, and clamoring for an audience with as much enthusiasm as if Jade and Mia were royalty. Maybe for Golden Springs, the family with the most money qualified for that role. The Coopers were definitely not Old Money, though. There was a crass pretentiousness that declared their fortune had been recently amassed.

Morgan made the rounds of the garden, stopping to chat with Anna. Then Dr. Henry and Patty Drewmoore approached, asking about Morgan's hand, and then Adelaide's condition.

"Dr. McCormick says she may have several more months to go," Morgan said. "Donkeys carry their foals forever and a day."

"Poor Adelaide," Patty said. "We'll all be glad when she delivers. Baby donkeys are so cute."

"It looks like the show is finally going to begin," Henry said.

Morgan hadn't even begun investigating when the press corps exited the back door onto the deck, escorted by Harlan Cooper.

She moved with the crowd toward the podium on the deck, until she noticed the side gate open. Camille herded Gayle and Farley through, glanced around, then latched the gate. Crashing Jade's press conference. Things were about to get interesting. Camille attempted to meld into the shrubbery in a bland rose-colored pantsuit that had probably done service at many a PTA meeting. It did nothing to flatter her dumpy figure. She looked panicked when Morgan walked up to her.

"I didn't know you were coming to Jade's press conference," Morgan said.

"I had to see what the excitement was about," Camille said. "Kids, go help yourselves to the snacks."

"I wonder if they have sushi," Farley said.

Gayle shaded her eyes and peered toward a white tent at the back of the garden. "I think I see a chocolate fountain."

The slender teen wore a snug pink tank top. Her jeans fit like pantyhose. She wobbled on top of the same stacked heels she'd worn Sunday. Camille waited for her children to leave, then turned to Morgan.

"Are you the door guard?"

"No. I'm here because Kurt invited me. I didn't crash the

party. I'm guessing you came in the side gate because you don't have an invitation."

"I had to see Jade. I need to know whether he even remembers Carlee."

"He does," Morgan said. "I talked to him a few days ago, and he seemed genuinely broken up about your sister's death."

"Oh, yeah. I'll bet. That Jade is a good actor. Everyone thinks he and Carlee were the couple of the century." She snorted.

"Really?" Morgan asked. "I haven't heard this side of things."

"Carlee was desperate to leave Golden Springs. You can probably guess why. These days people would call our family dysfunctional, but back then we were just the messed up Krugers. Jade was perfectly happy as a small-town boy with small-town dreams. When I heard he made it big time, I wanted to see what my sister missed out on."

Morgan doubted Carlee would have lived the high life with Jade Tinsley. Mia was the one who propelled Jade, almost against his will, to his current state of wealth.

A woman in her mid-thirties approached. "Camille? Is that you?"

Morgan listened as they reestablished an acquaintance that had begun in junior high. The woman was one of the tie-dyed set. Whatever motivation Camille had for crashing the party, the damage was done. She wasn't leaving any time soon. Morgan scanned the deck. Cooper was plying the press corps with drinks. Jade wasn't with him. He wasn't in the garden or under the food tent, either.

Morgan marched up to the back door like she belonged there. She glanced into the kitchen. One of the uniformed wait staff pulled the plastic wrap off a tray of cheese and crackers and headed for the deck. Morgan ducked out of the way, then scooted down the hallway, prepared to tell anyone who stopped her that she was hunting for the bathroom, even though there was an elegant wood-paneled bathroom trailer outside for the guests.

No one could mistake the double doors to the den for a bathroom, but Morgan opened one side a crack. The room seemed empty, until she noticed Jade's golden hair as he slouched in a chair facing the fireplace. Morgan froze. She hadn't thought out what she might say to Jade. Who killed your fiancée? Your wife or your brother-in-law? Sasquatch? You? She was snooping mindlessly, hoping clues would leap out at her. Morgan backed up and started to close the door.

"Hello, Mary."

She didn't correct him this time. "I'm sorry. I didn't mean to disturb you. You must be practicing your speech."

"I'll be reading from index cards. I can't memorize other people's words."

"Your father-in law's?"

"In a good part. Mia made her additions, too."

Morgan sat on the chair next to him.

"I suppose you think I'm foolish," Jade said, "letting other people run my life."

"No," Morgan said. "Not if you're happy."

Jade's handsome face crumpled in misery. In the silence, Morgan could hear the tick-tock of the grandfather clock. She waited until she was sure Jade wasn't going to burst out sobbing.

"If you're so uncomfortable about running for City Council, then back out. Don't make the announcement."

"And disappoint my wife's family? The Coopers have done so much for me. And Mia . . ."

"Better now than later."

Jade lowered his face into his hands. His broad shoulders slumped. Jade's emotions seemed out of proportion to the situation. Maybe Camille was right, and he was acting. But there might be another option. Morgan took a guess.

"This isn't just about running for City Council."

"No," he mumbled through his hands. Jade looked up, but not at Morgan. He stared at the closed curtains to the French doors. "It seems kind of funny that this opportunity came up right when you found Carlee. It's almost like, I don't know. It sounds silly."

Morgan waited while he sorted out his thoughts, hoping he had time before the Coopers interrupted to drag him off to fulfill their destiny.

"I don't know why I'm telling you this. You just seem like a good listener. Not judging my words. Just hearing them. I feel like I'm at a crossroads. Do I continue on this path that others chose for me, or do I strike out on my own? Everything in my life changed the day Carlee disappeared, and a part of me died. I know. How cliché, right? But from that day on, I've let people decide my life for me. Maybe if I knew what happened to her."

"Jade, did she have a reason to leave?"

He jumped to his feet, startling Morgan. "Stupid, stupid, stupid!" He paced around the room, shaking his clenched hands in the air. "It was all my fault. I ruined everything!"

"What was your fault?"

Jade looked at Morgan like he had forgotten she was in the room.

"Jade, I'm trying to figure out what happened to Carlee. If there's anything you remember—"

"Why should you care? You never even met her."

"I know Gerda. I know that Carlee's disappearance tore apart what was left of their family. Gerda has the same hole in her heart as you do." Morgan raised her hands. "The entire town was damaged. It's a mystery that needs solving. Maybe finding out what happened to Carlee could bring everyone healing."

"I would help you, if I knew anything."

He claimed to have ruined everything, and yet he didn't know anything? Maybe seeing a piece of evidence would shock his memory into gear.

"I found this." Morgan pulled one of the larger chips of ammolite out of her handbag. She held it out to Jade. "Did you give Carlee a necklace made with this type of gem?"

Jade took it from Morgan's palm. "No. I didn't give it to her." He frowned. "But it seems familiar." He closed his eyes. "I remember her wearing something like this. After we argued."

Morgan heard a scuffling sound in the hallway. She was so close to getting answers. She took the ammolite chip from Jade and tucked it in her handbag.

"Someone's here to take you to your press conference," Morgan said.

A guilty look passed over Jade's face. "And I'm hiding in the den, talking to a stranger about my ex-girlfriend."

"Maybe we can avoid a scene," Morgan said. "Is there another way out of the room?"

Jade pulled aside the curtain. The French door was open. Morgan slipped through and nearly stepped on the tail of a tiger-sized gray tabby. That was why the door was open, no doubt. The regal cat required entry and exit from the Cooper mansion at its own convenience. A thick, head-high evergreen hedge surrounded the small tiled patio. Jade dropped the curtain.

"Hi, kitty." Morgan bent to pet the silky-furred cat.

"Camille," she heard Jade say. "I didn't expect to see you here."

Oh, great.

"No, I'll bet not," Camille said.

The patio seemed secluded, but anyone could stroll through the wooden gate in the hedge. Morgan lifted a metal café chair and set it near the gap in the door. If someone wandered by, she could claim she was admiring the patio, or petting the cat, or serving as a witness when Camille avenged her sister's murder.

"I wasn't invited," Camille continued. "I imagine it would embarrass the high and mighty Coopers for the sister of your dead fiancée to show her face on your special day. But you know what? I don't care what they think."

"You're always welcome in my house," Jade said.

"This isn't your house," Camille said. "It's not even Mia and Chase's. What kind of game are you playing?"

He ignored her question. "I heard you came back for a memorial service."

"The one you won't attend?"

"I want to," Jade said. "More than anything. But it would hurt Mia."

"Don't you need closure? Or, oh, I get it. You don't feel any guilt. You just walked away unscathed. Unlike the rest of us."

Morgan's heart beat faster. She was going to hear the solution to the mystery, if no one caught her eavesdropping.

Hurry, Morgan thought. *Spill the beans, or the ammolite.*

"Of course I feel guilty," Jade said. "The last time I saw Carlee, we argued. If I could take that back—"

"You killed my sister, Jade."

Morgan held back a gasp. The gray cat wove between Morgan's legs and the chair's ornate metal legs, unconcerned about the human drama taking place in the den.

"You're as much to blame as me, Camille. You didn't have to tell her. You could have kept quiet. We're both guilty."

"I didn't have a choice."

"Don't give me that. You didn't even come home to help search for her. Sometimes I wonder . . ."

"You know how Golden Springs is." Camille's voice trembled with emotion. "The gossip. The judgmental old biddies just waiting for a person to mess up. I was nineteen and pregnant. There was no coming home."

The timeline clicked into place. Gayle's age. Her hair, as thick and golden as Jade's. Camille's exit from town right before her sister vanished.

"But I thought—I was told . . ." Jade's words tumbled into silence.

"You thought what?"

Morgan heard the creaking of the sofa, and imagined Jade sitting.

"So there was a baby."

"Is," Camille said. "My daughter. Gayle."

"I suppose you're going to tell me she's my kid." Jade's voice sounded hollow, like there was no strength behind the words. "Did Carlee know?"

"No. After the way she reacted to hearing that we'd slept together, well, telling her you got me pregnant would have killed her." When Camille spoke again, she sounded drained, too. "I guess it didn't matter in the end."

"Someone's here," Jade said.

The door to the den must have opened, because Morgan heard Mia's voice.

"Jade, they're ready for you."

A terrible moment of silence was shattered when the door to the den slammed, rattling the glass in the French doors. The cat jumped, then scampered away through the hedge.

"What's going on here?" Mia shouted. "What are you doing here?"

"Just saying hello to my old friends," Camille said.

"You don't have any friends here," Mia said, her voice a low growl. "You are not welcome here."

"Don't worry, Mia. My business is done."

"Then I'll see you out," Mia said.

"I have to get my children." She let the word hang there, perhaps to torture Jade, then added, "I'll let myself out."

"No, I insist," Mia said.

Morgan heard the sound of scuffling.

"Get your hands off me," Camille said.

"Ladies," Jade said. "There's no need—"

"Shut up, Jade," Mia said. "You're only making things worse. Like you always do."

"I'm leaving," Camille said. "Don't worry. I won't upset your pathetic little plans to take over this rat-hole of a town."

After a pause, Mia spoke. "God, Jade, what were you thinking, letting her in here? And right before your press conference. Here, use my eyedrops."

"I can't do this," Jade said.

"Leave it to a Kruger to destroy anything good," Mia said. "Those people all need to die."

Chapter Thirty-Three

Morgan slipped through the hedge gate and hurried around the house, emerging at the side of the deck. Kurt wore an insincere smile nearly matching the one on Harlan Cooper's weathered, sagging face. Cooper entertained the press corps with booze and tall tales while Marlene related anecdotes about an exotic vacation with the enthusiasm of a sleepwalker to the knot of people surrounding her.

Morgan climbed onto the deck where she had a decent view of the garden. She could see Camille weaving her way around raised beds thick with flowers, locating Farley outside the food tent. Mother and son scanned the garden, looking for Gayle. Even from her perch, Morgan could not spot the girl with the golden hair. She turned toward the kitchen entrance, thinking perhaps Gayle had sneaked inside the mansion. A sturdy woman in a white chef's jacket stood guard, her arms crossed over her chest and a frown creasing her face.

"May I help you?" the cook growled, in a tone that implied she had no intention of assisting Morgan.

"I must be lost," Morgan said. "This house is so huge. Which way is the bathroom?"

The cook pointed wordlessly to a bathroom trailer.

Morgan headed for the greenhouse instead. She skirted the edges of the party, which was growing a tad restless over the delay of the main event. The tempered glass greenhouse door creaked as Morgan slipped inside. Humid, earth-scented air washed over her. Morgan stepped as silently as she could on the pea gravel walkway.

The greenhouse contained plants selected for beauty, not utility. Artful arrangements of ceramic pots spilling over with flowers surrounded tiny round café tables and wrought iron chairs. Fountains filled the air with the soothing sound of splashing water. Artwork, metal sculptures, ceramic frogs and fairies filled every empty space.

A plastic cup of red punch, melting ice cubes floating like tiny icebergs, rested on a table. Morgan followed the sound of voices muffled by the foliage. She stopped abruptly and ducked behind a lime tree.

"These began as a mistake," Chase said. "I had the heat too high."

Gayle stood beside him, admiring glass icicles that looked cold blue, and yet would never melt in the heat of the greenhouse. They hung from a metal pole with tree-like branches, each bearing two or more icicles.

"When I began to throw the first pieces out, Mia asked me for them. Said there was a market for twisty strands of glass. Mia's always finding a market for something."

"I'm glad you didn't throw them out," Gayle said. "I think they're beautiful."

The teen smiled at Chase, then reached out to touch an icicle. Gayle seemed oblivious to the effect she had on Chase. Morgan watched, a queasy feeling in her stomach, as Chase's eyes roved over Gayle's young body, barely concealed in the tank top and skintight jeans.

"After she strung the first one up," Chase said, "I had to agree. When the sun hits them, and the fan moves them a little . . ." He demonstrated by running a finger across several.

Gayle made the appropriate ooh and ahh noises. Morgan was ready to intervene if the situation became more intimate, but

Gayle's attention was pulled away by a pot of flowers.

"These are amazing."

"Pedicularis groenlandica," Chase said. "That's the scientific name. They're also known as elephant-head flowers."

"I know," Gayle said in a near whisper. "They were my aunt's favorite flowers. Grandma Gerda told Mrs. Beatrice when she asked what flowers we should have at the memorial service."

Chase crouched beside Gayle, and Morgan was debating whether espionage was over, and it-takes-a-village parenting intervention was required, when the greenhouse door creaked open and rapid footsteps came down the pea gravel aisle.

"Gayle?" Camille called. "Are you in here?

Gayle and Chase jumped to their feet in an action that smacked of guilt. Morgan tried to edge away, but as Camille emerged from the greenery, Chase made eye contact with Morgan. Her cover was blown.

"What are you doing?" Camille shrieked. "Get away from my daughter!"

"Mr. Cooper was showing me his artwork."

Morgan wanted to scream. The oldest pickup line in the world was the artist luring a girl to his apartment to see his latest painting.

"I'll just bet he was." Camille grabbed Gayle's arm.

"Hey! You're hurting me!"

Morgan made her entrance. "Camille, I was keeping an eye on things."

"Why didn't you break it up?" Angry lines etched deep into Camille's haggard face. She resembled her mother, Gerda, probably more than she wished.

"Because there was nothing to break up." Chase glared at Morgan.

"It isn't lost on me how much Gayle looks like Carlee," Camille said. "You couldn't have my sister, so you go after her niece? That's just pathetic. Your entire family is pathetic, using Jade Tinsley like a prize racehorse to further your family's ambitions."

Morgan tried to interrupt, reaching for Camille's arm to lead her out of the greenhouse, but Camille slapped her hand away.

"He doesn't seem to mind," Chase said. "What? Did you think he'd spend the rest of his days pining away for your sainted sister? The golden girl, always first in her class, the prettiest, the most athletic. Is that why you went the opposite direction, dating every boy in school, being the party girl? You were jealous of Carlee, of the attention the whole town gave her."

Camille glanced at Gayle, who was soaking up every poisonous word.

Camille seethed for a moment, then pointed a finger at Chase. "You were jealous of Jade. Everyone knew you were infatuated with my sister, and she didn't even know you existed."

"We are a lot alike, Camille, you and me. You chased around, trying to get Jade's attention. Or was it your mother's? Me, wishing Carlee would notice me. Trying to get my own father's attention when he seemed to think he only had one child, his perfect daughter."

"You shouldn't be an artist," Camille said. "You should be a psychologist. You think you've got it all figured out."

Chase took a step toward Camille. "I wish I could figure it all out. I wish there were a way to heal all the hurts of the past." He reached out a hand. "We two, at least, can be friends now, surely?"

"So you can get your slimy paws on my daughter? No!"

"Mother!" Gayle's face flushed pink. "Chase was totally being nice. He didn't do anything weird. Why do parents always think the worst?"

Gayle sprinted down the pea gravel pathway, remarkably agile on her thick-soled sandals. The greenhouse door slammed closed behind her.

"Now see what you've done!" Camille yelled.

Morgan stepped beside them, hoping to cool the situation before violence erupted.

"Chase, your attention to Gayle may be innocent, but surely you can see how it might look to a concerned parent. A pretty young girl hanging around with an older artist."

Camille snorted.

"I'm practically a dinosaur," Chase said with a smirk.

"And Gayle does resemble her aunt. I never met Carlee, but I've seen photos of her, and Gayle looks just like her. Camille says you had a crush on Carlee."

"More like an obsession," Camille said.

"Every boy in town was in love with Carlee. I was one of many."

"Chase is as screwed up as anyone in this pathetic little town," Camille spat out.

"We can't change the past," Chase said. "But some of us have managed to let go."

"I changed my life," Camille said. "I moved away, and it was like I never existed in Golden Springs. I evaporated like fog. No one tried to find me, either."

"No one knew where to look," Chase said. "Or maybe they would have."

"I wouldn't have ever come back, either, if it weren't for Morgan finding Carlee's—" Camille's anger dissolved abruptly into tears. "I have to find my daughter."

After the greenhouse door banged shut, Morgan turned to Chase.

"I apologize," Morgan said. "I was looking for Gayle."

"No need to explain." Chase slumped onto a chair, the legs wobbly on the cracked cement paving stone. "I'll admit that Gayle looks just like Carlee. She's a beautiful kid. But I'm not a pervert. Gayle is perfectly safe with me."

Chase turned his focus to the elephant-head flowers.

"Where did you get those?" Morgan asked.

"You'd have to ask the gardener," Chase said.

"Carlee's favorite flowers just happen to be in your greenhouse?"

"My parents' greenhouse," Chase said. "I just live here."

His lack of concern made Morgan think he didn't know about the elephant-head flowers at the dugout. Which might mean he had nothing to do with Carlee's disappearance. Maybe.

"Was Mia jealous of Carlee, too?" Morgan asked.

Chase stood, brushing his hands together as though they had been soiled.

"What about all the guys who were infatuated with Carlee?" Morgan continued. "Were there any who might be jealous enough that if he couldn't have Carlee, no one else could? That he'd kill her?"

"I resent the implication, Mrs. Iverson. Neither my sister nor I killed Carlee Kruger. I suggest you stop playing amateur detective and mind your own business."

Chase Cooper stormed out of the greenhouse, letting the tempered glass door slam behind him. Morgan sat on the chair for a moment, replaying the conversation. Chase had not argued against Carlee's death being murder. Did he know something? As a witness? Or, despite his protest of innocence, as a perpetrator?

When Morgan left the greenhouse, the sun had dropped lower in the sky, and the air had chilled several degrees. Jade's speech was well under way. Considering he had not written them, he did a remarkable job of delivering the borrowed words with passion. Jade was an actor, she realized, living a life not of his choosing. Morgan wondered whether he was a good enough actor to cover up a murder.

In the den earlier, nothing Jade said made Morgan believe he killed Carlee. It seemed he had more motivation to murder Camille, who destroyed his relationship with her sister by confessing her affair with Jade.

Morgan wanted desperately to unload all her information on Kurt. She needed his perspective. The cold case was simultaneously weaving together and unraveling.

She moved through the knots of people clustered around the propane patio heaters. A woman standing next to Kurt wore a vintage overcoat just like his. No. It was his coat, draped over the shoulders of the lovely young thing huddling close to his side. Morgan felt a surprising stab of jealousy.

She imagined the painful emotion magnified by youthful hormones. Pregnant and scared, teenaged Camille might have killed her sister, hoping Jade would marry her. But Camille left town before Carlee disappeared. Had she come back long enough to kill Carlee?

After the speech, the hired help lowered three sides of the circus tent–sized food canopy and moved the patio heaters inside. Only the hardy remained in the increasingly breezy out-of-doors. The hardy, and the upset. Gayle slouched on a folding chair at the edge of the garden. Which meant Camille must still be on the grounds of the Cooper mansion. Morgan found her with Farley under the food canopy, the boy oblivious to his mother's anxiety as he loaded a sturdy paper plate with gourmet treats. Morgan worked her way to Camille's side.

"Gayle's outside," Morgan told her.

"I've been trying to find her for an hour," Camille said. "I'm beyond ready to leave."

"Come on. I'll show you where she's sitting."

Morgan wasn't concerned about protecting the Cooper public image, but she would do what she could to save the

Kruger family more pain. Gayle huddled on the chair. Her hair hung over her shoulders, shielding her face like a golden veil.

"Gayle, we're leaving," Camille said.

The teenager looked at her mother with red, puffy eyes.

"I'm not going anywhere with you." Gayle slid off the chair and onto her feet. She placed her hand on a low gate that led to the woods.

"Where do you think you're going, young lady?"

Gayle ignored her mother.

"You can't go off in the woods," Camille said. "Alone. Dressed like that."

Goosebumps covered Gayle's bare arms and shoulders. The teen turned, her hands balled into fists.

"Is this how Aunt Carlee was dressed when she ran away? She was probably sick of you and grandma. A couple of drunken party girls." Gayle wiped the back of her hand across her tear-damp face. "All those times you lectured me about behaving myself, and you'd done everything you warned me not to do."

"Yes, Gayle. Because I didn't want you to make the same mistakes as me."

"Our whole family is one big lie."

Gayle shoved open the gate and bolted down a trail. Camille started to chase after her, then stopped, defeated.

"She'll come back," she said to Morgan. "Won't she?"

"It's easy to get lost in the hills," Morgan said. "We should go after her."

"I'll go. You bring help."

She began to say something more, but her words were interrupted by a scream.

Camille flew through the gate. Morgan wanted to follow, but Camille was right. She should get help. A dozen people who heard the scream ran toward Morgan. Harlan Cooper bolted to the head of the crowd and blocked the gate. He waved his hands at the gathering crowd.

"If we all gallop off into the forest, we might obliterate the woman's tracks. I'll check out the situation and call if I need help."

Cooper pushed the gate closed and trotted up the trail.

"I'm not waiting around here," a hefty cowboy said.

When he chased after Cooper, four more men followed.

Kurt raced to the gate, a camera banging against his broad chest. He had his overcoat back. Morgan felt guilty for noticing, under the circumstances, but she was glad all the same. He spoke to Morgan before plunging into the forest.

"Find Doc Drewmoore. He and Patty were headed for their car. We might need him." Kurt shook his head. "I really hope we don't, but just in case."

Morgan reluctantly left the growing throng of people at the garden gate. A dozen scenarios played in her head, but the most logical one was that Gayle had tripped and fallen while running through the woods in her ridiculous shoes. In which case, Morgan's time was better served getting medical help. She sprinted through the garden and around the house.

Henry and Patty Drewmoore waited in a short line for the valet to bring their vehicle.

"Doctor, I'm glad I caught you." Morgan gasped for breath, then added, "A girl might need your help."

The valet pulled up with their car. The doctor retrieved a medical bag from the trunk and began to rapid fire questions at Morgan for which she had no answers. As they reentered the garden, the crack of a gunshot reverberated off the back of the house. Doc Drewmoore broke into a trot.

One of the men holding back the crowd saw the doctor and yelled, "Make a hole!"

People opened a gap just wide enough for Doctor and Mrs. Drewmoore. Morgan pushed her way after them. A short distance through the dense forest, a group huddled in the middle of the trail, some on their knees and others standing. Harlan Cooper paced circles in a thick bed of pine needles. Kurt's camera flashed again and again. Gayle had a borrowed suit coat wrapped around her shoulders. Camille stood next to her daughter, her hands clenched into fists at her sides.

"The doctor's here!" someone yelled.

People rose and backed away, except for one man who remained kneeling beside a body on the trail. He pressed a handkerchief to the prone man's shoulder. The man on the ground wore a beige canvas coat, and wild matted whiskers hid his face.

The mountain man.

The temperature dropped another ten degrees as the sun slipped behind the mountains. Morgan turned up the collar of her thin jacket against the chilly air creeping down her neck.

"Kurt," she whispered, "did you see what happened?"

"Big Foot grabbed Gayle, and then Cooper shot him."

"Is he alive?"

"Doc Drewmoore seems busy," Kurt said. "If the mountain man were dead, he wouldn't be trying to patch him up."

By the time Chief Sharp and Deputy Parker arrived, the mountain man was sitting up.

"Chief!" A man in a suit and tie waved one hand at Sharp while the other remained stuffed inside his jacket pocket. "Chief, over here."

He pulled a handgun out of his pocket, holding it by the barrel. He passed it grip-first to Bill Sharp.

"I unloaded it. Here are the bullets. All that were left in the gun."

Chief Sharp accepted the weapon and ammo. "Who did you shoot?"

"Not me. Harlan Cooper. He shot Big Foot. Doctor Drewmoore's giving him first aid."

"Who's getting first aid?" Chief Sharp asked. "Big Foot or Cooper? Never mind. I'll see for myself."

The forest was getting dark by the time Chief Sharp directed people back to the Cooper house. The mountain man trudged up the trail, his hands cuffed behind his back. A red-stained hole had torn through the shoulder of the stolen jacket.

Deputy Parker held the mountain man's arm, guiding him as he stumbled on the uneven ground. Doc Drewmoore followed. Chief Sharp grasped Harlan's arm, but there were no handcuffs on Cooper. Mrs. Drewmoore had her arm around Gayle's shoulders, which were covered with the borrowed suit coat. Camille moved to bring up the rear with Morgan, her face chalk white in the gloom.

As Camille approached, she muttered to Morgan, "See what all your meddling has caused."

Chapter Thirty-Four

The police chief herded the key players into the house. Morgan wished she could station herself at the French doors to the patio with the tabby cat again. Instead, she huddled near a heater in the tent while Kurt interviewed people and took more photos.

Lorina headed her way, a glass of pink wine in one hand and a plate of petit fours in the other. Her sequin-accented black western blouse dazzled in the lights of the tent.

"Morgan, have you got a minute?"

Kurt seemed to have forgotten he brought a date. Morgan had nothing but time.

"I don't know anything about—"

Lorina shook her head. "I'm not gleaning gossip about the shooting. I can already tell you how that's gonna go down. Harlan Cooper's guilty as hell, and he'll get off scot free."

"What else is he guilty of?" Morgan asked.

If he'd shoot a man in front of witnesses, he might be capable of murdering a young woman when no one was looking.

"You name it," Lorina said. "He's as crooked as a politician. If people didn't know him so well in this town, he'd be running for City Council himself. No one'll vote for him, so he's setting up his son-in-law as his puppet. But that's not what I wanted to talk to you about."

"I'm listening."

"This ain't gonna be easy." Lorina closed her eyes briefly as she took a deep breath. "Okay, here's the deal. Can you give Del a message?"

"I suppose so," Morgan said. "Depending on what the message is."

"Let the old buzzard know he was right."

"About what?"

"He'll know," Lorina said.

And that was it. The cowgirl strolled off into the dwindling crowd. Mia must have been waiting to catch Morgan alone. She stepped close and rubbed her hands in the warmth of the heater. Mia's cheeks were flushed nearly as red as the flowers on her dress.

"I hope you're happy."

"Me? I didn't have anything to do with your father shooting a homeless person."

"Isn't Sasquatch the man who hid Carlee Kruger's bones in the woods for sixteen years? Don't make him sound like the victim."

"How did the mountain man know to come here?" Morgan asked. "Did he get an invitation?"

"Apparently invitations were not needed, judging from the number of attendees who weren't on the guest list."

"Including me," Morgan said. "But I'm here with a member of the press who was invited."

"We should have been more specific." Mia glanced toward the tent opening as someone came in. A person of no apparent interest, because she returned her attention to Morgan. "Now that you've opened this can of worms, what do you intend to do with it?"

"Look, Mia, I just happened onto Carlee's remains. I didn't mean to stir up people."

"And yet you have."

The woman was already angry with her. Morgan decided to plunge in.

"Isn't it better for everyone to have closure? To finally know what happened to Carlee?"

"To stir up old emotions and animosities?" Mia asked. "Oh, sure. That's much better."

"Mia, I understand you weren't around when Carlee disappeared."

"Right. So if you imagine I had anything to do with her death, you're way off base. I wasn't around to pull the trigger."

Morgan's heart jumped to her throat. She swallowed hard. "Is that how Carlee died? She was shot?"

"Like the homeless man?" Mia laughed, but it was a bitter sound. She pushed angry words past smiling lips. She was more accomplished at acting than her husband. "If you dare accuse my father of murdering Carlee Kruger, I will sue you for slander. Anyway, I thought the prevailing theory was that she got lost in the woods and died of hypothermia."

Mia's mother waved a hand at her from the front of the tent. Without so much as a goodbye and good riddance, Mia left.

Morgan kept herself from putting her foot in her mouth again by stuffing it full of petit fours and exotic chocolates. Kurt finally finished, or perhaps he just ran out of interviewees.

"I'm sorry," he said. "This turned out to be more work than I expected. Are you ready to go?"

"I've done all the damage I could do for one day."

As they waited for the valet to bring Kurt's vintage car, he asked her, "Are you hungry?"

Morgan felt a little green around the gills from her sugar overload. "I may have nibbled too many gourmet treats to ever be hungry again."

"Oh. I was hoping to make up this lost day to you by taking you out."

"I'm exhausted, Kurt. But you're welcome to have dinner with Del at the rock shop. I'm sure he forgot to eat again, and we have leftovers."

"Okay. But I still plan to make it up to you at a later date."

"Deal."

Morgan filled Kurt in on her discovery that Jade was Gayle's father.

"I didn't learn anything nearly that interesting," Kurt said. "Just that every one in Pine County thinks Harlan Cooper is a sleaze bag, and yet they still plan to vote for his son-in-law."

"You were there when Cooper shot Big Foot. You must have more news."

"Del will want to hear the story."

When they arrived at the rock shop, Del had indeed neglected to warm up any leftovers for himself. He welcomed the chance for a helping of gossip with his meal. Morgan whipped up a batch of biscuits from a box mix to go with the leftover elk stew. She had a small bowl herself, which went a long way to counteracting all the sugar in her system.

"You seem skeptical of the whole Cooper-is-a-hero scenario," Del said to Kurt. "You must of seen something, because it sounds like he rescued that girl from Lord knows what."

"When Big Foot saw Cooper," Kurt said, "he started babbling something about doing what Cooper told him to. That was when Cooper pulled out his gun."

"So he can talk," Morgan said. "We were afraid the mountain man was mute, and even if the police caught him, he wouldn't be able to tell what he knew."

"Do you think Cooper was trying to keep the mountain man quiet?" Del asked.

"Hard to say," Kurt said. "Cooper is supposed to be a good

shot, and he just grazed the guy's shoulder. I don't think it was because he was afraid of hitting Gayle. After he pulled the trigger and Big Foot toppled, the rest of us had to tackle Cooper to get his gun."

"We aren't any closer to knowing what happened to Carlee," Morgan said.

"Unless the mountain man talks. He's at the hospital now, but Chief Sharp plans to lock him up when he's released. Attempted kidnapping. Why don't you drop your bombshell on Del, Morgan?"

"Everyone in both families has more than a few loads of dirty laundry. That whole happiest couple in the world scenario is the worst lie of all. Jade Tinsley is Gayle's father."

"Man, oh man." Del whistled. "That's a regular soap opera."

Morgan nodded. "Jade gets Camille pregnant. Camille leaves town. Carlee vanishes. Then a couple of years later Mia snares Jade. Not to mention Chase being obsessed with Carlee, and being ignored by her. They all had a motivation to kill her."

"But there's no proof Carlee was murdered," Kurt said. "And neither Camille nor Mia was in town when Carlee vanished."

"That's what they say," Morgan said.

"As I understand it," Del said, "the girl might have just wandered off in the woods and died of exposure."

"Just because people are hiding secrets," Kurt said, "doesn't mean they're murderers. Unless I learn something to dispute my assumption, the mountain man is still the most likely candidate if foul play is involved."

"Speaking of candidate," Del said, "how did the shindig go?"

"Like a finely oiled machine," Kurt said. "Too smooth. It's obvious the Cooper family has higher political aspirations, and they're all pinned on Jade."

"City Council today," Del said, "state representative tomorrow."

"I still think you should run, Kurt," Morgan said. "Jade doesn't even want the position."

"I'm not sure I'm ready to tangle with the Coopers. Besides, Jade Tinsley is a shoe-in."

Kurt gave Morgan a brief peck on the cheek, claiming he had an article to write and photographs to sort through. Morgan thought about the attractive woman he'd lent his coat to, and wondered if she was realizing too late how much she liked Kurt.

After he left, she remembered her conversation with the president of the gemstone society.

"I saw Lorina Dimple at the press conference," Morgan told Del.

"And why would that be of any interest to me?"

"She asked me to tell you something." Morgan paused to get the words right. "She wants you to know you were right. She said you'd know what that was about."

"I suppose I might," Del said. "Not that it changes anything." He had seemed ready to settle into his chair next to the woodstove, but now he stood and stretched. "Long day. We can all sleep a little easier. If a killer's been running loose, he's in custody now."

"I'm not so sure," Morgan said.

Thursday Morgan felt jittery, and wished she hadn't consumed three cups of coffee. She jumped when the phone rang.

"Hi, Sarah. Is everything okay?"

"We're fine, Mom. Are you okay? You don't sound so good."

Morgan relayed the story of Jade's press release, and Gayle's near-kidnapping.

"Golden Springs sounds like the Wild West," Sarah said. "That's not how I remember our summer visits with Uncle Kendall and Aunt Allie. Speaking of which, how did Mrs. Stonewall's bake sale go?"

"Beatrice raised nearly a thousand dollars, and I found five hundred tucked away for a rainy day, which brings us to a grand total of half of what Kendall asked for. Then some anonymous donors kicked in the rest. I wish I knew why he needs to come home so urgently. I'd call the FBI if he's in real trouble."

"That's federal," Sarah said. "Uncle Kendall might need the CIA. But I don't think it can be that bad. Otherwise they couldn't leave the country on a commercial flight."

"Good point," Morgan said. "I'd better send him the money so they can escape whatever it is they're running from."

After finishing that conversation, Morgan called the number Kendall had given her. A man answered who knew just about as much English as Morgan knew Spanish. She was afraid to give too much information, not knowing exactly what Kendall's situation was, but she managed to leave Kendall a message. Then she arranged the wire transfer. Would Kendall get the message? Would the money reach him? She had done what he asked. Now she could only wait and worry.

By late Friday afternoon, Morgan still hadn't heard from Kendall. She was hovering near the landline shop phone, and had her cell phone in her pocket, when Beatrice called.

"We're planning the memorial service," Beatrice said. "Gerda doesn't have any good photos of Carlee."

Carlee Kruger had been a beautiful young woman. It seemed odd that Gerda didn't have the typical class photos of her daughter, and the less typical glamour shots from her beauty pageants.

"Anna said Kurt has some photos in the files," Beatrice said. "Can you run by and pick them up after you close the shop? Anna said she'd be working late."

Morgan felt another little stab of the green-eyed devil, jealousy. Which was childish. Anna had already made her feelings clear. She wasn't interested in Kurt. Morgan decided she must be going off-kilter under all the stress.

"I'll pick up the photos," Morgan said.

She fought the urge to change into something more attractive than the worn Washington Warriors sweatshirt and stained jeans that were just fine for mucking out barn stalls.

Anna was ready when Morgan walked in the door. The photos sat in a file folder on her neat desk. Trevin had also found the negatives in the basement, a relic from the ancient days of film photography.

"You missed Kurt," Anna said to Morgan's unstated question. "He had to run some papers to the city clerk."

When Morgan arrived to make her delivery, cars filled the driveway and crowded the space in front of Beatrice's house. Parking was at a premium in Golden Springs. Morgan squeezed into a spot down the narrow, steep street, then hiked up the stone steps to Beatrice's front door.

Gerda was in a good mood, for Gerda, grousing a little less than usual. Camille was quiet. Gayle sat in a corner, hunched over her pink smart phone that matched the fluorescent pink of her long-sleeved T-shirt, tapping madly on the screen with her thumbs. The scooped neck of her shirt exposed an embarrassing quantity of pale flesh on the slender teen.

Beatrice held up one of the photos. "My goodness, Gayle looks exactly like Carlee."

Gayle seemed oblivious as the ladies studied her. A cascade of blond hair the same color as her aunt's, except for the purple and orange streaks, partially concealed her face. She finally seemed to feel eyes upon her, and looked up.

"What?"

Gerda sat next to her and reached for a hand that Gayle wouldn't give.

"You look so much like Carlee, it takes my breath away."

"Well, I'm not her, you know." She shoved her phone in a little pink bag slung over her shoulder and stood. She was halfway to the front door when her mother spoke.

"Where do you think you're going?" Camille asked.

"Mr. Cooper invited me to do some glasswork at the gallery." Gayle shoved her bare feet inside glittering pink open-backed sneakers.

"You are not going to that gallery," Camille said.

"I can if I want to. There's nothing here for me to do. Besides, that crazy homeless guy is in jail. I'm safe."

Gerda's face flushed deep red, and Morgan took a step back from what promised to be an epic explosion.

"You are a selfish child," Gerda said. "You do not understand that your mother fears losing you as she lost her sister."

It was Camille's turn now to reach for Gayle's hand, but the girl took a stumbling step backward. She grasped the glass doorknob.

"I don't know what you have against Chase. He's just being nice."

"You don't know anything about that family," Camille said. "I left Golden Springs to keep you safe from all this."

"Don't act so holy to me. There's nothing special about our family." She turned on her grandmother, which in Morgan's opinion was as dangerous as facing off with a pit bull. "Mom told me you were drunk all the time. That's why she left home. But I can't see why that made a difference when Chase told me mom was a drunk *and* a tramp."

Camille's hand snapped toward Gayle like a snake about to strike, but Gerda deflected the intended slap.

"We will break this curse here and now," Gerda said, all the old command returning to her voice.

Beatrice stepped into the fray, speaking to Gayle. "What

perfect world is it that you live in, child? A place where no one ever makes mistakes? That place doesn't exist."

"Aunt Carlee left," Gayle said. "Mom left. And I can leave, too."

Gayle jerked the front door open and ran down the stone steps. Camille lost it then, running to the door with a half-growl, half-cry in her throat. Beatrice and Morgan grabbed her arms.

"Let me go!" Camille wailed. "I have to stop her!"

"How?" Gerda slumped down on a chair, her face going pale as though the life had drained out. "It's happening again." She dropped her face into her hands. Her shoulders shook with sobs.

"I'll go after her," Morgan said. "You wait here in case she calls. Or comes back."

Morgan pulled her lilac-colored fleece jacket on over her sweatshirt, checked her purse for the pepper spray, and headed out the door.

Chapter Thirty-Five

The back streets of Golden Springs followed former walking paths and horse-drawn buggy lanes. It was a twisting, winding labyrinth.

Morgan lost Gayle when the girl ducked between two houses. By the time Morgan reached the alley, Gayle was nowhere to be seen. Morgan called Kurt to tell him what had happened. Her call went to voice mail. She remembered he was at City Hall, so she left a message, condensed into the briefest of news flashes, then called Bernie.

"Keep an eye out," she told Bernie.

"Do you want me to hold her for you?" Bernie asked.

"Emotional teenager, probably not," Morgan said, a little breathless as she walked. "Just call Beatrice's house if you see her. Let them know which way she's heading."

"I can't sit tight hoping Gayle wanders by. I need to help."

"I'm positive she's going to Jade's gallery." Morgan glimpsed a flash of bright pink going down the stone steps that led from Beatrice's neighborhood to Main Street. "I see her. Definitely heading to the gallery. Meet me there."

Gayle had disappeared again by the time Morgan reached the bottom of the steep steps. Morgan ran up the sidewalk toward the pedestrian mall and Jade's Aspen Gold Art Gallery. She caught up with Gayle as the teen rattled a gate that blocked foot traffic from cutting behind the gallery.

"Gayle, stop!"

The girl squeezed between gate and fence. Morgan had no hope of making it through the narrow gap. She dashed to the front of the gallery in time to see Lynn the salesclerk insert a key into the door's deadbolt lock.

"We're closed," the young woman said. "Come back tomorrow." She turned away from the door.

"Wait!" Morgan yelled. "A girl went around the back of the building. She said she was coming to see Chase. She threatened to run away from home. I have to talk to her."

"I didn't see anyone," Lynn said.

Morgan could believe that, the way the clerk kept her nose perpetually stuck in a magazine.

"If she came to see Chase," Lynn added, "she might've used the back door. His lady friends avoid the front door. In which case it's nunya, you know?"

None of your business. Morgan knew.

"It is my business when the 'lady friend' is fifteen."

Lynn's mouth fell open. She began unlocking the door when Mia swept out from behind the back curtain. She said something to the clerk Morgan couldn't hear, then came to the door. Mia turned the key and dropped it into a tiny black purse. Morgan pushed, but Mia had locked the door.

"What do you want?"

"I'm looking for Gayle." Morgan shouted through the pane of thick glass. "She said she was coming to the gallery. Her mother is worried."

Lynn hovered at Mia's elbow. Mia frowned at her.

"I'll handle this, Lynn. You can go home."

Lynn seemed reluctant to miss out on the drama, but Mia's scowl must have convinced her to back off. The clerk slowly gathered her purse and magazine from the checkout counter. Mia glared at Morgan through the locked glass door.

"Gayle?" Mia asked. "Is that the little Carlee lookalike?" Mia knew perfectly well who Morgan was talking about. Mia didn't wait for her answer. "She's not here."

"I saw her go through the gate. Maybe she's in the back room."

"I just came from there," Mia said. "I'm telling you, Gayle's not here."

"She just got here," Morgan said. "Maybe you missed seeing her come in. I need to talk to her."

Mia spun around on one designer heel. She and Lynn fussed around with the cash register and a vinyl bag, gathering the day's cash and receipts. When they both vanished behind the curtain, someone must have flicked off the light switch. All but the front window display went dark.

Morgan clenched both hands into fists and stared into the darkened gallery, infuriated. Chase's glasswork of purple elephant-head flowers caught her eye. Created from molten glass, they seemed as animated as the living flowers in the Cooper greenhouse. Carlee's favorite flower. He had a crush on her in high school. And now he had lured Carlee's lookalike niece into his back-of-the-shop love nest.

"Morgan, I'm here." Bernie grabbed a light post with one hand and gasped.

"Did you run here from the bakery?"

"It sounded like an emergency." Bernie pressed her face to the glass, fogging the gallery window with her breath. "Is Gayle in there?"

"Even if she is, Mia won't let me in."

Morgan walked to the gate, rattled the dry wood, and tugged on the chain. Short of kicking the gate to pieces, there was no getting through.

"Gayle slipped through here."

"Wow, you'd have to be really skinny to squeeze through that." Bernie took a step back, placed her hands on her generous hips, and looked up. "Hey, someone's up there."

Morgan moved beside Bernie and followed her friend's gaze. A figure ducked away from the window. Morgan caught a glimpse of long blond hair.

"That has to be Gayle." She grabbed the cell phone out of her jacket pocket and punched in Gayle's number. "No answer." She sent a text, not expecting a response. "Chase Cooper probably convinced her to ignore her phone."

"Seriously?" Bernie pursed her lips like she tasted something sour. "Gayle's just a kid. What a perv."

"A kid who looks like Carlee Kruger. The salesclerk said Chase's lady friends use the back way in. Come on."

Morgan tried not to skulk like a B-movie spy as she led Bernie past the gallery, down the sidewalk on Main Street, and into an alley paved with bricks. Other than the overflowing trashcans and flattened cardboard boxes sticking out of a Dumpster, it was charming. Morgan scanned the back of the gallery.

"Maybe we should call the police."

"I don't know, Bernie. Gayle went voluntarily. Unless we know for certain she's in trouble—"

The back door of the gallery banged open. Bernie grabbed Morgan's arm and pulled her behind the Dumpster. Lynn hurried to a dented little car covered with flower stickers. Mia jumped into a sports car. The tires squealed as she tore out of the narrow alley. Lynn followed at a much slower pace.

"Gayle wasn't with either one," Bernie whispered. "If she was inside the gallery, one of them would have noticed."

"There was enough time between Gayle going through the fence, and them leaving, that Gayle could have gotten inside without being seen. Especially if Chase snuck her upstairs."

They waited a minute, then Morgan tiptoed toward the scarred wooden door. Mia had been in a hurry, but she was not so rushed that she forgot to pull the door shut. Morgan tugged on the curved metal handle. Then Bernie tried.

"Hopeless. Now what?"

Morgan looked up at the three-story brick building. She knew how she would feel if it was her teenage daughter inside. She would have driven a tank through the front door, if need be, to rescue Sarah from the clutches of a devious older man.

"All that space can't be filled with paintings and art supplies," Bernie said. "I wonder if anyone lives up there."

A third-floor curtain fluttered.

"Was that Gayle?" Morgan asked.

"I couldn't see anyone. Maybe a cat peeked out the window."

Or Gayle had attempted to escape.

"Keep an eye out." Morgan ran her fingers around the cracked and peeling wooden frame of a ground-floor window. The panes, painted dark brown, were loose. Any old caulking had crumbled away long ago. Morgan pressed her palm to the glass and applied pressure.

"What are you doing?" Bernie whispered.

"Trying to find a way in."

Morgan pushed on a different pane. The glass cracked.

"Oops."

"If you're concerned enough about Gayle to risk a breaking and entering charge, wouldn't it be better to call Chief Sharp?"

"He might not get here in time."

"In time for what?" Bernie seemed to consider the options, and grimaced. "Euw. We'd better hurry."

"Is the coast clear?"

"I don't see anyone," Bernie said.

Morgan stooped to pick up a brick, then pulled her arm back. Bernie stopped her.

"Too noisy." Bernie tore the flap off one of the cardboard boxes protruding from the Dumpster. "Wrap this around your hand. It'll muffle the sound, and keep you from getting cut."

Morgan pressed her protected fist through the cracked glass pane. The brittle glass splintered into shards. She dropped the cardboard and groped inside for a latch, hoping there wasn't someone on the other side ready to grab her arm.

"Great," Morgan said. "It won't budge. I think it's painted over."

"Let me try."

Morgan stood guard while Bernie reached through the empty pane, contorting herself to reach the latch. Wood cracked loud enough to wake the dead, or at least draw the neighbors across the alley to their windows. Bernie pulled her hand out, holding a latch sealed shut with brown paint.

"I guess I don't know my own strength." She dropped the latch. "Must be from kneading all that bread dough."

Morgan pushed up on the window. Bernie joined her.

"It's no use. The thing is painted shut."

"Just," Bernie said, "a little." She closed her eyes and pushed. "More."

The wooden window frame shrieked as it rose. Morgan dragged a trash can under the window and climbed on top. The aluminum lid dented with her weight. Bernie offered a steadying hand. Morgan brushed broken glass out of the way and clambered through. The room was dim, lit only by the fading sunlight coming through the broken window.

"I'm in a storage room." Morgan spoke softly, not knowing whether people might be near. "Or maybe a work room."

"I'll never make it through the window," Bernie said. "I'll keep watch out here. I'm calling Rolf."

Morgan put her phone on vibrate and dropped it in her pocket. She inched her way through the room. This was not where Jade painted, but where frames were built and shipping crates assembled. The workshop smelled more of sawdust than oil paints and turpentine.

Light etched the outline of a door. She worked her way past stacks of lumber and a workbench with a vise, saws, and hammers, groping for the door. She turned the knob slowly and opened the door a crack.

The door opened into a narrow hallway. At the end was a steep staircase. To the right were two doors. One bore the single word "office," painted in neat block letters. Next to it was a colorfully painted door with "restroom" in lacey script. To the left was the curtain to the gallery, and a doorway that most likely led to the back door. Morgan tiptoed to the curtain and peeked out. The gallery was quiet, but she heard muffled voices coming from the office. Then shouting.

"—take care of it."

"And this is what happens." Harlan Cooper's voiced boomed off the brick walls. "You didn't take care of anything, as usual. And it's up to me to clean up your mess."

"I can take care of my own business."

"The only business you have is because of me."

Their voices lowered, and the next exchange was too muffled for Morgan to hear. She slipped into the restroom. Two stalls crowded the tiny room. There was barely enough room to stand at the sink. Faded fabric in a pine tree print formed a curtain around the sink. The soap and paper towel dispensers had seen a lot of use. The odor of bleach and the musty smell of mold filled the room. Morgan closed the restroom door. As her eyes adjusted to the cave-like darkness, Morgan could see light from the hallway seeping in around the door. She pressed her ear to the wall shared with the office.

"That family should have been run out of town years ago. And instead of letting security eject her from the premises—my home, need I remind you—you have a little chat with her in my den. The press conference was nearly ruined."

"I'd say that was your doing," Jade said. "You shot a homeless man!"

"I'm a hero," Harlan said, "saving a girl from a madman. I helped your campaign. But it's no good if you blow it by dragging all of your skeletons out of the closet."

"I didn't want to run for City Council in the first place. If Mia finds out—"

"She's known from the start."

There was a pause. Morgan tried to be silent, but her breath came in ragged gasps.

"How could she?" Jade asked. "I didn't know until Wednesday."

"Camille went to her high-school chum first," Harlan said. "Mia's always been a good friend to those in need. Especially when they can help her own cause. Mia had the good sense to bring the girl to me. I gave the distraught young mother-to-be more than enough money to have an abortion. Instead she kept the brat and used the money for a bus ticket out of town."

"Wait. You and Mia both knew I had a daughter?" Jade choked on a sob. "Why didn't you tell me? Everything would have been different."

"Right. You'd have been saddled with a bastard child. You'd never have become an artist, with your own gallery. You'd have been waiting tables or selling used cars, living from hand to mouth."

"I'd have had a daughter."

There was a long pause.

"That's cruel, Jade. You know Mia can't have children."

"That's what she told you and Marlene, to keep you off her back about producing grandchildren for you. I guess that's the one thing daddy's little girl wouldn't do for you. The one and only thing."

The door to the office banged open. Morgan tried to imagine an excuse for why she was in the gallery restroom after hours, but she heard another door slam shut. Had both men left? Or just one? If so, which? Morgan was not certain who she would rather face in this situation. Cooper seemed ruthless enough to kill to protect his political ambitions. But if Carlee found out Jade had an affair with Camille, resulting in her sister's pregnancy, they might have had a fight passionate enough to end in murder.

Morgan tapped out a cell phone message. Her spelling and grammar suffered as her hands shook.

Cooper knew jade is gayle father

Morgan suspected her text didn't make any sense, but Bernie responded quickly.

saw jade leave r u ok

That meant Harlan was still in the office.

hiding in bathroom Cooper is in building seen g?

no and no news – must be upstairs still

Morgan heard banging around in the office, drawers opening and closing. Finally, she heard the office door creak open, and footsteps in the hallway. They headed toward the restroom. Morgan only had seconds to consider hiding under the sink, with its protective curtain, but there was not enough room. Hiding in a stall seemed the best option, but if she latched the door, that would tip off Harlan that someone was inside. She pulled one stall door open wide, then dashed inside the other. She tugged the door closed but didn't latch it, then climbed on top of the toilet seat.

The light flicked on. The brightness after near total dark startled Morgan, and it took a moment for her eyes to adjust. Under the stall divider, she could see Harlan's alligator boots as he paused in front of the mirror. Then he turned to the open stall door. She heard splashing, then flushing, then the door banged open. He didn't wash his hands.

Morgan waited for the sound of the back door. Instead, she heard stairs squeaking. Great. If Chase had Gayle upstairs, how was Morgan going to reach her without alerting Harlan? Maybe it was time to call the police. Morgan had her doubts, though. She had assumed she saw Gayle's blond hair in the window. It just as easily could have been Jade's. Surely, if Jade had seen his daughter with Chase, he would have intervened. She might be on entirely the wrong track.

She clambered off her perch, her legs stiff. She went to the door, pressed her ear to it, trying not to think of all the unwashed hands that had touched it. She pulled her jacket sleeve over her hand to turn the knob. Harlan was still climbing stairs, going up all three stories.

Morgan slipped outside, flinching as the door creaked. Surely he would break up Chase and Gayle, if they were upstairs, and if he caught them doing something other than glasswork. He would not want his son involved with the Kruger family, an underage girl who could ruin the family's political aspirations. Especially a girl who was his son-in-law's illegitimate daughter. Chase was Gayle's uncle. Not blood related, but still, ick. Morgan shuddered at the thought that she might be too late to rescue Gayle.

The creaking stopped. Morgan crept up the first flight of narrow, steep steps. She paused on the second floor, listening. The stairs opened into a windowless room with old furniture, a mini fridge and a microwave. She tiptoed toward the light coming in from the front-facing windows.

Three canvases sat on easels. Paint palettes and brushes cluttered small tables. Jade seemed to have a factory-style production line going. The room smelled strongly of turpentine or some other paint thinner. She only saw one glass jar with brushes soaking, but the fumes were enough to make her dizzy. She struggled to suppress a cough.

Morgan stepped through the other door. The room was furnished with a twin bed covered with a faded comforter, a clothes rack, and a table with a lamp. Maybe Jade hid in the second floor apartment when he needed to escape his troubled life.

Or maybe this was where Chase brought the lady friends that Lynn had mentioned. If so, where was Gayle?

There was one more floor. Unfortunately, Harlan was up there.

Doubts paralyzed Morgan. Bernie was watching the back of the building. Could she have missed Chase and Gayle leaving? No way. But maybe they had exited through the gallery, while Morgan and Bernie were breaking in to the back of the building. Now the entire escapade seemed ridiculous.

Morgan listened for footsteps above her, but heard nothing. She stepped to the staircase. Looked up into the darkness. Dark. Why would Harlan Cooper be in a dark room? Was there another bed on the third floor? Maybe he had a spat with Marlene, and he was in the doghouse. Morgan checked her cell phone. No text messages.

Morgan stepped back into the second floor bedroom and tapped out a message to Bernie.

See anyone leave

no all quiet

Something scraped across the floor above Morgan, making a noise like a chair being dragged across the wood floor. She hovered at the bottom of the stairs. Morgan had nearly convinced herself to leave, when she heard the sounds of a struggle. Then a girl's cry.

Harlan Cooper was the perv.

Chapter Thirty-Six

Morgan punched 9-1-1 on her phone with shaking fingers. When the dispatcher answered, Morgan whispered, "Jade's Aspen Gold Art Gallery," then reached inside her bag for the pepper spray. Holding it in front of her at arm's length, she climbed the stairs, not caring how much noise she made. She pushed open the door at the top of the steps. Noxious fumes washed over her, stinging her eyes and filling her lungs.

The scene was not what she expected. An industrial painter's mask concealed Harlan Cooper's nose and the lower half of his face. Two round filters on either side of his mouth made him look like an alien insect. Cooper struggled to tie a shop rag to Gayle's face as she kicked, sending one open-backed sparkly sneaker flying. Her arms were tied behind her back.

"Let her go!" Morgan yelled.

He did, letting Gayle slump to the gritty wood floor. The teenager huddled in a heap, her orange- and purple-streaked hair fanning across the pink, long-sleeved T-shirt that hung off one shoulder. Morgan took three steps forward, keeping the pepper spray canister aimed at Cooper, her finger on the trigger. Harlan reached behind his back and pulled out a handgun. It didn't look like Del's revolver. Cooper's gun was black and boxy, all hard angles.

"I win," he said, his voice muffled by the respirator mask. "I suppose you have a cell phone. Like that's going to save you. Hand it over."

Morgan did. Her skin crawled as his fingers brushed her palm. He glanced at the phone, then mashed his thumb on the screen to end the call. Harlan tossed it on a spindly-legged table.

"We'll be long gone before the police get here. Hand me that, too."

Morgan gave him the pepper spray. He kicked the door closed, then threw the pepper spray on the table.

"Snooping and spying." Harlan's words were difficult to understand, muffled by the mask. Or maybe the fumes were getting to Morgan. "I've heard around town that you're a real busybody. Guess the rumors are true, for once."

"Let Gayle go. She's just a kid."

Gayle looked up from her seat on the floor. Tears streamed down her cheeks. Morgan felt her own eyes tearing up. The small room reeked of paint thinner. The only window was painted shut, like the one in the workshop. It was a wonder the entire building hadn't ignited.

"Did you hide from that incompetent clerk when she closed shop for the day?" Harlan asked. "I've been wanting to fire that girl for a while now."

"There's no way this will end well for you," Morgan said. "Half the town is looking for Gayle."

"I can imagine a dozen scenarios where I come out on top. The kid is a Kruger, after all. Everyone in Golden Springs knows they're just a bunch of misfits, drunks, and whores."

Gayle attempted yelling something through her gag, but she choked instead. Morgan started to kneel beside her, but Harlan waved her back with his gun.

"Your mother could try running away from her past," he said to Gayle, "but that doesn't change the facts. You're just a mistake. But mistakes can be erased."

"Harlan, no."

Gayle looked from Harlan to Morgan.

"Oh, didn't your mommy tell you?" Harlan asked Gayle. "She was part of a sick love triangle with her sister. Jade Tinsley is your father."

A growl forced past Gayle's gag. She struggled to stand.

"You want this over already?" Harlan aimed the gun at her. "I was hoping to drag things out a little longer."

"The chief will match the bullets to the one in the mountain man's shoulder." Realization hit Morgan, swimming into her fume-clouded brain. "You're the ATVer who shot at Rolf. Gerda's brakes. And mine. You did that. You wanted to kill the mountain man, but you missed. You tried to kill us all."

Morgan hoped his incompetence so far boded well for her and Gayle's survival.

"You're right, Morgan, on all counts. Except I wasn't planning on shooting you, and nobody's going to find you."

Gayle's phone sang a line of a pop song, and Morgan's phone buzzed, vibrating across the antique table. Harlan glanced at them, distracted for an instant. The muzzle of his handgun drooped, aiming at the floor. Morgan grabbed a brass floor lamp and swung it at Harlan's head. The cord ripped from the wall, pulling her off balance. The tattered lampshade grazed Harlan's face, hitting the respirator. He fell into a metal rack, knocking cans and bottles onto the floor.

"Gayle! Run!"

The girl slumped on her side. The room blurred like watercolors running down a rain-soaked painting. Morgan coughed. She needed fresh air, before she passed out. She thrust the lamp at the window. The painted glass cracked, bulging out but not giving way.

Harlan scrambled to his feet, straightening his respirator mask with one hand. He aimed the gun at Morgan, then at Gayle, swinging the black barrel back and forth. Morgan considered making a move when the gun aimed at empty space, but her head was too cloudy.

"Drop it." His voice rasped through the respirator.

Morgan released the lamp. It fell, the incandescent bulb shattering on the wood floor. Harlan reached for Gayle, dragging the unconscious girl across the room. He waved the gun at Morgan.

"Come on."

Morgan followed. He threw open the door. Fresh air. Morgan tried to draw a deep breath, but coughed instead, her lungs attempting to expel the chemical fumes. She fell to her hands and knees, her head spinning and her stomach roiling.

"Get up. Hurry!"

Halfway down the stairs, Harlan yanked off his respirator mask and tossed it aside. As they reached the bottom floor, Morgan heard pounding on the back door. Harlan waved the gun at her.

"You say one word, and I'll shoot you both," he whispered.

Morgan might have pointed out that whoever was at the door would call the police if they heard shots, but Harlan had a mad dog look in his turquoise-colored eyes. He was past reasoning.

Harlan turned the deadbolt and jerked the door open a crack. Morgan could only imagine what his jowly face looked like, pale and sweating, peering through the gap.

"What do you want?"

Bernie's voice stammered. "I—I was looking for—There's a kid. A runaway. I heard she might be at the gallery."

"You heard wrong."

Harlan slammed the door. Bernie's fist hammered on the thick wood.

"Hey! Open the door!"

Harlan ignored her, dragging Gayle into the workshop. Morgan froze, torn between staying with Gayle or escaping. Then she remembered that she didn't need the door. She and Bernie had broken the workshop window. She could overpower Harlan, take his gun away, and crawl out the window.

Just like an action-adventure movie heroine. One a couple of decades younger than Morgan, and in great physical condition. Morgan shuddered. The chemical fumes must have caused brain damage if she dreamed her escape scenario would work. Her pounding heart sent throbbing waves of pain through her head. She drew rapid shallow breaths. Each exhalation felt like fish-hooks being dragged through her lungs.

Calm down, Morgan told herself. *Stall for time.*

Help was on the way. Had to be. If Bernie realized what was happening. Morgan drew a breath, preparing to shout, hoping Bernie was listening at the window. She choked on a cough instead, doubling over, tears running from her eyes.

"Knock it off." Harlan's voice was a husky whisper.

From far away she heard Bernie's muffled voice.

"Morgan? Are you in there?"

Pain sliced through her head. Morgan watched, helpless, as the floor rose to meet her. White sparks engulfed her tear-blurred vision just before everything went dark.

Morgan felt sick, but she feared the gag in her mouth would make throwing up fatal. She swallowed several times. That only made it worse. The cloth tasted bitter, the chemical taste burning her tongue. Morgan struggled to bring her hands up to remove the gag, but her arms were tied behind her back. Consciousness made her aware of her cramped position, and the pain in every joint from being curled into a tight ball.

She tried to orient herself. From the intense fumes, Morgan guessed she was back in the upstairs storage room. Then the floor seemed to drop out from under her, and she was falling, momentarily weightless, until she landed. Her face scraped across the floor. But instead of gritty, hundred-year-old pine, this smelled like fresh sawdust.

The workshop. Shipping crates. She was inside a wooden box. Like a pine casket, only she wasn't dead. Not yet.

Morgan bounced again, landing hard. Then again. She heard an engine. She was in a vehicle. On a rough road. Her head banged against the wood. She tried to tuck her head in, envisioning a turtle, but it was no use.

She floated in and out of semi-consciousness until the bone-rattling motion stopped. An engine shut off. A vehicle door slammed. Footsteps crunched across gravel. Then her container moved, screeching across a metal surface.

Morgan felt weightless for an instant, then the container slammed hard to the ground. Her teeth snapped on the smelly rag, and with it, part of her inner cheek and tongue. The gag muffled her cry of pain. Then she was moving again, and she heard grunting and gasping from whoever dragged her container.

She tumbled, slamming from one side of her prison to the other until she stopped, upside down. Her neck felt like it would snap. Morgan tried throwing her weight the opposite direction, but her cage wouldn't budge. She heard another crate tumble down the slope next to her.

Morgan struggled to breathe, then not to breathe, as inhaling only drew burning fumes up her nostrils and deep into her lungs. She inched her way into an upright position, taking the weight of her body off her neck and shoulders. Cold seeped into the crate. And silence.

Morgan kicked her bound feet, thumping the inside of the crate. Somewhere near, there was a thump in response. Gayle was alive. Morgan uncurled as far as the confining crate allowed, stretching and pushing against the wood. A nail shrieked as it wrenched out of the crate. A thin line of pale moonlit sky shone through the crack. Morgan gathered her strength, then pushed again.

She kicked the crate, bucked and slammed into the sides. Morgan was past fear and well into rage. Harlan Cooper was insane. How could he imagine the people of Golden Springs wouldn't put things together? Dozens of people were already searching for Gayle. Morgan had called 9-1-1. Bernie had undoubtedly called the police, too. She would have seen Harlan leave the shop with the crates. In moments, the police would arrive and arrest him. With a sinking feeling, Morgan realized help would come to the gallery. Unless Bernie had followed them, no one knew where she and Gayle were now.

Footsteps crunched across the dirt. They dropped onto the ground near her crate. Morgan lay still.

Let him think you're dead, she told herself.

The steps moved away. She heard what sounded like a shovel scooping into the dirt, then dirt pelting the crate, sounding like hail on a metal roof. Probably covering up his tracks. The truck engine started. The sound disappeared into the night. Morgan allowed herself a moment to sob in despair.

Pull yourself together.

Crying wouldn't get her out of the pine box she'd been buried in. She tried to work the zip ties off her wrists and ankles, but the plastic only dug into her flesh. Morgan renewed her previous strategy, kicking and pushing until her feet were numb and her head ringing from banging against the wood. Finally, the side of the crate broke loose.

Dirt poured inside. In the darkness, she could only feel and hear the endless shushing of dirt. No one could hear her gag-muffled screams, but that didn't stop them from coming. The dirt stopped.

Morgan pressed her back against the crate, scared that any movement might send the dirt cascading inside again, burying her alive. Maybe she should stay still and wait for help to come. But one of the scenarios playing through her imagination left her and Gayle trapped in the crates, under the dirt, for days. Weeks. Forever.

She stretched her bound feet out, pushing against the crate. A shower of dirt rained down for a moment, then the moonlight shone though the crack again. Morgan choked on a sob of joy. She renewed her struggle, kicking and pushing, working her way toward the widening crack until her head emerged, then her shoulders.

Morgan threw all her weight against the crate wall, forcing it to open wide enough to worm her way out. A nail ripped the sleeve of her fleece jacket as she thrust her way through. She flopped onto the ground, then rolled onto her back. She was in a pit. Cooper had shoved dirt over one side. The crates weren't buried so much as hidden from the casual passerby.

Morgan backed up to her former prison and raked the zip ties on her wrists across a nail. She poked and scratched herself before the plastic finally snapped. Then she ripped the gag off her mouth, inhaling deep cold breaths of night air until she was dizzy from hyperventilating. Morgan reached into her front jeans pocket and pulled out her keychain. On it dangled a tiny pink pocketknife, a flashlight suitable for finding a keyhole, and several keys. She cut off the zip ties around her ankles.

Exhausted, but still riding the adrenaline that had kept her alive so far, she scrambled over the hill of fresh dirt, feeling for Gayle's crate. She shone the flashlight across the mound, but it offered little in the way of illumination. Then the feeble light glinted off the head of a nail. Morgan dropped her keychain into her jacket pocket and dug with her hands. The tattered bandage on her left hand tore off. Dirt stung her old wound, and the fresh scratches from the nails.

"Gayle, are you okay? Make some noise!"

When she had cleared away enough dirt, Morgan looked around for something to pry the crate open. A foot-long piece of rebar was too thick to fit into the narrow gap between boards. She found a stake, but the weathered wood snapped off when she tried to use it as a lever. Groping in the dark pit for anything reflecting moonlight, her fingers hit metal. The business end of a shovel, with the handle snapped off. Only a jagged bit of wood protruded from the blade.

Morgan pushed the shovel blade in the narrow crack between crate walls. After a few attempts, the end of the crate wrenched off. Morgan landed on her backside in the dirt. She rose to her feet and stumbled to the crate.

"Gayle?"

Fumes rolled out of Gayle's crate, choking Morgan. The girl had received a stronger dose of paint thinner than Morgan. She pressed the protruding nails over carefully with her sneaker before dragging Gayle out of the crate. Then she sawed at the zip ties binding Gayle's hands with her little knife. The blade had already dulled with abuse. When the plastic broke apart, Gayle's arms flopped to her sides. She didn't reach up to tear her gag off, and when Morgan tugged it away from her mouth, she didn't draw in gasping breaths of night air. Morgan brushed long golden hair away from Gayle's face.

"Gayle, you can breathe now." Morgan cradled the teen in her arms. "Please breathe!"

Chapter Thirty-Seven

The moon cast dim blue light into the pit. Morgan couldn't hear whether Gayle was breathing over her own ragged breaths and pounding heart. No phone. No help. Panic threatened to overwhelm Morgan, until she focused on the steps she'd learned in CPR class.

She rolled Gayle onto her back, then watched the teenager's chest for any rise and fall indicating breathing. There was no movement. In her current state of panic, would she notice something as subtle as respiration? She thumped Gayle's shoulder.

"Gayle, can you hear me? It's Morgan. I'm going to start CPR."

She tilted Gayle's head back to open her air passages. Suddenly the girl broke away from her, rolling on her side to cough.

"Thank God!" Tears of relief blurred Morgan's vision.

Gayle rose to her hands and knees, coughing, choking, and gagging. Morgan knew the pain she felt as the fresh, chilly night air worked its way into her poisoned lungs. At last, Gayle sat in the dirt, her legs splayed in front of her and her hands pressed into the dirt behind her. She closed her eyes and seemed to concentrate on drawing shallow, rapid breaths.

Gayle spoke slowly, as though each word took an effort to find, then push past her lips. "Where are we?"

"Good question," Morgan said. "Sit tight. I'm not going anywhere. I just want to see if I can tell where we are."

She crawled on top of a crate, sending avalanches of dirt into the pit. As she scrambled for ground level, her lungs felt raw with every gasping breath. Finally she stood, turning in a circle, and saw a moonlit field and stands of aspen and pine.

"I see lights. Maybe a ranch house. It doesn't look too far."

"Why did he do this to us?" Gayle whimpered in a raspy voice. "I don't understand."

"I don't either, Gayle. But we have to get out of here. He could come back. Do you think you can climb up here with me?"

Gayle shook her head, her golden hair appearing blue in the moonlight. "I can't." Stuttering sobs hiccupped from her, in between rattling coughs.

"We have to," Morgan said. "We don't have a phone, and Cooper could come back."

Morgan climbed back into the pit and helped Gayle to her feet. She had lost one shoe kicking at Cooper in the gallery. The other one was gone now, too. Morgan prodded the teen up the unstable mound of dirt. The girl's bare feet dug into the soil. When they reached the top, and she and Gayle both stopped wheezing, Morgan spoke.

"I think we're on the Dalton ranch."

The irrigated field in the distance, the barbed wire fence lined with pines and aspens, could have been any foothills pasture. A prospector's pit in the middle of a cow pasture had to be unique. Vernon had found one on his place, at the same time the ATVers shot at Rolf.

"Let's head toward that light." Morgan pointed. "That must be the Daltons' house."

Gayle shivered. Her long-sleeved, pink shirt had barely been adequate earlier in the day, when it was much warmer. Now she was barefoot, too, and her blue jeans weren't much thicker than pantyhose. Del would have an opinion about the survival capability of modern fashions.

"Here."

Morgan peeled out of her fleece jacket and handed it to Gayle. Her sweatshirt was warm enough, and she had socks and shoes. The teenager pulled on the jacket, zipping the front and shoving her clenched fists into the pockets.

The tiny pink knife, dull now, and the feeble light of a flashlight not intended to illuminate a distance farther than a few inches were Morgan's only survival resources. She had lost her purse during the fight at the gallery. Anything helpful, like a real flashlight or waterproof matches, were in her purse or her car's trunk.

"I want to go home!" Gayle burst into rasping sobs.

Morgan yanked the reluctant girl into a hug, more to warm her than to give comfort. At first Gayle tensed. Then she went boneless, soaking Morgan's shoulder with tears.

"Come on," Morgan said. "We need to get going."

They stumbled across the uneven, pathless field. The Dalton cattle had surely beaten a regular route to their watering trough and hayracks by the barn, but Morgan couldn't detect one in the dark. She swept her flashlight back and forth. It offered little help. Gayle yelped and fell to her knees. Morgan gave her a hand up.

"I stepped on something. My foot hurts."

"Gayle," Morgan said, trying to distract the girl. "Why did you go to the gallery today?"

"Chase texted me. He was going to teach me more about glasswork."

"Oh. A text message."

"Why?"

"I didn't think you'd go there to see Chase's father. I didn't see Chase anywhere in the building, and I was all over the place."

"That creepy old guy answered the back door." Fresh tears

flowed. Gayle wiped them away with a fist. "Why would Chase want me to go to the gallery if he wasn't there?"

"Think about it, Gayle. He sent a text message."

"But it was from Chase's phone." Understanding flashed across Gayle's face. "Oh. The old guy could have taken Chase's phone, just like he took ours." She stopped. "But where is Chase? Do you think he's okay? Maybe he's in that pit."

Gayle turned as though she was ready to head back to the prospector's pit.

"I'm sure he's okay. He probably doesn't even realize his phone is gone. You know how artists are when they're creating."

"You think so?" Gayle asked.

"Absolutely."

Gayle studied Morgan. The teen seemed to buy her story. Morgan had her doubts about Chase, and his role in their kidnapping. Now was not the time to share that with Gayle. She had enough trouble without throwing betrayal into her emotional stew.

Morgan handed Gayle the keychain. "Squeeze here to make it light up." She hoped giving the teenager something to do would keep her moving.

They stumbled across the pasture in silence for a few minutes, until Gayle stopped and crouched down.

"Something's out there," she whispered.

Morgan strained to see. A shape moved along the fence line. She tugged Gayle behind the spindly branches of a bush that had yet to leaf out. The form was too bulky to be Harlan Cooper, but traveling too fast for a drowsy grazing heifer.

"What is it?" Gayle asked.

"I'm not sure." Morgan put a protective arm around the teen, and this time the girl didn't flinch away. "I can't make out anything in—"

"Heeaaawwwwww!" A familiar braying shattered the quiet

pasture. "Hee aaww hee aw hee aw!"

Gayle screamed, and clutched Morgan so tightly, she couldn't breathe. She pried the girl's arms loose.

"It's my donkey," Morgan said. "We must be close to the rock shop."

She thrashed through branches and ran toward Houdini.

"What are you doing out here?"

Morgan grasped the donkey's halter like it was a lifeline. Gayle ran to join her, wrapping her arms around Houdini's neck even though they hadn't yet been introduced.

"Warm," Gayle muttered.

"Houdini has been sneaking over to the Dalton ranch on an almost daily basis. I thought we'd patched every escape route, but I'm glad we didn't."

"Will he take us home?" Gayle asked. "Can I ride him?"

"He pulls a wagon. I don't think anyone has ever tried to ride him." Morgan glanced at Gayle, shivering with cold and shock, her breath still coming in asthmatic wheezes. "Let's try."

Morgan kept her grip on the nylon web halter while giving Gayle a leg up. Houdini seemed startled, his big ears aiming back toward the strange human. Morgan stroked his neck, hoping to soothe away his instinctive aversion to allowing a predator to remain on his back.

"Gayle needs your help. She needs a ride to the rock shop. Can you take us home?"

She tugged on the halter and aimed in the direction of the light. Houdini took a step, then another. Gayle couldn't have weighed more than a hundred pounds, but the donkey trudged along as though she weighed a thousand. Then he stopped. Morgan pulled and Gayle nudged gently with her heels, but he refused to budge.

"Look!" Gayle pointed.

Tall grass rippled as a creature zigzagged toward them.

Houdini didn't seem alarmed, so Morgan guessed it wasn't a coyote. Dog burst out of the grass. His tongue hung out one side of his grinning mouth. He careened into Morgan's legs, nearly knocking her down. As she rubbed his head, his tail wagged so hard his back feet nearly went airborne.

"Here, boy," a male voice called, then a whistle pierced the air.

Morgan saw the glow of a flashlight, the white arc sweeping back and forth, and behind it, the silhouette of a sturdy man wearing a fedora.

"Kurt!" Morgan yelled. "Over here!"

Kurt broke into a run, slashing a noisy path through the grass. He threw his arms around Morgan, pulling her into a bear hug. For the first time in hours, she felt safe.

"Hi, Mr. Willard." Gayle's voice was as raspy as an old smoker's.

"Are you ladies okay?" Kurt shrugged out of his trench coat and held it out to Morgan. "You must be freezing."

"Gayle needs it more than me. Cooper nearly succeeded in poisoning her."

Kurt helped Gayle pull on the coat that was several sizes too large. Houdini grunted once or twice, but remained still as Gayle hugged the coat around herself. Dog danced in circles around them.

"Cooper tried to kill us both," Morgan said.

"And bury us alive," Gayle said.

"He tried to suffocate us with paint thinner." The story still had gaps in it, but Morgan knew one thing for certain. "I'll bet that's how he killed Carlee. You can still smell it."

She held out her sweatshirt sleeve for Kurt to sniff. He wrinkled his nose.

"Phew. Which Cooper was it?" Kurt asked. "Most of the family was on your suspect list."

"The old one," Gayle said. "Chase's dad. Do you have a phone?" Gayle's words trembled past her lips. "I need to call my mom."

"In the inside pocket of my coat."

Gayle wrestled around in the brown leather coat until she found the correct pocket. The phone emitted soft beeps as she rapid-fired a number.

"Hi, Mom?"

While Gayle stumbled through a tearful conversation with Camille, Morgan and Kurt led Houdini. Dog ran ahead, then returned, then ran ahead again, urging them to move faster. Morgan could see the outline of the low building now. The lights came from the rock shop, not the Dalton ranch.

"How did you find us?" Morgan asked.

"Half of Golden Springs was already searching for Gayle. Del asked me to pick him up so he could help search for the three of you, and I wasn't getting anywhere in town."

"Wait. I might be foggy from the fumes, but did you say three?"

"Bernie is missing."

The stars spun in the blue-black sky, and for a moment Morgan thought she would pass out. Bernie had been beating her fist on the back door of the gallery. Cooper wouldn't have let her walk away. And Bernie wouldn't have left a friend behind.

"That's why Cooper left," she said. "He had to bring Bernie here. Bury her with us."

"Where did Cooper take you?" Kurt asked.

"A prospector's pit. We should go back. Everyone's searching in town. If he's got Bernie, and she's alive—" Morgan choked on the last word.

"If Cooper went back to Golden Springs, the police might already have him in custody."

"If Bernie called them before Cooper got her." Morgan tugged on Gayle's sleeve. "You can call your mother from the rock shop. We're almost there."

Gayle reluctantly ended her call and handed the phone to Kurt. He punched in a number while they continued walking.

"Del, can you meet us at the road?" He paused while Del answered. "I found two of them." Another pause. "I'll call Sharp." A final pause, then, "No, the ATV makes too much noise. You'll see my flashlight."

Morgan tried to soothe Gayle while they travelled the last few yards across the pasture. She realized that for all the girl's whining earlier, Gayle had been holding herself together. Now that they were so close to safety, she teetered on the edge of hysterics, slipping into the shock people experience after a near-death experience. Houdini increased his pace. Whether he was aware of Gayle's trauma or just anxious to get back to the barn didn't matter.

Del met them at the fence. While Morgan and Kurt held the barbed wire strands apart, Del climbed through.

"Let's not waste any time." He grasped Houdini's halter with his left hand and turned him parallel to the fence.

"Where are we going?" Gayle pointed across the road. "The lights are over there."

"Houdini can't climb through the fence," Del said. "The gate is up the road just a bit."

Gayle's lips quivered and tears filled her eyes.

"Unless you want to walk," Morgan said.

Gayle shook her head and grasped Houdini's mane, standing up stiff as a bristle brush. Del headed up the fence line with the donkey and girl in tow, walking with more energy than seemed possible for the old cowboy. Morgan started to follow, but Kurt held her hand.

"Deputy Parker answered my call. He and the chief are in the middle of another case."

"What could be more urgent than this?"

"Suicide attempt," Kurt whispered. "Marlene Cooper swallowed a bottle of pills."

"Maybe Harlan Cooper tried to kill his wife," Morgan said.

"The fact is, we might be on our own for a little longer. The Granite Junction police are on the way to assist, but it's a long trip up the pass."

"Meanwhile Cooper might be headed to that pit with Bernie, and he's going to see Gayle and I are gone."

"Can you tell me how to find it?" Kurt asked.

"Hey," Del yelled. "Are you coming or not?"

"I can't explain how to get there," Morgan told Kurt. "But I think I could backtrack to it."

"Just tell me what direction," Kurt said.

Morgan shook her head. "I have to go."

CHAPTER THIRTY-EIGHT

When they explained the situation to Del, he grabbed Kurt's elbow and led him several paces away from Gayle and Houdini. Morgan followed, keeping her eyes on the girl. Gayle's legs hung over the donkey's round sides. Houdini lowered his head and snatched a mouthful of grass.

"You'd better take this." Del reached inside his jacket and pulled out his revolver.

"You might need it." Kurt kept his voice low enough that Gayle wouldn't hear. "We don't know where Cooper is."

"I have the attack donkey." Del pushed the gun at Kurt. "Take it."

Kurt raised his hands and took a step back. "How are you going to defend Gayle if you run into Cooper between here and there?"

It wasn't far to the rock shop as the magpie flies, but Del had to walk the donkey to the Daltons' gate, and then back down Hill Street.

"All right then." Del replaced the gun in his shoulder holster. "At least take this." He handed Morgan his heavy flashlight. "There's enough moonlight to get us to the shop. Guess I'd better hurry."

Morgan was afraid Gayle would be reluctant to leave with a stranger. The teen seemed more concerned about reaching the wood-burning stove and the promise of hot cocoa.

Dog seemed torn between following the donkey or Morgan

and Kurt. He ran back and forth between them as they parted ways, then settled on staying close to Morgan.

A wide swath had been trampled from the fence through the grass to the spot where Houdini, Dog, and Kurt had found Morgan and Gayle. A narrower path led them across the field, becoming harder to follow as the grass thinned. No wonder Vernon Dalton hadn't noticed the prospector's illegal pit on his property. He had little reason to spend time in this sparsely vegetated area of the ranch. His cattle no doubt preferred the more lush irrigated pastures.

As they backtracked to the prospecting pit, Morgan had more time than she wanted to consider what they might find. The options for Bernie's condition if she was in the pit were too horrifying to dwell on, so Morgan fretted about not finding her, and having wasted half the night in a fruitless search while Cooper escaped. Or wandering around in the chilly dark night while everyone in town celebrated his capture and Bernie's safe return. Anything to keep herself from imagining her friend in that dark pit, alone.

"He's here."

Kurt clicked off his flashlight and crouched behind a cinquefoil bush. Morgan clicked her flashlight off, too. She huddled beside Kurt while Dog squirmed at her side. She saw red taillights at the bottom of the low hill.

"Is that a crate in the back of his truck?" she whispered.

A head appeared above the edge of the pit. Even at a distance, Morgan could hear Cooper's curses.

"He knows you're gone."

"We've got to get Bernie," Morgan said. "She's in that crate."

Morgan started to stand, but Kurt pulled her down.

"We can't just go charging down there," he said. "Cooper has a gun, and he's quick to use it."

Morgan thought of Del's offer, and wished Kurt had taken

him up on it. But Del needed to protect a girl who wasn't in any shape to defend herself.

"We can circle around the fence line," Morgan said. "That will take us right in front of his truck. He won't see us."

"I want you to stay here."

"I can't hide and watch," Morgan said. "I have to do something."

Kurt reached for her hand. "You can go back to lead the police here."

That was the logical thing to do. Kurt squeezed her hand, then leaned close and gave her a brief kiss on the cheek. Morgan hugged him, holding on for a moment.

"Be careful," she whispered.

Morgan crouched low and watched the scene at the bottom of the hill, knowing her view would end when she headed across the pasture. Dog followed, his seemingly boundless energy winding down to trot protectively by her side.

Cooper cursed and kicked the crate, then shoved it to the edge of the truck's tailgate. He climbed down and tugged. Cursed some more. While he wrestled with the crate, Morgan could see Kurt creeping along the fence line.

She reminded herself that she would be more help showing the police where to find Bernie and Cooper than attempting to confront an armed homicidal man. Morgan jogged along the twice-trampled trail until she tripped and nearly fell. Her feet slowed, but her heart continued to race. Her lungs felt as though they were not pulling in any oxygen from the night air. After she dropped below the ridgeline, she turned her flashlight on. Dog trotted ahead, confident of the route. She followed.

Across the field, a light swept back and forth. A flashlight. Sure the Granite Junction police had arrived, Morgan waved Del's flashlight. The person broke into a run. Morgan turned and ran back toward the pit, Dog at her heels.

Her legs felt like they were moving in slow motion. She scrambled down the hill toward the pit. The crate lay in a broken heap behind the truck's tailgate. Bernie and Kurt stood together, their hands raised in surrender. Cooper aimed his gun at them.

"The police are coming!" Morgan attempted to yell, but her voice came out a hoarse croak.

Even if Cooper hadn't heard her words, he must have seen her. The gun aimed in her direction as she ran down the hill. Kurt made a move, but Cooper swung back toward him. Morgan waved her arms above her head, hoping to draw his fire. Maybe he would miss at this distance, and Kurt could get the gun away from him. At the very least, the police officer behind her would realize what was happening. Then it occurred to Morgan that she should have warned the police about Cooper's gun. She spun around, ready to run up the hill.

Am I that oxygen-deprived?

Stars danced in front of her eyes. Morgan wasn't sure whether they were the ones in the night sky, or ones formed inside her own head. She heard the sound of a gunshot at the same moment that she sat on the ground hard. A puff of dust exploded from the dirt beside Morgan as the bullet hit the hill instead of her.

A hand clamped around her bicep. Morgan yelped as someone jerked her to her feet. Dog growled, the short fur on his neck and shoulders rising in a primitive threat.

"Call your dog off," Chase Cooper said.

Morgan gasped. "What are you doing here?"

He didn't answer her. "Dad! What's the situation?"

Harlan Cooper's voice echoed up the hill. "About time you got here. I need a hand."

Chase gripped Morgan's arm and steered her down the hill. In his other hand he held a gun. She struggled to keep her feet under her. Dog slunk along at her side, the fur on his neck bristling. When they reached the truck, Chase pushed her toward Kurt and Bernie.

"Huh," Bernie said. "And here we had Chase pegged as a mere pervert. Turns out you're a murderer, too. Like father, like son."

"You aren't going to get away with this," Kurt said.

Cooper snorted. "This isn't the movies, reporter boy. No one's looking for you out here. They're all busy fighting a fire. Right, son?"

The fumes in the gallery's third floor storage room had overwhelmed Morgan. She had wondered then about the fire hazard. The fumes had been recent and deliberate.

"Vernon Dalton knows where this pit is," Morgan said, her voice raspy. "He'll think of it when news about all of us going missing reaches him, and he'll lead the police straight here."

"You won't be here. Now that my boy is here to help, we'll move you to a place too remote to be found until you're nothing but bones."

"Just like Carlee," Morgan said. "You killed her."

Chase took a step closer to his father. Morgan tried to read his expression, but between the moonlight and the burn scar on the right side of his face, she couldn't guess what he was thinking.

"Or were you covering up for Chase?" Morgan asked. "Of course. You pinned your political hopes on your son first, but when he put himself out of the running by committing murder, you turned to your son-in-law."

"Wow, that's twisted," Bernie said. "But you can't get away with killing the three of us. Not after shooting the mountain man in front of witnesses."

If Chase seemed emotionless, the talk was having an effect on Harlan. He pressed the back of his free hand to his forehead, wiping away sweat.

"Shut up!" Harlan yelled. "We're heading to the rock shop. Everyone knows Delano Addison is armed, and he's a hotheaded geezer. It's entirely believable that he'd accidentally shoot you thinking you're home intruders."

"All three?" Chase asked. "I doubt he could get off three good shots with his bum arm." He glanced at Bernie. "And no one would believe the baker committed mass murder."

Was Chase trying to convince his father to end his spree of kidnapping and violence, or was he trying to come up with a better plan? Morgan couldn't decide.

"Gee, thanks," Bernie said. "I'd like to think I'm incapable of being the monsters you two obviously are."

"That's the kind of sass I'd expect from you," Harlan said. "But the townsfolk all believe you're such a sweet girl. Chase's right. They'd never buy it. Morgan, now, she's an outsider. From a city. Maybe you snapped under the pressure of trying to keep your family's ratty rock shop open." He shook his head. "Not the snapping kind. The newspaperman? Also an outsider, and kind of an oddball. But the choice is obvious. It has to be a Kruger. That family's so messed up, it wouldn't be a stretch to believe one of them had it in her to slaughter a roomful of people."

"Gayle?" Morgan asked. "No matter how carefully you try to arrange the crime scene, no one will believe that. The police will figure it out. You're not as smart as you think. I know you're responsible for the pit behind us. You dug it looking for ammolite. You're the one trying to buy the Dalton place. Letting their cattle loose, knowing that if any of their herd was killed, it would be financially devastating. Trying to force them out."

"You two were on the ATVs," Bernie said. "You tried to kill my boyfriend!"

Cooper smiled. "You girls are brighter than I thought."

He seemed ready to tell all, so Morgan kept throwing out her hunches.

"You gave Carlee that ammolite necklace," Morgan said.

"Necklace?" Harlan glanced at Chase.

Morgan hoped they were going to spill the solution, the final details of Carlee's death, when Harlan spoke again.

"If Golden Springs wasn't full of busybodies, it wouldn't have come to this. That bunch of old biddies thinking Gerda and Camille needed some kind of a reunion." Harlan snorted. "None of this would be happening right now if they'd left well enough alone." He waved his gun at Morgan. "And you, playing amateur detective. Getting your friends killed."

"No one's dead yet," Kurt said. "We can end this without violence."

"Naw," Harlan drawled. "Hey, I like this scenario better. Try this one on for size. The Kruger brat gets shot breaking into the rock shop, and old Del kills himself when he realizes what he's done. The three of you disappear, never to be seen again."

"Kurt's right about one thing, Dad," Chase said. "No one's dead yet. By the time we take care of these three, and get back to the rock shop to finish the job, the police could already be there."

"They'll be too busy with that fire. It should be going pretty good by now, right?" Cooper waited for a reply, then turned to look at his son. "You did torch the place, like I told you to?"

"Dad, I don't see a way out of this. I've lived with knowing what you did to the Kruger family long enough."

"I didn't kill that girl."

"You told me it was an accident." Chase's voice trembled. "That Carlee fell. No one would believe you, and you'd go to prison. I was just a kid. I had to believe my father. Keep my mouth shut." He wiped his sleeve across his face. "I kept quiet for sixteen years. It's time now. Time to get the whole story out in the open. The truth. Quit hiding behind secrets." Chase held out his hand. "Give me your gun, Dad."

Harlan clutched his gun tighter.

"You've been whining about me playing favorites since you could talk," Harlan said. "Your sister was always more of a man than you. She didn't ever shrink back from doing what needed to be done."

"Are you saying Mia killed Carlee?" Kurt asked.

"Naw," Harlan said, "nothing of the sort. She only made the phone call telling Carlee that I knew where Camille ran away to. Said I could give her the address, if she'd meet up with me. And Carlee came, even after her sister had betrayed her. See what forgiveness gets you?"

"But Dad, why? I don't understand. What did Carlee ever do to you to deserve—" Chase shook his head. "No."

"Face it, son, you've got no potential. Jade, now, he could go all the way to the White House. Jade needed my help to escape those Kruger girls. See how well he's done with Mia? It's all been worth it, and everything was right on schedule. I can depend on my daughter, unlike her pansy-ass brother. Can't even commit a simple little arson for his old man."

Chase pushed words past his clenched jaw. "All these years I hoped your story was true, but you lied to me." His face twisted in anguish. "You did murder Carlee. So you could give Jade to Mia, like you gave her everything else she ever asked for. Is Jade the son you always wanted? The one who'll obey your commands? Live his life for you, instead of himself?" Chase pointed his gun at his father.

"Chase," Kurt said. "Don't."

But he ignored Kurt, his attention focused on his father with a white hot rage. Dog looked from one person to the next, like a spectator at a tennis match, then focused on Morgan, as though waiting for a signal. She didn't dare make a move.

Harlan kept his gun pointed in her direction, encompassing Morgan, Bernie, and Kurt as his potential targets.

"Drop your gun," Harlan said, "or I kill them."

Chase hesitated, then lowered his arm. "Okay, Dad. Slow and easy. See, I'm doing what you want."

Cooper watched his son. "Too little, too—"

Kurt lunged forward, tackling Harlan.

"Go, Dog!" Morgan yelled.

She grabbed Bernie's arm and pulled her down the soft mound of dirt inside the pit. They dropped onto their stomachs and peeked above the edge.

Kurt and Harlan wrestled while Dog pranced around them, nipping and growling. Chase grabbed his gun and aimed at the men, his shoulders dipping first to the left, then the right, as he seemed to wait for a clear target. Another shot went off, this one muffled. The wrestling stopped abruptly.

Kurt heaved Harlan off him. Blood stained the front of his shirt. Harlan lay face down, motionless.

"You shot him." Chase staggered back a step, his gun shaking. "He's dead."

"I didn't mean for—" Kurt began. "Chase, give me the gun."

"I didn't finish." Chase choked on a sob. "Didn't finish what he told me—"

Chase swung around wildly. He lifted his arm, aimed at the stars, and fired three shots. Then he let the gun slip from his hand and drop to the ground. Kurt picked it up. Morgan and Bernie crawled out of the pit.

Chase dropped to his knees beside his father, his shoulders shaking with silent, dry sobs. He rolled Harlan onto his back. Morgan knelt beside Chase. Harlan's turquoise eyes stared at the night sky, empty of life. Blood oozed out the hole left in his chest by one of his own hollow-point bullets. He was beyond the aid of CPR.

Kurt seemed to be the only one not in shock. His voice was calm as he called Deputy Parker, and then was transferred to the Granite Junction police, who were already at the rock shop. They had heard the gunfire and were racing across the pasture. Vernon Dalton appeared on his yellow palomino, his rifle glinting in the moonlight, as he guided the police to the pit. Questions flew. Answers stuttered past lips frozen with the chill night air and shock.

Through it all, Kurt remained unnaturally calm. Morgan wondered if his training as a reporter gave him that poise in the face of trauma. When he finally helped her off the truck's tailgate and led her to a police SUV for the ride back to Golden Springs, she wrapped her arms around him and gave him a quick hug. He felt as cold as a stone.

Chapter Thirty-Nine

The rest of the night and well into the next day, events blurred together. Questions, the ambulance to Granite Junction, more questions, and finally sleep, aided by something the nurse gave her. The greatest fear the doctors had, she learned later from Beatrice, was that she or Gayle would suffer brain damage from breathing the paint-thinner fumes. Although their exposure had been intense, it had also been brief.

Kurt called while she was asleep. He left a message that he would try his best to visit her later, but he would definitely be in Sunday to give her a ride home. His voice sounded mechanical, but Morgan told herself everyone sounded funny in voice mail. The next morning, she eagerly anticipated Kurt's arrival, surprised at how much she wanted to see him. But a stream of visitors arrived before she had any sign of him. First Bernie, Rolf, and Stacie. The baker had some cuts and bruises that had been bandaged up in the emergency room early that morning. The three of them clung to each other as though afraid of ever being parted.

Then the church ladies came with a bouquet of spring flowers containing no elephant heads, and get-well-soon cards with dozens of signatures. Teruko tucked a bear with angel wings into Morgan's arms. The nurse scooted them out for another check of Morgan's vital signs. Gerda and Camille entered her room next.

"I will never be able to repay you for what you have done for my family," Gerda said in her terse German accent. Her voice faltered slightly as she continued. "You saved my granddaughter. My words cannot express what I feel."

Camille wrapped an arm around Gerda's sturdy shoulders. "It's okay, Mom. Morgan knows what you mean." Tears spilled down Camille's cheeks. She pulled a tissue from the box beside Morgan's bed and mopped them up. "When I think of what that man put our family through—Maybe it's wrong of me, but I'm glad Kurt killed him."

"Kurt didn't mean for that to happen." Morgan reached for the woman's hand. "The gun went off while they were fighting."

"Harlan Cooper would have murdered five people before the night was over if Kurt had not stopped him," Gerda said. "He might have gotten away with it, too."

"He wanted me to get rid of my baby. And sixteen years later, he tries to kill her again." Camille started to say more, but she broke into sobs. Gerda wrapped her in a fierce hug.

"Gayle tells us she would not have survived without your help," Gerda said, the stiffness returning to her words. "Kurt Willard pulled the trigger and rid us of that monster, but that would mean little if I had lost another family member to a Cooper."

That fact remained to be processed. Maybe if Cooper had been a stranger, his death wouldn't have weighed on Morgan. She had spent a day at his home. She knew his name, his family, his connection to the community. How would Chase deal with the loss of his father? Mia would hate them all forever. Would the daughter face charges for her involvement in Carlee's death? And poor Marlene. Had she learned truths about her family that made it unbearable to live? Or was she complicit in their sins, and sought to escape justice in the coward's way?

Professor Esteban dropped by with flowers. The geology professor pulled a chair beside Morgan's hospital bed.

"Vernon Dalton called. He asked me to arrange a survey of his property."

"Looking for the ammolite?" Morgan asked.

"I took a quick look at the pit where the Coopers were digging," Esteban said. "There is no ammolite there, but I think there is a promising site closer to the road."

"That's good news," Morgan said. "The Daltons are struggling to get by. If they have valuable gems on their place, they could be the boost that helps them keep their ranch."

"If I am right, and there is a seam containing ammolite, it runs from the Dalton ranch, under the road, and onto your land. As long as I am conducting a survey, I should take a look at your property."

Morgan shook her head. "I don't know that I want anything to do with ammolite. It caused so much trouble. In the end, I didn't learn whether Harlan Cooper—" She paused. Tried to focus on the flowers on her bedside table, not the image of Harlan's dead eyes. "If he didn't know where the ammolite was, then someone else was digging it up."

The doctor returned and gave Morgan the okay to check out. Still no Kurt. The nurse pushed a wheelchair into her room. Morgan was dialing Bernie's cell phone, hoping she was still near enough to the hospital to catch a ride with, when Kurt rushed in.

"I was about to give up on you."

"Sorry I'm late."

He barely spoke as they rode down the elevator to the parking valet. His vintage car pulled up.

"Cool car, man," the valet said.

Kurt gave it a cursory looking over, then handed the valet a five-dollar bill. Morgan smiled. If he was still that concerned about his car, he must have recovered from their terrible night. He helped Morgan out of the wheelchair and held the door for her. From his grim silence, she was beginning to think he had decided to dump her in favor of the cute reporter from the *Granite Junction Times.* They were nearing the outskirts of the city before he spoke.

"I apologize. You must think I'm a terrible boyfriend, abandoning you in your time of need, but I knew half of Golden Springs would be looking after you."

So now he was her boyfriend. Morgan smiled.

"I had visitors this morning," Morgan said. "But I really wanted to see you."

"You'll forgive me when I tell you what I learned."

Kurt reached for her hand and gave it a squeeze. Warmth filled Morgan, and for a moment the stress of the past week dropped away. But Kurt stared straight ahead through his windshield as they drove up Topaz Pass.

"What's your news?" Morgan asked.

"Let's wait until we get to my house."

The silence became increasingly unbearable until they were settled in Kurt's living room, seated on an upholstered antique love seat.

"I went to the city jail to visit the mountain man," Kurt said. "His name is Evan, by the way. Doc Drewmoore said he's lucky to be alive. Under the heavy canvas coat he stole from Del, Evan wore his Kevlar vest from his time in the Army. A Sasquatch in a Kevlar vest." Kurt shook his head. "Evan's vocal cords are definitely rusty from lack of use."

Morgan started to speak, but Kurt held up a hand.

"Hang on. This might answer your questions."

He showed her the legal pad covered with page after page of Kurt's mixture of cursive and blocky print, and a loopy scrawl by Evan, alias Sasquatch.

"Evan Howe," Kurt said, watching Morgan's face. "Ring a bell?"

"Evan," Morgan repeated. "Big guy." She grabbed Kurt's sleeve. "No! The prom king?"

"It gets better. Or worse, depending on your perspective."

Then Kurt told her the story of the Golden Springs high-school student who returned from a brief stint in the Army after sustaining a head injury. His career as a soldier at an end, he decided to make his fortune digging gemstones out of the Colorado mountains. When he found gem-quality ammolite, he made the mistake of showing it to Harlan Cooper, a man he trusted. They entered into an uneven partnership, with Cooper blackmailing Evan into selling the fossil gems cheap because the ammolite came from private land not owned by Evan.

"The Dalton ranch?" Morgan asked.

"He didn't give me the specific location. I'm not sure he remembers where it is."

Evan's stash of ammolite went missing from his cabin near downtown Golden Springs. He confronted Harlan Cooper, who told Evan to just go dig some more. Evan suspected Cooper of stealing the ammolite, and was devising some way to shake himself of their business relationship.

Morgan couldn't stop herself from interrupting. "I think Chase was the thief. He must have known about Evan, stolen the ammolite, and made a necklace for Carlee."

"That could be. Through all this, Evan admitted he liked to drink a little. Cooper took him to a local watering hole one evening, and kept him supplied with whatever he wanted until closing time. Cooper tried to pry the location of the ammolite mine from Evan, but he wouldn't reveal it. They walked outside, and that's all he remembers. He woke up the next morning at the dugout with a hangover, a lump on his head, and a dead girl."

"Carlee," Morgan said. "Only Evan Howe didn't kill her. Cooper did. He set up Evan."

"And it worked," Kurt said. "Evan believes to this day that he killed Carlee. When Cooper 'discovered' him at the dugout, he told him he'd better stay out of sight or he'd be hanged for murder."

"Hanged? Really?"

Kurt turned to a page of the notepad. "That's what he wrote."

"Good grief. The poor guy must really be unhinged."

"He spent his life hiding Carlee and hiding from the law, convinced he'd killed the prom queen in a drunken rage."

"And the elephant-head flowers?"

"Evan remembered that Carlee had given a report in high school about them. He knew they were her favorite flower, so the first two years, he brought her a bouquet on her birthday. Later he transplanted the flowers to the dugout. He didn't live there, by the way. He thought of the dugout as her crypt."

Morgan shivered. "What's going to happen to Evan?"

"He seems happy hanging around the jail until his paperwork clears to be admitted to the mental facility. Chief Sharp even unlocked his cell, but Evan only leaves to get coffee from the chief's office and to play checkers with Deputy Parker."

"Poor Evan, if he thinks the chief's coffee is worth drinking." Morgan wrinkled her nose. "And poor Deputy Parker. Whew!"

"Evan cleaned up. His hair and beard are still a ratty mess, but he's gone through a few bars of soap. Evan asked about Hawthorne."

"Who?"

"The mutt's name is Hawthorne." Kurt shrugged. "I assured Evan we'd look after him until he's well enough to leave the hospital. If you don't want the dog, I'll take him."

"Hawthorne, hum? He likes running around." Morgan looked around Kurt's townhouse, full of antiques and breakables, and tried to imagine the rambunctious dog who couldn't seem to sit still living there. "I think he's better off at the rock shop for now." Kurt looked relieved. "Did Evan say anything about Chase Cooper?"

"According to Evan, Chase had nothing to do with Carlee's death."

"But he was drunk, and then unconscious. He didn't see what happened. And how could Chase not figure out what his father was up to? And Mia, and Marlene, his wife?"

Kurt shrugged. "Happens all the time. A family member is a paragon of virtue by all public accounts, while leading a secret life. Cooper murdered Carlee, and although he might be a sleaze in his business dealings, he might never have killed again, at least until the past threatened to topple his little empire."

"If I hadn't found Carlee, which set in motion Camille coming here with her kids, which drew Evan out of hiding . . ."

Kurt held up a hand. "A man would have gotten away with murder," he said, "and the Kruger family would never have found peace."

They sat in silence for a moment. Kurt seemed to have run out of words. His normally ruddy cheeks were ashen, his eyes full of pain.

"Camille and Gerda visited me at the hospital," Morgan said. "They're grateful you stopped Cooper. I think they will find peace now, thanks to you."

"I hope I can." He leaned forward in his chair, propping his elbows on his knees and resting his forehead in his hands. "I just keep playing that scene over and over in my head, trying to find another ending."

"I can't think of any way that would have ended without one or more of us dead," Morgan said. "There was no other ending."

Morgan spent the rest of Sunday at Kurt's townhouse. There was nothing romantic about their time together. Morgan suffered from a splitting headache all Sunday afternoon. She tried to focus as Kurt asked questions. He tapped on his laptop keyboard while they went over the events of Friday hour by hour, and minute by minute. While they waited for pizza to be delivered, Kurt made an announcement.

"I've decided to run."

"For the City Council seat?" Morgan asked.

"I registered at the last minute. I decided candidates shouldn't run based on who's most likely to win."

"I'm guessing Jade will drop out. The field of candidates will be more balanced."

Their conversation switched from murder to politics. Morgan was grateful for the change. After a pizza dinner, Kurt drove Morgan home. He gave her a chaste kiss on the cheek before leaving her with Del and Hawthorne.

The memorial service had been postponed from Saturday until Monday, allowing Gayle to attend. Kurt picked up Morgan and Del. As they drove to the church, Morgan still felt woozy, more from painkillers for her persistent headache than from the aftereffects of the paint thinner poisoning.

Kurt offered Morgan his arm as they walked into the church. She didn't care who stared, or which tongues started wagging. Holding on to Kurt Willard's arm felt right. She began to make her way toward Bernie, Rolf, and Stacie, but Anna waved them to the church ladies' pew. Beatrice turned to see who Anna was calling over, focused on Kurt, and frowned.

"I hope you realize that sitting with us carries with it certain obligations," she said, her tone all business.

Kurt glanced at Morgan, the alarm obvious in his raised brows and cheeks flushed a deeper red than usual. Morgan wondered what Beatrice had in mind. Conversion to the tenets of their faith? Becoming an elder of the church? Morgan felt a blush creep up her own cheeks.

"You have to wash dishes afterwards." Beatrice folded her

arms across her chest and leaned back into the stiff wooden pew, the hint of a smile tugging at the corners of her lips.

The Krugers were united in the front pew. Gayle nestled between her mother and grandmother in a tangle of intertwined arms. The teenager wore a remarkably boring pink sweater that covered her shoulders. The streaks of green and purple in her glorious golden hair were all that differentiated her from the enlarged photos of her aunt on the stage. Farley twisted around to look at the rows of pews behind him, gave a weak smile, and waved at Kurt.

Beatrice leaned close to Morgan. "The eleven-year-old never knew his aunt," she whispered, "but nearly losing his sister hit him hard. Camille almost had to tie him to a chair to keep him from joining the search. Poor little guy."

Poster-sized photos of Carlee Kruger on the stage were surrounded by arrangements containing spikes of elephant-head flowers. Pastor Filbury delivered a moving eulogy. Then people rose to speak, climbing three steps to the podium, fumbling with the microphone and crinkling papers or shuffling note cards. Somewhere in the middle of the grieving and the tears, the somber memorial turned into a celebration of Carlee's life.

As Beatrice returned from her turn at the podium, and her story about Carlee's first day in Sunday school, she squinted toward the back of the church. She slid onto her seat next to Morgan.

"It's him," she whispered.

Morgan turned to look. Jade Tinsley leaned against the wall, perhaps attempting to blend in with the woodwork. His hands were shoved deep in the pockets of black slacks. His white shirt was rumpled. Morgan prayed he wouldn't make some kind of scene that would disrupt the healing.

After considering him as a potential murderer, she wasn't quite ready to let go of her animosity. If he hadn't gotten Camille pregnant, Carlee wouldn't have been drawn into Harlan Cooper's trap. She hoped he was here at least partly to repent.

Jade noticed Morgan. He focused on her for a moment, his face taut with grief. He nodded and mouthed the words, "Thank you," then spun on one heel and left.

Kurt was a good sport about cleaning the kitchen, accepting the most manly apron available, and scrubbing the toughest casserole dishes. He disappeared while Morgan and the ladies wiped counters and put away the clean coffee mugs.

Bernie leaned through the kitchen doorway. "Morgan, Mr. Thompson just announced that the Cooper family made a donation to the historical park in Carlee's name. They're sending a blue spruce sapling over to the park later this week."

Just as fast as she'd appeared, Bernie left. Beatrice grabbed a chair as though she needed the support, then slowly sank onto the padded seat.

"Are you okay?" Anna asked.

"I was so afraid."

"What is it, Beatrice?" Teruko asked.

"The tree?" Beatrice looked at each of the kitchen ladies one by one. "The donation to the park? I thought the Cooper family might escalate their hatred of the Krugers after losing their patriarch. But perhaps the feud is over."

"Ah." Teruko sat on a chair beside Beatrice. "Yes, they sent peace offerings."

"I don't know." Morgan shook her head. "Marlene nearly killed herself, and Mia was such a daddy's girl, I can't see her making peace with the Kruger family."

"Perhaps Chase is behind the donation," Teruko said. "It is he who most needs healing. He kept many secrets that a boy should not have known."

"Did anyone else notice Jade sneak in the back of the

church?" Anna asked.

"No," Teruko said. "I did not see him."

"He left before the service ended."

Anna stopped, her eyes on the doorway. Kurt grasped the doorjamb with one hand.

"Are we done here?" he asked.

"No." Teruko struggled to her feet and tapped across the kitchen tiles in her stylish pumps. She reached for Kurt's hand. "We are not done until we thank you." Her voice wavered more than usual. "You saved Morgan, Bernie, and the Kruger girl."

"In a way," Anna said, "you saved Golden Springs. The town couldn't have survived another blow like Carlee's death. Not emotionally."

"Or spiritually," Beatrice added.

"I don't think you give yourselves enough credit," Morgan said. "In my four months here, I've learned how resilient you are."

"Don't speak as though you're an outsider," Anna said. "You're part of this town now, like it or not."

When she finally pulled herself away from the group hug, Morgan walked with Kurt to the church parking lot. He held the door for her as she climbed into his vintage Plymouth. He put the key in the ignition, but didn't start the car. Instead, he turned to look at Morgan.

"I thought this was a game when I started turning over rocks and poking sticks in dark holes," Kurt said. "I never imagined my amateur sleuthing would endanger you. Or that I'd end up . . . I wish it could have ended differently."

Morgan put her hand on Kurt's arm. "You had no choice. Harlan Cooper was a murderer. You acted, not even in self-defense, but in defense of other people." Morgan closed her eyes for a moment. "Hey, you didn't explain why you were walking across the Daltons' field with Houdini that night."

"I told you Del called me, wanting a ride into town to help search for the three of you."

"Yes." Morgan waited. There had to be more.

"When I got there, Houdini was kicking the barn door. Del said he'd never seen the donkey do that before. He opens pasture gates all the time, and even went through the side of the barn when Evan Howe had made an opening for himself, but the barn door was a first. I would have ignored the donkey, except that he seemed to be waiting for someone to follow him."

"Seriously?"

"I can't explain it, but I felt like I was being led. Del suggested I follow him. I didn't want to waste valuable time chasing a donkey when I needed to search for you, but then I saw a flash of light in the pasture. And we don't have lightning bugs here."

"That was my flashlight. It quit working before you reached us."

"By then I could hear Gayle crying, and both Hawthorne and Houdini zeroed in on you. There was no stopping either one of them."

"If you hadn't—"

Kurt interrupted. "But I did." He put his hand on top of Morgan's. "Please don't remind me I'm a hero. The entire town has been trying to throw that mantle on my shoulders, and frankly, it's pretty darned uncomfortable to have expectations that high to live up to. Before all this mess with the Cooper family blew up, I recall that I made you a promise. I was going to take you out after the press conference. We ate leftovers with Del instead. I owe you dinner."

Morgan smiled. "You do."

"And I know the perfect place. The only problem is, the restaurant is half a day's drive from here. Ah!" He held up his hand, pointing upward with his index finger. "I remember!

There's a nice bed and breakfast nearby."

"Oh. I'm, um . . ." Part of Morgan's brain tried to tell her things were moving too fast, but it was shouted down by her heart. "That sounds relaxing. Er, nice. I mean, yes."

Kurt leaned across the wide seat of the Plymouth. Morgan scooted closer. Their lips met. Her cell phone vibrated.

"My phone." She winced. The caller ID was an unknown number. "Considering all that's been going on, I'd better take this call." She held the phone to her ear. "Hello?"

"Morgan," her brother's voice boomed. "Allie and I are in Denver. We need a ride from the airport."

She placed a hand over the phone. "It's my brother," she told Kurt. "Hang on." She spoke into the phone. "When does your flight arrive?"

"Now," Kendall said. "We're here. How long will it take you to get here?"

"I was in the middle of something. Can you hang on for a minute?"

Morgan didn't wait for Kendall to answer. She covered the phone again.

"You're not going to believe this, but my brother and sister-in-law are at DIA. He needs a ride. Now."

"It's a conspiracy." Kurt closed his eyes for a moment, then shook his head. "I'll take you."

"I can't ask you to do that."

"You're not in any condition to drive. He patted the Plymouth's steering wheel. "After we drop them off at the rock shop, we'll head to the bed and breakfast. Kendall and Allie will need your room, right?"

Morgan thought about the awkward explanation she would need to make to her brother about her plans, then considered the situation he'd dropped on her, with no warning, once again.

She spoke into the phone.

"We're on the way."

"Oh, be sure to bring a car seat," Kendall said. Allie said something in the background. Kendall spoke to Morgan again. "Allie says to get one of the little ones. You're a mom. You know. For a baby. And hurry."

ABOUT THE AUTHOR

Catherine Dilts, a former flat-lander, writes amateur sleuth mysteries set in the Colorado mountains. She works as an environmental scientist, and plays at heirloom vegetable gardening, camping, and fishing. Her short fiction appears in Alfred Hitchcock Mystery Magazine. *Stone Cold Case* is the second book in the Rock Shop Mystery series. In her debut novel *Stone Cold Dead,* business is as dead as a dinosaur, but when Morgan Iverson finds the body of a Goth teen on a hiking trail, more than just the family rock shop could become extinct. Catherine loves rock shops because they are like geodes—both contain amazing treasures hidden inside their plain-as-dirt exteriors. Visit her at http://www.catherinedilts.com.